FUMBLED

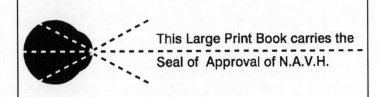

This Large Print Book carries the
Seal of Approval of N.A.V.H.

FUMBLED

ALEXA MARTIN

THORNDIKE PRESS
A part of Gale, a Cengage Company

LIBRARY OF CONGRESS CIP DATA ON FILE.
CATALOGUING IN PUBLICATION FOR THIS BOOK
IS AVAILABLE FROM THE LIBRARY OF CONGRESS

ISBN-13: 978-1-4328-6958-8 (hardcover alk. paper)

Published in 2020 by arrangement with Berkley, an imprint of Penguin Publishing Group, a division of Penguin Random House, LLC

Printed in Mexico
Print Number: 01   Print Year: 2020

This book is dedicated to the wives and the girlfriends.

To my Lady Ravens, thank you for turning strangers into family.

ACKNOWLEDGMENTS

When I began writing, publishing was something I couldn't even wrap my head around. Finding a publishing home at Berkley is the dream I never allowed myself to have. Kristine Swartz, thank you for being the most amazing editor ever. Ryanne Probst, Jessica Mangicaro, Erin Galloway, and Jessica Brock, thank you for everything you have done for me and my books. To the rest of the Berkley dream team, thank you for welcoming me and my crazy football books with open arms. I am forever grateful.

Jessica Watterson, thank you for being my agent. You are the champion every writer deserves to have in their corner. I could not have done this without you.

I have been overwhelmed by the kindness other authors have offered me throughout this journey. Helen Hoang, thank you for never ignoring my messages. Jasmine Guillory and Kristan Higgins, your support has meant everything. I'm so grateful for your lovely words and encouragement.

Phoenix and Shay, my mentors in Black Girl Magic. Watching you go after your dreams is inspirational.

Maxym, Tricia, Shannon, and Gwynne, your talent amazes me. Thank you for turning All The Kissing into what it has become. I love working with you all.

Natalie and Kim, who would have thought we'd be spending all these Friday nights together? You two, plus our crazy crew, have packed these three years with more memories than I could've imagined. I'm so lucky to call you both friends.

Lin, thank you for reading every piece of everything I send you. Without your encouragement, I'm not sure I would've ever been brave enough to put my words into the world. When I joined that mom group, I thought I'd get some advice on stretch marks; I never imagined I'd find a best friend. And remember I wrote this when you're writing your acknowledgments for what will no doubt be a best seller.

My family. Frannie, you never fail to be anything but a shining light in everyone's life. One of these days, I'm going to sneak my way into one of your trips! Grandpa

Jesse and Grandma Frankie, thank you for your support and encouragement. Derrick, thank you for taking over our circus when I had to disappear into the writing trenches. Your belief in me is everything and I love you. DJ, Harlow, Dash, and Ellis, you are my why. And even though I will ban you from ever reading beyond this page, I hope you're proud. I'm so grateful to be your mom.

And to every person who has watched, with bated breath, as your loved one chases their passions, knowing it might prevent them from coming home: Your quiet strength does not go unnoticed. You are the glue that holds everything together.

ONE

I'm on my knees.

In the back of a club, covered in a foreign liquid, and on my freaking knees. Plus, I'm pretty sure the coarse, dirty carpet beneath me might rub a hole through my lace stockings.

Some drunk asshole spilled whiskey all over my corset while trying to cop a feel. I'm pretty sure I've looked through hundreds of corsets and still can't find my size. Which, I guess, all things considered, is a good alternative for other reasons to be on my knees in a nightclub.

I never, not in a million years, thought this would be my life, but if life has taught me anything, it's to expect the unexpected.

And also, screw expectations. Expectations always leave you disappointed, broken, or — if you are really lucky, like me — all of the above.

"Hey, Poppy, Papi!" Sadie shimmies into

the room, over the piles of mismatched thigh-high stockings and red-sequined corsets, waving a flat iron over her head. "Sadie's here to save the day."

I met Sadie on my first day here. I crossed the threshold into what I was sure was going to be dark, depressing, and coated with daddy issues, only to find my own little rainbow, dusting anyone around her with glitter. Literally. I love her to death, but if you come within three feet of Sadie, you can expect to find glitter on you for the next five months.

"You're a godsend. Phil looked like he was about to have a coronary when he saw me. I guess there's a big group coming tonight and my smelling like cheap booze and having half a head of frizzy hair was almost the end of the world." I grab another corset and check the tag: size zero . . . again. "Ugh! Why am I the only person here not a size zero or two? I'm going to crack a rib trying to close this."

"Because you like wine too much." Sadie doesn't look at me as she plugs the flat iron into the only empty outlet in the room.

"Whatever. Red wine is a health food. My heart is strong as hell, thank you very much." Resigning myself to the fact that I'll spend the rest of the night unable to breathe or bend properly, I start to peel off my ruined uniform, but for some reason, the clasps are stuck. "Ohmygod. Halp!"

Sadie rolls her eyes, taking her sweet time to come and help me. "You are doing the absolute most right now."

"Am not," I whisper yell at her. The upper clasps opened fine, so both of my hands are working to keep my girls covered. "Can you hurry before someone walks in and thinks I'm trying to get onstage tonight?"

"You suck in and squeeze the top as tight as you can. I'll try and rip the bottom ones open." She's biting her lip, and I know if she were to let go, she'd be laughing in my face. "Ready?"

I appreciate her restraint.

"Ready." I nod.

"Go!" She pulls as hard as she can. Which, unfortunately for me, is much stronger than I was bracing for and I go flying.

Face first.

With the reaction time of a sloth.

Of. Course.

I say nothing when I hit the ground. I just lie there, unmoving, taking inventory of my face. Running my tongue along my teeth, all still there. Feeling for the wetness of blood dripping from my nose, all dry. Everything is intact.

13

Well, everything except my right breast.

And my pride.

But I lost that years ago.

"Holy crap," I moan. "I never thought I'd ever in my life say this, but thank God for thigh-highs." A pile of the lacy little buggers saved my face!

And then I hear it.

Sadie's self-control has left the room.

"Why didn't I have my camera on?" she manages to get out through her peals of laughter. "You should have seen your face going down."

She does her best slo-mo replay for me, complete with open-mouthed horror and wide-eyed fear.

"I kind of hate you right now." I fight my own smile. I'm secretly also bummed she didn't catch it on camera. I know it makes me seem like a nine-year-old, but watching people fall is a favorite pastime of mine . . . even when it's me. "You pushed me."

"That's what happens when you ask someone to undress you while wearing four-inch stilettos." She gestures to my weapon-adorned feet. "I accept none of the blame."

"You're a terrible friend. You could at least pretend to feel bad." I don't even try to stand up. I just lie on the floor and twist the clasps until they come undone . . . about four minutes too late. I'm half tempted to throw on my leggings and take my ass home.

Alas, the nearing empty gas tank in my car and electric bill that was fifty dollars more than normal pop into my head, reminding me I am a certified adult with certified adult problems. So my adult ass has to stay and serve adult drinks.

"Pretending is for porn stars, darling," Sadie says. "Now throw on a robe so I can fix your hair."

Ugh. My hair.

I don't hate much about my job.

But nearing the top of my hate list is burning my curly locks into submission. I've always loved my gravity-defying hair, but Phil — the club owner — has a strict "straight hair only" policy. I think it's bullshit and low-key racist, but I need a paycheck more than I need to stand on this Black Girl Magic mountain.

"How are the tips for you tonight?" I ask as Sadie yanks my head around, trying to get as close to my roots as possible without scorching my scalp.

"Not great." She avoids my eyes in the mirror. "But Phil put us on the VIP table tonight and they were walking in when I was heading up here, so things should get good."

"If it doesn't, let me know if you need one of my tables after they leave. I've worked overtime this week and my feet could use a slow night."

In reality, I could use every spare cent I can get.

But Sadie's been having a rough go as of late with her mom crashing at her place and giving her exactly zero extra dollars a month for rent and food. Plus, with prices skyrocketing in Denver, thanks to the thousands of marijuana enthusiasts moving in, she's struggling.

Something I understand all too well.

Supporting two people on this pay isn't what one would call a cake walk.

"Thank you," she says into my smoking tresses. "Maybe I could take one."

"No, *thank you.*" I reach my arm beyond me, blindly searching for her hand to squeeze. "I have to spend the rest of the night in a uniform a size too small. I'm going to look like a stuffed sausage. You're saving me from extra humiliation."

"Oh, stop it." She finally looks at me, her eyes lit with humor. "The only thing it's going to do is make your waist look smaller and your already massive boobs look even bigger. You're going to rake it in tonight."

"I can always count on you to look on the

bright side."

"That you can." She smirks at me and, as if by magic, conjures up a handful of glitter and throws it over my head.

I don't even attempt to brush it off me. This has happened to me enough to know glitter is like quicksand — the more you fight it, the more it sticks to you. Instead, I hang my head, resigned to the fact that I befriended a glitter-wielding psychopath.

Sparkly bitch.

If anyone tries to quote me, I'll deny it with every last breath, but I adore my waitress costume — not uniform, this is straight dress-up.

Well, when it's not crushing my lungs.

When I'm not at the club, I'm at home or school pickup in leggings, a T-shirt, and tennis shoes. I never, not in a million years, imagined myself working at a club, but I do take a secret pleasure in playing sex vixen. When I first started, I convinced myself it was an acting job. I have zero talent in the arts, but ever since I watched season one of *American Idol,* I've wanted to "gig." So that's what I told myself. Just going giggin'.

And it still works.

I'm one of the best waitresses here, and I consistently bring in the highest tips. Because when I walk in the door, I'm no longer Poppy Patterson: single mother and disowned daughter. Nope. I'm Serena. My stretch marks are hidden under my corset and thigh-highs. The mandatory red lipstick only makes my full lips seem even fuller. The metal piping in the deep V corset makes my waist smaller and my post-baby boobs perky and full. Not to mention, the sky-high heels I was convinced would grant me a workers' comp case make my short legs enviable even to someone who's five eight.

"I hate you," Charity says as soon as I step on the floor.

I jerk my head back. "What did I do?"

"Sadie said you couldn't find a corset in your size and you might go home." She sets her empty tray on the bar and uses her free hands to gesture the length of my body. "But you're still here lookin' like your tits are about to slap you in the face and Phil just pulled me from the high rollers."

The thing with Charity is, even though I've worked with her for the last two years, I still don't know how she feels about me. She either has the best, driest sense of humor, or she loathes me.

My heart says I'm her favorite person on the planet.

18

My brain, on the other hand, says she'd run me over if given the chance.

"If it makes you feel better, I can't breathe. There's a high probability of me spilling a drink all over someone tonight and getting fired."

"One can only hope." She points at the tray Nate, one of the bartenders tonight, is loading with shots and cocktails and throws a sideways glance my way. "VIP. You're up."

What a peach.

You'd think with a name like Charity, she'd be obligated to be kind.

She turns to leave and I call out to her back, "Thanks, Char-Char." She doesn't turn around, the slight stutter in her step the only indication she heard me at all. Maybe nicknames and Charity don't go together. Point taken.

The Emerald Cabaret is in an old building in Historic Downtown Denver. I never knew such classy clubs existed until I came here. It's almost like a speakeasy of sorts. The bottom floor is a steakhouse that costs a mint — not that I know from personal experience, I've never eaten there — and the upper two floors are the club. They had it remodeled so the third floor is the VIP section. It's completely open to the lower floor, and from what the performers have told me, they had to special order the silks for them to be long enough to do all the aerial tricks they do. There's also a private stage and a couple of private rooms I have no desire to ever step into.

Every night I take a second to appreciate the girls.

It is freaking art. You have to be strong as hell to do some of the Cirque du Soleil stunts they do. I swear, some nights I leave with my heart in my throat because of secondhand fear of these women flipping and twisting down the silk headfirst.

Most nights, though, I'm just in awe.

And thankful. Because of their skill set, we are filled with a certain kind of client. Besides a bachelor party here and there, we mostly serve the lawyer or businessman trying to have fun and make deals without seeming too sleazy. And not the football-playing variety. Something I made sure of before I accepted the job.

It was the only question I had during my interview, and Phil's firm (and angry) no is the reason I'm here.

And for two years, it's held up.

I walk up the stairs, feeling the strain in my calves that never seems to fade even though I've walked up them hundreds of times. I reach the top step and Dane, my favorite security teddy bear, lifts the velvet rope so I'm allowed to share breathing space with these very important people. I see Sadie clearing empty glasses off the table in front of the stage that Ruby (real name: Hannah) is *slaying* on. The silk is twisted around her ankle and going behind her head as she twirls and flips. I square my shoulders, put a little extra sway in my hips, and plaster a smile on my face. I take comfort in knowing I'm rocking the shit out of my sequined corset and my legs look fab in my sky-high heels and stockings.

This is my gig. I am Meryl. I am Julia. I am Sandra. I got this.

I repeat the mantra in my head on a loop until I round the table and take a deep breath to greet my new group of customers.

Then I see *him* and everything is forgotten.

Everything tonight, at least.

Not the bus ride across town. Not Mrs. Moore staring with disgust at my bloated midsection, telling me *he* didn't want me. Not all my dreams going down the drain.

Not the white-hot burn of rejection.

No, that's all crystal clear.

But where I am and what I'm supposed to be doing? Poof. All gone.

21

I grab the tray with my free hand when my shaking causes the drinks to rattle, and I start to back away. I can't decide on a pace, so it's an awkward dance of moving too fast and looking like I'm fleeing (accurate) or walking too slow and drawing attention to myself for looking suspicious (also accurate).

I have tunnel vision on Dane and the velvet rope to freedom when an arm brushes against my shoulder. Every tightened muscle in my body unravels like a jack-in-the-box and I spring forward.

"Shit!" I screech, throwing my hands in the air trying to stop it, but helpless as I watch my tray and all the drinks go flying in the one direction I need them not to go.

The liquid drenches the poor man from his too-long, light brown hair and thick beard covering his strong, square jaw to his chocolate leather loafers as the glass tumblers crash to the floor around him. The dark amber liquid dripping down his perfectly straight nose, despite the fact that he broke it in high school, is a vivid contrast to his ivory skin. All his friends manage to jump up — narrowly avoiding smelling like a distillery for the next year.

"What the fuck?" he roars, rising to his feet faster than someone his size should be able to and attracting the attention of every person on the third floor. Even the DJ scratches the record. "You've gotta be fuckin' kidding me!"

I'm frozen in place. Watching with horror and fascination as he shakes out his arms and legs, drying off with the efficiency of a wet dog. A wet dog with biceps straining against his checkered blazer sleeves and quadriceps about to bust the seams on his tailored-to-perfection pants.

"What was that?" He looks down, clearing the wet hair stuck to his face so he can see the klutzy culprit. And when he does, the change in his demeanor is instant. His green eyes triple in size, his back goes straight, and the almost man bun is long forgotten. "Poppy?"

"Hey, TK." I wave with both hands.

Then I run.

God.

I hate my job.

Two

I always considered wearing heels one of my weaknesses. After I was hired here, I wore them around the house for hours until I no longer looked like a newborn giraffe. I wasn't sure if it was worth it, considering the questions I had to dodge about why and how and where I was going to wear them. But as I take the stairs at the Emerald Cabaret two at a time and reach the back door in record time, I know it was probably one of the most useful exercises I've ever forced upon myself.

I hit the metal door running and it flies open and starts to close just as fast. I barely miss it clipping my shoulder before I hear it slam shut.

Freedom.

Hands on my fishnet-covered knees, I gulp in the warm Colorado air. Between the sobs threatening to escape and my desperate need for oxygen, it feels like I'm swallowing razors. I'm so hot, I feel like I might pass out at any given moment. My straightened hair is shot to hell, I can already feel the curls forming against my neck. But I still can't stop shivering. My stilettos wobble against the parking lot pavement, and I know there's no way I'm making it to my car.

I start to lower myself to the ground, careful not to go face first. I wouldn't call myself vain, but scraping my face against the pavement doesn't sound particularly pleasant.

I'm squatting, my fingers grazing the gravel, when I hear the squeak of the door opening behind me.

"Sorry, Sades. I don't even know what happened in there," I lie. I know exactly what happened. The thing — or more accurately, the person — I've been avoiding for the last ten years.

Instead of a response, a set of familiar hands whose touch I should've long forgotten grab my waist. They are stronger than I remember, maybe even bigger, but the jolt of recognition, and the resurrection of butterflies I thought had died years ago, is the same.

The messed-up part is, I'm not surprised by this turn of events. The eternal-optimist part of me was rooting for Sadie to push through those doors. The realist, been-shit-on-and-present-for-the-last-decade-of-my-life part of me knew it would be TK.

He lifts me with ease and sets me on my feet before turning me to face him, doing it so slowly, I'm not sure he even wants to be doing this. He always was too curious for his own good, at least some things never change. I keep my eyes closed, trying to prepare for what I thought I could avoid forever.

For what has now become inevitable.

"Poppy?" His deep voice disbelieving.

I screw my eyes closed tighter and take one last deep breath before opening them. *Act normal. Act normal. Act normal!*

I don't know what I'm doing. I just know I have to try to recover from that scene. Shoot the breeze and hope he leaves me alone.

Leaves us alone. Which shouldn't be hard; he's done it already.

But when I raise my chin to look him in his bright green eyes — the eyes I know so well — I damn near crumple onto the ground beneath me.

I'm so not ready.

"What the hell, Poppy?" His gaze travels the length of my body. But he doesn't look appreciative. He looks pissed. "What is going on? Why are you here?"

I remember everything about him. I remember the way he mumbles nonsense in his sleep the night before a big game. I remember the way he shies away from praise for anything other than football. I remember the way he dances like nobody is watching him even though he has zero rhythm. Everything.

But I guess he forgot I don't take being questioned or talked down to well . . . at all.

"I work here." I put my hands on my hips and tilt my head, trying my hardest not to show my nerves. "Obviously."

He narrows his eyes and I see his jaw clench under his thick, light brown beard . . . a beard that wasn't there ten years ago. A beard that only accentuates how his features have changed from teenage boy to very grown man. "You know what I meant. Why are you in Denver? But since you brought it up, why the fuck are you working here?"

It's a valid question.

He went to college thinking everything had been taken care of and my sights were still set on Northwestern University.

I never made it. I didn't even send in the application.

27

But I can't tell him why.

At least not now.

"I came to live with my aunt for my senior year and never went back." I shrug my shoulders and look away. It's not a lie, it's just not the whole truth either. "I work here because I have bills to pay and I like the hours. Though I doubt I even have my job anymore. Thanks for that, by the way."

The weight of consequences settles on me like a boulder to the gut. Not only did I spill drinks on TK and who I'm assuming are his teammates, but I ran away like a maniac and turned a little scene into a gigantic one.

Crap.

I'm going to cry.

I turn my back to TK, biting down on my bottom lip until the burning behind my eyes starts to fade. Then I start to count to ten.

"I'm not sure you losing a job at some nightclub is a bad thing," TK says, interrupting me.

I spin around on my heel, tears and calming practices long forgotten.

"I don't make millions like you! I need this job!" I try to go up on my tippy-toes to get closer to eye level, but my heels already have me at my maximum height. "I have bills to pay and mouths —" I cut myself off.

"I have responsibilities, TK. I know this isn't anyone's dream job, but it does what I need it to do."

"And you're telling me working at some club, wearing this" — he gestures to my barely concealed cleavage and my lace-covered thighs — "is the only way for you to do it?"

I'm not one to resort to violence, but the urge to slap him is almost too much for even me to resist.

"I'm not telling you anything because it's none of your business what I do," I snap.

The parking lot isn't the best-lit one on the block, but that doesn't stop me from seeing TK's face go red and his shoulders square up. Something else about him I remember, his confrontation position.

"Look." I gentle my voice, ready for this entire exchange to be finished. "I'm glad I got to see you, and I'm so happy you're doing well and living your dreams. Really. I couldn't be more thrilled for you."

I reach out and take his hands in mine, ignoring the way this single touch wakes up my body from its years-long hibernation.

"But you aren't part of my life and I don't need judgment from you when I get enough of it from everyone else. We haven't seen each other in ten years. We used to be close;

now we aren't. I'm sorry this meeting happened like this, but we aren't teenagers anymore. We lost touch. That's okay. You don't need to worry about me or what I'm doing. I have it all covered."

I thought this would do the trick. Placate him and he'd go on with his fairy-tale life and forget all about the teenage girlfriend he left behind to pursue his glory.

However, when I try to pull my hands away and make a semi-dignified exit, his hands tighten around my wrists and he's full-on glaring at me.

"We *used* to be close?" His voice is almost a whisper.

"Yes, used to be. We were young and thought it was more than it was." I know it's not the right answer as soon as the words slip from my lips.

TK drops my wrists like they're made of fire and takes three giant steps away from me. I'm not sure if it's for my protection or his.

"I fucking loved you!" His voice echoes off the brick buildings surrounding us. "You disappeared! You changed your number, left without telling a single person where you were going, and your asshole parents refused to say a word. It was like you never existed. And now I see you and you've been living

30

in the same fucking city as me for the last six years? What the hell, Poppy?"

He rakes his hands through his thick, long hair and rests them on top of his head, staring at me. Expecting an answer I don't have. I don't know if his outburst pissed me off or confused me. The TK I remember was the calm to my storm. Always thinking things through before giving anyone the satisfaction of getting a rise out of him.

Hell, I'm going to need at least a week to sort through everything he just said.

After who knows how long, he closes the distance he just put between us. I try to move back, really, I beg my feet to move, but I can't. I'm frozen in place watching his chest rising and falling as he approaches. My brain is telling me to run like hell, but my body is already crying out for him.

Traitor.

"There was no reason for me to reach out. I'm not the same girl you knew." I force out the understatement of the century.

"Bullshit."

He keeps coming toward me, and it takes every last bit of my restraint not to retreat.

"It isn't." I hate the way my voice wavers, the way my insides clench at his proximity.

"I've fucking missed you. I don't know why you ran from me up there, but seeing you is the best thing to happen to me in months." He seems like he's back to calm, but his emerald eyes have turned to onyx. One of his hands moves to the back of my neck while the other one falls to the base of my back. "But if you don't feel the same way, if you really don't want to see me, say so. I'll go back inside, pretend this never happened, and we'll go our separate ways."

Just say those simple words and this will be over. I've spent so many years being angry at him, this should be a relief. But I open my mouth and the words won't come. Because, dammit, I've missed him so much. He was my person and then he was gone. And ever since, I've been walking around with an ache in my heart so deep, I've become numb.

Maybe this is what I needed. Some sort of closure. A validation of what we had.

"I hate you." I say the words on an exhale and watch with avid fascination as confusion clouds his features. I know I should stop, but instead, I keep going. Rushing the words out before I convince myself otherwise. "But I've missed you."

"Fucking hell, Poppy." His voice is heavy with something I don't recognize and his fingers flinch against my neck.

Then before I have a chance to react, his

mouth is on mine.

It's not a gentle kiss. His soft, full lips press hard against mine, and his full beard scratches my face. My stomach flips and I get so light-headed I reach out and grab his shirt for support.

He bites my bottom lip and tugs, just like he used to. I'm not sure if it's the gentle pain of his teeth grazing against my lip that makes everything even more intense or if it's knowing that he still remembers what I like, but I gasp and he takes advantage of my open mouth, thrusting his tongue inside. Our tongues tangle, exploring and tasting . . . remembering.

I feel like I'm floating, the only thing tethering me to the earth beneath me are his hands. Electricity flows from his fingertips, burning his movements into my skin. It's painful and exciting and *wonderful*.

I don't know how long we stand here, him in his expensive suit, me in a sequined corset, tangled together, because it feels like time has stopped. After a while, our kiss becomes less wild and his soft lips touch mine once more. A sweet ending.

I wrap my arms around him and rest my head against his chest. His rapid heartbeat pounds under my cheek as he draws circles against the exposed skin of my back and I feel a sense of peace settle over me.

I've not been an angel since we parted ways. I mean, I'm grown and I have needs. I've had relationships and wild nights. But this? This kiss? It was better than anything I've had over the years.

"I like your suit," I whisper. "Sorry I threw booze on it."

"S'all right." He squeezes his arms around me. "I like your outfit too."

"It's too small. I almost broke a rib putting it on."

He starts to shake beneath me, and when I look up at him, he's laughing, his perfect lips, his deep Cupid's bow that I still dream about sometimes, are pulled up at the corners. His eyes, back to the bright green I adore, are creased at the corners, one slightly hidden by his long, silky locks. And it's all so much better than the anger he had directed at me only moments ago.

"Missed you," he whispers.

"Missed you too, Ace."

As soon as the little nickname I had for him in high school falls from my lips, the mirage around me crumbles to my feet. My back goes straight and I push away from him with a quickness not even I am prepared for. I stumble backward, swatting away his hands as they try to steady me.

"This is a mistake." My voice doesn't waver even though my insides are knotted and my hands are shaking. Most likely because, as much as I hate to say it, I mean every single word I'm saying. "You need to leave."

"What? What just happ—"

I cut him off. "Nothing. Nothing happened. I need to go. You need to go." I'm rambling. Panic courses through my veins, the slight breeze in the air causes goose bumps to break out up my arms and legs. "We can't do this."

"Like hell we can't." His deep voice rumbles with frustration.

He starts to walk toward me again, but as he does, the back door opens and Phil's glare finds me in a split second.

"You comin' back to work or what?" His tone indicates I don't actually have an option.

Not that I need one. I don't run again. I take a deep breath and ignore TK. I walk through the door with my head held high and TK's eyes burning a hole through the back of my head.

But I still have my secret.

One neither one of us is ready to talk about.

One that will stay where it's supposed to

if he listens to me and leaves me alone.

But like I said, my luck is crap and I need to prepare. TK isn't the only one in for a shock.

Ace is going to be pissed.

THREE

I didn't go back to work.

I took a detour to my purse and told Rochelle that VIP was all hers. Then I got the hell out.

"I can't believe you just left!" Sadie is still scolding me through the phone.

"My uniform got ruined. My replacement was small. Then I poured drinks all over the Mustang players Phil's been dying to get into the club." I recount the events she's already aware of, leaving out my parking-lot tryst. "I know when to call it quits. Nothing good was going to come from last night."

"Phil was pissed. Like more pissed than I've ever seen him. And you told Rochelle to cover for you?" Her voice goes up ten decimals. She hates Rochelle almost as much as Rochelle hates me. "You know that miserable bitch is the worst. She tried to steal my tips!"

"I'm sorry. She was the only person I saw

and I wasn't thinking straight." I attempt to placate her, more worried about the Phil part of what she's saying. "But Phil. How pissed would you say he was? Like he's going to put me in the shitty parts of the club for a few weeks or I shouldn't go back in because I'm fired?"

"He was going to fire your ass. He said it about a hundred times to the football players. 'Sorry about her. I promise, she's gone after the scene she caused.' " She mimicked his hoarse smoker's voice so well I might've laughed if I wasn't about to throw up.

"What do you mean, he *was* going to fire me?" I try to get her to focus on the important part.

"The guys didn't care. Honestly, they were laughing after it happened. The only thing bothering them was Phil. He might as well have dropped to his knees. It was pathetic, truly."

"You are vivid to a fault."

"Whatevs," she says. "Well then, the big dude with the hair came back. Which, by the way, has piqued my interest in the sport of football. If they are out there looking like him, my cute little ass is gonna be parked in front of a TV every Sunday."

"Sadie! For the love of God, tell me if I'm fired or not!" *And stop reminding me about*

TK's ass.

"Sorry. Geez." She sighs into the phone and starts talking before I hang up and call Phil my damn self. "So the big guy comes back. Moore or something. And Phil apologizes straight to him this time. Telling him you're fired, and I'm not shitting you, this Moore guy had just sat down, and as soon as Phil said it, he stood back up, looking like a fucking angry giant and just towers over him, saying, 'She is not.' Just like that. With this deep-as-shit voice, he tells Phil if he fired you, he'd make sure nobody came back to the club. Phil looked like he was about to shit himself!"

Sadie breaks into a fit of giggles. I, on the other hand, have to find a bench to sit on. TK went head to head with my boss so I could keep a job he made clear he thought was crap.

"Isn't that great?" Sadie says through her laughter.

"Yeah. Great." I don't know what to do with this new information, I just know I can't process it with her on the phone. "Listen, thanks for filling me in, but Ace's soccer practice is about to end, so I have to go."

"Sounds good!" she says, oblivious to the

crisis I'm having. "Tell him Aunt Sadie says hi!"

"Will do." I force cheerfulness into my voice. A skill I am way too practiced at. "Bye, babe."

I slide my finger across my screen, ending the call before she has the chance to say anything else.

Owing TK is not something I need on my conscience.

I'd rather get fired.

Dramatic? Yes. But also accurate. I had a feeling last night wasn't the last time I was going to see him and now I know it.

What I don't know is what the hell I'm going to do about it.

I don't think about it for long. Anger chases the confusion clear out of my system. The audacity of this guy. To come into my life and demand answers? Maybe my last week in DC didn't stick with him, but it altered my entire life. He went on to live his dreams and I ran from everyone I knew to create a life for the person he didn't even want. TK can screw himself if he thinks talking to my boss and doing the absolute bare minimum is going to earn him brownie points. We've spent too much time apart, with too many lies and too much hurt filling the voids, for this to end in anything

40

other than disaster.

"Mom!" My green-eyed ball of sunshine runs toward me, a soccer ball at his feet and a backpack that's too big bouncing on his back, and chases away every dark thought clouding my mind. "Did you see my goals? Coach said I'm starting on Saturday!"

"You know I saw them!" I give him a high five, just as excited and proud of him as he is of himself. "And I saw that new fancy footwork you had out there."

"Oh, you saw that, did you? Just a little somethin' somethin' I picked up watching videos on YouTube."

God. This kid. Too cool for his own good.

"A little somethin' somethin'? I can't with you." I'm fast losing my battle to stay serious.

"Yeah, you know I got those skills, Mom." He wiggles his eyebrows my way and I lose any semblance of a strict mom.

"I know." I nudge him with my shoulder once I stop laughing. "You get 'em from your mama."

"Suuuurrreee."

"What?" I stop cold in my tracks. "Ace, don't make me take your soccer ball and whoop you in front of all your little friends."

"Mom, you're not faster than me and . . ." He pauses and scrunches his cute little

41

nose. "No offense, but you're old."

"I'm twenty-seven, for goodness' sakes! That hardly qualifies me for an AARP card."

"A what?"

Dammit.

Now I feel old.

"Never mind." I reach over to him, slip off his backpack, and throw it over my shoulders for our walk home. "I'm not old, though."

"I was just kidding; I know you aren't. All the boys on my soccer team and my class have crushes on you. I told them it's gross, but they don't listen to me."

Oh great. I have a bevy of nine-year-old admirers and none of age. I don't know if I should be flattered or scaling back my volunteer hours.

"Tell them I have cooties." I elbow him lightly on his shoulder.

"Already did." He smiles up at me, his lone dimple on his left cheek appearing. "*Sooooo*, Mom."

Knew it. He doesn't flash the dimple unless he wants something.

"What do you want?"

"Well, I was thinking, I really like soccer and I think flag football is super fun." He draws out the words. "But I'm gonna be in fourth grade. Don't you think maybe it's time for me to play tackle football now?"

Crap. I should've known where this was going. Tackle football is the one thing he begs for all the time and the one thing I won't budge on.

"Ace. You know how I feel about tackle football. I'm not sure if I'm ever going to want you to play, dude."

"But, Mom! I'm the only one who still plays flag. All the kids are going to laugh at me!"

"Well, when you're twenty-five without brain damage, you can thank me then."

"I won't hurt my brain, Mom. I'll tackle the right way and my helmet will fit. I promise, I'll listen to the coach and be safe."

"Ace." I put my hand on his shoulder and guide him to a shady spot in the grass to sit. "I know if you played, you'd listen to your coach and try your hardest to tackle safely. The problem is, there's no safe tackle. No matter how you tackle somebody, your brain still rattles in your head, and, buddy? Your brain is too perfect to let anything hurt it."

"I just love football." His green eyes gloss over, like they always do during this conversation.

I've tried to shield him from football for more than the TK reason. I remember going to TK's games. I remember how vicious the hits were in high school and how the coaches and trainers would put the players on the field way too soon after an injury. And when the discussion about CTE — chronic traumatic encephalopathy — began, my fears grew tenfold.

Ace is the only person I have and I'll do anything I can to protect him . . . even if it makes me the mean mom. His friends' parents think I'm a judgmental asshole because of my "no tackle football" policy. They "joke" and call me overprotective and a helicopter mom, but I couldn't care less.

Ace is the reason my heart beats, America's favorite pastime be damned.

"I'm sorry, buddy." I wrap my arms around him and close my eyes when he nestles his head into my chest. I know it's not too much longer until he's too cool for mom hugs. "How about we walk home, change out of these stinky soccer clothes, and then head to Fresh for muffins and smoothies?"

He perks up as soon as he hears Fresh. "A large smoothie?" he asks, his green eyes peeking up at me from beneath his long lashes.

"Okay, but only because I think you are the best and I'm trying to bribe you."

A smile spreads across his face, all sadness over football magically forgotten. "I like it when you bribe me. How do I get a new bike?"

Smart-ass.

"Chores," I say, and he groans. "However, I might be swayed by straight A's when school starts."

"Fine." He leans away from me and extends his hand. "Deal."

"You drive a tough bargain, kid." I accept his hand and shake it. "Now let's go . . . because you really do stink."

He bites his bottom lip, but the crinkle in his eyes can't hide the laughter he's trying to hold in. I'm guessing this is because, even though he is a nine-year-old boy, he still has a sense of smell and knows I'm not lying.

I love our walks home. I love listening to Ace chat my ear off about who said what at practice and point out the funny things we see all the way home. But today I can't focus.

Stupid TK.

He had to crash into my life. No matter how hard I try to forget about seeing him — kissing him — my mind won't stop drifting back to him. And every time I laugh at something Ace says, my heart clenches and

I almost fall over with guilt.

I know I did the best I could with what I thought I had, but even that's not helping. The guilt I feel knowing TK has missed out on this amazing kid for all nine years of his life is enough to make me weep. TK was scared? Well, so was I. But when I didn't go through with it, I should've told him. I was just too afraid to be rejected again.

Breaking me out of my thoughts, Ace starts to sprint and shouts, "Race you!" the second we turn onto our street.

"Cheater!" I squeal, trying to catch him but knowing it's no use.

He might be a smart-ass like me, but when it comes to athletics, he's all TK.

"Ha! Losing your touch, Mom." He laughs in my face as I reach the gate I've been meaning to paint for the last year in front of our house a good ten seconds after him.

"What —" I put my hands on top of my head to try to slow my breathing. "Ever. You cheated and I'm in flip-flops." I try to save face.

"Yeah . . . sure." The little creep purses his lips and nods.

He deserves no response.

I pull open the gate, cringing a bit at how loud the squeak is getting and add WD-40 to the running grocery list in my head.

Just like every time I make my way up the walkway to our front door, happiness flows through me. There may be a lot of projects I'd like to get done to the house, but even so, I love it.

Our little bungalow in Denver's historic Five Points neighborhood is my most treasured possession, after Ace, obviously. With its violet shutters, turquoise flower boxes, and mint door, I'm sure any HOA-regulated neighborhood would have a coronary. It's everything I dreamt of when I was a Barbie-toting little girl, but so much more because it was Maya's.

When I was sixteen, pregnant, and terrified — and years ahead of what could've been a lucrative MTV opportunity — Aunt Maya was the only person in my life who didn't give up on me. Not only did she not give up on me, she took me in when my parents put me out, severing the final threads of an already strained relationship with her sister (aka Tiana Patterson, aka my mother). She was like my fairy godmother. I admired the life she lived. Always giving, never judging — the picture of grace and kindness. She brightened my life every day.

Then, when she passed suddenly two years ago, she left her house and her old but safe and reliable Volvo S40 to me and made it very clear she felt the same way about me and Ace as we felt about her.

Over the years, we became a package, the three of us.

And I miss her every single day.

"Ace!" Jayden, Ace's friend from school who fortunately — or unfortunately — lives at the end of our block, yells out before I can unlock the front door. "Can you come over to my house? My dad got me the new NBA game for my PlayStation; you can be Curry! And he said you can spend the night!"

Freaking Jayden.

Everyone knows nothing can beat out Curry and sleepovers . . . not even muffins and smoothies.

"No way!" Ace shouts back before turning pleading green eyes my way. "Can I, Mom, please?"

"Fine," I concede, even though I really want to force him to stay with me and enjoy some freaking mother-son bonding.

"She said yes!" He punches the air above him and takes off toward Jayden, who's waiting on the sidewalk in front of our gate.

"Wait!" I stop him before he gets too far. "You still have to change and shower before you go. Mr. Lewis is nice, but even he doesn't want to catch a whiff of your soccer pits."

"A fast shower?"

"As long as you wash everything thoroughly with soap, I don't care how long you're in there." If I've learned anything from being Ace's mom, it's that kids are disgusting. They'd rather be the parade leader to hundreds of flies than take a decent shower.

"I'll be there in four minutes," Ace tells Jayden before shooting through our open door, throwing off his clothes behind him as he runs.

"Probably closer to twenty," I amend to Jayden.

"Sounds good, Miz P." Jayden turns on a heel to walk back to his house but spins in my direction again before I can go inside . . . not like I ever go inside without watching him make it to his house. "Oh! And my dad told me to tell you to come over too."

I bet he did.

I fight the urge to roll my eyes, but since they are already twitching, I'm not sure my efforts are successful.

Lesson for all those interested: Don't sleep with your kid's friend's dad . . . especially when said dad lives five houses down.

Life mistake number 8,749.

Don't get me wrong, Cole wasn't bad, but so not worth the constant texts and awkward touching when our kids weren't looking. The latter becoming increasingly annoying and pervy.

"I have to work tonight, but tell your dad I said thanks for the invitation." My voice has risen about thirty decimals on the peppy-o-meter, but luckily for me, nine-year-old boys are oblivious to fakeness.

"Okay, Miz P. Thanks for letting Ace come over."

"You're welcome." I smile at the sweet kid who's at my house almost as much as I am. "You both better listen to your dad, 'kay?"

"We always do!"

"Suuuurrrreee." I shake my head and wave, knowing that's a damn lie. I like Jayden, but listening to anybody, especially his dad, isn't his strong point.

I stand on my porch and watch Jayden until he pulls open his front door and disappears into his house. I go inside, tossing my shoes onto the rug guarding the original hardwoods, and head to the kitchen to use the old rotary phone mounted on the wall. I have a cell phone, but there's something super satisfying about the twirling and clicking of an old house phone. Mrs. Duncan answers after the second ring and tells me

50

she'll be heading to Black Hawk to gamble tonight now that she's off babysitting duties.

"Live your best life, Mrs. Duncan."

"Child, I've been living my best life since you were only a twinkle in your parents' eyes."

I know she can't see me, but that doesn't stop me from snapping my fingers as I tell her, "I know that's right."

I place the phone back on the cradle and walk to Ace's room just in time to see him shoveling football cards and mismatched clothes into his backpack.

"Got everything?" I ask.

"Yup!" He zips up the bag and tosses it over his shoulders. "See ya!"

He starts to run, but I step in front of his door, preventing his clean break.

"Aren't you forgetting something? Maybe an 'I love you, best mom in the entire world'?"

He shakes his head and rolls his eyes but plays along with me anyways.

"Love you, Mom." He wraps his arms around me, giving me a quick squeeze.

"Love you too." I pull him in even tighter, talking to the top of his curly-haired head. "Don't forget your manners. Please and thank you and go to bed when Mr. Lewis says so. 'Kay?"

"I always do." He tells me what I already know.

"I know." I let him go and clear his path to video game glory. "I'll see you tomorrow."

"See ya!" He bursts into the hallway, out the front door, and is halfway to Jayden's by the time I reach the porch.

I wave to Cole when he lets Ace in and then hustle back inside and to my bathroom. Tonight might not be going as planned, but at least I'll have ample time to focus on my hair and makeup. Maybe if I look my best, Phil will have mercy and not stick me at the shitty tables.

Worth a try.

FOUR

As it turns out, Phil finds desertion to be the worst offense a person can commit. I guess he was in ROTC in high school or something. And even though he decided to defend our country by providing a high-quality night out instead of joining the military, he still stands strong behind these convictions.

I just hope he gets over this quickly because I've been here for three hours and I've made half of what I normally make in one. And without the perk of good tips, I'm about 1.26 seconds away from throwing my stilettos at him and quitting.

I'm also stuck with the most obnoxious bachelor party in the history of bachelor parties. Who has a flipping bachelor party on a Tuesday?

Bachelor parties on any given day mean drunk, dumb assholes. Tonight you can add loud and too handsy — which I *do not* handle well — to the list. But considering I almost lost my job yesterday, it's in my best interest not to cause a scene tonight, something Jacob, who I have not-so-lovingly dubbed Best Man Douchebag, is making very difficult.

"Hey, baby," he slurs. "Why don't you show us some of your moves?"

"I'm not a performer." I take a small step backward and point to the stage only ten feet away. "I think there are a few chairs open if you'd like me to go hold one for you."

"I know where the stage is. I'm drunk, not blind, woman." Jacob tries to wiggle his eyebrows at me, but it looks like he might be having a stroke. "Which is why I wanna see *yooouuu* dance."

"Sorry, I just deliver drinks." I also suffer from an ailment of zero rhythm, but that's really not the point at all. I turn to head back to the bar to get the order of tequila shots Groom Douche-bag called for.

These jerks better tip well.

I manage to take only two steps before a sweaty hand wraps around my arm and pulls me back.

"Don't be like that." His hot breath burns my skin and turns my stomach. "Just one little dance, maybe in the back room."

Disgusting.

I pull away, but before I can make my escape, his arm is around my midsection, pulling me back until his erection is pressing against my back.

Don't get fired. Don't get fired. Don't get fired.

I remind myself of all of Ace's activities and the back-to-school shopping I'll have to do soon as I search the room for Dane or Jerome or any of the flipping bouncers we have scattered throughout the club.

Of course, when I actually need one of them, they're nowhere to be found.

Who's deserting who now, Phil?

Dick.

Best Man Douchebag moves his hand up my arm and to my neck and I'm almost positive he's leaving a snail's trail of slime in his path. "Your skin is so soft," he yells, like his mouth isn't mere inches from my ear. "And I like your hair."

Then he does it. He buries his fingers in my hair and asks, "Is it yours?"

Oh no.

Hell no.

I raise my foot up while at the same time twisting sideways, bringing my elbow forward, preparing to break his foot and hopefully injure an internal organ or two.

But before I can strike, commotion in front of us causes him to drop his grip on me.

"No fucking way!" the one guy in the group who's managed to keep a semblance of self-respect yells. "TK Fucking Moore."

Oh, give me a break!

My eyes snap to him, giving him the dirtiest look I can manage.

I hold his eye contact, not wanting to be the one who looks away first, but while I'm being stubborn, I notice a few unwanted details. Details like how, God help me, he really is the perfect male specimen. His long hair is pulled back into a bun — which, over the years, has become my panty kryptonite — and his beard, though still thick, looks like it's been trimmed since last night. His tight black sweater outlines every hard ridge on his chest and his jeans are snug enough to showcase his muscular legs but loose enough to seem as if he's not trying to look like sex on a stick.

Ugh!

Since when do quads turn me on?

Why? Why couldn't he be balding with a beer belly from a drinking problem?

But even looking so damn fine, why the hell is he here? To screw with me . . . again?

I drop a hand to my thigh and pinch it as

hard as I can to remind myself not to shove my heel right up his ass.

"Are you shitting me?" Jacob, who seconds before wouldn't leave me alone, stiff-arms me out of his way. "You're the man! The Mustangs gonna bring it home this year?"

"That's the plan," TK mutters, his stupid, gorgeous eyes never leaving mine. "Mind if I steal your waitress for a second?"

"Not a problem, man. Don't blame you, she's hot as fuck." Jacob grabs my arm — again! — and guides me toward TK, but this time his fingers bite into my skin a little deeper. It's not that the pain is excruciating, but it does surprise me, which makes me flinch. And when I flinch, Jacob's alcohol-glazed eyes narrow in on his grip and a smile starts to form on his psychotic lips.

Best Man's not looking at my face, so he misses it when I try to murder him with a look and the way my lips pull back, revealing all my teeth, like a dog about to attack. TK, however, does not.

With a speed and strength I didn't know he was capable of, TK moves me to his side and then his warm, not sweaty, and — begrudgingly — comforting hand is wrapped around mine.

"Whoa there, Sparks," he whispers in my

ear. "Glad to see your fire never went out."

He doesn't let go of my hand as we navigate our way through the douche brigade.

"I swear to God, TK." I yank my hand out of his grip once we've put some distance between us and the bachelor party. "Why are you here? I am not in the mood to deal with your bullshit tonight."

"The way I saw what just went down, you should be thanking your lucky stars I showed up when I did." His lips curl under his mustache and the jerk laughs. Laughs!

Wrong response.

"Actually." I stop and poke him in the chest with my finger, wishing it was something sharper and I could inflict some damage. "You're the reason I was stuck over there!" I poke him again. "I had it covered, I didn't need you to save me."

"Poppy." He says my name like some joke I'm not aware of. "I wasn't saving you. You think I forgot the way your eyes glaze over and you seem to grow ten inches when you're pissed? I saw that and decided to step in and save the son of a bitch from getting his ass kicked in front of all his friends — not that he didn't deserve it. Plus . . ." He shrugs and his pectoral muscles taunt me. "I figured your boss might not look fondly on you desecrating his customers."

He's right, I would've been fired and most likely facing assault charges. I just can't let him know I know he's right. "You could've grabbed a freaking bouncer!" I point to Jerome, who's too busy flirting with Rochelle to notice anything on the floor. "But no, TK 'Football God' Moore just had to save the day, didn't he?"

"You think I'm a god?"

He would only hear that part.

"I really can't stand you." I close my eyes and throw back my head, sending up a silent prayer not to go to jail tonight. "*You* think you're a god. And what are you doing here again?"

"You think I'm a god!" he sings out, drawing even more attention to himself. "I brought some of the rookies. Mini camp is in a week and they were bored and sad and missing their mommies, so I figured, what can get your mind off your mom better than scantily clad women?"

"You're ridiculous." I roll my eyes so hard, I worry for a second they might get stuck in the back of my head.

TK has always been fun and playful, something I see in Ace every time he's with his friends. Always the center of attention, making everyone around him laugh and smile. I used to crave being on the receiving end of his silliness, now I'd pay him to leave me alone.

Except he's loaded and I'm not, so I don't offer him my tips.

"Come outside with me for a bit?" he asks, oblivious to my wanting to end him. "I ordered them a ton of food and bottle service, so they'll be fine on their own for a while." He looks up to the third floor and rubs his hands against his jeans.

"I don't think so," I say. "Phil's still pissed about yesterday, I don't think taking extra breaks is in my best interest tonight."

And I don't trust myself to be alone with him. I'll either kiss him or choke him . . . but I'm not sure which one.

"It's fine," he reassures me. "I talked to Phil when we came in. I told him I'd recommend this place to all my teammates, but I needed to talk to you without him interrupting this time."

My mouth falls open and I put my tray on the unoccupied table beside us.

"You can't do that." I put my hands on my hips instead of wrapping them around his throat like I really want. "Seeing you once in ten years does not give you the right to come into my work and talk to my boss about me."

"Please, Poppy." He tucks a stray piece of

hair behind my ear. "Yesterday didn't go well. I just want to talk to you without the running and screaming. Just for a minute."

"I'm busy." I pick up the tray, prepping for my escape.

"Please," he says again. "I promise, after we talk, I won't come back again."

I would like it if he didn't come back again.

I inhale deeply, thinking it might be a mistake before I even agree. "Just for a minute."

"Thank you." He smiles and the wrinkles around his eyes — another thing he didn't have ten years ago, something else I find extremely attractive — deepen.

I don't respond.

I don't know how to.

Instead, I turn on my heel and walk to the exit, already regretting saying yes.

We walk out the same door we went through last night and move to the same spot. Exactly the same, but something is different.

Last night, we were high on shock and anger. Tonight, something else is lingering around us.

Maybe it's the echo of our kiss. The warm June breeze mimicking TK's touch against my cold, exposed skin.

Or maybe it's all the secrets we're holding back, physically attacking us. Pushing us together before they rip us apart.

"Go out with me." TK breaks the silence.

"What?" I ask even though I heard him loud and clear.

"Come out with me," he repeats.

"TK, no." I shake my head, moving away from him.

"Poppy, yes." He moves toward me, closing the distance I tried to create.

"I told you yesterday, I'm not the same girl you knew." I gesture to my costume, something I regret as his gaze follows my hands, his eyes heating, lingering on my bare legs. "You don't really want to go out with me. We didn't have a real ending. You want closure and I understand why, but we don't have to date to do it."

"Wrong, Sparks." He reaches for my hair and tugs it lightly, forcing me to look up at him. "This isn't about closure."

"It is." And if it isn't, it will be soon. I might not have social media or follow football, but I'd have to live under a rock not to know TK's acquired quite the reputation during his time in the League. I can't, nor do I want to, compete with the women he has at his beck and call. The only thing I need to focus on is telling him about Ace.

"No. It. Isn't." He still keeps his grip in my hair, but now his other hand is at the base of my back, bringing me even closer to him. "The thing is, I thought I had closure. You left. I went to school. It was closed. But then I see you yesterday, wide-eyed and scared, fuckin' scared to see me. And when I went after you, I found you."

"It's not like I was hiding." I gesture to the open parking lot. "I wasn't hard to find."

"That's not what I meant," he grinds out. "I *found* you, Poppy. As soon as I touch you, something in your eyes settles. I know you don't know it, because it's the only part of your body you don't have guarded, the one place this mask you're wearing doesn't hide. But I saw it, and without you even knowing it, you told me you're still mine. I don't know what happened while I was gone, but I'm gonna fix whatever is broken."

"TK." I close my eyes, not sure how to feel.

"Open your eyes, Poppy." He lets go of my hair and lifts up my chin, dusting his thumb across my cheek as he goes.

"I'm not yours and you can't fix me," I whisper.

"I know I fucked up. I was a stupid kid, and when I left for school, I was selfish. But

63

a lot changed in the time we were apart. I grew up." His voice is gentle, but it feels like a warning. "I know what I want and I protect and fight for it. And right now, I want you."

This is my chance. *Tell him about Ace, get it over with!*

I open my mouth, Ace on the tip of my tongue. But before I can say anything, TK's mouth is on mine, erasing all the reasons to tell him about Ace right away.

His tongue coaxes mine, twisting and tangling, and I feel it straight down to my core.

He pulls away, biting my bottom lip before he lets go and takes a step back. I feel the loss of his body pushing against mine as soon as the breeze hits my face. But when I look up at his face and the way he's looking at me?

Holy shit.

It takes my breath away. Nobody has looked at me like that for . . . well . . . for ten years.

"See?" he asks. "Settled."

He's right.

I hate it when he's right.

"When's your next night off?"

"Sunday." I don't know why I tell him . . . besides never wanting him to stop touching me and everything to go back to how it was before my life exploded into a million pieces.

"Sunday night then." He tugs on the end of my hair, smiling when I narrow my eyes and shake my head free. "I'll pick you up at your place."

" 'Kay." I try to keep the panic of TK knowing where I live from showing. I guess I'm successful because there's only a quick peck on my lips before he takes his phone out of his back pocket, unlocks it, and shoves it into my hands.

"Call your phone, then save my number."

" 'Kay," I say . . . again. Because not being awkward for ten minutes is too much to ask.

I do as he asks/demands/suggests, knowing with every digit of my number I should hit the Delete button and end this for real. But I don't. Because, again, why wouldn't I take up an offer to potentially blow up the nice, secure life I've created for me and Ace?

I hand him his phone, my number now his most recent call, and hope I'm not ruining three lives by doing so. He looks at it, the bright glow of the phone illuminating his face. I take the moment to stare at him, to notice the different shades in his beard — the same colors that highlight Ace's hair each summer — the way the lines in his

forehead deepen when he raises his eyebrows, a look, I've noticed, he does often.

He taps the button on the side and it goes
dark, not giving me enough time to avoid
getting caught staring at him.

"You can stare all you want on Sunday, I
know I will."

I forgot how well he disguises his smooth
as sweet . . . and I forgot how easily I fall
for it.

"Whatever." I half roll my eyes, so not
committed I can't even convince myself I
mean it.

I head back inside, half because I need to
go back to work, half because I no longer
trust myself to be around him. He follows a
step behind me the entire way and I feel his
gaze burning a hole into my ass as I walk.

The dim lights and loud music are a
welcome distraction when we step onto the
floor. I walk straight to the bar, ignoring the
look on Sadie's face, and pick up my tray. I
do, however, chance a quick glance at TK
as he walks past me, heading back to the
third floor.

Sunday, he mouths.

This time I don't fight the smile spreading across my face. *Sunday,* I mouth back.

Maybe this will be good. We can recon-
nect, remember why we used to be so good

together, and then I'll tell him. It could take some of the sting out of the blow.

Or maybe not.

FIVE

"You better fucking spill!" Sadie, finally out of patience, yells in sync with her makeup and garment bags hitting the floor in my entryway.

"Mouth!" I scold, but she's having N.O.N.E. none of it. I've been dodging this for days and I'm out of evasive moves.

"Oh, hush. You already told me Ace was at a soccer sleepover. We're grown as fuck and I will cuss if I want to." Color starts to rise in her porcelain cheeks. They're getting so red, they almost match her fire-engine hair. "You've been avoiding me since Tuesday and I want to know what the fuck is going on!" She stomps her foot and glitter falls from her jeans, dusting my hardwood floors.

I throw my head back and groan. "We're going to need wine." I knew we were going to have this conversation tonight, so I made sure my wine selection was on point . . . even though Sadie will only drink Moscato.

It's the biggest point of contention in our friendship.

"Really?" Her brows knit together and she drops her hands from her hips, forgetting her anger. "Didn't you just meet him?"

"Sadie." I grab her hand and drag her through my living room and into my kitchen.

My house, while small, is packed with personality. My kitchen is my favorite room.

Maya had been talking about remodeling the kitchen for months before she passed. She kept putting it off and putting it off until it was too late. And on top of everything sucking, walking into the dated kitchen she hated but thought she had time to change sucked even more.

So I decided to do something about it. Now, even though Maya left me some money, I tucked the vast majority of it into Ace's college fund. The rest went to her funeral. Which meant doing the kitchen had to be finished not only in stages but on a seriously tight budget.

Luckily for me, I live in the age of Pinterest and free classes at the local Home Depot.

I did the counters first. I found out you could fake butcher block countertops by using pine panels. Considering my kitchen is the size of a postage stamp, the grand total came to under a hundred buckaroos. Cole let me borrow his tools, and in a day? Voilà! New countertops. A few months later, I painted the top cabinets a bright white and the same mint color as our front door for the bottoms. A few months — and some very large tips — after I splurged on a white subway tile backsplash. It cost too much money and I regretted it for weeks, but now it's my favorite part. Then, last month, I was bored on the Internet and stumbled upon a stainless steel side-by-side refrigerator on Craigslist for a steal!

Yeah, sure, my appliances don't match yet, but give me a couple of years. It's going to be fab.

I don't have to say anything to Sadie as we walk in. This is a practiced routine of ours. We are so good at it, in fact, that if navigating the kitchen were an Olympic sport, we'd get the gold every time.

She grabs two wineglasses with different-colored stems, even though I drink red wine like a grown-up and she drinks juice like a boozy toddler. I hand her bottle over to her and tuck mine under my arm as I pull the wine opener I glued a magnet to off the fridge and swing the door shut.

Once we both have full glasses, not that

quarter-of-a-glass crap some people pull, we move to my living room and plop down on Maya's worn-to-perfection charcoal sectional.

"So . . . ," Sadie draws out, staring at me over the edge of her wineglass. "You ready to talk?"

I take a large gulp of my Malbec. "No." I need a minute for this to kick in before I spill the beans.

"Then I'll start." She puts her wineglass on one of the coasters Ace made me for Christmas three years ago and tucks her legs underneath her. "TK Moore. Starting wide receiver and known party boy of the Denver Mustangs."

Shit.

I should've started.

"Sad—" I start, but stop when Sadie does a superaggressive zipper motion in front of my mouth.

"No." She points in my face, the redness coloring her face again. "I gave you tons of chances to tell me and you didn't. So I went looking in other places and now you get to hear what *I* found out."

I settle back and swallow another mouthful of wine.

"So . . . TK. Football and parties." She picks up where she left off. "Two things you avoid like the plague. And not only does he party . . . he *parties.* The only reason all those Mustang players were at Emerald Monday night is because Rochelle partied with him over the weekend and promised him all sorts of shit if they came to us."

Oh my god.

I might get sick.

Rochelle? Out of everybody in the entire state of Colorado, TK and I have *her* in common?

Disgusting.

Rochelle has hated me since my first day at the Emerald Cabaret. I'm not sure why, I just know she does. And if she has her eyes set on TK — which, let's be honest, who wouldn't? — and saw him talking to me? I'm more screwed than I ever dreamed.

And considering I already dreamt I was pretty screwed . . . this is really bad.

Every word coming out of Sadie's pink-painted lips twists my insides tighter and causes the throbbing in my head to become so extreme I'm willing to do anything to make her stop talking.

"TK is Ace's dad!" I blurt out the secret I've been keeping since my parents sent me packing.

"What?" she screeches, leaping off my couch like a jackrabbit. "You said you didn't

know who Ace's dad is!"

She repeats the lie I told her.

"I lied." I put my glass on the coaster next to hers and hug a yellow throw pillow next to me. "TK is Ace's dad. He was the only person I'd ever slept with up until a couple of years after Ace was born."

"Are you insane?" she asks, but seeing as I'm not quite sure, I don't answer. "Your baby daddy is one of the highest-paid guys on the Mustangs and you're dropping drinks to sleazy dudes in decent suits to pay your fucking bills? And then . . . he has the audacity to show up . . . after doing whatever he did with Rochelle and cause a scene at your job. And then, after all of that, you agreed to go out with him? I repeat . . ." She stops pacing, drags her hands through her long, wavy locks, and pulls them out so she looks like she stuck her finger in a light socket. "Are you insane!" She screams the words, but I don't flinch, and in my re-action, she finds her answer. "You never told him," she whispers.

"I couldn't."

"Poppy . . . what . . . why?" She picks up her wineglass and chugs what's left, like this subject is mentally draining for her. "How could you not tell him?"

"I tried."

She plops on the couch beside me and doesn't say a word. She just purses her lips and aims her judgmental side-eye my way.

"I mean, I did tell him . . . initially." I sit up straight, on the defensive even though she's silent. "I sent him a text message saying I was pregnant. He didn't respond so I took the bus all the way to his bougie-ass neighborhood, trekked my way past all the rude old people who looked at me like you're looking at me now, and when I got there, his mom told me TK didn't want a baby. She said he had a future to protect and it didn't include being a teen father. Then she handed me a check for five hundred dollars to get an abortion." I shrug, trying to downplay the exact moment my soul was crushed.

"What a bitch." Sadie says the understatement of the century.

"That's not even the end of it." I pull the pillow closer, probably misshaping it for the rest of time. "I called him when I left, hoping to talk to him, hear his words. And a girl answered his phone. I was sixteen and pregnant and he already had another girl answering his phone. I didn't call him again. I sent him a text saying I'd get the abortion, but when I got to the clinic, I panicked and ran. I just never told him I changed my mind."

This is the first and last time I've told this story. I hate how weak it makes me look. How pathetic. Being a strong single mom is one thing. Being a broken, stupid girl, pregnant by a guy who she loved but didn't love her back, is another.

"We need refills." She points to my glass with a little bit left. "Drink."

I do what she says, mainly because I was going to do it already but also because that's Sadie for you. Always prepared for a glitter bombing, but not so much for ten years' worth of mental baggage.

She nabs the glass out of my hand and hightails it to my kitchen and returns with bottles instead of glasses.

"Sades, I can't get drunk before he gets here," I protest . . . but still take the bottle from her hand.

"I know. But this is a lot, I might need to take your bottle after I finish mine."

"So I guess I'm doing my own makeup?" I ask.

"You're a big girl. You should've thought about this before you dropped a nuclear bomb on me." She waves the bottle around like a magic wand. "You know I don't have the coping abilities to deal with this."

Touché. I did meet her in a club. I bet a therapist would have a field day with us.

We sit on my couch in silence, both lost in our thoughts, a dangerous place.

Sadie speaks first. "Did you really think he wouldn't want to know?"

"I don't know." I want to say yes, continue the lie I've worked so hard to convince myself of. "TK was fun. Everyone knew it. Hell, from the look of things and what Rochelle told you, he still is. He told me his decision and I didn't think it was fair to force mine on him."

"But you didn't even give him a chance to step up." She raises her voice a bit. "You didn't give Ace a chance to know him."

I know who she's getting mad at.

And I know it's not me.

But that doesn't mean I don't have to close my eyes and count to ten before I respond to her.

"I am not your mom, Sadie." My tone is gentle but firm enough that she snaps out of whatever flashback she was stuck in. "I was a sixteen-year-old girl. He didn't want a baby and my parents kicked me out of the house without so much as a farewell. I did the best I could with what I had. And Ace is happy. He's spent the last nine years of his life rooted in love and stability, something I couldn't have guaranteed for him if TK was in our lives."

"I'm sorry." She puts the bottle on the table and grabs my hand. "You know I think Ace is the shit and you're the best mom ever. But now TK knows you're here. Are you going to tell him?"

I take my free hand and grab my bottle of wine. "I have no idea."

Then I finish the bottle.

SIX

"Damn, Poppy, it must be said, you wear your work uniform well, but nothing can compare to those jeans," TK tells me as I walk toward him after I knock down all the bowling pins . . . again.

About an hour after the wine had magically vanished, TK texted me and told me to dress casual and to wear socks — a wardrobe request I found odd until I realized my feet would be in rented shoes. Punch Bowl Social is a restaurant/club/arcade/bowling alley I've wanted to try for years but never did on account of its being always packed and my having a nine-year-old.

It's packed again tonight. However, when you're TK Moore, they figure shit out.

I wish I wasn't impressed . . . but I hate waiting and it was really freaking impressive.

"Oh no." I shake my head, the laughter

coming often and easily. "Don't try and throw my game by complimenting me, and also, don't be that guy."

"What guy?" He raises his eyebrows and looks more adorable than a man with long hair and a beard should be able to. "What did I do?"

"The creepy guy." I tug his beard, unable to keep my hands off it. "Who needs to shave and watches girls' butts from behind his overgrown facial hair."

He doesn't pull away and I don't let him go, so I'm able to see the glint in his eyes up close. "I lost track of how many times you just insulted me."

The little touches started as soon as I sat my butt down in his blacked-out Range Rover. His fingers would graze my thigh after he changed the radio station. I'd grab his arm when he said something that made me laugh . . . which was all the time.

This is our second game of bowling and I'm kicking his butt. It's almost unnerving how well this is going. I thought it'd be awkward, like at the Emerald Cabaret. But it turns out, when I'm dressed in regular clothes and we aren't hanging out in a parking lot, things are just as easy as they used to be.

"Oh my god!" A shrill voice from over my

shoulder causes me to jump and let go of his beard. I don't have to turn around to see who the intruder is because she shoulders her way in between me and TK before I even have a chance to move. "TK Moore! You are seriously the *only* reason I watch football. Well" — she flips her long, clearly dyed blonde hair over her shoulder and it slaps me in the face — "your pants are."

I start choking. Whether it's from a stranger's hair getting in my mouth or her desperate pickup line, I'm not sure. What I am sure of is it being enough to pull TK's annoyed face from hers to mine.

"You all right there, Sparks?"

I shake my head. "There's hairspray in my mouth and I don't own hairspray." I cringe and resist wiping my tongue with my fingers, considering they were just inside bowling ball holes.

I start to have a mini meltdown. I jump up and down, shaking my hands and head, whining with my tongue hanging out of my mouth. The perp is standing in front of me, not even acknowledging my presence, but lucky for me, TK turns around and grabs his glass of water, a stack of napkins, and comes to me.

He puts a hand to the back of my head. A hand, I should note, so large he palms the entire backside of my head, wild curls and all. I not only feel but see him shaking with laughter as he brings a napkin up to my mouth and wipes my tongue. I try to narrow my eyes in his direction, but I can't. Because I'm laughing too.

"Here." He hands me the glass of water after my tongue has been wiped clean. "Have a sip."

I take the glass, but I don't have a sip.

No.

I gulp every last drop down and then go get my Shirley Temple off the table and finish it too.

Dramatic?

Maybe.

But her hair was *in my mouth*!

"Ugh." She groans. "It's not like I don't wash my hair."

"Why are you still here?" I ask, narrowing my eyes at the Barbie wannabe.

I don't intimidate her in the least, though; she just rolls her eyes and hands me her phone, the camera app open.

"Take a picture of me and TK." She takes a step back and — showing way too many teeth — wraps her arms around his waist, dropping her makeup-covered face onto his light gray tee.

I don't want to do it.

And I can feel it building from the depths of my soul.

I'm gonna lose my mind.

I mic-drop her phone and make my way into her personal space. "Look here, you stu—" I start, but don't finish because TK has managed to pry the skank off him and is now pulling me away.

"We're going to eat now," he says over his shoulder. "Have a good night, ma'am."

If I wasn't so pissed we had to leave the bowling game I was winning, I would've laughed at her crestfallen face at being called "ma'am."

I don't laugh.

But I do scrunch my nose and stick my tongue out at her.

Whatever. We can't always be winners.

I shake my wrist free of TK's grip when I lose sight of the witch and move beside him.

"Do they have any tables ready?" I ask, putting the previous situation behind me. "It looks really busy."

"I slipped the hostess a hundred when we walked in to keep a table open for us."

"Damn, Moore." I let out a long whistle. "Who you trying to impress?"

I laugh, bumping my hip into his. I remember asking him the same question on our first date when he came to my front door dressed in a suit jacket . . . to go to the movies.

He stops walking and turns to me, looking me dead in my eyes, and says, "You."

It takes my breath away. How can he pack so much meaning into three letters?

Ace.

The thought of him forces me to break eye contact.

"Come on." I tug on his hand. "I'm starving and I want to see *the* TK Moore work his magic."

"I'll show you my magic later," he whispers into my ear before his teeth graze it, sending shivers down my spine.

Jesus, Mary, and Joseph.

I almost just came in the middle of the restaurant.

I'm still standing in the same spot when I hear my name. "Poppy! You coming?" TK yells a few feet away from me and I don't miss the way he smirks over his choice of words.

"Ass." I roll my eyes.

"Later," he says.

I shake my head and stop talking. I bet he'll have an answer for anything I say.

He wraps his arm around my shoulder, pulling me into his side and kissing the top of my head. I'm not a huge PDA fan, but something about the sweetness of his gesture makes my heart clench inside my chest.

Ace.

I close my eyes, trying to force him out of my mind for just one night. I'll tell TK, I reassure myself. Just not tonight.

The hostess shows us to our table. It's tucked into what might be the only quiet corner in the entire place. I say thank you, followed by TK, who I see slide another bill into her palm. I try to ignore it, but a part of me who has zero business getting mad does. I've been struggling for years and he just threw away two hundred dollars so he didn't have to wait his turn.

"So," I say, when he slides into his side of the booth, unaware of my hidden resentment. "What're you gonna get?"

"Meatloaf," he answers, not even looking at the menu. "Always the meatloaf."

I stop myself right before I blurt out that meatloaf is Ace's favorite meal too.

"I make a great meatloaf," I offer instead. "It was my aunt Maya's recipe. It's the best."

"You'll have to make it for me one day." He taps my leg under the table with his foot, which reminds me of something, and I grab on to it like a dog with a bone to get off the subject of his coming to my house.

"Crap! We left our shoes!" I start to move out of the booth to go get them. I was wearing the Tory Burch flats I'd been pining over for years that Ace (well, Sadie) bought me for my birthday.

"It's fine." He motions for me to sit. "I told them before we sat down, they said they'd bring them to us."

Shoe delivery.

Another Mustang perk, I guess.

"Oh," is my lame response. "Thanks."

"Not a problem." He smiles, those green eyes so much like Ace's drilling a hole through my heart. "You have to get a punch."

" 'Kay." I flip over the menu to look at the options even though I'm not sure it's the best idea considering I'm already down a bottle of wine tonight. But clearly, I'm not the ambassador of good decisions. "They all look good," I tell him at the same time the waitress approaches.

"Can I start you with something to drink?" she asks, looking at me instead of TK, and I want to kiss her for it. I was starting to think I'd become invisible standing next to him.

I don't kiss her, or answer her for that matter, because TK orders for me.

"We'll have one of each punch," he says.

Eyes wide, I whip my head in his direc-

85

tion and a stray curl slaps me in the face.

"Do you know what you want to eat yet?" he asks, either oblivious or ignoring my look of shock. "Or do you need a couple of minutes?"

"Um, I'll have the burger, medium-well, please." I hand her my menu.

"And I'll have the meatloaf," TK orders when she turns back to him.

"Three punches?" I whisper yell after she walks away. "Are you trying to get me drunk?"

"Maybe." His lips curl up under his mustache. "How else am I going to get you to do karaoke?"

"Oh no!" I laugh at the thought of my ever doing karaoke. "I'll have to be blackout drunk for you to ever get me on a stage!"

"Then I'll have to order more," he says.

And I have a feeling he's not joking.

Seven

TK was not joking and I am drunk — with a capital D.

I drink wine, never hard liquor, and the punch hits me harder than I'd anticipated.

I'm also having more fun than I can ever remember having.

"You're lying to me!" I reach for his hand on the table. "That did not happen!"

"Swear to God." He holds up both hands in surrender. "She showed up with fucking Bundt cakes."

He's telling me about the time Lydia flew to Denver without telling him during his rookie season and went to the training facility to meet his new teammates.

"The guard at the gate had to call to get me because she refused to leave. My coaches were nice while she was there, but I got fined five thousand dollars for leaving to get her."

"Your mom's insane." I might be laughing, but I could not be more serious.

"She just loves hard." He defends her honor, which is sweet, but also bullshit. "She loved you too. She was just as sad as me when you left."

At that, my back goes straight and the happy drunk in me disappears.

"She hated me and was thrilled to see me go." I think back to her gloating face as she handed me the check and I feel the heat rising up my face. I went through a phase where I wondered if she would've been more supportive if I had been a blue-eyed blonde — and white — like her. But I realized it wasn't a racial issue — it was a crazy one.

"She was not."

I take a deep breath and try to collect my spinning thoughts. "New subject." Even though I'm not thinking my clearest, I still know this is not a safe topic for me.

"Wanna go play games?" he asks.

My shoulders sag with relief and I nod my head. He gets out of the booth before me and comes to my side, offering a hand to help me up.

He looks like such a badass — long hair, thick beard, huge muscles with tats spilling out from his sleeves — but he's such a gentleman.

I stand up, and instead of letting my hand go, he winds his long fingers through mine, holding on tight as we weave through the crowd. He stops for pictures when a few groups recognize him, but he never lets them give me the camera, and even though I try to move out of every shot, he keeps me firmly at his side.

"You know they're gonna Photoshop me out of those pictures when they get home, right?"

"I doubt it." He looks down at me, barely missing a drink tray as he does. "They'll probably look at it, see how hot you are, and take me out."

"You are so full of it!" I laugh, but my cheeks heat at his compliment.

We break through the crowd and into the hallway leading to the arcade. The walls are painted a bright teal but there's a break of white-painted brick with the words "i love you so much" in red graffiti.

"Picture?" TK points to the graffiti.

I bite my lip and nod, unsure why, after all the shit we've shared, *this* makes me turn into a shy schoolgirl.

He stops a couple of girls walking past us and asks them to take our picture. We both hand them our phones and TK pulls me fast and tight into his chest. I look up at him, laughing so hard my side aches, and he looks down at me, lines crinkled around his eyes, smiling just as big as I'm sure I am.

We don't even turn to look at the girls with our phones before they're handing them back to us. It's clear they have no idea who TK is, because they just seem annoyed that they agreed to do us a favor. Not honored that the almighty TK Moore directed his attention their way for a moment.

I like them.

We follow the girls to the stairs, me behind them, TK insistent on walking behind me.

"Such a good view, Sparks," he says when we reach the top floor.

I don't say anything this time. I just roll my eyes and keep walking . . . maybe with a little extra swing in my hips.

"Oh!" I jump when I see the arcade games and turn to TK. "Wanna play Ping-Pong?"

"If you want, but . . ." He pauses and his face changes. The smile disappears and he tenses up. "This isn't gonna be like bowling. I am going to kick your ass."

I slap his shoulder and a supersexy snort slips out. "In your dreams, buddy."

If I thought TK let me win at bowling, the way he kicks my ass at Ping-Pong and every other video game the arcade offers would've proved me wrong.

"Whatever," I pout after losing another game of Ping-Pong. "I still kicked your ass at bowling."

"Keep clinging to that." He leans down to kiss me, and like the sore loser I am, I turn my head so his lips hit my cheek. "Will a milkshake make you feel better?"

"Yes," I answer, and let him kiss me this time.

What can I say? Ice cream can always get you back in my good graces.

We walk back to the restaurant and I'm not shocked to see they saved our table for us. Or at the fact that TK offers up another money-filled handshake upon this discovery.

"Two chocolate milkshakes, please," he orders when our same waitress comes back.

"Sorry I beat you so bad." He sounds sincere, but the smile confirms his lies.

"You're so full of it." I roll my eyes and pretend to be annoyed, but I'm pretty sure he knows I'm full of it too.

"I'm having a lot of fun." He reaches across the table to hold my hand again. "I wasn't lying when I told you I missed you. I want to see you more."

I've been so focused on living in the moment, I blocked out everything waiting for me at home. And if I'm honest with myself,

I kind of wanted tonight to be a disaster. I wanted to reassure myself that I made the right decision by keeping Ace a secret. But the more the night goes on, the more I'm questioning every decision I've made.

When I got pregnant with Ace, I was young, scared, and alone. And even though TK was still a kid and didn't have the wealth and power he has now, he came from money. I've always been able to justify my reasoning for keeping him away by imagining TK and his family as comic book villains. Thinking that TK just moved on and was a massive, egotistical asshole who would've only harmed Ace made it easy.

As a mom, you'll do anything to protect your kids, even things that everyone from the outside looking in deem as wrong. But sitting here with TK, and realizing he's not the bad guy I had living in my head for the past nine years, has clouded my judgment.

The alcohol had been enough make me forget about my real life for a bit, but listening to him being so honest with me while I'm lying to his face makes me feel like the scum of all scum.

Ace's face, the one he makes when he sees his friends with their dads, pops into my mind. The way he conceals the sadness behind a mask of kid joy when he gives me the Father's Day present he made at school taunts me.

"We have mini camp this week, but when it's over, come over."

"I have to tell you something." I pull my hands away from him and tangle them in the bottom of my shirt.

"Oh." He looks confused, not understanding the sudden change in my demeanor. "What is it?" he prompts when I don't continue.

"I have a kid." I blurt it out before I can change my mind.

I watch him physically recoil, his back colliding with the pleather-covered seat. "Um. Wow. A kid? That's . . . that's really great, Poppy."

Poppy. Not Sparks. He's already checking out.

"Yeah," I tell him, pushing myself to tell him everything. "He's a really great kid, the best, actually."

"I'm sure he is, you're his mom."

"Thanks." My fingernails are digging into my palms and I focus on the biting pain and instead of the look of horror on TK's face. "He's nine."

I search his face for some kind of acknowledgment. For anything that shows he knows. But instead, he doesn't say anything and forces me to lay it all out there. "His name is Ace and he's yours."

There.

I did it.

Ripped off the Band-Aid and it didn't hurt nearly as bad as I thought it would.

Or so I thought.

I blink and the look of horror is gone.

Even through his beard, I can see the deep red coloring his cheeks. His eyes are so narrowed the green has disappeared and his hands are bunched fists against the table.

"Are you fucking kidding me right now?" he whispers, the softness of his voice only accentuating his anger. When I don't answer, he slams his fists against the table. The wrapped silverware jumps with me and the salt and pepper shakers fall over. "Are you fucking kidding me!" He stands up, leaning over the table, screaming in my face.

"Ace." I use the nickname I've been avoiding calling him.

"Don't you dare," he snarls. "I can't believe you'd pull this shit. I know I have to deal with accusations like this, it comes with the territory. And for six fuckin' years I have. I let them roll off my back. I don't let people get too close and I keep my eyes wide open. Do you know how hard it is to never open up, to never trust someone?

94

Then I see you again and I think I can let my guard down for a night . . . one night! And then you pull this? You?" He points a shaky finger at me. "You find me and think what? That you found your meal ticket? That you can pin some kid on me?"

"What?" Now I'm the one pulling away. "Pinning a kid on you? Ace is yours. Just because I didn't go through with the abortion *you* wanted doesn't mean you get to act clueless in all of this."

I had a lot of scenarios in my head. Most of them did not end well. But not once did I think TK wouldn't believe Ace was his.

"Abortion? You're so full of shit." He's still leaning over the table, trying to intimidate me with his size. "You work at a fuckin' club, Poppy. It's clear you're not living your best life. I'm back and you see your chance." He smiles, but there's nothing friendly about it. "What? You get knocked up when I left for school knowing I'd find somebody better than you?"

It would've hurt less if he'd punched me in the face.

I blink more times than is normal and try to pick my jaw up from the table where it is no doubt resting.

I don't even know this person in front of me. When we dated, TK was the calm, even-tempered one in our relationship. Where I would jump to conclusions and occasionally — maybe more than occasionally — lose my ever-loving mind, TK always measured his responses. Every word that passed through his lips was well thought out and calculated. And on the rare occasions when we did fight, he would walk away before he *ever* said anything that would hurt me. So this TK, the one who seems to let every mean, hurtful, spiteful thought fly out of his mouth, is a stranger.

"Now you're just trying to be mean, TK. I get you're upset I didn't tell you I changed my mind, but you're pissing me off. I'm not gonna sit here so you can insult me all night."

"Then go." He points toward the entrance we came in through. "Get out of my face with this bullshit."

I try to tell myself that something isn't right, that something else is going on, but it doesn't work. I feel the burning behind my eyes start to build, which only makes me angrier.

Do not cry. Do not cry. I hold eye contact with him until the tears evaporate, no doubt from the heat of the rage boiling beneath my skin.

"Screw you, TK. I didn't even want to tell

you about Ace. I was giving you the benefit of the doubt of being young and dumb. And even though it was fucked up, you deserve to know you have a son almost as much as he deserves to have a dad." He opens his mouth to say something, but I keep going. "But let me be clear: In no way will you be allowed around my son like this. He is pure and he is loved and he is untouched by bullshit. We're fine without you. If you don't want him, it's your loss."

"I can't believe you're keeping this shit up right now." He sits back down, raking his fingers through his hair. "My mom told me not to meet up with you."

My jaw falls to the floor. Lydia Moore. The bane of my existence.

"Yeah, I lied when I told you she liked you," TK says, reading me all the way wrong.

"Like I give a single shit if your awful mother likes me." I grab my purse from beside me and throw it over my head. "But it's good to know you're finally big enough to make a decision on your own."

"You're so full of shit right now, I can't even believe it. Find some other sucker to pin your kid on." The asshole laughs.

I scoot out of the booth and stand next to TK, ignoring the crowd around us. Even

97

though I'm standing and he's sitting, we're still eye level. I block him into his seat and keep my voice low and even. No way is he getting me to act out in public. "Screw you, TK. You didn't want him. I went to your house after you were too chickenshit to even respond to the text I sent you saying I was pregnant. I went to your house. I called you, pregnant and heartbroken, and you had some other girl answering your phone. I was sixteen. Sixteen, scared, and alone at a clinic with your mom's money." I don't let go of the eye contact. He can choose not to believe me if he wants, but he's going to have to work hard to convince himself I'm lying. "You wanted to know why I moved? It's because my parents kicked me out when I told them I was pregnant. You went off to college, living your fairy tale, not even thinking about me or even trying to find out if you had a kid. Now you act like I'm the one in the wrong? This is why I ran when I saw you. I didn't want to see you. I didn't want to tell you."

"What are you even talking about right now?" He shuts his eyes and brings his fingers to his temples, pushing on his pressure points like his head is the one about to explode.

I ignore his question and point a finger in

his face, just wanting to say what I need to say so I can get the hell out of here. "You're going to think on this and one day you'll realize what a massive asshole you're being. But before you come apologizing, think really hard. If you want to be a dad, I won't stop you. But you come to fucking stay." I wait for him to acknowledge anything I've said, and when he doesn't, I prompt him, "Got me, Moore?"

"I . . ." He lifts his palms and tilts his head to the side. Maybe he had more to drink than I realized. "What?"

I don't respond. I turn on my heel and walk straight to the door. I hit Broadway with my shoulders back and my head held high and walk until I can't see Punch Bowl Social anymore. There's a group of teenage boys messing around next to a bus bench, and the mom in me wants to ask them about curfew, but the woman who just had her heart stomped on ignores them. I sit down on the bench and dig out my phone, hoping there's an Uber nearby.

The bus comes before Sam, my Uber driver, does. And sitting on the bus bench, again. After being rejected by TK, again. I let the tears I've been holding in for ten years fall. For me. For my sweet boy. For the family I've always wanted but will never have.

On a cold metal bench on Broadway, I give up all hope.

EIGHT

By the time Sam drops me off at my well-lit bungalow, I've realized one thing.

TK's rejection means nothing.

I've been doing this alone and I still will. I don't need his support or money or love. I don't need shit. Ace is a fantastic kid and I did that. Not TK. Not his mom or my parents. Me. And when he comes home in a few hours, he'll still have me.

And one day, when Ace is old enough and he asks about his dad, I'll be able to tell him I told TK. My conscience is clear. TK gets to live with this, not me.

Not one thing changed.

So screw TK and the Mustang he rode in on.

I kick off my flats and grab my phone before dropping my purse on the floor. I drag my ass to my room and collapse on my bed, still in my clothes. This is why I don't cry, this is why I don't feel. I feel like

I've run a marathon, it's freaking exhausting.

I unlock my phone and pull up the one contact I know will answer my call no matter the hour.

"Chello." Sadie yawns into the phone after the third ring.

"I told him." I waste no time with preamble, there's no point.

"No shit?" she says, sounding much more awake. Apparently life drama is the gossip equivalent to caffeine for Sadie. "How'd it go?"

"Well, I had to hike down Broadway and catch an Uber home, if that tells you anything."

"That bad, huh?"

"Understatement of the century," I say, swiping the stupid tears falling down my stupid face.

"Was he pissed you changed your mind or that you didn't tell him? Is he getting lawyers?" Her voice rises from curious to panicked in a matter of seconds. "When is he going to meet him? Are you going to need a lawyer too? I have a little in savings to help pay for one."

"No." I don't know why I didn't wait to call her. I have not recharged my emotional stability batteries enough to deal with this conversation.

"No what?" I hear her sheets rustling. "He isn't going to try any custody stuff?"

"Well, since he thinks I'm lying about Ace being his so I can get some of his money, I'm going to assume he's not interested in a shared custody agreement."

She gasps into the phone and is silent for about ten seconds. "Are you fucking kidding me?" she screams. I have to pull the phone away from my ear, afraid she might've ruptured my eardrum. "Why would you lie about that? And he found you and asked you out, not the other way around!" She's still screaming.

"I mean, I understand him having questions. You don't see someone in ten years and then they say they have your kid, who wouldn't have some? But he straight up called me a gold digger. He didn't ask to see a picture. He didn't ask when his birthday was. Nothing." I take a deep breath, willing myself not to get worked up again. "I guess it's good. He's not who I remember him being, and if this angry man is who he turned into, I don't want him in Ace's life. It's better he doesn't want in from the go."

"You're right," she says, but it's lacking any conviction. "Anyways. I was reading a

103

study on Facebook and it said lesbians raise the best kids. We can get married and raise Ace together. It's obviously the only answer."

I snort. "Obviously." I stand up and peel off my jeans, something that would've been easier without all the alcohol I had tonight. "One problem."

"What?" she asks, her voice full of curiosity.

"We aren't lesbians." I mean, I love her, but I also love penis.

"Semantics."

"You're insane, but thank you for listening to me rant and offering up an alternative solution. It was a bad one . . . but I still appreciate it."

"Maybe we could be sister wives without the husband?" she suggests.

"That's a plan I can get behind." I laugh a real laugh, which feels nothing short of a miracle after the debacle of a night I had. But it just goes to show I was right. Nothing changed. I have Ace. I have Sadie. And I have myself — and also a very reliable vibrator. What else do I need . . . besides sleep? "Thank you for listening to me bitch."

"Anytime," she says. And I know she means it. "*Aaaaand . . .* if you're still feeling down, I can always swing by and glitter dust you."

"Dear God, no. Keep that crap to yourself."

"Just a suggestion." Even though I can't see her, I know she's shrugging her shoulders, thinking I'm the weirdo for not wanting to find glitter in my hair for weeks. "See you at work?"

"Yup." I look at the clock, T minus about seven hours until Ace is back, and seventeen until work. "Later."

"Later," she repeats, and ends the call.

I take off my bra and head to the bathroom.

And what's waiting for me in the mirror is not the uplifting moment I need. My hair still looks fantastic, it's out to *there* and my curl definition is amazing. My face, on the other hand, does not. Red and swollen eyes, black smudges down my blotchy cheeks, and my lips are already starting to chap from how much I chewed on them.

I turn on the hot water, and when the steam starts to billow up, I throw my washcloth underneath the faucet. I pull it out of the water and drop it twice before I can wring it out. I lay it on my face and take comfort in the heat against my skin. I take it off and put it under the water one more time, this time, when I bring it to my face, I wipe off the remnants of mascara and tear stains.

I put on face lotion and my head scarf and turn off the lights before I climb into my bed with too many pillows. I pull up the covers, and when I close my eyes, I silently pray that, at least in my dreams, I won't have to be alone.

Maybe there, somebody will want me.

Somebody could love me in my dreams.

Someone with green eyes and a beard I didn't get to touch nearly enough.

NINE

The weeks after our date crawled by.

Mustang players obviously got the memo about the Emerald Cabaret being the place to be. Every night I dreaded walking into work, bracing for another run-in with TK. Thanks to the little bit of good luck I still have on my side, so far he's skipped the outings.

It's been a month and I'm just starting to be able to breathe easy when I show up for work each evening. Rochelle only asked once how I knew TK, and since he hasn't come back, she hasn't asked again. She's just taking full advantage of the players who do come . . . and my refusal to wait on them.

It's messed with my tips a bit, staying out of VIP, but my sanity is worth so much more.

Plus, training camp is starting soon, so I won't have to worry about them coming for a while.

"Ace is looking great out there." Cole pulls my thoughts from work to the soccer field in front of me.

"So is Jayden." I try to look up at him, but the sun is settled right over his head and not even my sunglasses can help me out. I get out of my pink soccer mom chair to stand next to him. "I hope they end up on the same team."

I'm letting Ace try out for competitive soccer this year. Jayden played last year, and other than video games, soccer is all they talk about. It's going to cost a mint, but he's not talking about football anymore, so I'll take what I can get.

Plus, with school starting soon, I can get a part-time job during the days as well.

"Me too. It'll be good for the boys and for us."

Ummm . . .

"For us?" I ask.

"Yeah, you know." He shields his eyes with a hand over his forehead . . . even though the sun isn't in his eyes. "Carpooling and stuff."

"Oh yeah," I agree, not mentioning the fact that I've never missed a game or a practice. "That'll be helpful."

"Which, speaking of, did you walk or drive today?" Cole asks.

Smooth.

Except not at all. I mentally slap myself again for sleeping with him. One moment of weakness and years of awkwardness.

"We always walk, unless the weather's insane."

"Oh, cool. Maybe we'll join you next time," he invites himself.

I don't want to be a bitch, but no.

If Cole and Jayden join us, Ace is going to talk to Jayden the entire walk, which defeats the purpose of us walking together. "I mean, you're always welcome, but it's kind of our time together," I say.

"We wouldn't want to intrude." He shoves his hands in his pockets. "We were gonna drive down to Bonnie Brae and get some ice cream since this is the last tryout if you guys want to come with."

Dammit.

It looks like Cole has discovered my weakness.

I love wine, but I adore ice cream. And Bonnie Brae ice cream is the best in Denver. They make all their ice cream in the shop and have these chocolate, sprinkle-covered cones that are downright sinful.

"I actually cannot say no to that offer," I say, and he laughs at my very serious declaration. "But would you mind if I ran home first? I made chicken in the Dutch oven and I need to take it out."

"Not a problem." He reaches over and rests his hand on my lower back.

Lucky for me the crazy soccer parents are paying attention to their kids instead of Mr. Touchy-Pants. You'd think after working at the Emerald Cabaret for as long as I have, I'd be an expert in the art of rejecting unwanted touches. And I am . . . at work. Outside of it, it's this weird gray area where I want to be assertive but not a bitch. Even though I taught Ace when he was two to keep his hands to himself, I've come to learn it was a lesson many men missed.

I'm trying to think of a polite way to get him off me when another hand taps me on the shoulder.

I turn my head and am greeted by the most beautiful and unwanted sight on the entire planet Earth.

Trevor Kyle Moore.

"You've got to be kidding me," I accidentally say out loud.

"Nice to see you too." He smirks.

I roll my eyes.

Asshole.

"Holy shit. You're TK Moore!" Cole says.

When you hate a person, you want the entire world to hate him. And out of every-

110

thing I hate about TK, everyone else adoring him is what I hate the most.

But at least Cole drops his hand.

"Why are you here?" I ask.

"You know TK Moore?" Cole asks. But he doesn't sound as excited anymore. I guess a superstar football player is only exciting before you realize he might be your competition.

He just doesn't realize I have no desire for *either* of them.

"No," I say at the same time TK says, "Yes."

"Sorry, Cole." I turn my back to TK. "I'll be right back."

I look at the soccer field and take a deep sigh of relief when I see tryouts are still going strong and Ace isn't the least bit focused on the sideline.

I walk away from the field without looking back at TK, assuming he's following behind. "What are you doing here?" I point an accusatory finger in his direction when we stop a good distance away from prying ears.

"I came to see my friends." He gestures to a couple with a stroller NASA could've designed. There's about a football field's length between us, but as soon as I look in their direction, they wave, not even attempting to be discreet in their curiosity. "They live right outside the park."

I focus my gaze a little harder. "Is that Gavin Pope?" I ask, even though I know the answer. Gavin Pope is F.I.N.E. fine. He was the only reason I peeked at games the single season he played for the Mustangs. "I thought he was in New York now."

"Yeah, and his wife, Marlee. They're here for the off-season," he says, but I knew that too. It had been all sorts of scandalous when they hooked up. I couldn't tell the difference between the gossip columns and sports sections for months. "They head back to New York next week, I was saying bye."

"Well." I shrug. "I don't want to keep you from them." I turn to leave again, but while the desire for my exit is high, the execution is low.

TK grabs my hand and stops me from going. "Wait."

"No." I snatch my hand back. I guess I am good at that outside the club. "You said everything you needed to say the last time we talked, and honestly? This isn't a good time for me."

I glance over his shoulder and my heart rate kicks up about two thousand percent when I see the boys circled around their coach in the end-of-practice huddle.

"I want to apologize." He ignores the

panic I know is written across my face. "I shouldn't have said some of the things I said to you. I was upset, but that's no excuse for the way I behaved."

He's got that freaking right.

"Cool. Apology accepted." I rush the words out, still focused on Ace's wild curls in the huddle. "I have to go."

"Aren't you going to apologize?" he asks.

Oh my God.

Was he always this big of an idiot?

"No!" I turn and shout, drawing more attention to us when I want to do the opposite. "Ugh. I mean yes. I'm sorry. I'm sorry about this entire mess, I should've told you years ago."

"You're still sticking with this story, Poppy?" His shoulders slump and the corners of his mouth turn down, like he's sad I failed a test I wasn't aware I was taking. "I didn't mean to judge you about having a kid and I'm sure he's great, but it's messed up that you're pinning him on me."

I feel my jaw tighten and the migraine only TK seems capable of giving me starts to appear. I'm ready to tell him where he can shove his nonjudgment when I hear the faint sound of a whistle. I look back to the field and I see boys running in every direction to their parents scattered around the field, but my eyes go straight to the sun-kissed mop of curls on the head of a smiling boy with emerald eyes on me.

"Shit," I whisper. "Fine. Sorry. It was messed up." I turn to him, imploring him to leave. "Is that what you wanted to hear? I said it, now can you go?"

I'm close to falling on bended knees to get him gone.

But it's too late.

"Mom!" Ace yells right before running into me just short of full speed.

I catch him with an oof from me and laughter from him.

"Coach said he'll e-mail the parents Monday about what team we make!" He's so excited to tell me the news, it takes him a minute to register that we have company. His green eyes widen as soon as they land on TK. "Holy crap!"

"Ace!" I scold . . . even though I say way worse every single day. "Mouth!"

"Sorry, Mom." He bites back his smile before looking back to TK. "Are you TK Moore?"

It's like watching a slow-motion car accident. I don't want to watch, but I can't look away.

Ace is staring at TK in awe. Born in Denver, Ace is a Mustangs fan through and through. It doesn't matter if I try to distance him from football, the Mustangs are his team and there's nothing I can do to change it. So being this close to one of their star players? It's like he's at the pearly gates and Jesus himself has greeted him.

TK, on the other hand, looks like he's been punched in the stomach. His green eyes are wide, no doubt taking in an identical pair staring back at him with his nose, single dimple, and sun-bleached highlighted hair. I always knew Ace favored TK, but seeing them together? The similarities are even stronger than I thought.

"Y-yeah, man." He stutters his answer, his eyes flying between me and Ace. "I am. And you're Ace." He recovers enough so Ace doesn't notice the internal freak-out he's having.

"You know my name?" Ace turns to me, his eyes glossed over from blissed-out joy.

"Your mom was telling me about you." TK carefully schools his features. "She said you're a big football fan."

Ace starts to answer, but I cut him off.

"Why don't you go stand by Mr. Lewis and Jayden," I say when he manages to rip his attention from TK. I can't watch this any longer. My heart doesn't know whether to break or explode and I can't chance melting down at the park. "We're gonna run home and then go get Bonnie Brae with them."

"Bonnie Brae? Can I have a sprinkle cone?" Ace asks.

"Only if you hurry over to them."

"Sweet!" His smile turns megawatt and he punches the sky above him, his curls flying across his sweat-covered forehead. "Nice to meet you, Mr. Moore," my polite boy says before shooting across the park, back to Jayden, who's on the grass, pulling off his shin guards, and Cole, who's watching me with a keen interest.

I start toward them, eager to leave this scene in the past, but I stop dead when I hear TK behind me.

"He called me Mr. Moore," he whispers.

I will myself to keep walking. *Ignore him.* I told him Ace was his and he didn't believe me. I can't deal with his emotions right now, not when I have my own set of messy ones brewing a nasty storm.

"He has my gap," he says a little bit louder.

This gets my attention.

"What?" I turn to see him still watching Ace.

"The gap in his front teeth. I had that gap. My dad did too. I was in braces from fifth grade until my freshman year."

"Yeah, the dentist told me we needed to find an orthodontist." Something else trying to push me to the brink of financial ruin.

"He looks just like me, Poppy." He pulls his gaze from Ace to me, and even though I want to stay mad at him, I can't. He looks crushed. "You weren't lying."

"I wasn't." It takes every last morsel of restraint, but I don't roll my eyes or punch him in the throat.

"He called me Mr. Moore," he repeats.

"I know."

"He doesn't know I'm his dad?"

"Honestly, TK?" I don't want to sound cruel, but I'm having a hard time stomaching the scene in front of me. "Why would he?"

He doesn't say anything. He just watches Ace again.

After a few beats of silence, I leave him to his feelings and walk away.

I turn my back on him, missing it as his beard catches his falling tears.

TEN

"Are you helping close again?" I ask Sadie with my purse on my shoulder and the doorknob in my hand.

"Yeah." She shrugs. "I told Nate I'd close out the cash registers at the bars for him."

Where I take any excuse to go home, Sadie will cover whatever task you throw at her so long as she doesn't have to go to hers.

"Call me when you get home, yeah?"

"Okay, Mom." She rolls her eyes, but I know she'll call.

"You better." I pull open the door and wave behind me. Rochelle is still in the dressing room with Sadie, but I don't acknowledge her. She'd have something bitchy to say back. And after everything with TK this afternoon, I'm not sure I have the restraint it would take not to resort to an all-out cat fight.

"Bye, guys," I shout to everyone on the floor as I head out the back door to the parking lot.

The parking lot, though never well lit, seems extra dark tonight . . . or maybe dark is just the new filter for my life. The lamp-post I parked under is out, and every gust of wind, every whisper of a car in the distance, causes me to jump and move a little quicker. I hate this creepy-ass back alley lot. I start to dig in my purse, cursing all the receipts and loose change acting as key camouflage. When they appear by what feels like magic, I get in and lock the doors before I even start the car.

Call me a scaredy cat if you want, but I've watched too many episodes of *Dateline* to try to be brave.

I'm turning the key in the ignition when a knock on my window sends me jumping so high the only reason my head doesn't hit the roof is because my knees slam against the steering wheel.

"Roll down the window," TK says.

"Jesus Christ!" I yell before the window is down all the way, the sound of my pulse still echoing in my ears. "Are you insane? You almost gave me a heart attack!"

"Sorry," he says even though he doesn't seem sorry at all. "We need to talk."

Fan-freaking-tastic.

As if today hasn't been long enough.

I knew this needed to happen, but couldn't he have waited a few years or something?

I hit the locks and let out a sigh. "Get in."

I close my eyes, dropping my head against the back of my seat. I hear the door open and feel my car dip under his weight, but I don't open them until the door closes.

I throw my car into gear and reverse out of the parking lot without a word. I have an idea of what's about to happen, and there's no way in hell I'd chance someone from my job witnessing even a second of it.

"Where are you going?" TK asks.

"No idea. Just getting out of here." I twist the volume knob and turn up the radio while I drive. TK doesn't object — I think we both need a minute to get our heads together.

I end up pulling into the parking lot of an abandoned warehouse I'm sure someone will turn into lofts soon. It's more than a little bit creepy, but the feeling of a murderer looming in the shadows seems like a fitting atmosphere for the two of us.

I turn off the radio, but neither of us says anything.

TK breaks the silence. "I talked to my mom."

Well, crap.

That's not what I was expecting.

"She denied knowing you were pregnant."

"Surprise, surprise." I don't even try to keep the sarcasm out of my voice. "Of course she denied it, TK."

"I don't believe her."

My head jerks back and the smart-ass response I was preparing falls away.

"I told her I needed space while you and I figure things out, because, Poppy?" He takes a deep breath, and I brace. "I want to get to know Ace."

Now this is no surprise.

After I turned my back on his red eyes earlier, I knew this was the only outcome. But still. Hearing the words? Panic and elation collide in my gut while bile rises up the back of my throat.

"I want that too." Even against the silence of the night, the words are weak. Forced. Even though they're the truth.

"How do we do it?" he asks.

We? This is your circus, buddy. That's what I want to say, but this whole adult, choose-your-words-carefully thing has really gotten to me. So instead, I whisper, "I have no idea."

He's in the same clothes he was wearing earlier, but his chino shorts are covered with wrinkles and his tank is misshapen along the hem. His hair, which was pulled up, is now framing his face, and I can't miss how red his eyes are even from the gentle glow of my dashboard.

I want to reach out to him, offer him the comfort I have no business giving him.

"Training camp starts next week." He pulls at the bottom of his shirt and I see why the hem is ruined. "Can we do it before then?"

We.

My entire time as Ace's mom, it's always been me. Just me.

God. Even the pronouns are changing.

"I think I should tell him alone," I say. He starts to object, but I keep going before he can say anything. "All he knows about you is you don't know about him. That's all. You aren't the only one who'll be shocked by this. I have to work tomorrow, but I have Monday off. I'll tell him in the morning and you can come over for lunch. But let him react to the news alone. I don't want him to feel ambushed."

"No." He takes a deep breath and releases his shirt. "I mean yeah. You're right. That's good."

I don't know if I'd go all the way to good, but at least it's a plan.

"So he really doesn't know about me?"

"No. I told him the basic stuff. We met in high school. You left for college and we lost contact. Then I found out I was pregnant, but you never knew. He doesn't think you abandoned him or anything."

"That's good, I guess."

"Yeah," I say.

I don't know what to say or do. Can I leave now that we have a plan? Do I need to tell him more about Ace? Do I wait and let Ace tell him what he wants him to know?

"Do you still have my address?" I ask him the first thing that comes to mind.

He nods his head but still doesn't speak and I don't know what else to say. I move to put my car into Drive so we can get the hell away from each other, but TK finally finds his words.

"I don't know what to think, Poppy."

Well, crap.

"I know." I don't even feel the tears build before they fall this time. I turn my head to the window, not wanting TK to see. "You're not the only one."

"I don't know what to believe," he says.

"What do you mean?" I ask, not understanding his train of thought. "What's there to believe?"

"I never knew you were pregnant. I never got a text or told my mom I wanted you to have an abortion. I really don't know what you're talking about and my mom said it never happened." He pushes the heels of his palms into his eyes. "I know she can be overprotective, but she'd never not want to know her own grandkid. Still, why would you make up this entire story if it weren't true?"

The world falls from beneath my feet. Every single stone I've laid, every inch of the walkway I've paved for me and Ace, vanishes. And what's left . . . what's real? Well, nothing is there.

"Holy shit." I breathe out the words, picturing Ace's face when I tell him about TK. I thought I was protecting him from a dad who never wanted him. But seeing TK? Putting together the pieces of the puzzle I've been collecting since we met? The excitement at seeing me, the anger toward my leaving, his insane and confused re-action of my telling him about Ace, and the heartbroken man he was seeing Ace today.

We were played.

I know in my heart of hearts TK had no idea about Ace.

Everything makes sense and it knocks the air out of me.

What am I going to say to Ace? We've been a few miles away from his dad for the last six years, and I kept it from him. Will he ever trust me again? Will he ever run to me, carefree and happy? Or am I stealing his childhood, robbing him of his innocence? Will I break something I'll never be able to repair?

Tears clog my throat and my breathing becomes ragged.

All I ever wanted was to protect him, and now I'm going to be the one to ruin him.

Sweat breaks out on my forehead and a rush of heat consumes my body. My stomach flips and I just manage to unbuckle my seat belt and open my door before I empty the contents of my stomach all over the broken concrete outside.

I don't dare look at TK as I unfold myself from the driver's-side door, avoiding the mess I've made — literally and figuratively. I slam the door shut and walk toward the empty street. Hoping a little distance from him is what I need.

It doesn't work. The harder I try to relax, the more frantic my breathing becomes. Rapid in and out. Shallow and useless. I put my hands on top of my head, trying to open my lungs, desperate for the oxygen that's evading me. A car turns onto the street and its headlights dance in front of me as it passes.

"Poppy." TK's voice echoes in the back of my mind. "Poppy!" he yells again . . . or doesn't. I'm not really sure.

The streetlights above me move farther away. My body sways, still fighting to take one deep breath.

My head spins. My vision swims. Everything in the tunnel in front of me starts to fade. I reach out and try to grab on to something, anything, but nothing's there . . . until TK's arms wrap around my waist, holding me on my feet.

"Are you okay?" He asks the question he has to know the answer to.

I don't speak right away as I clench my eyes shut and will the world to stop spinning. When my legs start to feel like they are filled with bones and some muscle again and I'm not worried my stomach is going to revolt all across the pavement . . . again, I push out of TK's grasp. "I am the complete opposite of okay, but I don't factor into this decision." I walk back to my car, assuming he's following, and sit in the driver's seat. "The only person who matters in all of this is Ace."

A lesson TK will be learning all too soon.

ELEVEN

When your life is on the brink of exploding into smithereens, sometimes you just have to take comfort in what is familiar.

Tomorrow, I have to put on my big-girl panties and tell my kid something that might cause him to need a lifetime supply of therapy. So tonight, even though I'd rather be home, drowning my fears in ice cream and wine — or wine-infused ice cream, if that's not a thing, somebody needs to get on it stat— I'm at work. Where, unless TK decides to ambush me again, I know what to expect. I plan on losing myself in the monotony of taking orders, climbing stairs, and serving drinks. I'll let the rhythm of the music draw me in and I won't think about tomorrow until I get home. Work, tonight, is a freaking godsend.

"Who's Ace with tonight?" Sadie asks, our eyes locking in the mirror in front of me.

"Mrs. Duncan." I shimmy my shoulders

offbeat — even though there's no music — trying to force peppiness into my voice. Fake it till you make it, is what I always say. "I'm telling you, you better be prepared for some big tips tonight. I've never been so excited to work. Plus, Cole's out of town, we're opening together, and you haven't caused my hair to combust into a poof of smoke. This is shaping up to be a great night and I'm going to take advantage of it."

"You know there are two things I'm always prepared for." She unplugs her flat iron from the outlet next to her and holds up her index finger. "One, money." She adds her middle finger with a flick of her wrist. "And two, glitter."

As if to prove that my positive attitude for the night is going to pay off, I dodge the handful of glitter she releases before it can embed itself into my scalp or adhere to my skin.

"Like a ninja!" I laugh . . . but not too hard. I don't want her to plan a sneak revenge glitter bombing later.

I make my way to the floor, waving to Sandra as she heads into the "entertainment" dressing rooms. They have better lighting and more comfortable chairs than we do. But since they are swinging around on oversize scarves and flipping headfirst toward possible death, I guess they deserve it.

Leaving the well-lit hallway and entering the dim, smoky (even though smoking isn't allowed) club always leaves me feeling a bit disoriented. My poor eyes aren't what they used to be and they struggle to focus with the flashing lights being tested on the stage.

Once they do adjust, I see Rochelle standing across from Phil having a very animated conversation. I didn't think she was scheduled to open with us, but seeing the mood she's in right now, I plan on working even harder than I normally do to stay away from her. I spin on my heel and, as silent as possible, make my way behind the bar, careful not to let my heels click against the clean-for-now tile.

Too bad for me, I must have used all my ninja stealth with Sadie because I make it only three steps before Rochelle's crazed, overlined eyes find me.

"I cannot believe you!" she screeches, her arms flailing and her skinny legs struggling to keep her upright.

I feel the wrinkles form on my forehead as I raise my eyebrows. "Ummm . . ." My eyes shift between Rochelle and Phil, both of whom are staring at me like I'm in deep shit. "I have no idea what you're talking about."

"Don't play stupid, Poppy," Rochelle spits, and starts to walk my way, her long black hair whipping back and forth in sync with her ample cleavage. As she gets closer, I notice her bright blue eyes are now a striking shade of red. I'm not sure if it's the reflection of the red lights in the club or the Devil making his presence known.

"I'm not playing anything. I have no idea what you're talking about." I use my gentle mom voice on her but take comfort in the bar between us and the rows of glass bottles behind me in case I need a makeshift weapon.

"Really?" She tilts her head to the side and purses her lips. "Then let me refresh your memory."

She reaches into her fake Gucci purse and I know it's risky seeing as she could very well be digging for a weapon, but I wonder if her lips are natural or if she's had lip injections. She really does have great lips. Too bad she uses them to spew garbage.

After a minute or two of digging and loose receipts falling to the floor, which really messes up the dramatic effect of the scene she's acting out, she pulls out her phone. She taps in her password — 123456, because she's a genius — and her fingers dance across the screen before she shoves the phone in my face.

It takes me exactly three seconds to realize what I'm seeing and four to realize a positive mind-set can only take me so far.

On her phone, underneath the bold, hot-pink script declaring the website *Baller Notice,* are pictures — yes, multiple — of TK and me in the parking lot behind the Emerald Cabaret. The photos are grainy, but even so, there is no denying that it's him as he stands next to my car or him climbing into the passenger seat. There is even one of him with his arms wrapped around me in the abandoned parking lot that I'm not sure I could even find again if someone asked.

Fuck. My. Life.

"I did all the work to get him in the club." Rochelle's perfectly plump lip curls up in disgust. "Not only did your ass steal his table and tips from me, you went ahead and pursued him outside of the club too!"

"It . . . it's not like that. I mean, yeah, I guess, but . . ." I stumble over my words, trying to peel my eyes off the screen. "This has nothing to do with you."

"Bullshit! This has everything to do with me!" She stabs herself in the chest with a sharp, pointed fingernail then aims it in

Phil's direction. "And Phil and everyone in this club!"

"What? How?" I put her phone on the bar top between us, not chancing getting too close. I've been to the zoo with Ace too many times to stick my hand in the cage with an angry lion now. "Besides enjoying my immense embarrassment, I still don't see what this has to do with you."

"TK hasn't come back," she says, calm and collected, like the wild beast I was just talking to a minute ago was a figment of my imagination. "He hasn't been back in weeks. Neither have the other players. I called TK and he told me you're the reason he stopped coming in." She slams her case-protected phone onto the glass bar top. "These pictures were posted this morning. He came to see you last night but won't come inside anymore. Three years! Three years I worked here, trying to get these big-money ballers to come in and you ruined it for all of us in a month!"

I remember when he said he didn't answer numbers he didn't know. I hate the thread of jealousy that starts to unravel knowing they spoke. "TK answered your call?" I voice my thoughts out loud, which I realize is a mistake when Rochelle screams so loud, the bottles on the shelves behind me start to rattle.

"Fuck you!" She reaches over the bar, her hands outstretched and aiming for my neck.

"Rochelle." Phil finally makes himself useful and moves from the spot his feet have been glued to. "Relax."

Once he reaches her, he spins her around and pulls her in for a hug, wrapping his arms tight around her, locking her arms at her side.

A human straitjacket. Clever, Phil.

"You need to leave," he says in her ear.

I turn around and start to fidget with the bottles of vodka to give them a bit of privacy during this strange, yet personal, moment.

"Poppy." Phil gets my attention.

I turn around, prepared to see Rochelle's retreating form heading to the exit, but when I look at him, I'm met with matching glares.

"Go home, Poppy," Phil says, his voice steady. "I'll have Sadie clear out your locker and bring you your stuff."

The floor falls from under my feet and my stomach starts doing somersaults. "Wh— What?" I try to swallow down the bile rising up the back of my throat. "What do you mean?"

"Rochelle is right," he says, a blank expression carefully laid on his aging face. "I've

133

been fighting to get Mustang players in this club since I started it. It finally happened, and just as soon, you ended it —"

"But —" I try to break in, desperate to keep my job. The job that has allowed me to be a class mom and keep clothes on my son's back.

"You're a great waitress, but even the money you bring in can't make up for the business you lost the Emerald Cabaret. You know the rules. I don't care about your personal life. I don't care if you date a client as long as it doesn't affect my bottom line." His eyes soften a bit as he watches the tears roll down my face. "I like you, Poppy, I really do. This isn't personal."

I think about telling Phil about my past with TK. Telling him about Ace and everything that has transpired between us is on the tip of my tongue when Rochelle — or more specifically — the Cheshire Cat grin she's now sporting catches my attention out of the corner of my eye. And in a split second I realize I'd rather lose my job than give her my secrets. I close my eyes, take a deep breath, and compose myself.

"I understand." Shoulders squared and back straight, I walk from behind the bar and toward the exit.

Not another word is uttered as I make my

walk of shame in stilettos and a corset to the parking lot. I climb into my Volvo, my head held high and cheeks dry.

On the scale of crappy things that have happened to me, this is at the very bottom.

Screw Rochelle and screw Phil too.

I'll get a new job.

And I'll never straighten my freaking hair again.

TWELVE

I come to but I don't open my eyes.

I scrunch them tight, trying to pinpoint what part of me hurts the most. I may have indulged in one or two glasses after I got home. Lucky for me, nothing hurts . . . besides maybe my pride.

I grab my phone to check the time and see that I have two unread text messages. One from Sadie asking what in the hell happened and one that kicks my adrenaline into overdrive.

> I'll be over at 2. Let me know if that doesn't work for you.
>
> -TK

Oh my God. TK. Today. Crap!

I check the time and mentally break down how long I have until TK gets here — which takes longer than I'd like to admit — and then I shoot out of bed like my mattress is on fire as my ears strain to hear if Ace is up and about.

Thankfully, the only sound is from the air conditioning struggling to keep me in my preferred frigid temperatures.

On summer break Ace sleeps like a log and I make no effort to curb the habit. With my hours — or my old hours, I should say — it works out for the best anyway. And today, of all days, I need a moment alone to prepare.

I go to grab my robe off the hook behind my door, but I step on something before I get to it. I look down and see my corset spread out on the floor. Instead of moving it, or throwing it in a fire, I stare at it for what feels like a really long time. It looks so ordinary lying on my rug. The sequins look lackluster without the club lights bouncing off them and the underwire's misshapen in places. Why would I ever miss that? I kick it beneath the bed. Out of everything happening in my life right now, that dingy thing doesn't even make the list.

I make the short trek to the kitchen. If anything, this news I'm about to bombard Ace with deserves a good breakfast . . . and maybe that new bike he was asking for.

I check my fridge and pantry and thank the heavens that even though I've been avoiding the grocery store, I still have everything to make Ace's favorite breakfast.

I think it's the smell of bacon wafting through the hallways that brings Ace to the kitchen. His green eyes widen just like I saw the night before on his burly counterpart, and his dimple pops through when a toothy smile covers his face.

"Crepes and bacon!" He runs and high-fives me after I set his plate on the table, the nine-year-old equivalent of a bear hug. "Thanks, Mom!"

"You're welcome, buddy." I try to match his smile, but the nerves twisting my insides into knots prevent it. He's too focused on the grape jelly and cream cheese–stuffed crepes covering his plate to notice my strained smile and watery eyes.

I wash dishes while he eats, knowing damn well that anything I eat won't stay down. Plus, it gives me a minute to rehearse what I'm going to say one more time.

"You're not eating?" he asks from the refinished kitchen table.

"Not really hungry, I had coffee."

Most days my breakfast consists of only coffee, so this doesn't set off any alarms. I bet he's just happy he gets extra crepes. He might only be nine, but he eats more than me ninety percent of the time. The impending teenage years already have me cowering in a corner. He's going to eat me out of house and home.

When I've procrastinated for as long as possible, I wipe my hands on the dish towel Ace made for me in kindergarten with his tiny handprints and sloppy penmanship, and sit at the table with him.

He's humming in between bites, long, sun-bleached curls bouncing across his forehead and eyes sparkling with happiness from something as simple as crepes. He's oblivious to the atom bomb I'm about to detonate, and I wish I could avoid this forever.

I mean, what if I tell him about TK and then TK bails? Everyone leaves. Especially ones who've never had to think about anybody besides themselves. I'll be okay if TK ghosts, I've gotten over him before, but Ace . . .

I stop myself before I let my train of thought go any further. I will not burden Ace with my fears. This will be great.

Please let this be great. Please don't let his sparkle disappear.

I chant the pleading prayer in my mind over and over until his last bite is gone.

He moves to take his plate to the sink, but I put my hand on top of his to stop him.

He tilts his head to the side, no doubt shocked that I'd ever stop him from cleaning up after himself.

Here we go.

I take a deep breath and resist the urge to close my eyes. "We have to talk."

I guess even at nine, those are dreaded words. His fingers flinch beneath mine, and he starts to chew his bottom lip, a bad habit he inherited from me.

"Did I do something?" His voice trembles and I want to kick myself. I haven't even told him anything and I'm already messing this up.

"No, buddy." I link my fingers with his and give him a squeeze. I don't know if I'm doing it for his comfort or mine. "It's about your dad."

There.

I know ripping off the Band-Aid wasn't all too successful with TK, but fingers crossed history doesn't repeat itself.

"What?" He jerks his arm and I tense my fingers around his, unwilling to let him go. "My dad?"

"Yeah, bud, your dad." I keep my eyes on him, fascinated by the mix of emotions marring his beautiful face.

"Wh-what about him?" He stumbles over his words.

"I saw him." I wait for him to say something . . . anything . . . but when he doesn't, I continue on. "I told him about you and he wants to meet you."

"He does?" His eyebrows rise to his hairline and a wonder-filled smile takes over his face.

Shocked excitement for him.

Painful guilt for me.

I made him doubt himself. My decision made him doubt his worth . . . his ability to be loved.

"Yes, he does. You're the most amazing person I've ever met, anybody would be lucky to have a second around you." It's a fierce declaration, true on every level.

His smile turns shy. His own biggest critic, he's never been one to bask in Mom's attention.

"He's coming over today —"

Ace cuts me off. "Today? What time?"

"He'll be here at two."

He looks at the clock and then closes his eyes, no doubt calculating a countdown in his head. "I gotta go clean my room!" He pulls his hand from mine and pushes away from the table, the old legs dragging against the hardwood floor.

"Ace." I stop him just short of sprinting out of the kitchen.

"Oh." He shakes his head and reaches for his dirty plate. "In the sink. Sorry."

"Not that." I pull the plate from his hand again. "I have to tell you who he is."

His brows furrow. "Ummm . . . okay?"

He clearly thinks I'm insane.

"Your dad is . . ." Why is *this* part so hard? "TK is your dad. TK Moore."

I don't know what I was expecting, but sheer bliss was not it.

"That's why you were talking to him after my practice!" he shouts. "Oh my god! TK Moore!" His hands fly to his hair then out in front of his face, then back to his hair. "Wait until my friends find out!"

I want to stop him. *Don't tell your friends. We don't know how long he'll be around.* But I don't. I might be scared TK will bail, but those are my insecurities and there's not a chance in hell I'm screwing Ace up about his dad any more than I already have.

Ace continues to punch the air while dancing around the tight kitchen. I can't remember the last time he's been this happy.

He just found out his dad is Superman. Why wouldn't he be thrilled?

But I can't help wondering, how long until he thinks I'm the villain who kept him from his hero?

142

THIRTEEN

As the day goes on, I can feel the shift of energy in the house. The hairs on the back of my neck stand straight from the static energy the nerves are creating. Ace asks a few more questions — if his room looks okay, if it'll be all right for him to mention football — before he retreats to his sports-covered room. At one thirty, he comes out of his room, dressed in the Jordan outfit I found at Ross before summer started, and sits next to me on the couch. I give him the remote, but he's too focused on the empty street in front of our house to even notice.

At two o'clock sharp, TK's Range Rover glides to a stop in front of our house. I leave Ace, whose knee hasn't stopped bouncing since he sat down, on the couch while I greet TK.

"Hey." I open the door as TK walks up the uneven pathway to the porch, plastering a smile on my face I'm ninety-eight percent sure makes me look like a murderous clown.

But it's the effort that counts, right?

"Hey," he repeats, his eyes shifting around like I'm going to bombard him with a village of children. "How are you?"

"We're good." I answer for Ace even though it might not be true.

"Good . . . that's good." One of TK's hands is holding an oversize plastic bag, the other one is in his pocket, but even through the thick fabric of basketball shorts, I can still see it fidgeting. "You look good."

"Thanks," I say even though I know he's lying.

I look a hot-ass mess. I didn't even try to put on makeup. I thought if I acted casual and nonchalant about the whole thing, Ace would too. Also, if I let a few tears slip without makeup on, there won't be a faded spot on my face traced with bleeding mascara.

I move out of the doorway and motion to the living room like a *Price Is Right* model. "Come on in."

He doesn't say anything and I watch as he transforms right in front of me. He closes his eyes and his long fingers flex around the bag handle. He inhales a breath so deep, I'm surprised there's any oxygen left over for me. He exhales and rolls his neck from

144

left to right and back again and kicks out each leg three times. I bet this is what he looks like in the locker room before a game. Then his eyes open, his shoulders relax, and a genuine smile from under the thick beard — dammit to hell, I still want to dig my fingers into it — appears.

All hints of nerves gone, he walks past me and into my living room.

And straight into Ace's life.

No turning back now.

He walks to the middle of the room and stops cold, no doubt taking in the beauty that is Ace. I ignore the butterflies rioting in my stomach, walk past him, and stand between the two of them.

I watch as they both stand in silence, checking each other out. After a minute, they're both wearing matching smiles and expressions of awe. The fear I've felt since I walked out of that clinic dissipates and excitement takes over. I'm able to forget my guilt for a minute and bask in the goodness of Ace and TK together.

TK holds out the bag he's been clinging to. "I hope you're a Mustangs fan."

"I am." Ace takes his time reaching for the bag. I think he's afraid to look too eager, not only wanting to be the cool nine-year-old he always is but wanting his superstar dad to think he's awesome too.

TK slides the bag onto Ace's wrist, and Ace's eyes widen as his arm falls under the weight of the bag.

Ugh.

Just great. The bribery begins . . . bribery I have no feasible way of competing with.

Ace turns and runs to the couch, where he promptly dumps out what I assume is every Mustangs item TK was able to get his hands on. Including, but not limited to, a Moore jersey, socks, hats — baseball and the knit variety — a stuffed Mustang that Ace might be too old for, and a hoodie I wish was a few sizes bigger so I could steal.

"Awesome!" Ace turns and stutter-steps in TK's direction.

TK sees his hesitation and takes it upon himself to close the distance between them and wrap Ace in his strong arms.

My heart squeezes and then proceeds to explode into a million glittery pieces inside my chest.

"Glad you like it." TK ruffles Ace's mop of curls but takes another minute before he completely releases him.

"Wait until I show Jayden, he's gonna flip." Ace starts putting his new goodies back in the bag. Well, not the jersey. That he puts on over the shirt he's already wearing.

146

"His dad buys him a new jersey every season and he always tells me about the Mustangs games he gets to go to."

"Who's Jayden?" TK asks.

"My friend." Ace states the obvious but continues on before I have to supplement information. "He lives down the street and hopefully we'll be on the same soccer team this year. When I saw you the other day, that was our last tryout." At the mention of soccer, his green eyes almost pop out of his skull. "Mom!" he shouts even though I'm only a few feet away. "Has Coach e-mailed you? Check your e-mail!" he keeps yelling, not giving me a chance to answer.

I grab my phone off the coffee table and punch in my password when my hands are too sweaty for the fingerprint technology to work.

I open my e-mail and skim over what feels like hundreds of ads, trying to ignore Ace bouncing on his toes and biting his nails — a habit I fear I'll never be able to break — until I see it.

DENVER ELITE TEAM ROSTERS

"It's here!" I shout.

Huh? So I guess that's where Ace gets his loud tendencies from.

"Did I make it? Did I make it?" Ace asks.

"Hold on." I motion a finger at him. Scrolling through the names.

Denver Elite Soccer Club will have four teams for their Boys U10 division — Gold, Silver, Bronze, and Copper.

They start from the bottom.

"Hurry, Mom." Ace rushes me, like I'm going slow for dramatic effect. "Did I make it or not?"

"There are so many names, I haven't gotten to you yet." But as soon as I say it, I see what I'm looking for: Ace Patterson. "Team Gold, baby!" I cross the short distance between us and pull him into a hug.

"Team Gold? Really?" Ace asks, not yet returning my hug. Like I would ever trick him about this.

"Yes, really!" I squeeze him extra tight and lift all seventy pounds of him with my legs. "I told you you're amazing. I knew you'd make it!"

I put him back on the floor, unable to hold him any longer. And the news finally sets in.

"I did it!" His feet leave my rug again — but this time of his own accord — as he jumps Tom Cruise on *Oprah* style onto my couch. "I'm on Team Gold!"

I raise my hand for a high five, but he

ignores my hand in front of his face and turns to TK, giving him the high five instead.

I mean . . . Damn.

"That's awesome, dude!" TK returns the high five with genuine excitement. "Congratulations!"

"Thanks!" Ace jumps off the couch. "I've played soccer since first grade, but this is the first year Mom let me try out for competitive. I can't believe I made it."

I watch the two of them, bonding over sports, over the good news Ace has been hoping to hear since I gave him the go-ahead to try out, and I check my hurt.

This is the way it should be. The way it always should've been. And once I get over my initial reaction, I go soft at the realization that this is the first big moment Ace gets to share with both of his parents. It's the first time in a long time I get to share my pride and happiness over Ace with another person.

I feel my smile growing and decide to give them some time to themselves. That's what today was supposed to be about anyway.

I turn to leave, thinking of all the chores I've ignored since school let out, and decide to attack the mounds of unfolded laundry piling up.

This dad thing is already proving to be very beneficial.

I don't even make it out of the living room when TK calls to me. "Poppy, put on some shoes."

I turn back to him, my eyebrows raised at his demand. "Why?"

"Our kid just made Gold. We have some celebrating to do."

"Poppy?" TK asks when I don't make a move or even whisper a word.

But it's impossible.

Our kid.

That's what he said — *our kid.*

Melt me like a freaking Popsicle.

I nod at him, still incapable of speech, and slip on the flip-flops I left on the floor next to the chair.

"Mexican food?" TK asks, and I watch as Ace lights up.

"Mexican is my favorite!" Ace turns to me, aware that I exist again. "Did you tell him that?"

I give him the God's honest truth. "Nope."

"She didn't tell you?" he asks TK.

I guess my answer didn't satisfy him.

"Nope, Mexican food is my favorite, so I was just hoping. Looks like we have a lot in common already." TK holds up a single finger. "We're both superstar athletes." He

150

adds a second finger. "We have great taste in food." Third finger. "We both cheer for the Mustangs every Sunday." Fourth finger goes up. "We're ridiculously good-looking." He adds his thumb. "And . . . most important of all . . ." He drops his hand before pointing a finger at me. "That lady is crazy about the both of us."

I wasn't prepared for those words to come out of his mouth, and because of that, there's no holding back my laughter . . . or the accompanying snort. Ace and TK are laughing too, so much so that every time I think we're almost done laughing, we make eye contact and the laughter starts all over.

I wrap an arm around my midsection and wipe the tears from the corners of my eyes with the other. "Still full of yourself, I see." I stand firm in my position as anti-ab-workout, but I'd imagine this is what I'd feel like after doing a couple hundred sit-ups. "Are we gonna eat or what?"

"Food is always a yes." TK pulls the keys from his pocket. "Let's hit the road."

I look at Ace, who is still standing next to TK, and something inside me that's been broken for so long, something I didn't even realize was still aching, fuses together. He's always been a happy kid, but right now? He's blissed out.

151

"Cool car!" Ace says to TK as soon as we hit the sidewalk.

"Thanks." TK beeps the locks. "Wanna sit shotgun?"

"Yes!" Ace shouts, lunging for the passenger door at the same time I yell *"No!"* and block his opening.

"Back seat until twelve," I say to anyone who will listen. Which, at this point in time, I'm not sure is TK or Ace.

But they both hear me.

I know this because, at the exact same time, they both mumble out a defeated-sounding "Moms."

"Yes, moms." I use sarcasm to deny my current need to turn into a gooey, gushy mess again. "We keep you safe. You're welcome."

Then, with me back in the front seat of TK's Range Rover and Ace safe and buckled in the back seat, we take off on our first-ever family excursion.

Only nine years late.

FOURTEEN

Two hours.

It took me two hours of identical orders, laughter at the same crappy jokes, and obsession with football and *Ninja Warrior* to realize that sometimes nature is indeed stronger than nurture.

"No way!" Ace shouts from the back seat, like TK isn't only a foot away from him. "I can't believe you like that movie too! Mom hates it."

"Because it's terrible, and sitting with the only two people in the world who like it isn't going to convince me otherwise."

"Poppy," TK says beside me, his voice deep and serious. "They brought Kevin into the new millennium. We got to see how he handled himself with modern technology."

"*Home Alone 1* and *2* were perfect on their own. But *3* was pushing it, although at least the kid had a different name. However, *4* was just a disgrace."

"It's the best one!" Ace says at the same time TK says, "You're a sequel snob."

"It wasn't —" I close my eyes, inhale through my nose, and throw my hands up in the air, as if summoning the Holy Spirit itself to talk me down. "No. No, I'm not debating the merits of *Home Alone 4* with you guys."

Ace dissolves into a fit of giggles on TK's black leather seat. I don't know why their bad taste is so amusing to him.

TK lets out a deep, throaty chuckle. "You're a nut." Then his hand comes off the steering wheel and he squeezes my thigh before sliding it down to my knee and back to the steering wheel. I don't know if it's reflex or if he meant to do it, but I do know my thighs now feel like they've been plastered in cement with how tight I'm squeezing them together.

"Yup." I force out a laugh that sounds more like I have a hair in my throat. "You know me. Nutty Poppy."

Holy crap.

I did not just say that.

I close my eyes, hoping it will create a chasm in reality and I can go back in time and learn how not to be a socially awkward adult.

When I open them and sneak a peek at

154

TK, his chest is shaking and his lips are pulled in between his teeth to keep his laughter silent.

So I guess the chasm thing didn't work.

I narrow my eyes at him even though between the dark sky and — what has to be illegal — tint, it's almost pitch black inside his fancy Range Rover. But I keep my mouth shut since I clearly cannot be trusted when it opens.

He makes a right onto my street and comes to a stop outside my little bungalow.

"Home sweet home," he announces.

"Can you spend the night?" Ace asks. "We can watch *Home Alone*!"

"It's Monday night, bud." I turn my head and gentle my tone, he's been on cloud nine all night and I hate to be the bearer of bad news. "He probably has work."

"I don't." TK rushes the words out. "A sleepover and a movie sounds good, but only if it's okay with your mom."

"Please, Mom." Ace sticks out his bottom lip and clasps his hands together. A move that should've stopped affecting me when he was four but still manages to sway my decision making.

"It's fine with me," I say.

"Yes!" Ace jumps off the seat and high-fives TK.

"But!" I continue on, only louder. "Tomorrow you need to read at least two chapters of your book."

"Okay, I will," he says with the biggest smile he's ever had about reading.

"And . . ." I turn my head to look at the two of them. "No *Home Alone 4.*"

"Deal," they both say with wicked smiles on their faces, making me almost positive I'm going to regret this.

"He's knocked out." TK startles me out of the book I'm reading.

I close it and lean forward on my elbows. "I'm honestly shocked he lasted as long as he did."

I watch as TK crosses my kitchen. His hair down, swaying with every step, and bare feet padding across my kitchen floor. The ease and confidence he exudes make it so he fits in whatever environment he's in.

Like he belongs here.

My heart stutters and I shut down that train of thought. TK reappearing in my life has forced me to acknowledge how my feelings for him have never faded. I may have slept with other people, had a few almost-relationships, but now that I'm being honest with myself, I can recognize how I sabotaged every "relationship" I've had over

156

the past ten years.

Under the table, I kick out the chair across from me and watch as TK folds his oversize body onto my IKEA furniture. I hold my breath, not sure he — or my poor chair — isn't about to meet his demise.

The chair creaks and groans under his weight, but thankfully my screw-tightening skills hold up.

"He's a fantastic kid." TK leans back in the chair, propping his hands on the table and kicking his long legs to the side. "You've done a great job, Sparks."

I try to school my features to not let him in on just how much his words make me feel. When Maya was around, she'd tell me I was a good mom, but since she's been gone, I've been trucking along, trying my best and hoping I don't screw Ace up too bad. This parenting shit is so hard and I question every single decision I make. Having TK tell me I'm doing a good job is enough to set my sinuses on fire with unshed tears.

Also, he called me Sparks.

"Thank you," I whisper, and fiddle with my fingers. "That really means a lot."

"It's true." He grazes his fingers across the back of my hand. Electricity surges up my arms and down my spine, leaving goose bumps in their path. "The way he looks at you. How respectful and polite he is. It's obvious to anyone around you that you're a great mom."

"You have to stop complimenting me or I'm going to cry." I pull my hands from the table and tuck them between my thighs. "You don't want me almost passing out again."

TK laughs even though it was a terrible joke. "You're right, I wouldn't want that again."

We sit at the table, neither of us saying anything, and I'm one hundred percent okay with it. Some people hate silence. I'm not one of them. Bad news can't be delivered without words. Sometimes quiet is the only way to maintain peace. It's the noise that brings chaos.

TK doesn't appreciate the quiet like I do. He fumbles around, tapping his foot and creating a beat on my table with his hands, before sitting up straight in his chair.

"We still need to talk, a lot has happened."

See?

Chaos.

My stomach lurches and my palms start to sweat. No good has ever come from "we need to talk." And hearing those words come from TK's mouth is quite literally the nightmare I've had every day since Ace was born.

"About what?" I ask like a freaking idiot. The list of what we need to talk about is so long, we'd have to kill hundreds of trees to get enough paper.

"About what happened when you were pregnant, what happened when he was a baby . . . hell, Poppy. What happened last week!" He takes a deep breath and leans forward, like his words alone didn't riddle me with anxiety, now he's added serious body language. "What happens in the future?"

My stomach flips and my back goes straight. Everything in front of me blurs and my fingers start to tingle.

Oh no.

This.

This is what I was afraid of. I cannot . . . no. I will not lose Ace.

"No," I say.

"No?" His eyebrows scrunch together. "No what?"

"The future," I repeat his words. "No, you cannot take Ace from me. I won't let it happen."

"What the hell, Poppy?" His jaw tightens along with his fists, the veins in his muscular arms becoming more pronounced. "I just told you I think you're a great mom. You really think I'm that big of an asshole to try and rip a kid away from his mom?"

Do I?

"You have zero right to get angry right now." I point a deliberate finger across the table. "I don't know what to think. I don't know you anymore and the side of yourself you showed me when I told you about Ace didn't instill a sense of confidence in me." I don't want to be a bitch, but I'm also not going to mince my words to protect his fragile feelings. "You've spent the last ten years of your life having shit handed to you on a silver platter. You pass out hundreds like they're Tic Tacs so you don't have to wait in line. Are you really expecting me to not think you won't spend thousands on a lawyer for my kid? Seriously?

"All I know is Ace is the only person I have, and if you think for a split second I won't go to the ends of this earth to keep him with me, you're out of your mind." I roll my neck and raise my eyebrows. "Got me . . . Trevor?"

His jaw clenches again, making his beard twitch along with it, something that shouldn't, but does, turn me on. Which only pisses me off more.

"Don't call me Trevor." He narrows his

160

green eyes and leans across the table. "And I have every right to be angry. That's my kid in there too!" He points toward Ace's bedroom. "And I missed out on nine years of his life! If anyone here has the right to be mad, it's me." His teeth grind together, keeping what was meant to be a yell quiet enough not to wake up Ace.

"Oh yeah? As opposed to me? My family abandoned me when I left that clinic still pregnant. I finished high school a year late and any hopes of college went down the drain." I stand up so fast I send my chair flying from beneath me. It squeaks against the hardwood, no doubt making marks as angry as I am. "Ace is the *one* good thing I have in my life. He's the *one* thing that makes every sacrifice worth it. If you think you can ride in here with bags of toys and your superstar status and steal him from me, you're out of your mind."

TK, across from me, expression blank, takes his time standing. Every movement, every breath he takes, is completely measured. And though I hide it with narrowed eyes and a hand on my hip, it scares the shit out of me.

God, I hope I didn't just poke a bear.

He steps to the side of his chair and carefully pushes it back to the table. Once it meets his apparent standards, he starts to move. Shoulders tense, feet sure, he makes his way around the table and right into my space.

Stubborn (and quite possibly stupid) as ever, I hold my ground. I don't waver and I sure as hell do not retreat. I roll my shoulders back and stand tall, hoping my attitude makes my five feet three inches seem more intimidating.

It doesn't.

I know this because all six feet plus of TK keep coming toward me and don't stop until his chest damn near brushes my nose and his head is creating a shadow over my head. "Why'd you stop talking, Sparks?" he mumbles into my hair. "You had so much to say a minute ago."

"Stop calling me Sparks," I grind out, but don't look up at him.

"Why?" He puts both hands on my back. "You like it."

"I do not," I half lie. I don't like it, I love it. But I'm mad at him now.

"You do." He drops his head deeper into the mass of curls covering my head, the end of his beard brushing against my cheek. "Want me to tell you how I know?"

"No." It's one word, but I put as much feeling into it as I can without daring to move a millimeter. Not trusting myself when I'm being not only consumed by TK's presence but actually cocooned by his body.

"Because." He continues on like I didn't speak, pulling one hand from my back to take hold of the hair that was hanging over my shoulder.

I clench my eyes shut and dig my finger-nails into my palms to try to distract myself from the feeling of TK's mouth as he drags his lips through my hair until his warm breath pulses against my ear.

"Whenever I call you Sparks, I see your pupils dilate and your nipples harden. I see the goose bumps dot your arms. But most of all . . ." He stops talking but doesn't let up. No, instead, he traces the line of my ear with his tongue, nipping at my earlobe when he reaches it. "I see the way you squeeze your thighs together, trying to find the relief you've been craving since I saw you in the parking lot."

Could he be more infuriating? The cocky, sexy jerk.

"That's not true," I whisper because I have no energy to yell. Because all my extra energy is in use so I don't come this very moment.

"You're lying . . . Sparks," he says.

And with my chest pressed against him,

my bare arms hanging at my sides, and his hand resting against my spine, I know he can not only see but feel my reaction to the stupid nickname. His deep laughter beating against my neck confirms it.

"Sparks," he says once more, like driving me mad is his new favorite pastime.

"Screw you." I try to pack it with some force, but instead, it sounds like pleading . . . like an offer.

"Soon." He nips my ear again, drops his hands, and steps back.

The space he creates is just as confusing as everything else between us. Giving me my first opportunity to breathe, I both welcome and resent it.

"But what I was trying to say before you snapped about the future was that I have to report to training camp on Wednesday," he says, cool as a cucumber. Like the scene that has me shaken to my core — or wet to my drawers — didn't happen.

I close my eyes and shake my head, trying to follow the conversation. "What?"

"Training camp starts on Wednesday. We check in to the hotel in the morning and can't leave for two weeks," he explains, and I try to follow. "I don't want to go that long without seeing you guys, but I didn't want to bring it up in front of Ace in case you weren't feeling like coming up there."

"Umm . . . okay." I nod so he can see I'm listening.

"If you can come, I'll get you passes and put your names on the list so you can watch camp and I can see Ace after practice." He shrugs his shoulders, and for the first time since he went alpha-male extreme on me, I can see how nervous he is bringing this up. "I think they have a pretty nice setup for the families. Lots of kids come, Ace should have fun."

"No, I mean yeah." I trip over my words like a bumbling fool. "That sounds good."

"And since it will be a few days before I can see you guys, I was thinking I could watch Ace for you while you work tomorrow night."

My back goes straight as I aim my gaze at his feet. "Oh . . . work . . . about that . . ." I try — and fail — to keep my wits together. "I sorta don't work there anymore."

"You got fired!" he shouts.

My head snaps up and my eyes widen at his outburst. "Ace!" I whisper-shout at him. "Don't yell."

"Sorry," he whispers, even though he doesn't actually look sorry. "But what the hell happened?"

"Well, actually . . ." I stutter around my

words, trying to figure out the best way to deliver the news. "You happened."

His eyes go wide and color fills his cheeks from beneath his beard. "What?" he grinds out, and I can tell it's taking everything within him not to shout. "Please explain this to me."

"Somebody posted pictures of us from the parking lot the other night on some gossipy website. They were grainy and not great, but it's clearly us and we're clearly behind the Emerald Cabaret. And unfortunately for me, your friend Rochelle not only knows me but hates me," I say. TK's entire body is stiff in front of me and I swear I can feel the anger vibrating off him. "She told Phil I'm the reason you and your teammates stopped coming in, so he fired me for losing clients."

I know my tone is off, a single mom shouldn't sound so laidback about losing her only source of income, but I can't seem to make myself care. I know I can't afford to be unemployed for long, but it's not an emergency yet. Plus, I really couldn't work at a nightclub forever.

A career it was not.

"That bitch," TK whispers. "She fuckin' played me."

Since it sounds like a conversation he's

having with himself, I don't say anything.

"Fuck, Poppy, I'm so sorry. I swear, I didn't mean for this to happen." He rakes his fingers through his hair. "I didn't even know who it was when she called the other morning. I never save numbers in my phone. She asked if we could hook up sometime and she'd treat me and some of my teammates to VIP for a night. I just told her I was seeing someone. I never mentioned your name, I swear."

Did he say he was seeing someone?

"You're seeing someone?" I ask, not caring at all about anything else he said.

"Um, yeah?" His eyebrows scrunch together. "I mean, I wanted to see where this would go with you before I knew about Ace and I still want to . . . if you do, of course."

"I mean . . ." I plaster my arms to my sides to avoid pinching myself. "I'm open to it," I say, pleased with my answer. *Way to play it cool, Poppy.*

"Good," he says, a smile pulling up at the corners of his mouth. "And since you're looking for a job, my friend Brynn owns a restaurant called HERS and I think she's looking for help. If you're interested, I can call her and put a good word in."

"That's sweet, TK, but I can find a job by myself." Even though HERS is right down the street and looks like the coolest place ever.

"Who said you couldn't?" There's an undercurrent of annoyance lacing his words. "I know you can do everything on your own, but you don't have to now."

I like doing things on my own. There's a comfort in knowing that the only person who can let me down is me. But if I'm going to try to let TK in, really in, I guess this is the best place to start. Plus, I'd really like to work at HERS.

"Okay." I take a deep breath, like somehow I'm agreeing to more than a job referral. "It'd be great if you could call her for me."

"Good, then we're set, I'll call Brynn tomorrow and get the passes set up." He reaches out, twisting a strand of my hair around his finger. His eyes drop to my mouth. I hope it's because he can hear the silent pleading coming from it and he'll touch his lips to mine. Instead, the corners of his mouth pull up, deepening his smile lines. "Night, Poppy."

"Night, TK," I whisper, the words all air and begging.

He drops his head and touches his lips to mine before turning his back on me and retreating to my living room, where he turned the couch into his bed for the night.

I watch him go. His full, firm ass, the tightness of his quads, the graze of his sun-kissed hair against his muscular shoulders taunting me as he moves. I watch with intense focus things I never once noticed in another man. Every inch of TK calls to me . . . turns my insides into liquid.

As soon as he's out of sight, I give up trying to hold myself upright and slide down the wall until my ass is safely on the kitchen floor, which this close up, I realize, needs to be mopped.

But I can be Cinderella another day.

One when TK hasn't reappeared in my life, bringing back ideas of true love's kiss and happily-ever-afters.

FIFTEEN

I check my phone for what feels like the billionth time, hoping to see a text from TK.

Before he left on Monday, he promised to give Brynn a call and then text me with her number. I mean, I know training camp starts today and he was probably busy packing or something last night, but he was so insistent that he'd reach out to her that I thought he'd get back to me right away.

Still no text.

"Dammit," I breathe out before putting my phone on the table with a little too much . . . enthusiasm.

"Swear jar!" Ace shouts with a mouth full of scrambled eggs and points to the embarrassingly full mason jar on the kitchen counter. Though, to be fair, most of the contributions came from Sadie.

"Fine," I pout, pushing out of my chair to go pay my fine. "And don't talk with food in your mouth."

"So," Ace says in a way that clearly indicates he's about to ask for something. "I know Mrs. Duncan is supposed to watch me while you work tonight, but Jayden is coming back tonight and I was wondering if I could go over there instead?"

Crap.

"About that . . ." I smile a smile that I know is showing too many teeth to look natural. "I don't have to work anymore."

"Why?" Ace drops his fork onto the table, his green eyes filled with worry. "Did you get fired?"

Yes.

"What? No!" I lie. "I just decided I wanted a job where I could work during the day instead of all night and then I'm too tired to hang with my best guy."

"Really?" Ace still looks skeptical.

"Really." I ruffle his hair. "And guess what? I already have a meeting at HERS, you know, that place right next to Fresh. If I work there, I can bring home smoothies every day."

His face lights up and I see my mistake immediately. If possible, always lead with smoothies. A rookie mistake, really.

"Awesome!"

"Right?" I smirk and grab his now empty plate off the table for him. "And since I

171

don't have anywhere to be, I was thinking maybe we go see that new superhero movie you've been talking about and go to dinner tonight."

"Burgers?"

Predictable.

"We just had them yesterday," I groan.

"What about Mexican?" he asks. His eyebrows hide under his loose curls and he rubs his greedy hands together. "Chips and guacamole?"

"Deal." I know we just had it too, but there is no such thing as too much Mexican food.

I send TK a text asking for Brynn's number before I hop in the shower, but when I get out, he still hasn't texted me back.

On a whim, I decide to walk to HERS and introduce myself to Brynn. It's so out of character that when I look in the mirror to put gel in my hair, I'm shocked to see it's still my reflection looking back at me.

I don't repeat the mistake I made earlier when I ask Ace to go to HERS with me. And even though I just fed him, I still lead with smoothies and muffins. As expected, he jumps at the opportunity . . . after bargaining a large smoothie out of me.

"Fine," I concede, convinced this kid of

mine is going to be a lawyer of some sort when he grows up. "But you have to get the vitamin boost instead of the energy one."

Kid has more energy than anyone I've ever met. That caffeine boost they use gives me a major parenting disadvantage.

"You drive a hard bargain." He reaches for my hand. "But deal."

I look at his extended hand and laugh. "I'm sorry, but are you nine or thirty-five?"

"A very mature nine, thank you." He pushes open the front door, decked out in the Mustangs gear TK brought him.

I lock the door behind us and cringe again when the gate I still haven't fixed screeches.

"You really need to fix that, Mom."

"Yeah." I roll my eyes at his obvious suggestion. "Thanks for the advice, Ace."

"No problem." He ignores the sarcasm in my tone and skips away.

I try to keep up, but I'm too worried about scuffing the one nice pair of flats I own to chance it. Ace gets to HERS a full minute before I do.

"All right, dude." I lean into him when I reach the front door. "I don't think this will take long, I just want to introduce myself and then we'll hit Fresh." I fish my phone out of my purse and hand it to Ace. "Read a book, play a game, but turn the volume all the way down. Got it?"

"Got it, coach." He salutes.

Little smart-ass.

I pull open the door, relieved it's unlocked. Seeing as this wasn't the most thought-out plan and I didn't want to talk myself out of this brave endeavor, I left the house before even googling their hours.

"We're still closed," a peppy voice shouts from the back.

I look to Ace for any kind of support, a smile, a high five, anything, but he just shrugs, his eyes focused on my phone, and walks to a cozy-looking couch in the corner.

"I — I actually just wanted to introduce myself to you." I move to the open door the voice came from, and when I peek in, a gorgeous blonde is sitting at a desk covered in papers. "Are you Brynn?" I ask.

"I am." She shoves her chair back and stands when she sees me. "And you are?"

"Hi." I start to wave, then cut it short and extend my arm to shake her hand, then cringe at how awkward I must look. "I'm Poppy Patterson."

Her eyes go wide, causing lines to mar her otherwise Photoshopped face. "Poppy Patterson?" she repeats, her smile turning from sweet and welcoming to deranged and a little frightening.

"Ummm . . ." I drag out the word, unsure if I should answer or back away slowly. "Yeah?" I answer because she might be a bit of an oddball, but I'd still like to work for her.

"Like Poppy Patterson?" She bounces on her tiptoes and claps her hands together. "*The* Poppy Patterson?"

"Uh, I don't know if I'm *the* Poppy Patterson, but I've never met anybody else with my name." I tug one of the curls by my face, losing the battle not to fidget.

"Are you TK's Poppy?" she finally clarifies.

"Oh!" My shoulders slump and I let out a short bark of laughter. She's not insane and TK at least called her. "Yeah, sorry. He never texted me back, I didn't know he called you."

"He didn't," she half shouts at me, still vibrating with excitement.

"Uhh . . ."

Annnnnd I'm back to confused.

"Wait until I tell Marlee I met you! She's going to flip!" She turns back to her desk and grabs the phone covered in a "Smash the Patriarchy" case. "She said she saw you at the park, but you were far away. I get the first good look and she's gonna be so jealous. You're stunning, by the way. Not that

175

I'd expect much less from TK. He drives me insane, but he's hot."

"Thanks?" I don't know if it's necessary for me to respond — she's having a pretty lengthy conversation without me — but it seems like the polite thing to do.

"Marlee," she says into her phone, her eyes focused on me. "No. Stop talking. Guess who I'm looking at right now?" She pauses. "No." Pause again. "Nope." She singsongs and winks, like I'm a willing participant in this game. "Okay, okay. I'll tell you because you're never going to guess. Standing right in front of me at HERS is none other than Poppy Patterson." She pulls the receiver away from her ear, laughing, and I hear the scream from the other end.

"Mom?" Ace asks, peeking his head into the room, no doubt concerned with the noise levels echoing throughout the small restaurant. His eyes shift between me and Brynn, who has gone silent, which is alarming considering her earlier reaction. "You okay?"

"Yeah, dude. Everything's good," I rush out. "Just play on my phone for a little longer."

" 'Kay." He doesn't look convinced, but he turns and pulls the door shut behind him.

"Sorry about that," I say to a still-silent Brynn, whose eyes have nearly tripled in size since I looked at her ten seconds ago.

"Holy shit," she breathes. Whether it's to me or Marlee, I'm not sure. "A mini TK with better hair." She tears her gaze from the closed door and looks at me. "I didn't know a TK with better hair was possible." She blinks a few times, shaking her head as if to jar her brain back into action. "Shit. I'm being so rude. I'll call you later, Mars." She nods to whatever's being said but only says, "Bye," before hanging up and putting her phone back on her desk.

Meeting people I don't know is always a special kind of uncomfortable hell for me, but this seems like a whole new level . . . even for me. I don't know what to say and I want to find TK and wring his freaking neck for not calling Brynn and warning her I'd be coming in.

"I'm so sorry for just dropping in like this. TK said he'd call you and tell you I was coming."

"Please, you are not the one who should be apologizing right now." She raises both hands in front of her chest, as if surrendering. "And I swear, TK is one of the most forgetful people I know."

This information takes me aback for

multiple reasons. One, TK has remembered every last detail of everything Ace has told him since he came to my house that first meeting. Which is a lot. Ace never shuts up around TK. Two, the TK I know and have known since I was teenager was my personal recorder. Whether it was something my parents said in passing or notes for our chemistry test, he remembered it all. It's why he was a straight-A student. It used to drive me crazy. I'd study for hours and barely get a B, and he'd glance at his notes and ace his tests.

It's why I started calling him Ace.

"He said you might be hiring?" I ask, bracing for the instant letdown.

"I am," she says, her smile morphing from apologetic back to excited. "I guess TK doesn't forget everything."

"I know I'd need to do a real interview, but I'd really love to apply. Not only is this place right down the street from my house, but I've heard nothing but great things and I'd love to be a part of it."

This is all true. I'm not trying to butter her up . . . well, not totally. HERS is a bar owned by a woman and marketed toward women. The waitresses aren't dressed in cleavage-revealing tees, and there aren't men taking up all the seats and oxygen, man-splaining and acting like you should be grateful to be in their space.

And after working at the literal opposite for the last two years, HERS is my version of heaven.

Also, working in pants would be a welcome change.

"Do you have restaurant experience?" she asks.

"Umm." I hesitate.

I know I need to be honest, I'll have to provide my work history after all, but I'd hate for her to think less of me. For the look of disgust and superiority I've became so well accustomed to from the women who'd occasionally tag along with their boyfriend to the club, to make an appearance on Brynn's welcoming face. But I know I don't really have a choice. I pull at the hem of my shirt with both hands and avoid eye contact. "Yeah, I waitressed at the Emerald Cabaret for the last two years."

"Two years?" Brynn repeats, but I can't decipher the tone in her voice. "Good for you, girl. I know you were killing it there. I went a while ago, the waitress uniforms were so cute, I went home and ordered a sequined corset from Trashy. Spent three hundred dollars and wore it once . . . alone

179

in my bedroom. It wasn't a good look on me."

I find that hard to believe. Brynn is basically a supermodel. I'd put good money on everything being a good look on her.

"Trust me, once in your bedroom is more than enough. Wire piping isn't the cornerstone of comfort." We both laugh at the truth in my words, but I still reconsider giving my uniform back. I was the only one who wore my size, so it's not like they'll miss it.

"Yeah, and I'm all about comfort." She stops and bites her lip, her eyes moving to the ceiling before dropping back to me. "Listen."

My stomach clenches as I fight the urge to retreat. She was nice about my nightclub past, but here comes the gentle letdown.

"I think I'm a pretty good judge of character. I hired Marlee on the spot and that worked out well for me," she says.

My breath gets stuck in my chest, a sliver of hope poking out behind the gloomy cloud of dread that's always following me around.

"And my gut is telling me you're good people. If it's not too late notice, why don't you come in this weekend right before we open, about ten, and stay until after the lunch rush? We can see how you like it."

"It's not too late," I promise, feeling a relief so heady my knees go weak.

"Great!" She bounces on her toes again and I think she's genuinely excited for me to work with her.

"Thank you so much, Brynn." I give her a hug, forgetting in the moment how much I hate touching strangers. "You won't regret this!"

"I know I won't." She hugs me back, clearly not sharing my distaste for affection.

Now, I'm sure we are not only wearing matching psychotic smiles, but have matching pitch as well.

I lean in for one last hug when Brynn's arms go straight and she pushes me back.

"Oh!" Her eyes widen and drop down to my feet. "There's not really a dress code here, just dress how you're comfortable, but just so you know, I wear tennis shoes." She points at her red Chuck Taylor–covered feet and I want to weep.

"Tennis shoes at work?" I pull her in for another hug. "I will never let this job go."

Even if I do keep the corset, I decide in this moment, the heels must die.

I make sure to add lighter fluid and wood for my fireplace to the running grocery list in my head. Tonight, the spiked, five-inch Devils will meet their doom.

"See you soon." I wave and walk out of the office.

Ace's concern for my safety must've been fleeting because he's so into whatever he's doing on my phone that he doesn't even notice me walk out of the room.

"Come on, dude. Large smoothies and a dozen muffins to go." I snap my fingers, causing him to jump off the couch. "We have some celebrating to do."

SIXTEEN

"Answer, answer, answer," I whisper into the receiver as the phone rings in my ear and I pace back and forth in my room.

This is the third attempt I've made to call TK since I left HERS. I know he's busy and my new waitressing gig isn't the most exciting news in the world, but after blowing off sending me Brynn's number last night and not responding to my texts or answering my calls, I'm getting a complex. I've been racking my mind, going over what we said before he left, wondering if I did or said anything to piss him off. But I can't think of anything.

"Yo," TK answers just before I give up hope and hit the End button.

"Hey!" I say, and cringe at the volume of my voice. I haven't even started at HERS yet and I feel like Brynn's already rubbing off on me. "What are you doing?"

"Leaving meetings from this morning's

practice, about to grab some lunch before more meetings and more practice." There is something off with his tone. He seems almost annoyed to be on the phone with me. The knot in my stomach tightens and I sneak out of the living room without Ace noticing. "Do you need anything?"

"Uh, no. I just wanted to tell you about my morning."

I stop and wait for him to say something . . . anything, but I'm only met with silence.

"Me and Ace went to HERS and you're now talking to the newest waitress!" I dance in my room despite the chilly reception on the other end, too excited to not be unemployed to fight it.

"Shit, I can't believe I forgot to send you her number," TK groans, and I can picture him with his head down, his hair falling in front of his face, concealing his look of frustration. "Congratulations, though. I knew she'd hire you."

"It's not a huge deal, but thank you. I think it worked out better, you not calling," I reassure him, even though I'm still a little annoyed at his forgetfulness over something that was actually really important. "It forced me to step out of my comfort zone."

"I can push you out of your comfort

zone," TK says, all traces of the grumpy, brooding guy I was talking to pushed to the side by the horny teenager I remember all too well.

"TK!" I scold him, heat flooding my cheeks. "You can't say stuff like that."

"Why?" he asks, and I don't answer. "I'm alone. Is Ace by you?"

I glance around my empty bedroom. "Well . . . no . . ."

"Poppy." TK's voice has an edge to it and I give up trying to predict where his moods are taking him. "You know how many women I've wanted to explore a relationship with since I got drafted?"

I try to think back to our earlier conversations, but I can't remember the exact number. "Not many?" I figure it's a good guess because there's no way he's stupid enough to bring this up if it wasn't the case.

"None," he corrects me.

Jaw to the freaking floor.

None?

Why? How is that even possible?

"It's possible," he says, reading my mind in the same freakish way he was able to when we were younger. It creeped me out when we were kids, and it still creeps me out.

"There had to be at least one."

"Not. Fucking. One." He stresses each word. "I don't know if you know this or not, but people consider me a catch."

"You are?" Obviously, I know this is true. He's funny, hot, and rich. But he also has a ginormous ego and I'm not adding to it.

"Yeah, I am." He knows I know. "You might not want to hear this, but I'm gonna tell you anyways. I came into this league at twenty-two. I was single with seven figures in my bank account. I was looking for fun only. I didn't even hook up with most of the women who took me back to their place."

"Okay. I call BS on that." I glance at my closed door, straining my ears to make sure I don't hear Ace's impatient footsteps coming to get me.

"We have enough real shit that's happened between us to deal with. I'm not going to add to it by lying to you about something stupid."

I know this too.

"I know," I whisper, feeling bad for even joking about it.

"I know," he whispers back, and if I close my eyes tight enough, I'm convinced I'd feel his arms wrapping around me. "Remember when I told you that I made sure nobody trapped me?"

"Yeah." As much as I wish I was able to

186

forget every word he spewed the night I told him about Ace, the opposite happened. It's like everything that came out of his mouth was etched onto my brain.

"I kept my distance. I never got close enough for anyone to catch feelings or want it to go further than a good time," he says. "I'm the fun guy. The player they can brag to their friends about. I've never given anyone expectations of more."

I scrunch my nose, thankful he can't see my face. I try my hardest not to work out the math of his confession.

"I'm not sure I understand why you're telling me this."

"Because." He sighs, his giant hands no doubt working their way through his long locks. "I need you to get where I'm coming from. I don't take women home. I don't save their numbers in my phone. And I don't say lines.

"I know we're different people who've lived different lives, but you can't question everything I say to you. Yes, I'm here for Ace, I already love that kid. He's the shit and I don't want to miss out on another minute with him." He stops and I blink away the tears that pop up hearing him talk about Ace. Then more words come. "But he's not the reason I want to explore things with you. If anything, he's the reason we should stick to just trying to be friends. But even when I was mad because I thought you were lying about him, I was still dreaming about you. Spending the day with you guys was the happiest I have been in years. Being with you makes me feel like myself again. And you're so fucking beautiful that even though it's only the first day of camp, I'm already getting yelled at in meetings because I can't focus when all I think about is when I get to be with you again. When I'll be able to touch you . . . kiss you again."

Holy crap.

I mean . . .

I was not expecting that.

At all.

Thank God I'm standing in front of my bed, because after all of that? My legs lose the ability to keep supporting me.

I don't know how long I lie on my bed not saying anything. Ten seconds? A century?

TK calls my name, and I have to squeeze my eyes shut to clear the lusty haze clouding my vision.

"Sparks?" he repeats himself.

I sit up, smoothing my shirt and clearing my throat. "Yeah. Sorry."

"You good?"

"Yeah." I glance down at my shaky hands. "I'm good."

"So you understand where I'm coming from?" he asks, laughter — and cockiness — evident in his voice.

Pull yourself together, Poppy!

"Yeah." I pinch myself on the arm. "I understand."

"Good," he says, sounding all happy-go-lucky, not moody, or tired, or like a Sex God, and I wonder if maybe he developed some extra personalities to go along with all the muscles he's amassed over the years. "So are you and Ace coming to practice on Friday? Tell Ace we're wearing full pads. It's gonna be a good one."

"We'll be there." I try to sound normal, but instead I sound like an overexcited cartoon character from a show Ace stopped watching years ago. "Like Ace would ever let me off the hook. You don't need incentives, seeing you is enough. Even though . . ." I smile up to my ceiling. "He was talking about Maxwell Lewis a lot last night."

"Well, shit," he mumbles into the phone and I can almost hear his grin. "Now I have to embarrass poor Maxwell at practice tonight."

"If that's possible. I don't even watch

189

football and I know how good he is."

"Now you're just trying to piss me off." He laughs into the phone. "I'll see you guys soon, yeah?"

"Yeah," I whisper, feeling shy all of a sudden.

"Good. Later, Sparks."

"Bye, TK." I hang up before he can say anything else.

I throw my phone on the bed next to me and grab a pillow, bringing it to my chest and squeezing my arms around it as hard as I can.

TK unravels me in ways I thought impossible. I've lived such a guarded half-life for so many years, he's a shock to my system. TK is a double espresso after years of no caffeine. He's a blood-curdling scream after years of silence.

He's sunshine after living in darkness.

I heard everything he said to me, panty-baring proof withstanding, I felt every word as it passed through my receiver. And I want to fall into his arms with abandon. I want to dive into one of my favorite books and believe I'm as deserving of a happily-ever-after as the badass heroine fighting for love.

And I'm trying.

As much as I want to let go of all my fears, they keep popping up unwelcome in my mind. I don't know if I was an asshole in a past life or something, but I know not to stay excited for something for long. Besides Ace, nothing good in my life lasts.

So as excited as I am to explore things with TK, I can't help but sit and wait for the other shoe to drop.

I bring the pillow up to my face and let out a frustrated scream, full of anger and self-loathing for making even the simplest decision in my life a problem.

TK cares about me.

I care about TK.

We both care about Ace.

Simple.

But, man, am I making this complicated.

SEVENTEEN

"Hurry up, Mom!" Ace shouts through the
house. I don't even need to look to know
he's standing in front of the door with every
piece of Mustangs gear he owns on. Which,
thanks to TK, is quite a lot.

Ace is buzzing with excitement. All he's
been able to talk about for the last few days
is training camp. And not just to me. I am
pretty sure anyone who has encountered
him since TK came over has heard not only
about his other newly discovered DNA
contributor but about his impending trip to
the Mecca for Mustangs fans, the Mustangs
training facility in Dove Valley.

I close my eyes and count to ten before
answering, hoping I'll be able to disguise
some of the dread in my voice. "Hold on,
I'm coming!"

Nope, didn't work.

Even though TK has been in camp for
only a couple of days, I've enjoyed the

closed-to-the-public aspect of it. TK has made sure to call Ace every night and tell him about how practice is going and which rookies to watch out for. They'd chat for a while, Ace would go to bed happy, and I didn't have to stand around in the summer sun with women I don't know and probably won't like.

I wish we could do that today. But apparently opening day is the biggest deal ever to Ace so we're trekking to the freaking suburbs to stand outside with maniacs who took the day off work to watch grown men tackle each other into an early grave.

What is that, you ask?

Do I have a piss-poor attitude about this?

Why, yes. Yes, I do. But I'm allowed to be jaded.

I give myself a once-over in the bathroom mirror one last time and it pisses me off that I do. I don't know why I care. TK and I are "exploring" things. I'm not his girlfriend yet. But even so, I might have spent longer than necessary making sure my curl definition was on point and my bronzer was just enough. I don't have any Mustangs gear, but Ace demanded I at least wear my orange razorback tank. Orange is my color. And my brown skin does look phenomenal against my white denim shorts.

"Mooooommmmmm!" Ace calls again. Thankfully, he can't see me roll my eyes and stick out my tongue before I round the corner.

I was right. Ace is like a walking billboard for the Mustangs. Jersey, hat, basketball shorts, and socks, all Mustangs. He looks ridiculous but I don't say anything. The gleam in his eyes is breathtaking, and even though I'd rather spoon my eyeballs out of my head than go to training camp, his joy makes this worth it . . . I guess.

"Here, I'm ready." I grab my purse off the hook next to the door and slip on my flip-flops. "Did you get sunscreen on?"

"Yes, Mom."

Unlucky for him, I do see him roll his eyes. "Excuse me?"

"Sorry," he corrects himself. "I just really don't want to miss anything. I mean, this is opening day! Noah tried to go last year and they couldn't even get in, that's how crowded it was."

I try to think of any other reason to stall, but I come up empty-handed. "All right then, let's get a move on."

I don't even finish before he swings the back door open and sprints to the garage.

I guess we're doing this.

Ace is a child, and because of that, I will

not give him the satisfaction of being right.

We should've left at least thirty minutes earlier.

Parking is a nightmare and the volunteers in orange vests who are supposed to be able to tell me where I can park are zero help. Obnoxious people who might already be drunk are crossing the streets without looking and definitely not at crosswalks. And I'm pretty sure Ace has learned some new, creative blending of curse words.

I'm about two seconds from taking our asses home when I see police officers who look as miserable as I feel monitoring the front gate of the Mustangs facility. They are Ace's last chance at watching practice today. If they can't tell me where the hell I can park, I'm leaving.

I roll down my window and yell out to them, ignoring the cars waiting behind me because, well, screw them. "Excuse me, sir? Can you tell me where I can park?"

"There's paid parking all around, but it's probably full by now. Maybe if you head that way, you can find something." He takes his time walking up to my window, probably doing what I'm doing and trying not to yell at me for his misfortune of getting stuck here today.

"Yeah, I've seen all of that. But I have this

195

parking pass." I wave the stupid parking pass that doesn't have directions to the lot where the freaking parking pass is valid. "Do you have any clue where it's for?"

His eyes go wide and the once-over he gives me makes me super uncomfortable but also glad I took the ten — fine, thirty — extra minutes to get ready. "That's for the player and family lot. Turn right into here and we'll open the gate for you."

"Oh my god. Thank you so much," I say before he can retreat. "Finding this lot was about to make me go crazy. I swear, I might kiss you."

"Ew, Mom!" Ace groans from the back seat. It's the first thing he's uttered since I accidentally snapped when he told me to watch my language.

Not even out of the car and I'm already embarrassing him. Today's gonna go well.

"No problem, ma'am." The officer is clearly uncomfortable and color rises in his cheeks as he turns to walk back to the other officer manning the gate to parking freedom.

I turn right and they wave me through without having to say another word. Which, whatever. He called me "ma'am." I think saying I want to kiss you is much kinder than making someone feel a hundred years old.

As soon as we pass the gates, it's like we've entered another world. Gone are the Hondas and Toyotas of the world. I'm surrounded by blacked-out Mercedes, BMWs, and Range Rovers. I've always taken pride in our Volvo. It's a solid car. One I'd never be driving if it weren't for Maya, but holy hell, it looks like a freaking hoopty compared to the other cars. I glance in my rearview mirror and see Ace with his face plastered against the window. Where I'm wearing an expression of horror, Ace is in awe. So I push through my urge to flip a U-turn and bust back through the gate and instead just park as far away from the other cars as possible.

"All right, dude. You ready?" I hand Ace his lanyard with the laminated family pass hanging from it.

"Yes!" He snatches it from my hand, throws it over his head, and is out of my car before I can even pull the key from the ignition.

I open the door and follow Ace across the parking lot faster than I wanted. The heat radiating up from the pavement and through my flip-flops is like the Devil's way of encouragement. Any hint of morning breeze must have faded while we were driving in circles, searching for parking.

When we reach the sidewalk, there's a woman with a bright smile and a headset on to greet us.

"Hi there. I'm Jane, what's your name?" She reaches a hand out to Ace, whose smile shows he's the only one of us excited to be here.

"I'm Ace," he answers, and for the first time all day, I can hear the nerves in his voice.

"Hi, Ace." She shakes his hand, her smile never dimming, before she moves it to me. "And I'm gonna guess you're Mom?"

"I am." I shake her hand. "Poppy Patterson."

"Poppy," she repeats. "I love that name."

Most people repeat both names and say something like "Well, that's a mouthful" or something just as annoying. And that's before they find out my middle name is Penelope. Jane's genuine and kind reaction to my name warms me to her instantly.

"Like I told Ace here, I'm Jane and I'm the manager of the family program for the Mustangs. Since we haven't met before, I'm going to go ahead and assume this is your first time at training camp?"

"It is."

"Well, great! Is your Mustang player one of the rookies?"

198

"My dad's TK Moore," Ace answers loud and proud.

I never could've imagined how fast Ace and TK would take to each other. There was no awkward waiting period. TK has no problem calling Ace his son, and Ace clearly has no problem telling the entire world TK's his dad.

Me, on the other hand, I'm still adjusting to everything. And by the way Jane's jaw damn near hits her shoe, it's an adjustment for her too.

"Oh wow!" She shakes her head as if jarring her brain back into place. "I should've known that, you look just like him."

I'm glad I have my sunglasses on because Ace beams so bright at her words, it would've blinded me without them. "Thanks!"

Ugh. Like looking like me wouldn't be even better? Brat.

I clear my throat and pull her shell-shocked face back to mine. "Where are we supposed to go?"

"Oh, I'm sorry!" Her painted smile is back on her face. "Just follow this sidewalk and you'll come to a set of stairs. Once you go down the stairs, you can go two ways. Right will take you toward the field. We have tents set up behind the fields for you to watch

199

your players at camp. There's food and drinks available and fans so you don't die from heat exhaustion. If you go left, that will take you to a gate so you can join the rest of the spectators. There are games and bounce houses for the kids. Just make sure you don't lose your family credentials. Without them, you won't be able to come back in. After practice is over, the players will have an hour or two of free time in which they'll be able to see you before heading back to the hotel for team meetings."

I take in the bucket of information she just dumped on me and pray I can retain it all. "Left, spectators. Right, family. Got it." God. Is there an option three for isolation?

"And if you need anything else, I'll be right around here, so just holler at me."

"Will do." I try to smile, but the knots in my stomach make it impossible. I wasn't even this nervous my first shift at the Emerald Cabaret. Why does this seem so intimidating? "Thanks, Jane."

"Yeah, thanks, Ms. Jane," Ace says like they're old friends.

This time, as we start moving, Ace doesn't sprint forward and we walk together.

I guess this is it. No more procrastinating.

Time to see what this NFL crazy world is really like.

EIGHTEEN

It doesn't take long before two perfectly maintained fields appear in front of us. The steady hum of noise grows into a roar, and we're specks in the middle of a sea of blue and orange. Navy blue helmets with an orange stripe down the center bob around in groups spread across the fields. Wearing full pads and uniforms, the players are ready to put on a show for the thousands of fans who braved the traffic and heat to catch a glimpse of their favorite athletes.

Ace's steps stutter beside me as we approach the set of cement stairs leading down to the madness.

Sensing his nerves starting to take over, I squeeze his hand in mine. "You ready?"

"I guess so." The enthusiasm he's been toting around for the last week is almost completely diminished, which means one thing — I have to act like an actual grown-up and ease his fears, even though I feel like throwing up or running away . . . or maybe both.

"Then move it, Patterson." I walk down the steps, pulling him with me. "Which way are we going to go?"

Please say left. Please say left. Please say left!

"Ummm . . ." His eyes shift from side to side between the overwhelming crowd fighting to get the best view of the field and the calm of the white tent, where a few small children are running around in circles just outside the makeshift door. "Right."

Mother sucker! I bite the inside of my cheek and nod my head, turning on a rubber heel toward the tent of affluence.

We make it to the tent, and I can feel that when Jane said they had fans, she meant they had an industrial air conditioner. A cool breeze blasts out of the opening, causing goose bumps to cover my bare arms and legs, and even Ace rubs his hands along his exposed arms.

I walk inside first, too focused on Ace's hesitant steps to notice eyes swinging our way and the quick lull in the conversation floating around. As soon as he steps inside, a group of kids, mostly younger than him, run right to him.

"I'm Jagger. What's your name?" a boy

who's probably around seven and wearing jean shorts and a Mustangs jersey like I've never seen before asks him.

"Ace." He answers the question I hope he's prepared to answer all day.

"Hi, Ace," Jagger says, his brown eyes smiling and his brown skin flushed even in the chill of the tent. "We're gonna go play tag, do you wanna play with us?"

Ace looks to me before he answers and I nod my head encouragingly even though I want him at my side.

"Sure," Ace says. The smile that disappeared moments ago returns full force. He yanks off his family pass and shoves it in my hands before he runs off with his new friend and leaves me alone.

Well, damn.

I look around the tent, now very aware of being alone and new. It's like high school all over again . . . but worse. Even though the air conditioning has me wishing I brought a sweater, my palms are sweating and my cheeks are flaming hot.

The front of the tent is open, giving everyone a clear view of the practice fields. There's a table in the corner covered with sandwiches, salads, chips, and all sorts of goodies. Considering I'm already on the verge of emptying my breakfast all over the floor, I skip it, but I do grab a bottle of water from one of the many fully stocked coolers lining the back "wall." Plastic tables and chairs are scattered about and cheers from outside fill the space, giving me the false hope of flying under the radar.

I find an open table near the back of the tent and take in the scene in front of me. It's like watching a Bravo TV show being filmed live. Women with their hair straightened or curled to perfection move from table to table, giving air kisses and hugs to old friends. Their glossed lips, contoured faces, and false lashes are a stark contrast to my bargain bronzer and drugstore mascara. And don't even get me started on their outfits. The few who are wearing Mustangs gear have their shirts cut and sewn into body-hugging masterpieces. Designer jeans cover every set of legs, and I'm the only person in the room in flip-flops. High heels and red-bottom soles bounce in the plastic chairs as they animatedly fill each other in on their off-season adventures. Diamond rings wink and sparkle from every angle . . . even in the shade.

Listen, I know I'm no schmuck, but these women could give anybody a complex. It's like I've walked into a Christian Siriano fashion show. The women are all different sizes and races, but they are all freaking stunning. I thought I was coming to football practice, not freaking fashion week.

I don't fit in with the soccer moms and I won't fit in with these women either. I'm happy with my Target flip-flops and discount shorts. I don't want to be one of those women who judge other women based on their clothes. The kind of woman who guards herself under Gucci and Chanel armors.

"And what's your name, sweetie?" A voice with a strong Southern flare startles me out of my wealth-filled trance.

I look up to see the tiniest woman with the biggest, blondest hair I've ever seen. Her bright pink lips are framing teeth one bleaching appointment away from glowing in the dark, and the diamond-covered hoops in her ears are nearly as big as her head.

"Poppy." I smile big and stretch out my hand, faking the confidence I do not feel. "Poppy Patterson."

"I'm Dixie Thompson," she tells me while shaking my hand and not at all discreetly checking my very empty ring finger. "Your first training camp?"

"How'd you guess?" I let out a bitter laugh.

"We all had a first, which is a blessing in

itself." She sits in the empty chair beside me and leans in close. "My husband's Chad, Chad Thompson, he's an offensive lineman." She keeps going when my eyes don't light up with recognition. "This is his twelfth season with the Mustangs."

I shrug my shoulders, offering her an apologetic look. "I don't really follow football."

"Well then." She pats my hand resting on the table. "Nothing we can't fix. I'm from Texas and my daddy was a high school football coach, so I grew up under Friday night lights. If anybody can fill you in, it's me."

That's nice of her, I guess.

"Thanks."

"Are you here with someone from the front office?" she asks, clearly trying to connect the dots as to how someone with no football knowledge is sharing this space with her.

"Ummm . . . no." I move my hands under the table to hide the fidgeting. "TK Moore."

Her eyes damn near pop out of her head and her jaw is on the table. She stares at me, saying absolutely nothing for about ten seconds longer than is socially acceptable before half asking and half screaming, "TK?," drawing the attention of everyone within fifteen feet of us.

"Ummm . . ." I bite my bottom lip, unable to focus on Dixie with damn near the entire tent staring at us.

"Well, bless your little heart. Isn't that just special?" She smoothes her face into a smile that doesn't look natural or happy.

"I guess so?"

She pushes away from the table and unfolds herself from the cheap plastic chair that's probably burning a hole in her jeans. Her hair, which must be responsible for at least forty percent of the deterioration of the ozone layer, never moves. "Nice meetin' you . . . Poppy, wasn't it?"

I only nod, not at all understanding the direction this conversation went.

"Poppy," she repeats, looking down her nose at me. "Enjoy your day."

She turns on a heel that puts my work stilettos to shame and saunters her tiny self to a table filled with more wide-eyed beauties, who don't even attempt to hide their interest in wanting to be filled in on TK Moore's guest.

What in the world was that about?

"Ignore Dixie, she thinks she's queen supreme and her guard goes up whenever she thinks someone is a threat." A gorgeous brunette with the sharpest bob I've ever seen sits in the just-evacuated seat before I even have a chance to get a grip on what happened.

"Umm . . ."

"I'm Charli Easton." She points to the field diagonal from where we're sitting. "Number eighty-seven, Shawn, he's mine."

"Poppy." I half wave, still recovering from the whiplash Dixie gave me.

"So . . ." She pauses, a smile wide on her face, but unlike the Southern pixie, there's no calculating glint in her eye. "TK, huh?"

"Umm . . ." She's going think there's something wrong with me if I don't start stringing words together soon, but how do I answer that? "It's complicated."

I almost laugh at the gross understatement. "Complicated" doesn't even begin to describe the saga that is Poppy and TK.

"The good stories always are." She leans back in her chair, making herself comfortable. Well, as comfortable as you can get in a plastic folding chair.

I take a long sip of my water. "Isn't that the truth."

"What are we talking about?" a curvy black woman with loads of long black hair almost down to her ass says, taking the empty seat to my right.

"I was just introducing myself to Poppy,

here." Charli talks across me. "How are you holding up so far?"

"Girl." She leans back into her seat with a flair one can only learn by watching daytime soaps. "These damn kids are going to kill me. If not now, then from liver failure later. When I tell you I'm almost up to a bottle of wine a day, I am not lying. Little demons. They won't stop wrestling and pretending to be Daddy. Cute until they're breaking shit and almost breaking bones. I'm already ready for the season to be over. Anyways . . ." She sits back up and looks at me, flicking her wrist in a mini wave. "I'm Lavonne, but you can call me Vonnie. Sorry about that little rant, but I figured if you're gonna be my friend, you might as well know what to expect from me from the beginning."

I might love Vonnie. Some may say it's too soon and I'm too young to know what true love is, but she had me at wine and demons.

"I always make sure I have a bottle of wine stashed in the house," I tell her, feeling happy for the first time today that I decided to come. "So I totally understand."

"You have kids?" Charli leans in, her voice hushed and her eyes wide.

"One, Ace." I point to Ace, who's still running around, having the time of his life. "The one with the perfectly highlighted mess of curls, he's nine."

"I was wondering who the little cutie keeping my crew entertained was. They've usually scared off most of the other kids by now, but they're loving running around with him," Vonnie says.

Pride wells up in my chest the way it always does when Ace is mentioned. "He's a good kid."

"Mine are the ones in the Lamar jerseys." Vonnie points to Jagger, the one who stole Ace from me, and two other not-so-little boys with matching haircuts. They look like they could be triplets and my respect for her multiplies. "Wait." She pauses, squinting her eyes at Ace as he runs away from her boys. "Is that a Moore jersey?"

"Ummm . . ." My hands start to fidget underneath the table again. I pinch my thigh to avoid biting my lip and looking even more nervous than I already do. "Yeah."

"Wait," Vonnie repeats as she and Charli both lean in closer. "You and TK are a thing?"

"You didn't hear Dixie announce it to everyone?" Charli asks Vonnie, like she's annoyed to have to go over these details when there's a much bigger, juicier story to be told.

"You know I ignore Dixie's ass whenever possible." Vonnie looks from Charli to me. "Which is all the damn time. That woman works my damn nerves."

Considering my one experience with Dixie, that's not hard for me to believe. "I can see how that could happen."

"Yes, Dixie is insane. Everyone knows this," Charli whisper yells at both of us. "But what nobody knows is if TK has a son."

"Oh yes." Vonnie purses her lips and nods her head, the same look Maya's church friends give when spilling church tea. "Good point. Is Ace TK's?"

How did this become a paternity interrogation?

"I mean . . ." I look between the two women at my sides. I'm not ashamed, but it's also not really their business. But on the other hand, since I had Ace, I've become a pretty decent judge of character, and I'm ninety-nine percent sure they aren't asking for gossip ammunition. And letting my guard down a couple of inches can't hurt too much . . . right? "Yeah. TK and I went to high school toge—"

Vonnie and Charli both cut me off before

I can explain further.

"No more," Charli says.

"Yeah." Vonnie agrees and only ups my confusion. "Most of these women are the shit, but there's a small handful who you do not want to overhear your business."

"Cough, Dixie, cough." Charli points to the table where Dixie and five other women are sitting.

Vonnie puts an expectant palm in front of me. "Give me your phone."

"Oookay . . ." I give it to her because she doesn't seem like the kind of woman to take no for an answer.

She fiddles around on it for a couple of minutes before giving it back to me. "There. I entered my number, my address, and made an appointment for you to come over tomorrow for lunch."

I open my mouth to interrupt, but I don't get a word out.

"No excuses. You come, drink wine, and chat. Ace and my boys can run around and play. It's a win-win." Damn. She's good. I thought I had mom authority down, but she's putting me to shame.

Still one problem, though. "I'm actually supposed to start working this weekend. I can do Sunday night, though, if you aren't already busy."

"The only plans I have for the next two weeks are trying to not lose my mind. You coming over will greatly increase my odds of survival. Plus, Sunday is the first preseason game. Come over early and we can watch it together." She grabs her soda off the table and twists it open. "What about you, Charli? Can you make it Sunday?"

She shrugs her shoulders. "I did have some pretty exciting plans with my DVR, but they can wait a night, I guess."

"This bitch." Vonnie rolls her eyes and tries to sound irritated, but the smile tugging at the corners of her full lips reveals her true feelings.

"So Sunday?" I confirm.

"Sunday." Charli nods her head. "I'll bring dessert and you bring details. Like, all of them."

Well, shit.

What the hell did I get myself into this time?

NINETEEN

I hate to admit it, but I'm kind of dreading the whistle blowing and this day ending.

Admittedly, I pay zero attention to the football being played in front of me, I'm much more interested in the women beside me. Vonnie and Charli are hilarious and I feel guilty for the preconceived notions I had when I first stepped foot into the tent.

Charli, whose name I learn is really Charolette, is getting her master's in business from the University of Denver. Vonnie has her law degree but decided to take a break while Justin is playing. She started sharing her struggles adjusting from being a part of the workforce to a stay-at-home mom, and I guess she is Internet famous . . . which I also learn is a thing. You know people can make a crap ton of money from YouTube videos? What in the actual world and sign me up. Please and thank you.

"How much longer until it's over?" Ace

comes over to me for the first time since he went running off with Jagger. His face is beet red and glistening from the sweat he's gained over the last two hours of relentless playing.

I glance at my phone, which I realize is pointless. "I have no idea," I tell him before turning the question over to the experts around us. "Do you know?"

Vonnie glances at her rose-gold watch. "It should wrap up soon, I'd guess ten or twenty more minutes."

"Thank you," Ace answers. He starts to turn on his Nikes, ready to report his findings to the rest of his football offspring crew, but my hand on his wrist stops him.

"Why don't you sit down for a minute? Have some water and cool off? You've been playing really hard and it's hot."

"But, Mom," he tries to negotiate, "practice is almost over and I can rest the entire ride home."

"Ace." I raise an eyebrow and point to the coolers behind him. "Water."

"Fine."

"That's a good idea," Vonnie says before spotting her boys in the crowd. "Jett, Jax, Jagger! Come get some water before your dad comes to see you!" she yells, her booming voice gaining their attention and instant obedience.

The three boys run into the tent, grabbing water bottles and seats at the table next to Ace. I watch the four of them and it never fails to amaze me how easily friendship comes among children.

My attention is ripped away when I hear a sickening crash and the crowd yells out a collective "Oooooohhhh!"

I turn to the field to see the cart that has been sitting idly behind the end zone speeding onto the grass. My eyes immediately search out TK, making sure he's not the player writhing in pain on the forty-yard line. When I find him on the sideline, taking a knee with the rest of his teammates, relief so heady floods my system that tears cloud my vision and my limbs feel like they've been filled with cement.

An eerie silence falls over the tent that was only moments ago buzzing with laughter and gossip. My eyes shift around, trying to find the woman who is partnered up with the injured player. My heart physically aching in my chest at how helpless she must feel watching her loved one lying on the field. But I don't see anyone. No woman running onto the field, nobody crying at a table, surrounded by other wives and girlfriends trying to comfort her. Nothing. Just quiet observers who all share the same relieved expression that it isn't their loved one.

"What happened?" I whisper to Charli, who is quietly tapping the screen of her iPhone.

She lifts her eyes from her phone, a look of sadness replacing the funny, free spirit I've talked to all afternoon. "He was trying to make a tackle but went in with his head down. It wasn't pretty." She glances at her phone again, her frown increasing. "Rookie free agent." She turns the screen to me, showing me a kid, maybe twenty-two years old, smiling wide at the camera, his blue eyes sparkling and his cheeks flushed with excitement that his dreams might finally become a reality. A look I remember TK wearing whenever football came up.

"I hate this sport." The words fall out of my mouth before I have a chance to stop them. I clench my eyes shut, feeling like an idiot and hoping I didn't just burn the only bridges I've built. "Shoot. I'm sorry, I didn't mean . . . it's just . . .." I fumble around my words, not sure how to recover.

"No." Charli grabs my hand. "I hate it too." Her voice is hushed, but Vonnie hears her.

"So do I," she agrees. "Justin and I fight

all the time about whether or not the boys will play."

"Ace isn't playing."

Vonnie's eyes widen at my declaration, whether in surprise, admiration, or disbelief, I'm not sure. "And TK's good with that?"

"He has to be," I say. "It's nonnegotiable."

"Good for you, girl." She purses her glossed lips. "Justin has been playing in the league for eleven years. It's obviously been good to us and he loves it. But I see the way he limps when he doesn't think I'm watching or the way he's starting to forget little things more and more. It's a fucked-up sport."

Charli doesn't say anything, she just nods her head, her eyes still trained on the scene playing out on the field.

Then, almost as fast as it happened, the Mustangs rookie is loaded up on the back of the cart and making his way off the field. To everyone's relief, his arms are moving animatedly as he talks to the trainer sitting next to him. The crowd cheers and the chatter around the tent returns as if nothing happened. On the field, the players circle around the coaches at the fifty-yard line before clapping once and yelling "Mustangs" in unison.

The poor rookie is long forgotten as fans

make a mad dash to the newly opened autograph section. A few volunteers in bright orange vests and matching navy blue collared shirts guide a group of about fifty children to the gated-off area in between the end of the field and the front of our tent. "Everyone get a spot along the fence and have your jersey or ball ready for the players to sign," one volunteer tells the children, who are wearing expressions of either pure bliss or complete disinterest.

"Ayden! Ayden! Move to the front!" a dad screams at his kid from the general fan area. "No! Pay attention! Get over, move!"

"Oh yes," Charli says, seeing what must be a look of complete horror on my face. "Some of the Mustangs Kids Club parents are insane. Listening to them go nuts is a yearly tradition for me. Kind of like hanging the stockings at Christmas, except instead of the promise of Santa, these poor children will get a visit from a therapist."

"Is it really that serious?" I ask, staring out at the crowd, trying to find poor Ayden's crazy dad.

"To some of these people, absolutely," Vonnie answers for Charli. "Come on, let's take these boys to run off the rest of their energy on the field."

"That's allowed?"

"Trust me," Vonnie says, pulling me toward the tent exit, where Ace and her boys are trembling with excitement. "The personnel here are amazing. And they know a happy wife is a happy player. They keep them away from us for three weeks, so they know better than to limit our access when we do have a chance to see them."

"All righty then." I nod my head, not willing to go against Vonnie in anything. "Would you mind Ace going down with you? I think I'm just gonna hang back here." You know, out of the sightline of thousands of Mustang fans.

"No, you're coming with me." She tugs my hand. "I need someone to talk to, otherwise a fan is going to call me over and rope me into a conversation I don't want to be in."

"Fine," I grumble, sounding an awful lot like Ace does when he doesn't get his way.

"You girls have fun. I already warned Shawn the only place he'd find me is in my air-conditioned car." Charli waves us off.

"See you soon." I wave back, feeling a foreign sensation of excitement thinking about our upcoming plans.

"Go, boys." Vonnie gives all four boys the permission they've been craving and they dart down the small set of steps and onto

220

the field. Jagger, Vonnie's seven-year-old, and the most experienced training camp veteran, runs to the sideline and snags a couple of footballs for them to play with. They all take off to the field opposite us, where the two kickers aren't practicing drilling the ball through goalposts.

The hot Colorado sun and dry summer air grope my sunscreen-less body. I dig my knockoff sunglasses out of my cross-body purse. I might have a nasty sunburn later, but maybe the glasses will stop all the wrinkles caused by squinting too hard from permanently settling on my face.

Vonnie and I are talking about a lot of nothing, watching the kids running around, when a pair of strong hands settle on my hips.

"Sparks," TK says before turning me to face him.

I saw TK Moore running around on the field. His thick thighs flexing with his long strides as he raced down the sideline and leapt into the air with heights that defied gravity, his ass looking like a shelf in those padded white pants. But here, only inches in front of me, I see TK.

I see the same TK who would run to me after every high school football game, his green eyes alight, happiness almost tangible.

And a pang of longing, of sadness at missing out on years of his career, sharing this joy with him, shoots through my heart.

His hair is pulled back into a loose ponytail, and even though I know it's brown, it looks black from either sweat or water dumped on his head . . . probably sweat. His beard is noticeably longer and scruffier than it was just a few days ago, and even though I know he's sweaty and smelly, all I want is to feel it under my fingertips and against my face. He's never pale, but his skin is noticeably more tan since I last saw him, though Ace and I still have quite a few shades on him.

But it's his jersey and shoulder pads in his hands, leaving his chest and abs exposed, keeping me tongue-tied. I don't know if he really has no clue what he looks like topless or if he's messing with me to get a reaction, but I don't think I could summon the energy to care either way. He's not flexing, yet his abs are on full display. All six, hell, maybe eight of them carved out of stone underneath his tan skin glistening with the sweat of a hardworking man. Covered by just a sprinkling of chest hair trailing off under the waistband of his pants settled so low on his hips, the sexy V of his is summoning me to the promised land.

222

All in all, he's a freaking masterpiece.

"Poppy," he says, his voice shaking with laughter. "My eyes are up here."

"Yeah." I glance up at him, not even a tiny bit ashamed to be caught ogling him. "But the rest of you is down here."

"Well." He steps in closer, letting his equipment fall to the ground behind him. "Can't say I'm not happy you're enjoying the view."

"Whatever." I roll my eyes, but I don't deny it. I don't know if it's the sun or TK making me so much hotter, I just know the pull to touch the man in front of me is too strong to ignore.

"You look good." His voice drops to a whisper even though the screams of the fans calling out for autographs make it impossible for anyone else to hear our conversation. "I almost fell over when I saw you walk down the steps in these." His fingers graze the tops of my thighs right where my white denim shorts stop.

"These are the only shorts I have."

"Lucky for me, I guess." One of his hands moves to my lower back, pulling me in so close I can feel his sweat dampen my tank top.

"Good." I exhale the word.

TK's lips curve up into a knowing smile.

Not cocky.

Sweet and hopeful. Like I'm not the only person wanting to cross this line, wanting to pretend we don't have years of strife to overcome, that right here, we're just like every other couple happy to see each other . . . to touch each other.

He tilts his head to the side, silently asking for permission. In answer, I lift my chin and roll onto my toes. His lips part, showing off the smile I know braces perfected, right before he drops his head, touching his mouth to mine in one soft, perfect kiss that causes my knees to go weak.

"You looked good out there," I say, once I've caught my bearings.

"Thanks." His hand lingers on my back and I'm not eager for the contact to end. "Did you have fun?" He's watching me, concern evident. I guess talk of some of the cattier wives gets around.

"I actually had a lot of fun." I continue on when he lifts a single, disbelieving eyebrow at me. "No, really." I point to Vonnie, who's having a very animated conversation with her husband. "I sat with Vonnie and Charli, they're hilarious. We're actually getting together Sunday and watching the game."

He drops his eyebrow, but I can't read his expression anymore. A thought that hadn't crossed my mind all day pops in. We aren't a couple — what if he doesn't want me making friends with these people? They are his co-workers, after all.

"Shoot." I wince. "I don't have to go over there if you don't want. I know we haven't really discussed details, but I don't want to overstep any boundaries here. This is your work and I —"

TK cuts me off by dropping his mouth to mine once more. Out of all the interrupting techniques in the world, I have to say, I find his kisses the most enjoyable and effective.

"Go." He says the one small word like it's the most obvious thing in the universe.

"But they're your teammates' family —"

"Poppy, are you or are you not my girl?" he asks, cutting me off. "If I didn't want you here, you wouldn't be here. You're here because I want you making friends with my friends. I want our lives to become so intertwined we can't figure out where one starts and the other ends. I want you and Ace around as much as I can have you around. I want you both."

Oh my god.

Did he just ask me to be his girlfriend?

"Did you just ask me to be your girl-friend?" I try to bite back the smile threatening to consume my face . . . and fail miserably. "I mean, last time you asked, you wore your best button-up and khakis. Is sweaty and kind of bossy your new version of romantic?"

"Poppy." He says my name like he's already regretting making me his girlfriend. "Are you going to make me grovel in front of my teammates? Because if you do, I'm pretty sure they'll never let either one of us live it down."

"Well, lucky for you, I appreciate the sweaty, shirtless method." I let my eyes take him in, in all his glory once more. "So, okay. I guess I'll be your girlfriend."

I feel the heat creep up my cheeks, and I don't know if it's from suddenly feeling shy or flustered by how good he looks standing in front of me.

"Okay," he repeats, moving a mass of curls out of my face. His smile is so bright that, even with the beard, I swear I can see that lone dimple on his left cheek. He starts to lean down again, but this time *he's* the one interrupted.

"TK!" Ace yells, bolting across the field and hurtling his little body into TK, probably hitting him harder than some of his teammates did today. "You were *awesome* out there! That one catch? Holy cow! You went up so high and with one hand!" Ace jumps up, doing his best imitation of his new hero. "It was so cool, you have to teach me!"

"Thanks, dude." TK rumples Ace's curls, the same look of pride I have whenever I'm near Ace or hear his name written all over his face. And if anybody had questions about these two, they're answered in this moment. "You have to come over to my place. I have a football launcher in my backyard so I can practice without having a quarterback. I'll tell you all the family tricks, but you can't tell anyone . . ." He bends down and leans into Ace's ear conspiratorially. "Only us Moore men can know the secrets of greatness."

Ace doesn't say anything, he just stares at him, jaw slack, eyes wide, as if Jesus himself had just appeared on this field and told him all of life's greatest secrets.

"Ace!" Jett yells across the field with his hands on his hips, not at all impressed by TK or the other Mustang players making their way to the locker room. "Come on! I can't let my loser brothers win!"

"Jett Damon Lamar, you better not let me catch you calling your brothers losers again!" Vonnie booms out. Not only is her tone one not to be questioned, but she used his full name.

Not stupid, Jett is quick to shout, "I won't. Sorry, Mom."

"Can I go play?" Ace asks TK.

"Course, dude." TK leans in again, whispering just loud enough for Vonnie and Justin to hear, "But you better not let Jett's loser brothers win."

Justin barks out a quick burst of laughter. Vonnie, on the other hand, does not look amused. "You see?" She looks at me. "You see why my boys are so crazy? They have these big-ass man-children egging them on. And that one" — she aims a pointed-tip fingernail TK's way — "is the biggest jokester of all. You sure you want to deal with all of that?"

TK has always been that way. One time, in study hall, he snuck into Mrs. Hanson's room during lunch and planted fart noise machines all around. Mrs. Hanson's face got so red I was sure her head was going to explode. TK had in-school suspension for a week. I don't know if it's comforting or disturbing to know he's the same way ten years later.

I look over at TK, lifting an appraising eyebrow. "I think I'll risk it."

"Can't blame you," Vonnie says. "TK, you're a pain in my ass, but you are fine."

This time, it's me and TK laughing and

Justin standing there catching flies.

"What?" Vonnie purses her lips. "Look at him. Over there all topless, trying to impress Poppy. I'm supposed to be immune to all that?" She draws air circles around TK's abs. "I'm married, not dead."

"Put your shirt on, asshole," Justin yells, chucking a black Sharpie that only just misses TK's head. "Out here lookin' like fuckin' wilderness Fabio."

"Aww, shit!" TK runs in place and brings a fist to his mouth. "You got jokes, Lamar? You mad 'cause you're fifty-five and still haven't shaved?" He drops his hand and turns to Vonnie. "Tell your man that women don't find jealousy attractive."

"Women don't find jealousy attractive, babe."

"Whatever," Justin pouts. "I'm gonna go shower. We don't have meetings for a couple of hours, you and the boys want to grab something to eat?"

"If you think I've been dirtying the kitchen, cooking a nice dinner, only for those boys of yours to tell me they don't like it and want chicken nuggets while you're gone, you are mistaken. We're eating out no matter what. The only question here is if you're coming or not."

"Damn, Von," Justin groans. However,

even the reporters on the sidelines could see the smile he's doing a terrible job of disguising. "You could at least pretend to miss me. Treating me like this in front of TK. You know he never shuts the hell up."

"Boy, bye." Vonnie laughs. "You better take your stinky self to the shower and meet me in the parking lot in twenty. The boys snacked all practice long, but you know they'll probably be whining about being hungry again in less than thirty minutes."

Boys.

Glad to see Ace isn't the only miniature, never-ending food pit.

"I'll be out in fifteen," Justin counters, leaning in and planting a quick, sweet kiss on Vonnie's forehead. And for just a second, all the sass drains from Vonnie's body and I watch her eyes go soft as she looks up at her husband.

It's an oddly private moment to take place in the middle of such a public event. And I feel a little guilty for watching, but I know that even if they were circled by hundreds of screaming fans and flashing cameras, they wouldn't notice any of it.

I don't know if it's because, in my heart, I knew after I left TK, I'd never have something like that again, but seeing happy couples used to cause jealousy to course through me. But now, standing next to TK and hearing Ace's peals of laughter, it's not there.

I've been so nervous to let TK back into our lives. I said it's because I don't want Ace hurt, but if I'm honest with myself, it's my heart I'm worried about. I know the kind of man TK is, and he's a good one. I know he will never bail on Ace. What I don't know is, after all his time as a party boy, star football player supreme, if he's ready to settle down. It might seem fun to play family man now, but how long until the novelty wears off and he wants his VIP club status back? I locked my heart away and convinced myself I was fine with a lifetime of one-night stands and flings, and I was fine until TK trotted his sexy ass back into my life. One glance at him, dripping with booze, angry eyes and all, and I knew he had the power to break down the walls I'd spent ten years building up.

I just didn't know he'd do it so fast.

And it terrifies me as much as it thrills me.

"Sparks, you good down there?" TK's damp skin brushes against my bare arm and his padded legs bump into my hip, breaking me out of my thoughts.

"Really?" I pull my sunglasses to the top

of my head, giving him an unobstructed view of my glare. "A short joke? That's what we're doing right now?"

"Who?" His green eyes go wide and he moves a callused hand to his chest. "Me?"

"Oh, don't play innocent with me, Moore. I'm not Vonnie, I'm not falling for any of . . ." I gesture to his glistening, tanned, lightly dusted with chest hair, rock-solid chest. "This nonsense."

Lies.

I want to lick him.

"You're a shit liar, Sparks." He smirks, totally cocky this time. And I'd be lying if I said cocky TK isn't my kryptonite.

"I know." I don't even try to lie because, well, because TK is topless, smirking, and leaning down like he's about to kiss me.

He doesn't kiss me.

"You and Ace want to go eat?" he asks.

"Sure." Truth? I always want to eat.

Or drink.

Or eat and drink.

But mainly, right now, I want to do anything with TK and Ace. I want to soak up enough goodness with them both so that when this ends, I'll have enough memories to get me through.

"Cool. Let me shower real fast." He leans down and gives me a quick kiss on the cheek. "Yo, Ace!" he shouts across the field. "While you're beating them, think of what you want for lunch."

"Burgers!" Ace shouts back, needing zero time to think about it.

"I can't stand your ass," Justin grumbles, shoving one of TK's shoulders.

TK laughs, fighting to catch his balance from the unexpected assault. "You all love me," he says to Justin, but winks at me.

I shake my head and roll my eyes but he knows I'm full of it too. TK is one of those annoying people who makes a friend with every person he comes across. That stupid smile, his inability to take anything too seriously for too long, his hotness. Even when I wanted to hate him, I couldn't. Even when I was trying to guard my heart, he made it impossible.

It's the worst.

And kind of the best.

And totally where Ace gets it from.

TWENTY

"Did you have fun?" I kick off my flip-flops, too exhausted even to attempt to put them in my closet.

"Fun?" Ace repeats like he can't believe I have the audacity to ask such a ridiculous question. "It wasn't just 'fun.' It was the best day ever! TK introduced me to like every player on the team, even Maxwell Lewis!"

Maxwell Lewis is the veteran safety for the Mustangs. Most kids are obsessed with quarterbacks. You know, the big plays and jazzy touchdowns. Not Ace. Besides TK — for obvious reasons — Ace is all about defense. My laptop browser is always filled to the brim with YouTube clips of interceptions and pick-sixes. Ace has forced me to watch multiple clips, and I'd be lying if I said the guy didn't impress me too. Plus, from the three seconds I spoke to him, and the five minutes he indulged my kid by answering every question Ace had in his arsenal, Maxwell seemed like an even better human being.

He's also smokin' hot.

Ace didn't notice that.

"I can't wait to go back to school! Everyone is gonna be so jealous." Ace collapses onto the couch. "Especially Hunter, he never stops bragging about his family's stupid season tickets." He closes his eyes, but the smug smile that doesn't belong on his sweet face never fades.

I'd tell him to stop, but after seeing him with his twin all day, it's nice to recognize he still picked up something from me. Even if it is vengeance and pettiness.

"Am I right to assume you want to go again tomorrow?" I waste my breath on a question I already know the answer to.

"Duh!" His eyes fly open and he's off the couch just as fast, bouncing up and down. "I want to go every day!"

"Duh," I repeat after him. "Why'd I even ask?"

"I don't know. Moms do weird things." He shrugs his shoulders like he didn't just insult mothers across the globe. "Is it okay if I see if Jayden's home? I want to tell him all about today and give him the extra hat TK gave me."

I shouldn't feel guilty about the way things have gone down with Cole. I told him from the very beginning I wasn't looking for a relationship. But men never believe me when I tell them I want to keep it casual. I don't know if they think women are incapable of catching feelings or men possess a magical penis that casts a spell on our poor, unsuspecting vaginas, but they always end up shocked when I'm not pounding on their door and begging for a ring.

Cole is no different.

And knowing Ace is going to go over there, and I can guarantee with a great certainty, spend the entire night talking about TK? It makes me feel awful and awkward — awkful? — and I'm already enough of that without these added circumstances.

"That's fine, but you need to shower first." I wonder how old boys have to be to care about personal hygiene enough not to need to be reminded to take a shower?

"Deal!" Ace shouts, and starts to run to the bathroom.

"Wait!" I shout after him, and thanks to his socks and speed, he slides straight into the wall, bounces off, and lands on his butt. "Are you okay?" I ask once my laughter has died down a bit, because, you know, straight

236

Mom of the Year right here.

"Yeah." He cringes, rubbing his tush. "What were you gonna say?"

"Never mind." I wipe the tears from the corners of my eyes. "I can't remember now."

"Moms," he mutters, rolling his eyes to the back of his head.

" 'Kay." I wave away his bruised and stinky butt. "Shower. Now."

I'm waving to Cole right after Ace goes into his house when a familiar car turns onto my street. The bass from a rap song, which, if it were the clean version, would likely have only two words in it, booms from the windows. It's a stark contrast to the custom paint job that consists of more glitter than actual paint and the rhinestone-encrusted license plate holder that I'm certain has to be a road hazard.

"Hey, girl. I didn't know you were coming over," I say to Sadie as she opens her door.

"Oh, don't you even 'Hey, girl' me right now!" she shouts, her cheeks nearly as red as her hair and the long, pointed acrylic nail aimed at me. "I can't believe you!"

I take a hesitant step back. Sadie on a rampage is a dangerous thing, and getting glitter out of my curls is impossible. "Um . . . what?"

She puts her hands on her hips and stomps one platform-heeled foot on the cracked cement sidewalk. "Did you have a fun morning? Do anything exciting?"

Oh. Shit.

But how? We just got home!

"I was going to —"

"No," she says, cutting me off. "I'm not doing this out here. The emergency rosé is in the trunk." She waves her hands in front of my face as she walks past me, opening my gate with her foot. I accidentally inhale a strong whiff of nail polish and glue that makes me a little light-headed. "I was at the nail salon when I found out and left without properly drying my nails, so you have to grab it if you want it. And by that, I mean grab it, because I have a feeling I'm going to need wine with this conversation."

I follow her direction because . . . well . . . glitter bombs . . . and the guilt of my best friend finding out about me and TK from anybody besides me has me feeling so awful I'd do just about anything to make it up to her.

I walk into my house and she's already on her favorite corner of my couch with two glasses on the table and holding her phone — which might as well be a freaking gun with the way she's waving it around — in her hand.

"Fucking training camp!" she screeches as soon as I turn the deadbolt on my door. "Not only are you apparently on speaking terms with TK again, you're going to training camp and kissing on the fucking field!"

"Whoa." I plop down on the couch and twist open the cap on the wine. "Since Ace isn't here, I'm not going to make you put money in the swear jar."

"Poppy, I swear to God, if you don't —" She stops when her voice starts to quiver and swipes her hands across her cheeks.

Oh crap.

Sadie doesn't cry.

She masks her pain in pink and glitter and sarcasm.

But she doesn't cry.

"Oh my god. No. Don't cry!" I shove the glass of wine into her hand.

"Why wouldn't you tell me about this?" she asks. The hurt in her voice is enough to cut me.

"I was going to, I swear. It just happened so fast," I try to explain, even though now that she's in front of me, I know I should've reached out. "The day before Phil fired me, TK saw me at the park during Ace's soccer tryout. Of course, this happened at the end of practice because the only luck I have is the bad kind, and Ace ran up to us. When TK saw him, he finally pulled his head out of his ass and realized I wasn't lying. Then that night, he showed up at the Emerald Cabaret when I was walking to my car. We talked and set up a time for him to meet Ace."

With every word that comes out of my mouth, the glassy sheen of tears coating Sadie's eyes starts to fade and they widen in sync with her jaw dropping.

"Wait . . . so Ace saw him too?" she asks, blindly setting her glass on the table.

"Yeah, he was so starstruck. But the thought of TK being his dad obviously didn't even cross his mind . . . even when TK was staring at him like a freaking weirdo." I roll my eyes and shake my head, thinking back to how uncool TK played that meeting. "Anyways, someone saw us . . . or more specifically, saw TK and snapped some pictures. Rochelle found out about it and told Phil that the Mustang players weren't coming in because of me and that's why he fired me."

I see the puzzle pieces starting to shift into place for her, and I keep going when she doesn't say anything. "So TK came over on Monday to see Ace. He brought Ace a truckload of Mustangs gear and we went out to eat. They hit it off. They love the same food and movies. TK was clinging to every word Ace said like he couldn't get enough of him and Ace thinks TK hangs the stars." I fight to keep the hearts out of my eyes and my voice from turning to mush, but I know I fail enormously when Sadie slumps into the cushion and holds her hand over her heart. "TK ended up staying over . . . no, not in my room," I clarify when she sits up straight and her mouth opens to no doubt ask if we slept together. "But we talked that night and he invited us to training camp and oh!" I remember that I haven't even told her I'm not longer unemployed. "He knows the owner of HERS —"

"That cute-ass restaurant down the street?" she asks, cutting me off, a giddy smile on her face as she bounces so hard on my couch that the cushions around her fall to the floor.

"Yeah, that one." I'm pretty sure my smile matches hers. Good news isn't something I'm usually privy to, so I'm enjoying this immensely. "So Brynn, that's her name, Brynn, she hired me on the spot when I went in the other day!"

"Shut up! That's amazing! You have to tell me when you work so I can come see you . . . and try a cocktail or two." She's been hounding me about trying HERS out one day, it's just when I had days off, I never wanted to go out. So my new J-O-B benefits both of us. "So what else?"

Damn. I thought that was a lot. "What else is there to say?"

"What do you mean, 'What else is there to say'? Are you insane? The most eligible bachelor in Denver just helped you get a job, invited you to training camp, and has been hanging out with your son." She crosses the small space between us and grabs my face so hard, I'm ninety percent sure I'll have finger indents on my cheeks. "Your son together with TK!"

"Sadie." I drag out her name as I peel her hands off my face and bring them down to her sides, not letting go because, clearly, this topic has stolen the little bit of self-control she has. "Calm down."

"How the fuck can I be calm? How are you so calm? TK Moore is your baby daddy and now he's actually *your baby daddy*! Are you even going to work at HERS? Are you going to move in with him? Are you going to become one of the lunching bitches who takes tennis lessons?"

"First of all, please never say 'baby daddy' again." Gross. "And anyway, he's always been Ace's dad. Ace is nine. TK's DNA didn't just magically jump into Ace while he was sleeping the other night."

Sadie opens her mouth to interrupt, but my death stare and squeeze of her hands halt her words.

"To answer your other insane questions. Yes, I'm going to work at HERS. I haven't even started yet, how could I already be thinking of quitting? No, I'm not moving in with him. And definitely no to becoming a lady who lunches and plays tennis. TK is back for Ace, not me," I reassure her. Even though I might take back the no-tennis declaration. I really would like to learn how to play, it looks like a lot of fun.

"But you are going to start collecting child support, right? Because your baby . . ." She stops when I accidentally emit a low growl. "I mean, Ace's dad is loaded. You've been doing it on your own for nine years, it'd be nice if he helped out."

"I really haven't even thought that far ahead. Child support means court, court means lawyers, lawyers mean money I don't have much of." I take a deep breath and whisper my fears out loud for the first time. "Things between us are going really well. I don't know if I want to rock the boat. If he were to go to court for custody, who are they going to give it to? The single mom who didn't inform the father about their child? Or TK Moore, Denver's golden child whose house could probably swallow my house without chewing? I just don't want to take any chances."

"I don't agree because you deserve a helping hand." Sadie wiggles her hands free from mine and pulls me in for a hug. "But I understand. Fingers crossed he does the right thing without you having to ask him."

"Now . . ." I point to the wine sitting untouched on my table and try to change the subject. "Ace is gone and I did a lot of peopling today, let's drink and see if there are any new episodes of *RuPaul's Drag Race* on."

"That right there?" Sadie says, grabbing her glass of wine. "That's why we're friends."

Not the highest standards, but hey, I'll take what I can get.

TWENTY-ONE

"Hi, Miss Jane!" Ace calls out as he darts past her and runs straight to the stairs leading to the Mustang practice fields.

This journey out to Dove Valley almost made the mayhem of yesterday fade away.

Almost.

There is still a big crowd and more than one drunk idiot stumbling across the street, but the masses didn't come out in full force this evening. Plus, knowing where to park kept my stress levels from rising above a four.

"I take it he enjoyed himself yesterday?" Jane asks with a smile that makes her already kind face even warmer.

"You could say that," I say. "You could also say it was the absolute best day of his life, which is what he's told anybody who'd listen to him for the past twenty-four hours."

"That's just wonderful." She tucks her clipboard under her arm and claps. "What about you? Did you have fun?"

I think for a minute before answering, "I did." I tell her the truth and I'm still a little surprised by my answer.

Jane's smile is smaller this time, but there's understanding and quiet support in her eyes. "I thought you would."

I return her smile and make my way to the family tent. The hesitation and fear I felt yesterday are missing and in their place is excitement at a chance to talk with Vonnie and Charli and watch Ace run wild with his new friends.

And to see TK in his football pants, but that's a given.

I walk through the opening in the air-conditioned tent and spot Charli and Vonnie sitting at the same table we were at yesterday. I also note that Dixie and her friends, all wearing caked-on makeup, cleavage-revealing tank tops, and skintight jeans, are at least in flats today. I mean, they're covered with the intertwining C's of Chanel and G's of Gucci with coordinating handbags slung over their shoulders, but at least I'm not the only one not rocking five-inch heels.

"Hey, girl!" Vonnie calls across the tent, drawing Dixie's attention my way. I watch with avid fascination as her smile transforms from actual happiness to a plastic one that does nothing to conceal her disdain toward me.

I aim a smile almost as fake as hers in her direction before waving to Vonnie and maneuvering around tables.

"Hey!" I flop onto the hard, plastic-backed chair. "I didn't know if you guys were going to be here."

"Me and my crew will be at every practice unless there's been a grave or critical injury." She lifts a water bottle to her red-painted lips. "I need them to work out their energy someplace that's not my just-been-cleaned house . . . because, I swear, all I fucking do is clean up for them to make an even bigger mess."

"And I'm bored." Charli shrugs, her gleaming chestnut hair not moving out of place. "I binged all the good shows the first couple of days they were gone. Now all I have to do is study and who wants to do that?"

Next to Charli, Vonnie purses her lips and rolls her neck, a look I'm already well acquainted with. "You do," she says, attitude kicked up about a hundred levels.

Charli scrunches her nose and shrugs her shoulders. "But do I really?"

"Yes," Vonnie says. "You do. You've worked

your ass off for this, and you do not want to be known as 'Shawn's wife' for the rest of your life. You're going to want him to be 'Charli's husband' at some point." Vonnie casts a quick glance over her shoulder toward where our boys can be seen running and falling all over the place. "Trust and believe. This 'football wife' shit gets old real quick. I can't wait to go back to work."

I nod my head in agreement even though I have never been a football wife nor have I graduated from college, but Vonnie does put forth a convincing argument. She's probably an amazing lawyer.

"Uggghhhh," Charli groans, and aims her sunglass-covered eyes at the field, where the team is taking part in some delicious stretching. "You're right," she agrees, though begrudgingly.

"I know," Vonnie says before her eyes follow Charli's to the field. "Good God Almighty, thank you, Jesus." She lifts her hands to the heavens in praise. "That man of yours is so damn fine."

I look for Charli's husband, but I can't see the numbers since they're all bent over, touching their toes. "Where's Shawn?" I ask, not wanting to miss this show.

"Not Shawn," they tell me in unison.

"She's talking to you," Charli says, a smile

pulling at her lips.

"Not that Shawn's not fine too, but that damn TK? Lord. I don't know what it is about him."

"You don't need to explain." Charli reaches into her purse and pulls out a pack of Red Vines without ever looking away from the field. "Shawn has caught me staring at TK more than once."

"You guys are crazy." I laugh and take a Red Vine when Charli puts the box in front of me. "How can you even tell which one he is?"

"Don't play with me." Vonnie pulls her sunglasses low on her nose, her narrowed eyes and a perfectly arched brow directed my way. "You can't tell me you don't know which one of them is TK."

She's right.

I spotted TK as soon as I stepped on the concrete steps and haven't lost sight of him since.

"Well, yeah, but —" I start, but I'm cut off before I get a real word out.

"Exactly. Between his hair falling from his helmet and his ass filling out those pants better than anyone else in the league, he's impossible to miss." She pushes her sunglasses back into place. "Much to the dismay and ego bruising of everyone else on the team."

"Maxwell looks pretty good too," Charli pipes in.

"You're right." Vonnie points to Maxwell when I strain my eyes, trying to catch a glimpse of him with his hands flat on the ground in front of him. "Ebony and ivory. Fine and *fine.* Can I get an amen?"

"Amen," Charli calls, still focused on the field.

I finally spot Maxwell, who is only two rows over from TK, and enjoy the show.

Then I mentally reprimand myself for sitting here, snacking, talking with friends, and openly ogling these men the same way the men at the club judged me.

And dammit if I don't go right back to looking.

It's crazy how after just one practice, a scene so foreign yesterday feels familiar and welcoming today.

I walk out to the field with Vonnie and Charli. Vonnie forbade Charli from leaving us this time and Charli didn't fight too hard. We're laughing at a story Vonnie's telling us about Jagger when I glance over her shoulder and look directly into a phone as the flash goes off in our direction. The photographer is a woman probably around my age, with blond highlights scattered through her brown hair and a Mustangs jersey I'm positive she found in the children's department stretching past its limit across her very ample chest. She's with a group of five other women, all in similar outfits, all with phones focused on the huddles of women waiting for their players to come say hi.

"What's wrong?" Vonnie asks when my laughter dies. She follows my gaze to the sideline and rolls her eyes so hard, I worry they won't come back down. "Ignore the groupie brigade." She brushes them off with a flick of her wrist.

"Somebody posted pictures of me and TK kissing yesterday." I avoid eye contact, feeling the familiar heat creep up my cheeks.

"Which website?" Vonnie asks.

My eyes go wide and fly to meet hers. "Which website?" I repeat, horrified at the notion of there being multiple forums discussing my love life. "You mean there's more than one?"

At this, Vonnie and Charli look at each other for a split second before dissolving into a fit of laughter.

"Yes," Charli says, wiping under her eyes for falling tears. "There is more than one."

"And that's just sites designated to athlete gossip." Vonnie continues on like a camp counselor trying to scare the kids with ghost stories. "Then you have all the little side forums and Facebook groups sharing pictures and trading stories."

"But . . ." I struggle to form a cohesive sentence. "Why?"

"You're so sweet." Vonnie pats my shoulder, turning to look at the group of women who are meeting our gazes head on. "Because for them, this is a game. Some people collect football cards and autographs. And some" — she motions to the women in front of us — "collect dicks and chlamydia." She smiles sweetly and waves before turning us back around.

"Those are the women who watch *WAGS* and *Real Housewives.* They see the red bottoms, designer bags, and mansions," Charli tells my poor, scandalized soul. "They don't see the guys who get cut after training camp and never play again or the heightened chances of substance abuse and gambling. They don't see the women who dedicate their lives to raising their kids and following their husbands from state to state, only to have to become a caregiver when their husband gets diagnosed with Alzheimer's or ALS at forty."

"Damn, Charli," Vonnie says. "I was just

warning her about groupies. You gave it all to her."

Charli shrugs. "She can handle it."

I'm not sure I agree.

"Well, shit," Vonnie says, squeezing my hand. "I'm not sure *I* wanted to hear all that."

"Oh, whatever!" Charli shakes her head, not making the slightest effort to hide her laughter. "You've been at this longer than either of us. You're the one who schooled me!"

"I know I did." Vonnie lets go of my hand and shoves Charli's shoulder. "But shit, I don't want to think about these scary-ass stories all the time. Retirement is my light at the end of the tunnel. I can't have you messing with that dream when it's this close to becoming a reality."

"Not sorry." Charli sticks her tongue out right before Shawn runs up behind her and swoops her into his arms, causing a high-pitched scream and a girly giggle that seems almost foreign coming from Charli.

I turn to give them a little privacy and look around for TK.

When I find him, he's taking a selfie with Miss Tiny-Jersey.

Just my luck.

I don't want to watch. I don't feel threatened — honest, I don't. More like morbidly curious. The group of iPhone-wielding friends circle around TK. Hands coming from every direction to touch his shoulder, graze his hand, and one even "trips" and uses his chest to stabilize her skanky body. After she trips, TK takes a comical step back before moving down the line to grown men who fawn all over him.

The group of women make a circle, their smiles so big I'm sure they must crack their foundation. They fan themselves off, exaggerated hand motions no doubt describing how it felt to touch *the* TK Moore.

Gag.

It's as amusing as it is pathetic.

Then one of them turns her head and sees Maxwell and Peter Bremner, the rookie quarterback, coming her way, and all thoughts of TK are thrown out the window.

"TK!" a familiar voice shouts.

"Ace!" TK yells back, running our way and dropping his gear by my feet before picking up a nearby football and shouting, "Go long!"

Ace takes off down the field, his nearly completely blond curls with how much time he's spent outside blowing behind him as he creates his own wind machine, looking back over his shoulder at TK every few steps. TK makes a sudden movement, pointing the football to a hard left. Ace pivots with grace and sprints, following the route with a speed that even impresses me. TK launches the ball, sending it spiraling across the field a little in front of Ace. But with a determination and talent I didn't know he possessed, Ace leaps into the air, diving over the low-cut grass beneath him. He stretches his arms in front of him as far as possible and cradles the ball in his hands before gravity kicks back in and he slams into the ground.

"Holy shit!" TK says to nobody in particular, and it almost gets lost in the applause breaking out from the sideline. The crowd, apparently, finding this father-son moment as captivating as I do.

"I thought you said Ace didn't play football?" Vonnie asks, watching TK run across the field to high-five Ace.

"He doesn't," I answer, but don't look at her. My vision is locked tight on Ace, TK, and the few other players who drifted over to congratulate Ace on what may be the play of the day.

"Shit, girl," Vonnie whispers beside me.

My eye starts twitching. "I know."

A second later, Ace is lined up next to TK and across from a player I don't recognize.

TK pulls the ball back, standing up straight from his squared position, and watches Ace stop and go, trying to beat his professional opponent. He spins to the right this time and TK throws the ball right into his chest.

Even from a hundred yards away, I see Ace's eyes light up and his love of soccer start to fade.

"Holy shit." TK jogs up to me, his eyes still on Ace, who's running routes with Justin now. "Are you watching him?"

"I'm watching," I say, sharing none of TK's excitement.

"He's amazing. I wasn't half as good when I was his age." He keeps going, pride evident in every word. "When does his football season start?"

I knew we'd have to have this conversation at some point, I just hoped it wouldn't be in front of thousands of strangers. "It doesn't."

He swings his head in my direction, his brows knit together like I'm speaking German. "What do you mean?"

"Ace isn't playing football."

"You didn't sign him up yet?" he asks, trying to make sense of what I'm telling him.

"No, TK." I rub my hands together to try to stop them from fidgeting. "I'm not signing Ace up for football ever."

TK's back goes straight, and even through his thick beard I see his jaw tick. "Why not? Do you not see how good he is?"

"He's your kid, TK. He's the best athlete I've ever seen." This is the truth — there hasn't been one sport Ace has played that he isn't amazing at. "But I made my mind up about football a while ago and he's not playing."

"You care to explain why?" he grinds out, color rising up his face.

"It's too dangerous. The risks aren't worth it."

For some reason, this seems to calm him down. His shoulders relax and his lips turn up at the corners . . . which makes my back go straight.

"I get that you're a mom and you don't want him to get hurt, but he's a boy. He's supposed to be rough and get hurt sometimes." He keeps going, oblivious to how angry he's making me. "I'll get him the best helmet and teach him tackling techniques, he'll be fine. You don't need to coddle him."

Oh no he didn't.

"No."

His head jerks back and his smile flees. "No?"

"You heard me, TK. The answer is no."

257

"You're being ridiculous." He rolls his eyes, only further pissing me off. "He'll be fine."

"I'm sure since you play football, you think you know everything there is to know about it, but I'm not bending on this." I plant my fists on my hips. "This isn't some decision I made willy-nilly because I'm afraid he'll get a boo-boo. There have been so many discoveries about the long-term effects of concussions caused by football. I know football is America's thing, but a game isn't worth his health."

"I told you I'll get him a good helmet. He won't get a concussion." He keeps his voice low, but it does nothing to disguise the anger lingering in each word.

"Helmets don't make a difference." I fight the urge to slap the patronizing look off his face. "Our brains aren't connected to anything. They are free floating inside our heads. So every single hit you take, your brain rattles around and hits your skull. Every hit, TK, not just the bad ones. And each of those hits adds up and causes damage. Then there are the inevitable concussions that come with the sport on top of those little knocks he'd be taking every day. I'm not letting it happen."

The hardness behind his eyes has softened, but he doesn't say anything.

"I've talked to Ace about it. He loves football and he hates that he can't play — a feeling I'm sure has grown being around you. So I really need you to not fight me on this, TK." I grab his hands and hold them as tight as I can. "I know how much you love football. I mean, it's your freaking career! And I might hate watching you get hit and I dread knowing you will probably get hurt, but I'm not asking you to quit. I just need you to back me when it comes to Ace playing."

"This is important to you." TK says what might be the understatement of the century.

"It's Ace's health, so yeah, it's important to me." I pull my lips into my mouth.

"Then I won't mention it to Ace, and if he brings it to me, I'll back you," TK says.

Relief floods my system. I close my eyes and draw in a breath so deep, I go a little light-headed. "Thank you."

I don't care how sweaty and gross he is, I pull my hands from his and wrap my arms around him as tight as I can.

TK hugs me back and drops a kiss on my forehead.

"You hungry?" he asks.

"Always." I tip up my head and watch as a smile crosses his face.

"Then let me get showered so I can feed my woman."

"Sounds good," I manage to say without jumping up and down and screaming.

Because it doesn't sound good. It sounds like the best thing ever.

We had a disagreement. I told him it was important to me. Now he wants to feed his woman . . . and I'm his woman!

Every time I think he can't get better, he gets better.

He's not taking a hammer to my boundaries, he's using a freaking bulldozer.

TWENTY-TWO

I love HERS and I love Brynn.

I thought I'd liked the Emerald Cabaret. But after working at HERS for two weeks, I knew I'd been lying to myself for two years.

At HERS, I don't have to coach myself when I approach a table. I don't have to lie about my name or flirt with a scumbag looking to get his kicks. I don't have to pretend I'm someone else to make it through the night. And I don't report to a misogynist who thinks my worth lies between my legs.

Plus, with Brynn being best friends with Marlee Pope, HERS was already a hangout spot for Mustang wives. Charli and Vonnie insisted on coming over and quizzing me on the menu . . . which they knew by heart.

Too bad for me, tonight's preseason game is a home game, so Charli and Vonnie aren't keeping me company. Brynn asked if I wanted the night off, but since I've been here for only a couple of weeks, I couldn't take her up on it.

Ace was damn near crushed when I told him I had to work and we couldn't go. So when Jagger asked him where our seats were and Ace told him, with — I'm assuming — tears in his eyes, Jagger ran straight to his mom. To which I was scolded mercilessly for not asking Vonnie to take Ace to the game in the first place.

I now know why her boys are so well behaved. Vonnie is scary as fuck when she's mad.

She picked Ace up this morning and is keeping him until tomorrow. I told her she didn't have to, but with one glance my way, I shut up and gave her my kid.

"You're doing a really great job," Brynn tells me as I finish cleaning up after my last table. "The customers love you, and you picked up on the menu faster than any other waitress I've had."

I try my hardest not to bask in her praise, but I can't help it. "Thanks, Brynn." Smiling so wide my cheeks ache. "I love it here."

"Good, because I'm not planning on letting you quit." She takes the rag from my hand. "It's starting to slow down in here, why don't you head out and watch the rest of the game at home?"

"Are you sure?" I ask, not certain I can deny the appeal of a night in a quiet house.

"Positive." She smiles, her blue eyes even sparkling in the dark. "Get out of here and watch your man kick some Steeler ass."

"You don't have to tell me twice." I laugh and head to the back room to grab my purse. "See you tomorrow." I wave as I head out the front door.

I take a cautious step outside, bracing for whatever weather Mother Nature felt compelled to deliver. You never know what to prepare for here, but lucky for me since I left my car at home, it's beautiful out. After growing up in humid-as-hell DC, I'll never stop loving the dry Colorado air. Yes, I go through way more ChapStick and spend a little more on hair products, but it's so worth it on nights when I can enjoy a walk without my clothes sticking to my body. Tonight's one of those nights I have to close my eyes and whisper my thanks to Maya for not giving up on me . . . for making this life possible for me and Ace.

I round the corner to my house, reaching into my purse and pulling out my keys and phone. My phone is blazing with notifications — one missed call and five text messages. All from Vonnie. My heart rate picks up, a cold sweat breaking out across my

263

forehead until I unlock the phone and I'm met with silly selfies of Ace, Jagger, Jett, and Jax stuffing their faces with hot dogs and ice cream. They're all dressed in blue and orange and sporting matching face paint.

I stare at the pictures, going back and forth between each one, making them bigger, letting them shrink back to size. And something in my chest settles. Ever since I left DC, I worried about the day I'd have to tell Ace about TK. Then, ever since actually telling Ace about TK, I've been bracing for the moment he tells me he wants nothing to do with me for keeping him from his dad. But as I look at these pictures, all I see is a little boy who has been loved his entire life and just got a whole lot more love.

I push open the still-creaky gate and add on yet another thing to my to-do list, when I'm met with darkness. I swear, I just put a new lightbulb on my front porch last month. I start to type out a response to Vonnie when I trip on something in front of my door. I turn on the flashlight on my phone to see what's blocking my doorway, and when I do, I see the most gorgeous arrangement of flowers. And it's huge.

My heartbeat stutters in my chest. TK's first home game of the season and he sent me flowers?

I'm falling for him so freaking hard.

I pick them up from the ground and unlock my door. Barreling through my entryway, I damn near skip to my couch. I set down the flowers as gently as my giddy fingers will let me and grab the remote to turn on the game, something I never, in a million years, thought I'd do.

"Touchdown Mustangs!" the announcer yells as soon as the picture comes into focus. "Rookie quarterback Peter Bremner connecting with the second-year receiver Avery Sheppard for an easy catch. I'd say these guys aren't fighting for a roster spot, they're fighting to dethrone one of the starters."

Since TK's spot is set in stone, he only plays the opening quarter of preseason games alongside the other starters. Nobody wants the guys with guaranteed money getting taken out before the season even starts. Plus, it gives the new guys a chance to shine. Each team starts training camp with ninety hopefuls reporting to the small hotel, and when it's over, only fifty-three players are left standing. There's a reason they say NFL stands for Not for Long. Making a final roster is a huge accomplishment.

I turn up the volume to see the football sail through the goalposts for the extra point. Even though — without TK on the field and Ace badgering me to watch how tight so-and-so covered his man — it doesn't really matter how loud the volume is. The chances of me paying attention for the rest of the game are slim to none.

I slip off my flat ankle boots, letting them fall onto my favorite rug. If Ace did this, I'd be yelling at him right now. But I'm grown and pay the bills, so I can do it. Plus, nobody is here to see it. So nanny nanny boo boo.

My feet have the slight ache all waiters have at the end of the night, but considering I used to do this in heels and have to trek up stairs, it almost goes unnoticed.

Almost.

The commercial break ends and a drone flies above the stadium, giving everyone at home a bird's-eye view of TK's office. The field is a startling shade of green, and considering Denver has had watering restrictions since I moved here, it doesn't take me long to work out they're playing on turf. The thought of those little black rubber beads that will no doubt find their way into every crook and cranny of my house makes me cringe. Between TK and Sadie, my poor floors don't stand a chance.

The Mustangs' kicker takes a running start and drills the ball across the field and into the end zone, where the Steelers' player catches it and promptly takes a knee. Whistles blow and sprints wind down to jogs as the men exit the field and more players take their place. The announcers talk about the new coaches and their different strategies and my attention is already lost.

Lucky for me, I have flowers to focus on.

I loved them in the dark, but in my well-lit living room, they're even better. The arrangement has peonies, roses, hydrangeas, and tulips of all different colors. There have to be at least two-dozen roses alone, and I try to focus on the beauty and how special they make me feel instead of him spending hundreds of dollars on something that will die in a week or — more realistically with me tending them — a couple of days.

Whatever.

I've kept my kid alive for almost ten years — let's not lose sight of what's really important here.

I turn the vase around, wanting to look at the flowers from every angle, when I notice the little white envelope.

I start to laugh before I even lift the fold.

TK is more Kevin Hart than Shakespeare. He can have romantic moments, but he's not romantic. Or at least he didn't use to be. He just sent me flowers, so maybe this is his way of showing me he's changed. Maybe he's going to court me.

Courting sounds like fun.

I bet Prince Harry courted Meghan.

I shake my head, clearing my mind of princess thoughts, and pull out the note written in unfamiliar handwriting. You'd think the florist would use a printer, or at least entrust the note writing to a more penmanship-conscious employee.

I miss you. You left without so much as a goodbye. I know you don't want people to know about us, but he can't give you what you need. Only I can do that. Poppy, my Serena, you'll be mine. I'll make sure of it.

Yours —

I drop the note and watch as it floats to the floor. Its graceful motions, swooping from left to right, taunting me.

My first instinct is Rochelle's messing with me. Maybe even Phil since I still haven't returned the uniform. But almost as quickly as the idea pops into my mind, it fades away. Both of them are way too cheap to send flowers like this. Sadie would, we've bought impressive, no-reason gifts for each other more than once. But she knows what a

268

scaredy cat I am and she'd never do something like this knowing I'm alone.

A shiver runs down my spine and another thought crosses my mind. I walk to the front door, my paranoid steps slow and measured. I flip the switch to my porch a few times to see if maybe I just forgot to turn it on. But when nothing happens, I resort to my handy iPhone flashlight. I crack open my front door, leaving the top latch on, and aim the light straight to where my porch light is supposed to be.

But isn't.

The blood freezes in my veins, and without thinking, I slam my door shut, turning all my locks in a frenzy. I turn off all my lights and the TV, and I move around my house guided only by the flicker of streetlights coming through the cracks in my blinds. I check to make sure all my windows are still locked, and when I'm positive I'm in complete lockdown, I crawl to my front window and lie on the floor under it, listening for any noises like a harmless guard dog.

Game forgotten and so thankful Ace isn't here, I spend the rest of the night googling alarm systems and pushing old *Law & Order* episodes out of my mind. The good news is alarm systems have gotten cool and super high-tech. I can't imagine having one and not feeling safer. The bad news, however, is they are so expensive, I can't imagine ever having one at all.

Unless I work . . . a lot of hours.

I don't know if it's the thought of how much I need to work to feel semisafe in my own freaking house or the adrenaline leaving my system, but my eyelids weigh a hundred pounds and my room feels miles away. My bed is calling my name, and I try to get up, but after a few minutes of my muscles refusing to budge, I decide the hardwood floor isn't too bad.

TWENTY-THREE

Boom boom boom.

My dream has bass.

Boom boom boom. "Poppy!"

My dream sounds kind of pissed off . . . and like TK.

My eyes fly open and I bolt up.

Which is a mistake.

"Ouch." I grab my lower back and it feels like the hardwood floor spent my entire nap punching me.

Out of the corner of my eye, I see the screen on my phone light up. I'm not old, but I'm not a teenager and I maybe (definitely) read on my phone too much, so it takes my vision a few seconds to adjust and make out the name on the phone.

TK.

I shake my head. God forbid he be the tiniest bit patient.

I swipe the screen and forgo a greeting. "I'm coming."

271

"Finally," he mutters, and I contemplate revoking my offer. "I've only been banging on your door for the last twenty minutes. The cops are probably going to show soon."

Shoot. He's been here that long? I scramble off the floor, feeling a tiny bit bad but trying not to let him know I'm feeling that way. "Drama king."

"Just open the door."

I twist open the locks, unlatch the door, and pull it open. But not because he told me to, I was going to do it anyway. "Bossy."

"Whatever." He flips on the light switches in my entryway/living room. "Where's your phone?"

"Right here." I wiggle my fist full of phone in his face and look at the screen when his face hardens.

Fifteen notifications.

Oops.

"Crap." I cringe, seeing the ten missed calls from TK, three phone calls and two texts from Vonnie. "Is Ace all right?"

The panic I felt earlier starts to return, sweat breaks out on my forehead, my fingers tingle, and my eyes fill with inexplicable tears. I ignore the text messages Vonnie sent and hit her contact before I think better of it.

Not that it matters because TK swipes the

phone from my hand and disconnects the call before the first ring. "Ace is fine. He just wanted to tell you about the game. I saw him after, they were having the best time, and Vonnie has it covered. They were going . . ." He trails off, his gaze straying over my shoulder and redness traveling up his neck, hiding behind his beard. "What are those?"

Oh crap.

I didn't throw away the flowers.

For one, the arrangement is so big it wouldn't have fit into the trash can in my kitchen in the first place. Second, there was no chance in freaking hell I was walking my happy ass to the alley behind my house, alone, to throw them away.

"What's wrong?" TK's looking at me instead of the flowers — my lack of response must have gained his attention back. The hard set of his jaw softens and he wraps his big, strong, *safe* arms around me and pulls me into his chest.

"I thought they were from you," I whisper into his chest, thinking if football fails, he should market himself as an alarm system. "I don't know who they're from."

"Was there a card?" He burrows his nose into my hair, which I'm sure looks fabulous after resting on the wood floor for however many hours I was down there.

"Yeah, but there's no name."

TK drops a gentle kiss on my forehead, stepping around me and into my living room. After poking around the flowers and looking on the coffee table, he finds the card on the floor.

I watch with avid fascination as a myriad of expressions cross his face. First humor, since I've told him about Sadie and so has Ace. I'm sure he's thinking it was a joke. Then there's confusion. His eyebrows knit together, causing the cutest wrinkles to crease the bridge of his nose and deep lines to settle on his forehead. Then anger. The red that had faded comes back with a vengeance. This time the red doesn't hide behind his beard, you can see it through the thick scruff covering his cheeks.

"What the fuck?" he asks like I know something, his eyes flying back to the scratchy penmanship.

"I don't know." I take a deep breath. Partially to tell TK something I know is going to set him off, also because saying it out loud makes this real. And it's scary enough already. "There's something else."

He sticks the card into his pocket, and for the first time I notice how freaking hot he looks. His long hair is pulled up in a bun on the crown of his head, the highlights the sun has provided him with streaked through would cost me hundreds of dollars, and his emerald eyes are magnified beneath glasses I'm not sure he even needs. His big body is wrapped like a present in a tailored-to-perfection, brown plaid, double-breasted suit I'm convinced would look ridiculous on anyone else. The bottom half is just as good. Slim-cut pants suction to his thick, muscular thighs with his navy socks peeking out right above his loafers.

"Poppy." He snaps his fingers in front of my face. "Are you okay?"

"Yeah, sorry." I shake my head to clear it. "I like your suit."

"Thanks." His lips curve into a smile he's trying hard to fight. "What else did you want to tell me?"

"I don't really want to tell you. It's just, you know." I shrug. "You're here and you see the flowers. And it will probably be good to tell you. You'll be able to tell me I'm over-reacting and —"

"Poppy." TK interrupts my rambling. "Spit it out."

I want to stomp around my living room and flail and pout on my bed, pissed that nothing in my life can be drama free for long. But since society frowns on temper tantrums from anyone above the age of three, I settle for sticking out my tongue.

"I found these when I tripped on them walking to my door. I didn't see them because I thought I forgot to turn on my porch light." I hesitate, feeling unease prick at my skin and my back go straight. "But I never turn off that light, so I thought maybe it died already, even though I just changed it like a month ago."

TK's posture matches mine, and I know as much as I want him to tell me I'm over-reacting, he isn't going to.

"So I checked my light after I got the card and the lightbulb's gone." I rush the words out, hoping TK understands because I'm not saying it again. "I think whoever brought the flowers took it."

This time, TK doesn't get red or tense up like he wants to punch something . . . or someone. No. This time he goes ghost white and takes a step back like someone punched him.

And let me tell you, this scares me more than the note ever did.

"Are you okay? Do you need water?" I grab his hand and walk him to my couch.

"Am I okay?" He looks at me with wide eyes. "You were walking home alone to your empty house where someone not only

276

knows where you live but left you a note and tampered with one of the few safety measures you have. What if this person was waiting on the side of your house? They could've pushed you inside and nobody would've known. Fuck!" he shouts, *now* looking like he wants to punch something. "What if Ace was here?"

"I know," I tell him. Because I do know. It was just one of about fifty worst-case scenarios playing on a continuous loop in my head.

"So not am *I* okay . . . are *you* okay?"

I try to avoid looking at him. I try to internalize everything, not wanting to look weak. Not wanting to feel scared.

But then TK does what he used to do when we were kids. What he would do when I'd get in another fight with my mom over whatever she decided to fight with me about that day. He pulls me into his chest, one arm drawing circles on my back, the other hand tangled in my curls, his fingertips massaging my scalp, and says nothing. No more questions. No expectations. Just the simple comfort that comes with silence and his hands on me.

"I'm freaking the hell out," I whisper, my voice so hoarse from unshed tears I almost don't recognize it myself.

TK says nothing. His fingers tense against

my back, but the circles he's drawing on my back don't stop. Maybe he's waiting for me to say more and maybe there's more I should tell him, but those five words have drained me.

I zone out. Loving the silence and the calm that can exist only in moments like this one, when time comes to a standstill. Everything that happened tonight, hell, everything that's happened the last ten years, fades away.

TK speaks first, probably because he knows if he doesn't, we'll be here all night. "You should go get some sleep, I'm going to go —"

"You're leaving already?" My back goes straight and my entire body tenses. I do a horrible job of disguising the panic, but to be fair, I wasn't trying to.

"No, you didn't let me finish. I was going to say I'm going to go throw away the flowers." TK takes a step back but never stops touching me. "Do you think after what went down tonight, I'd leave you?"

If I didn't know him so well, I'd think he was fine. He looks fine, his facial features carefully schooled into a mask of impassiveness. But the whiskers on the left side of his beard move just enough that I know his jaw ticked three times — not once, not twice, but three times — and he is either annoyed, insulted, or both.

"I mean . . ." I pause, trying to find the right words to explain. It's not that I thought he'd leave, I just didn't know if he'd stay. But that doesn't make sense in my own brain, so I know it won't make sense to him. "Ace isn't here and we haven't spent this much time together alone in a long time. I just . . . I wasn't sure."

"Well, be sure." He drops his hands from my back and links our fingers together. "Because I'm here to stay."

Butterflies flood my stomach, and I bite the inside of my cheek to prevent my smile from overtaking my entire face.

Because I know he's not just talking about one night.

Twenty-Four

"I like your room." TK's standing next to my bed, taking off his clothes, and I'm in bed, fully clothed, trying not to stare.

"You haven't seen it yet?" I focus on each word leaving my lips, making sure I don't accidentally ask if I can lick him or something else equally inappropriate.

"Nope. You banned me to the living room. Ace took pity on me, though, and let me sleep on his trundle."

My eyes go wide and I pull my lips between my teeth. "You slept on his trundle?" I ask, unable to hold back my laughter. TK sleeping on Ace's tiny little trundle is the funniest thing I've heard in a long time.

Ace's trundle is broken. It gets stuck halfway under his bed and leaves half a twin bed to sleep on. I can't even sleep on the thing!

He turns to me, his eyes sparkling, no doubt understanding why I'm so tickled by this discovery. "Yeah, I lasted until I heard him snore and then snuck to the couch. Which, by the way, how does a kid that small snore so loud? I don't understand how it's possible."

"Oh my god! He is the loudest snorer ever! It's why I kicked him out of my room when he was five. Between him sleeping sideways and snoring like a freight train, I got no sleep." I throw back my head, laughing so hard I have to wipe my cheeks for a few tears. "I looked like a zombie. I went through so much concealer, I had a secret stash hidden under my bed."

Then the laughter stops as fast as it came when a sensation I've never felt in this bed happens. The other side — the empty side — of my bed dips.

TK's large, shirtless body unfolds on top of my comforter. His basketball shorts rode up while he was sitting and his legs dusted with hair are on full display. Both hands are behind his head and his eyes are closed. He's relaxed and not flexing, but somehow, his stupid muscles are still noticeable. When I try my hardest to flex my abs, you still have to poke through a layer of fluff to feel anything. He's just lying here and I can count all eight of his six-pack.

Show-off.

"Damn. This is a comfy-ass bed." He stretches, arching his back.

"It's old. Maya got it for me when I was pregnant with Ace." I lie down, trying to divert my eyes from the man beside me. "I told her I only needed a twin. I already felt like a mooch, pregnant, poor, and crashing in on her, but she told me a queen was the minimum I should lie on. I was lucky she didn't listen to my objections. I swear, my belly got so big it would've hung off a twin and then Ace was born and didn't leave my bed until I kicked him out for snoring."

I smile at the memory of a tiny Ace in his co-sleeper lying next to me, the sweet little baby noises he'd make and his tiny little hands sneaking their way out of his blanket no matter how tight I'd swaddle him.

I turn my head and TK's turned onto his side, watching me with an expression I've never seen.

"Sorry," I say, realizing I've been rambling on about a mattress. "You know I talk a lot when I'm tired."

He reaches a hand across the small gap between us and rests it on my hip. "Don't be sorry," he whispers, his eyes trying to communicate something I can't decipher. "I want to know about everything I missed, even your mattress."

"You do?" I'm not sure he knows what he's asking for. Everything is a lot.

"Every night since I saw you guys at the park, I lie down, and no matter what's going on or how shitty my day was, my mind always drifts off to you guys. What you're doing while I'm alone. What little traditions you have, just the two of you, that I missed out on. I wonder if you're glad I'm back or if I'm intruding on your life and making things harder for you."

"I've been doing the same thing since I got on a plane and moved to Denver. I wondered what it'd be like for you to be there with me cheering at Ace's soccer games and tucking him in at night, what it would feel like for us to be a family." The words fall from my lips before I have a chance to think about them. I scoot closer to him, closing the small gap between us, until I feel his breath against my skin. "I tried to hate you, I really did. But it never worked."

He slides one arm under my neck, his hand going to my hair and giving it a gentle tug. He forces me to look at his face and not his chest like I have been. "You know I never stopped loving you, Poppy, don't you?"

The air around me goes static and my

breath catches in my throat, all while my heart threatens to beat right out of my chest.

He continues on. "Because I didn't. And now, seeing you with Ace, seeing what a great kid he is? I love you even more. I know you might not be ready to hear this, and that's fine with me, but I need to tell you. I need you to know how sorry I am for being such a royal fuckup when we were kids and how thankful I am you're the mother of my child."

He's wrong about one thing. I am ready to hear it. I've been ready since the day I left.

I close my eyes and burrow my face in the crook of his neck. But when I go to say it back to him, the words catch in my throat.

I've loved TK for as long as I can remember. Hell, I loved him when I hated him. And for some reason I'm not sure even I understand, I can't tell him that. I know he means the words he is saying and I know he thinks he wants to stick around forever, but I also know how hard this parenting gig is. I've already bogged him down with so much, I don't need to throw my feelings on top of everything.

Instead of talking, I move my hands from their tucked position in between us and onto his bare chest, pushing up to his shoulders and stopping behind his neck. I pull his head toward mine, fully aware I'm starting something I don't think I'll be able to stop.

Something I don't want to stop.

TK reads where this is going. This close to him, I get to watch as the green of his eyes disappears. His eyelids lower, his pupils dilate, and it's clear he wants to go where I'm taking him. Yet he still pulls back an inch and studies my face. "Are you sure you want this? I don't need you to lick my wounds, I promise I'm okay with you not saying you love me. I don't want you to regret this."

Dammit.

I really do love him.

"I'm sure." I pull him closer again. "And it's not your wounds I want to lick."

He groans and I smile.

"Fuck." All restraint thrown out the window, he rolls me flat on my back, nudges his knee between my thighs, and then crashes his mouth onto mine. His beard scratches against my chin, but it doesn't bother me. Instead, it sparks every nerve ending in my body, magnifying the most inconspicuous touch.

My mouth opens to his without a second thought and he takes the invitation. There's no teasing, no softness, just a relentless attack I cannot get enough of. When he nips at my bottom lip, my back arches off the bed and he slides his hands up the back of my shirt with an efficiency I can only admire.

I'm so overtaken by emotion, by sensation, I know nothing in this entire world could pull me out of this moment.

Until TK starts to lift the hem of my shirt . . . with the light still on.

I pull my head back and push his chest, breaking us apart and missing his mouth before it's even gone. "Turn off the light," I groan before going for his mouth again.

"No." He shakes his head and the corners of his mouth tip up.

He leans back in, pulling at the hem of my shirt again, and this time I push him back a little harder. "TK." I stare at him, trying to convey the importance of a dark — preferably pitch-black — room. "Please turn off the light."

Up until this very moment, this has never been a problem for me . . . for multiple reasons.

For one, I never actually cared about what the men I slept with thought, assuming I was probably never going to see them again, and if I did, it'd be with clothes on.

Two, find me one person without a single imperfection. It doesn't exist. Everybody has something they are a little insecure about.

And last, we've always been here for *my* entertainment, thank you very much.

But I'm playing by a different set of rules with TK. I do care what he thinks. He's only gotten hotter since the last time we had sex — bigger muscles, better facial hair, even his freaking voice got deeper!

I, on the other hand, had a baby . . . and then nursed said baby. Sure, TK can probably tell my hips are a little bit wider and I'm still carrying the last ten pounds of baby weight — Ace will be thirty and I'll still reference weight I'd like to lose as baby weight. But what he doesn't know about are the faded, but still noticeable, stretch marks lining my stomach and thighs and probably ass if I ever wanted to torture myself and look. And let's be honest, push-up bras are magic. In clothes, my rack looks better than ever. But as soon as the bra disappears, so do any remnants of perkiness. I am a long ways away from the cute, unmarked sixteen-year-old girl he remembers. And I'm too turned on to have it ruined by a look of disappointment at my weathered and altered body.

"Why do you want the lights off?" he asks again.

"Never mind. I'm tired anyways." I try to push him away and roll from beneath him, both of which I fail at so spectacularly, it would be comical if I wasn't on the verge of tears.

Angry tears this time.

And angry tears are always acceptable.

"Get off of me, TK." I slap his bare chest . . . and then I do it again when he doesn't so much as flinch.

"Why do you want me to turn off the light?" He leans in like I'm not the rabid dog he's turning me into.

"I said get off of me," I snarl, pushing harder at his chest, which I'm now convinced is made of stone.

"Poppy." He rolls back onto his knees and settles between my legs, dropping his hands on top of my thighs, which are now framing him. "It's an easy question. Why do you want the lights off?"

I'm short, so I'm used to people literally looking down at me, but this way? Lying in the middle of my bed with TK's giant self looking mighty comfy propped up above me, staring down at me like he can see straight into my soul of darkness, I'm feeling extra vulnerable. "Does it matter?" I

288

snap, moving my hands to cover my eyes. The eye contact is too much for me.

"Yeah." He pulls my hands from my face. "It does."

"Why?" I yell. "People have sex in the dark all the time, TK. It's not like I'm asking you for some crazy, kinked-out shit."

"Because . . ." He squeezes my hands tighter and I brace, because if he thinks he needs to give me extra comfort, I'm not going to like what he says next. "I think you're trying to hide your body from me."

Heat floods my cheeks, and I turn my head to the side, clenching my eyes shut. "Please get off of me," I ask again, this time my voice cracking, and I hate myself for initiating this entire scene.

"But what I don't understand is why," TK continues on like I didn't speak. "Your body changed?" He lets go of one of my hands and uses it to turn my head back to him. "I know it did. Last time we were together, we were kids. Now you're a woman . . . a woman who carried our child." He brushes his thumb across my lips. "I hope when you finally let me lift this shirt, I see some stretch marks."

I think it's the shock, or maybe total disbelief, that causes me to open my eyes.

I've tried really hard over the years to be

one of those "these are my tiger marks" warrior moms, who embraces every change pregnancy bestowed upon her body. But I'm not.

I don't harp on them every time I strip down to take a shower or get dressed, I just don't show them off. I haven't been caught in a bikini since the summer of '07. And TK being an Adonis and all, I'm not too hyped up for him to bear witness to the road map of the forty pounds I gained.

"I'm serious," he says, never dropping eye contact.

I roll my eyes and purse my lips. "You are so full of it."

"Poppy, really listen to me, please." He lets go of my hands and moves from between my legs to the unused side of my bed. He leans over and, with what seems like no effort at all, lifts my still-carrying-baby-weight ass and drops it right in his lap.

This position almost feels more intimate, but also more equal, so I don't fight it. "Talk."

His eyes go soft, as if he's looking at me for the very first time, and he tucks a piece of hair behind my ear. "If I could do anything, I'd go back in time and be there for you and Ace. I wish I could've seen you pregnant. Your tits were probably phenomenal . . . Your ass too."

I tell him the heartbreaking truth. "They were obscene." Boobs as big as your head are really freaking painful. My back will never fully recover from pregnancy.

"I wish I could've seen your stomach and watched the changes as they happened. But that can't happen, so all I have, the only thing I can see, are the changes that stuck around." He leans in so close, I can feel his every breath against my mouth. "I don't know if you think I'm expecting to see the girl I was with last, but I'm not. I'm dying to see, and worship, the woman you are now. The woman who has busted her ass for the last nine years raising our son by herself."

Well, crap.

How do I say no to that? Especially when I want to say yes.

"Okay." I nod. "You can leave the light on."

"Are you sure?" TK asks like he didn't just full-court press this issue.

I inhale a deep breath before answering, "Yes."

"Good." He smiles, his white teeth gleaming against the dark beard framing his mouth.

I bite my bottom lip and try to stop my

hands from fidgeting as he lifts the hem of my shirt, raising it one agonizing inch at a time. He pulls it over my head and I close my eyes trying to calm my breathing. His fingertips dance across my shoulders, pushing the already loose bra straps down my arms.

My eyes are still shut when I hear a sharp intake of breath.

And I don't open them when TK's hands grip my hips and his forehead rests against mine.

"Poppy." His voice is husky and his breathing sounds like it does after a hard practice. "Please look at me."

It takes me a minute to do it. To prepare for whatever I'm about to be met with.

But when I open my eyes, I realize I could've spent my entire life preparing for this moment and I still wouldn't be ready for what TK gives me without a word.

It's a look of adoration I've only seen in movies. It's every single guard or layer of protection TK is always carrying, removed. There's no humor, no defenses, nothing but TK looking at me as if I'd hung the stars and the moon for him.

"You're so beautiful it hurts." He grinds out each word.

I shake my head. I suck at accepting

compliments and right now I can't even begin to try. Emotions — words I refuse to speak — are clogging my throat and I'm afraid if I say anything, everything I'm fighting to keep in will fall out.

"I need you to believe this. I need this to penetrate that thick skull of yours." His fingers on my hips flex, his fingernails digging into my skin. "You're fucking stunning. You're gorgeous here." He leans in, dropping a chaste kiss on my lips. "And here." He rolls us back over to our original position. His hands slowly travel up my sides, goose bumps following their path, until they cup my breasts. His thumbs graze my nipples. It's the smallest, gentlest touch, but it's like I've been shocked with a defibrillator. Electricity floods my system, sending my heart rate sky high and my back clear off the mattress.

TK takes full advantage. His mouth clamps around my nipple, sucking hard, then teasing it with a swirl of his tongue before moving to the neglected one. I can't control my breathing or the pulsing between my thighs. As much as I want to thread my fingers into his hair and hold him to me, they are tangled in the sheets, tethering me to the bed because I think I might float away if I let go.

You'd think I hadn't been touched in years by my reaction. And I guess, thinking about it, I haven't. I've been through the motions, but I've never felt this before — like I might actually, physically die if TK stops touching me. Luckily for me, I don't think he has plans to stop anytime soon.

I pry my eyes open and watch as his mouth leaves my breasts and drops a trail of kisses down my stomach.

"And definitely here," he whispers, but the word echoes in my mind. He lifts his head and traces a faded stretch mark below my belly button with his finger. His touch is so light it causes goose bumps to rise all over my body. He stares at the line for a moment before a small smile pulls at his mouth. He pops open the button on my jeans with ease and pulls down the zipper just as fast. "Let's get these off of you." I lift my hips, eager to assist in this mission, while he yanks them — and my underwear — clean off in one magician-worthy motion.

"Knew it." He sidles up between my legs, looking up at me from beneath his lashes. "Every bit of you is perfect."

Heat rises in my cheeks again, but this time it's from lust, not embarrassment. "TK." I try to close my legs, needing something to relieve the pulsing desire lighting up my body like a Christmas tree.

"Tell me you believe me, Poppy," TK says. His hoarse voice is the only indication he's suffering through this wait as much as I am.

"Please," I whine. He has reduced my verbal skills to one-word responses.

"I want to." He grabs my thighs and kisses the insides, making it impossible to find any relief. "Tell me you believe me."

"Yes," I force out between my ragged breathing. "I believe you."

TK doesn't speak.

And holy shit. Whoever said actions speak louder than words was not lying.

His huge hands pull my thighs apart as wide as he deems necessary and finally — FINALLY! — he dips his tongue between my thighs.

I collapse against my pillows and the world goes black, which I'm pretty sure is because my eyes roll to the back of my head.

My entire body is primed and ready to go not only from the kisses and attention he's peppered me with for the last who knows how long but from our very first encounter in the alley. My body has been yearning for him for months. Well, if I'm honest with myself, I've been yearning for his touch for years.

Which is why, when his mouth closes over

me, his beard brushing the sensitive skin of my inner thighs, it only takes approximately 1.26 seconds before my insides clench. My toes curl and my lips go numb as the orgasm literally builds from head to toe.

I push off the bed — or I levitate, who really knows — and watch as TK devours me like I'm the best thing he's ever tasted. He's not doing this out of obligation, my pleasure is his pleasure, and knowing that I'm turning him on is the catalyst to the earthshaking, body-breaking orgasm that rips through me. My hands fly to TK's head, digging into the hair I love even more at this very moment. I don't know if I'm holding him to me or pushing him away as I ride the waves of ecstasy flowing through my body, but I do know TK doesn't let up, which is why my insides tighten with another orgasm.

"Oh . . . my . . . god . . . TK." Each word more moan than anything else. "I can't." I arch my back and dig my feet into the mattress to try to pull away, unsure another orgasm like I just had won't rip me apart at the seams.

I get nowhere and TK doesn't stop.

No.

TK grabs my already shaking legs, lifts my ass clean off the bed, and drapes my thighs over his shoulders. I'm helpless in this position. I can't pull away, I can't move toward him. Nothing.

Except feel.

"Give it to me, Poppy," he growls out before dropping his mouth back down and slipping a single finger inside me.

That's the end for me.

A scream I'm pretty sure only dogs can hear is torn from my throat as the tension building in my core explodes. Aftershocks leave me lying on the bed, my body convulsing, as I come back down to earth. Every inch of me tingles and I'm pretty sure if I had the spare energy to open my eyes, sparks would be shooting from every pore.

"You good?" TK asks, his beard tickling my neck.

"I'm dead," I say between harsh, deep breaths. "You killed me."

"And I can do it again." I don't even have to look at him to see the smug smile on his face.

"There's no way I can . . ." I stop myself, remembering that was only the appetizer and I want the entrée. "Never mind." I roll over, opening my eyes. I bring my hands to his chest, moving them down . . . down . . . down. Until I reach his . . . "Wait." I sit up straight, not needing to look hard since the lights are still on. "You still have on pants?"

"Yeah." He answers my rhetorical question.

"Obviously." I roll my eyes and send up a quick prayer to the God of Sexy Times he won't ruin the mood. "Take them off!"

I don't mean to yell, but holy hell! You can't make a woman come her brains out twice and not be prepared for the next stage of the game. It's in the Sex Rule Book or something.

"Damn." He holds up his hands in surrender and smirks, still looking cocky . . . in the wrong way. "I'll get right to that, ma'am."

"I will hurt you, TK."

I'm revved up on lust and emotion. I am not the one.

But then he does drop his pants. And maybe I am the one because Holy. HOT.

I mean . . .

DAMN.

"Penises aren't supposed to be pretty," I say, not making eye contact . . . not even close.

"You've seen it before." He walks to his discarded suit jacket and pulls his wallet out of the inside pocket. He flips it open, and before I know it, he has a foil packet in his hand.

"I haven't seen it like this." I somehow remember how to speak as I watch his hands roll the condom over his impressive manhood. I clench my thighs together again, amazed I still have feeling down there.

TK moves to the bed, his quadriceps flexing with every step. The cuts at his hips point down to his erection, which is standing tall and swaying in a way so hypnotizing, I'm not sure I'll ever be able to break free of his spell.

Not that I want to.

"Come here," I whisper, grabbing his hand as soon as he sits on the bed and pulling him on top of me. With my free hand, I try — and fail — to wrap my fingers around him.

I don't close my eyes this time and neither does he as I guide him to my opening. Ever so slowly, he pushes in, letting my body adjust one inch at a time until he's buried inside me.

He flexes his hips but pulls back when I flinch from the bite of pain it causes.

"Are you all right?" he asks. His arms are shaking on each side of my head, and with the light on, I can see the beads of sweat building on his forehead.

I take inventory of my body before I answer. I tilt my hips upward, the discomfort I felt only seconds ago beginning to fade. "Yeah." I reach up, locking my hands behind his head and pulling his mouth to mine. I open my mouth for him and he slips his tongue in without hesitation and I can taste me on him.

Any remnant of discomfort dissipates and need replaces it. "Go, TK." I nip at his bottom lip. "Please."

That's all the convincing he needs. It's like I flipped a switch and the tender, gentle man I was just with turns uninhibited.

And I love it.

He slams into me with abandon. His strength gives it to me in ways I've never experienced before. It's not long until he's moved me up the bed, my head hitting the headboard in sync with every thrust.

"Fuck yes," he growls before pulling out, flipping me onto my knees and slamming back into me from behind.

My back arches into him as I try to meet him thrust for thrust. The only sounds filling my small house are our heavy breathing, moans, and his thighs slapping against my ass.

That familiar pressure starts to build, and my body goes solid, I clench around him as he continues his glorious assault.

"Come on, baby." He wraps my hair

around his fist, pulling my head back. "Get there." he says into my ear, his damp skin brushing against mine before dropping his other hand to my sex.

I feel him *everywhere.*

"Oh my god!" My knees give out beneath me as I come . . . again.

It's fast and so intense, everything fades away. I hear TK call out his release, but he sounds so far away. I think he's whispering something, but it's impossible to hear over the roaring in my ears.

"Holy shit," I tell my mattress after my breathing has returned to normal, TK's weight still resting on top of me. "That was amazing."

"That was better than amazing, Sparks," TK says into my hair before rolling off me. "That was fucking life changing."

Damn straight.

This might not be a forever thing, me and him, but it is a right-now thing. And so, for now, I'm going to take advantage of every second I have left with TK.

I smile to myself, enjoying the aches I know are going to be fully present in the morning.

Then I fall asleep.

With the light still on.

TWENTY-FIVE

"Look who finally decided to join us." TK smirks, pushing a large Fresh cup across the table. "I wasn't sure what you ordered, but Ace said it's always a vanilla latte, so that's what you got."

"Are you feeling okay, Mom?" Ace asks, handing me a Fresh bag I don't need to look in to know it's a blueberry muffin. "You never sleep this late and you look different."

I'm fine. Your dad just put it down so hard last night . . . and again this morning.

"Yeah, dude. I just had a long night at work. I guess I was more tired than I thought." I give him an answer that won't leave him emotionally scarred for the rest of his life. "When did you get home anyway?"

"Like an hour ago." Ace shrugs. "TK picked me up from Mrs. Vonnie's house and then we stopped at Fresh on our way home."

Ace has his back turned before he finishes talking to me, so he misses it when my eyebrows try to take cover under my hair-line.

"You picked him up?" I turn to TK, not sure how I feel about this.

His shoulders tense in a way that lets me know my tone isn't as happy-go-lucky as I hoped it was. "The vets got excused from training camp today," he tells me for some reason. "I dropped my stuff off at my place and Justin and Vonnie live right around the corner from me. I figured since I was right there, there was no need for you or Vonnie to go out of your way."

"I don't mind picking him up." I reach for my coffee and train my eyes on the floors I need to mop to avoid looking at TK. "You should've called me first."

"I did, four times," he says matter-of-factly.

Crap.

I close my eyes and draw in one of the deep breaths Sadie is always telling me to take after she goes to her once-a-month yoga class.

"I . . ." I pause, trying to think of an excuse to leave. "I forgot to brush my teeth."

I spin on my fuzzy slipper before TK can call out my lie, and I head straight to the bathroom.

Once I'm in the small, outdated room, I

slide down the door, not even flinching when my shorts-clad legs rest against the cold tile floor.

I don't understand what the hell is going on with me.

All I ever wanted was a reliable partner who cared about Ace just as much as I do. And now I have him, and he's TK of all people. It's so much more than I ever even let myself dream. And the first time he does the smallest thing on his own, like giving our son a ride home, I freak out!

Again, what is wrong with me?

I don't know if it's all the crap with the flowers, the things TK said to me — or the way he touched me — last night, or what, but I'm a straight-up disaster.

I swipe the tears falling down my cheeks and resist the urge to scream. It's like I'm incapable of accepting good things in my life. I want to be the person who just says thank you when TK does something kind. The type of woman who says "I love you" back to the man she's loved her entire life.

But that's not me.

No.

I'm the kind of person who thinks TK had to pick up Ace only because I was being irresponsible and overslept, knowing my kid might need me. The person who cries on a bathroom floor thinking of how much it's going to hurt when this illusion finally blows up in my face.

So much for enjoying this while it lasts.

"Poppy?" TK knocks on the door.

I clear my throat and scramble off the floor. "Yeah?" I ask, but it's too high and peppy to sound anything but forced.

"Can I come in?"

"Umm . . ." I look in the mirror, viciously wiping away the tear marks lining my face. "Sure."

I open the door when I look only a little bit like hell.

"What's up?" I try to step into the hallway with him, but TK pushes into the bathroom instead.

Now even with Ace, it's a tight squeeze if we both need to be in the bathroom at the same time. With TK's giant ass, I feel like we're at risk of running out of oxygen.

"That's what I was going to ask you." No nonsense and straight to the point. "Why were you crying in the bathroom?"

"Crying in the bathroom?" I purse my lips and arch a single eyebrow. "I was not."

"Poppy." He tilts his head to the side and narrows his eyes. "It's your move. You don't like people to see you upset so you hide in the bathroom. You missed half of homecoming sophomore year in the bathroom because that one chick had the same dress as you."

"It wasn't just because she had the same dress, TK! Victoria was at the store when I picked my dress. She did it on purpose because she was skinnier than me and had the hots for you. It was an intentional jab!"

Bitch. The dress looked better on me anyways. Orange is my color. She blended into it from all the fake tanner she used.

"So you don't deny hiding in the bathroom?"

"It wasn't because I was sad," I defend myself, though not well. "I was pissed and I couldn't fight her because I paid for my makeup and hair. I was not letting her ruin it."

"So you're pissed now?" he asks, using my words against me.

Sneaky son of a . . .

"No, I'm . . . I mean . . . I'm not pissed," I stutter.

"So you are sad."

"No!" I throw up my hands in the air, already exhausted by this conversation. "I'm not pissed or sad. I'm just . . . I don't even know how to say this."

"Just say it."

"I'm just not used to people helping out

with Ace, that's all." I tell him the simplest version of the garbage running through my mind.

His eyebrows scrunch together and he shakes his head ever so slightly. "Isn't having help a good thing?"

"Yeah . . . no . . . I don't know." I want to sit back down on the floor, but there isn't enough room for my legs and TK's feet. "I just like doing stuff for him and I feel like a crap mom for sleeping through your calls."

"He's my kid too." All of a sudden there's an edge to his voice that wasn't there seconds ago. "Maybe I like doing stuff for him and it has nothing to do with you as a mother." He rubs the back of his neck, and I swear, I can hear his teeth grinding.

"I know that." I draw out each word. "Why do you think I'm in the bathroom trying to sort out these irrational feelings on my own?"

I wait for some kind of response, any acknowledgment I spoke at all, but I don't get one.

And to be honest, he's too grown to pout.

"Listen." I stand up straight, using my "I mean business" mom voice. "I think we both need to understand this is an adjustment for both of us. I get you want to spend time with him and make up for time lost, but you need to understand that I've had him to myself for nine years. Learning to share isn't easy for me."

That gets through to him.

"You're right." He drags his large, callused hand across his face. "This isn't even why I came to talk to you."

"It isn't?" I ask, my eyebrows shooting up to my hairline again. I swear, a few more days with him and I'm going to have to make a Botox appointment. These surprise lines are gonna settle at some point.

"No." He reaches out, lacing his fingers in mine. A move that both makes me melt into him and causes my back to go straight in anticipation of what he's about to say. "I didn't sleep much last night."

"Probably would've been easier if you turned off the light," I offer.

Helpful? No. Funny? I think so.

I laugh.

TK does not.

"That wasn't why." He rolls his eyes and fights a smirk I can tell is tugging at his lips beneath the beard I love even more after last night. "Like I was saying, I didn't get much sleep thinking about you and Ace being alone in this house with the . . . flower incident." He drops his voice to a whisper for the last two words. "Then after Coach dismissed us from the hotel this morning and I went to my house that's way too big for one person anyways . . ." He trails off.

The hairs on the back of my neck stand up, knowing where he's going with this. I want to cut him off, but I don't, if by chance I don't really know where he's going with this.

"I was thinking you and Ace could move in with me," he finishes, looking as hopeful as Ace does every time he asks to play football or to get a puppy.

Neither of which will ever happen.

"We can't move in with you." I don't try to soften my answer.

"Yes, you can. My house is huge. Ace already has friends down the street." He starts ticking off the items on the list he must have built in his head. "It's actually in a safe neighborhood."

I think not.

"This is a great neighborhood, thank you very much." I pull my hands out of his grip. "And I don't care how many reasons you have why we should move in with you, it's not going to happen."

"School starts in a week, the same school he's attended since preschool. The soccer field for the soccer team he just made is right around the corner. His best friend lives at the end of this block." I resist the urge to shake TK, I'm so irritated to even be having this conversation. "This is the only home Ace has ever known. I might not be the perfect mom, but I pride myself on providing him with this kind of stability." TK starts to speak, but I keep talking. "I'm sure your house is amazing. Bigger and newer than this one, but that's not the point. We cannot uproot his life. Especially now, when he's still adjusting to the crazy bombshells that were dropped on him this summer."

"I didn't mean to insult you. This is a great house and I told you Gavin pretty much lives next door when they're in town, so I know it's not a bad neighborhood. I don't know why I said that," he half apologizes, which I guess is better than no apology at all.

"It's fine. I might say things I don't mean occasionally too."

This makes him laugh for some reason.

"Occasionally?" He reaches for my hands again and pulls me into his chest.

"Maybe more than that," I amend, fighting back my own laughter.

My temper has always been a bit — how should I describe it? — touchy.

"I'd say so," he whispers into my hair.

We stand in my bathroom, cuddled together for what could be hours but is probably only a few minutes. Both of us taking comfort in the other, letting the weird emotions we've both been feeling settle around us. I'd worry Ace would start to get concerned . . . or grossed out . . . but he has full remote access and probably hasn't even realized we're gone.

"Well." TK's voice cuts through my thoughts. "If you won't move in with me, I guess I'm gonna have to move here."

My head is facing the mirror, so I get a firsthand view of my eyes tripling in size and the color draining from my face.

"Y-you . . . you'll move? Here?" I stutter. A speech pattern, I'm learning, is becoming a staple of mine around TK.

"Yeah." He looks at me like it's the most obvious thing in the entire world. "At least until all this stuff with the light and flowers is worked out. It'll be great. Ace can stay in his house and school. I can spend more time with both of you. You won't have to be alone here. And I won't have to worry."

"Yeah . . . it'll be great," I repeat after him.

But I don't know if it will be great.

Playing house is a long ways away from the "enjoy him while I have him" vision I had planned. I want him and Ace to bond and have a relationship. What I don't want is to become dependent and hooked to a situation that's bound to fail.

And if last night was any indication, this is going to leave me completely and utterly screwed . . . in more ways than one.

TWENTY-SIX

"He what?" Vonnie damn near shouts, drawing the attention of the table behind her.

"He moved in." I slide another martini in front of her and a glass of red wine in front of Charli. "Last Monday."

"Last Monday?" Now Charli's shouting. "As in seven full days ago and you're just now telling us?"

"It all happened really fast." I shrug, not wanting to go into full detail in a room full of strangers.

"She just told you about TK?" Sadie slides her rhinestone-encrusted butt onto the barstool next to Vonnie, pointing a hot-pink acrylic nail my way. "Did she tell you about the maybe stalker she has?"

"*What?*" Vonnie and Charli scream in unison.

I narrow my eyes at Sadie before turning to both Vonnie and Charli. "I don't have a stalker." I try to calm them down. "I know you just met her, but Sadie is very dramatic. Always keep that in mind when listening to one of her stories."

"I do have a certain flair for the dramatics," Sadie agrees. Then, as if to prove my point, she raises a fist above her head before opening it and letting glitter rain down on her. I roll my eyes, thinking about how much longer it's going to take me to sweep up tonight. Vonnie and Charli, however, stare at her with wide-eyed wonder, like a child seeing Santa Claus . . . or me if I ever meet Beyoncé. "But, and correct me if I'm wrong here, Poppy, but someone who is not TK did drop off a giant bouquet of flowers on your doorstep, right?"

"Well, yeah but —" I say, but Sadie cuts me off before I can continue.

"And the note in the flowers didn't have a name, right?" she asks even though she already knows the damn answer.

"People forget to write their names all the time!" I defend the creep.

"That's true," Sadie agrees, swiveling her chair to face Vonnie and Charli. "But do they also say things like, 'You'll be mine. I'll make sure of it.'? And mention your real name as well as the alias you used at the club?"

After getting the job at HERS, it was

easier to tell Vonnie and Charli about my past employment at the Emerald Cabaret. When I did spill, they didn't balk, instead, their reaction was much like Brynn's. I guess they had both gone with Justin and Shawn after TK introduced the club to the team. Obviously, I wasn't working the night they went. But in a crazy twist of events, Sadie was and they loved her. So merging my friends ended up being easier than I ever expected.

"But —" I try and fail to defend myself.

"*Tsk tsk tsk,*" Sadie says, cutting me off. "I'm asking Vonnie and Charli, not you."

I give her my best stink eye and stick out my tongue. I don't know why I introduced them.

"Girl." Vonnie looks at me, concern written all over her face. "Why didn't you tell us about this?"

"Wait, wait, wait. And here's the kicker," Sadie says before I can answer . . . again. "Whoever left the note took out the light-bulb from her porch light."

Welp.

I guess I can cross Sadie off my Christmas list this year . . . and forever.

Freaking traitor.

"What the fuck, Poppy?" Charli asks, her face a little paler than it was a few minutes

315

ago. "This is really scary. Did you call the police?"

"No." I avoid eye contact, focusing on putting the finishing touches on Sadie's cotton candy martini.

"I'm just going to put it out there," Vonnie announces in the no-nonsense tone I've come to know her for. "When I was in law school, I studied some scary-ass cases. Stalkers always escalate. You need to report this. They might not be able to make an arrest, but you want this on record if something else does happen."

I set the pink, sickly sweet martini in front of Sadie instead of throwing it on her like I really want to. Sadie picks it up, taking a small sip before aiming a gleeful smirk my way. "But tell me again how dramatic I am, Pops."

I roll my eyes and turn to Vonnie, not giving Sadie the satisfaction of admitting she's right.

"I know. TK's been saying the same thing." My shoulders sag under the weight of defeat. I hate being wrong almost as much as I hate TK and Sadie being right. "But nothing else has happened and I'm hoping I can just ignore it away."

" 'Mmmkay," Vonnie says over the rim of her French martini (with a splash of champagne, 'cause she's classy AF). "Why don't you go watch a *Law & Order: SVU* marathon and tell me how all the women who ignore hypermasculine men with stalker tendencies end up?"

"Gah." I fall onto the bar, which is probably in the employee handbook under "Things Not to Do." "Fine. If something else happens, I call the police."

"That's all we ask," Charli chimes in, looking like her bronzed goddess self again. "Now to a slightly less terrifying topic, did Jane e-mail you about the Lady Mustangs meetings?"

"The third Wednesday of every month," I say at the same time Sadie asks, "What the hell is a Lady Mustang?"

I point to Sadie, who, I hate to admit it, looks like the Little Mermaid with the bar lights bouncing off the glitter in her red hair, and say, "Also, what she said."

I don't see her coming, but when I look over my shoulder, Brynn is behind me with three bottles of vodka in her arms, a shit-eating grin on her face and a twinkle in her eyes. "Did I just hear Lady Mustangs?"

"Ummm . . ." I hesitate, not understanding her enthusiasm. "Yeah."

She shoves the vodka on the shelf, causing the other bottles to wobble dangerously around it. Once her hands are free, she unties my bedazzled (courtesy of Sadie) money pouch and directs me to the other side of the bar. "You're off." She pushes my ass into the empty seat next to Charli. "Because one needs no responsibility and lots of alcohol when first learning about the Lady Mustangs."

"Oh shit." Sadie drains the rest of her martini. "I think I'm gonna need another one, too."

Brynn reaches for the red wine Charli's been sipping but stops short. "Nope," she says to nobody. She walks down the bar, her long legs crossing the distance in record time, grabs a bottle off the top shelf and a shot glass off the counter. When she's back in front of me, she slams them both on the bar top. "This calls for tequila."

"Oh lord." I stare at the shot glass only half an ounce away from being a tumbler and watch with wide eyes as Brynn fills it to the rim. "It can't be that bad!"

I don't know if I'm telling her or trying to speak it into existence, but when Vonnie stays silent — not common — and Charli pushes the shot closer to me, I know I'm in for a hell of a story.

But upside! At least we aren't talking about me anymore.

TWENTY-SEVEN

The tequila gods hath sent Brynn to earth to punish me.

It's the only plausible reason I can come up with as to why she not only let me, but encouraged me, to drink five monster shots of tequila followed by three Skinnygirl margaritas.

After learning about Marlee Pope's induction into the Lady Mustangs, which resulted in the Mustangs organization hiring Jane and creating the Family Programs department, aka the WAGS babysitters and liaisons, I couldn't have been more thankful my reunion with TK happened three years AM (After Marlee). And while I was shocked to learn about the wives leaking information to the press and spreading nasty rumors about girlfriends, I was not shocked to find out Dixie was front and center in all the drama.

You just can't trust someone with hair as

big as hers.

No.

That's a lie. Her big hair is both mysterious — how the hell does she get it so high? — and fabulous. We've all seen Dolly, right?

It's the unmoving forehead that really freaks me out. I mean, what's the point? Nobody is telling George Clooney to fill his wrinkles. Just another bullshit, unrealistic standard we hold women to. Anyway, sorry, not the point. The point is Dixie seems like a bitch and I was happy to learn my bitch-o-meter wasn't broken.

A plus for me, Brynn is so into the Lady Mustangs and all that comes with them, she closes down HERS every third Wednesday of the month during football season and lets them meet there. This way she can stay in the know without relying on anybody's faulty memory — her words, not mine.

So while it might end up being awful, at least it's convenient.

Once the tequila fully invaded my system, Charli and Vonnie volunteered to see me home and Sadie called an Uber to pick her up.

Sadie might make questionable life decisions almost daily, but she doesn't ever drive if she's had so much as a single glass of wine.

Once she threw herself into the front seat, her boobs damn near falling out of her scoop-neck tank and causing her Uber driver to turn bright red and stutter for almost a minute straight, they took off and so did we. Luckily Vonnie stopped drinking when the Lady Mustangs story began, saying she needed to be sober to insure the quality of the information I was being fed.

When we pulled up to my house, the porch light was on and TK was standing in the doorway before I was out of the car.

Now, this part is kind of a blur — I can't remember if Vonnie and Charli hit on or threatened him. I'm pretty positive he ended up carrying me to bed. In fact, considering the not-at-all-sober state I was in, me lying in my bed and not sprawled out on the floor is all the proof I need that TK deposited me here.

Noise coming from outside my closed door sends my pounding headache into overdrive. I'm not a doctor, so I don't know the technicalities about what happens during a migraine, but when I close my eyes, I can almost see my expanding brain thrashing against my skull.

I'd cry out in pain, but my mouth is so dry, I think my tongue might be stuck to the roof of my mouth.

I thought leaving a club and working at a respectable establishment would prevent events like last night from happening.

Guess I was wrong.

I crack open my eyes, but the sun pouring in through the bargain blinds I ordered from Groupon sends a shooting pain through my head so sharp I have to swallow back the bile threatening to ruin my favorite sheets.

I try to close my eyes and go back to sleep, but the noise inside my house has steadily been rising in volume. There are multiple voices, two I recognize, others I do not.

I hide my head under my pillows, determined to sleep until I feel human again, when the pounding in my head hits even harder.

Wait.

Not in my head.

Actual pounding outside my window. Followed by the unmistakable and never more unwelcome sound of a power drill.

"What the hell?" I say into my pillows.

This time, when I open my eyes, the sun is blocked out, thanks to the pillow barrier over my head. I lift it off my head at a snail's pace, and even though I'd rather be surrounded by a cloak of darkness, I'm supergrateful to see a tall glass of water and a bottle of Advil on my nightstand.

Maybe this living-with-TK thing will work out after all.

I sit up, clenching my eyes shut to try and combat the pulsating torture I've inflicted upon myself, and reach blindly for the medicine that — fingers crossed — will return me to my human state. I crack open one eye, count out four pills, and toss them in my mouth. I gulp the water, washing down the pills, then keep chugging until the very last drop is gone.

Too bad for me, they really are just pain relief and not a magic potion to quiet the world around me and let me recover in peace. I know this because all the noise still hasn't stopped. In fact, it might be even louder.

Because why the hell wouldn't it be?

I roll out of bed.

Literally.

I put out my arms, trying to catch myself so my face doesn't slam into the floor, and I guess I'm semisuccessful. Only semi because my lower body moves with the grace of a dead fish and my knees hit the ground so hard, I'm sure they'll be a lovely shade of purple tomorrow.

I grab my nightstand and pull myself up, mentally preparing to start my day and power out of my room before I can change my mind.

What I had envisioned as me barging out of my room, demanding to know what nonsense was taking place in my house, ends up being more of a hobble into my living room filled with people I don't know, being ordered around by my nine-year-old son.

I almost call it a day and go back into my room until I can wake up tomorrow, calling for a redo. But Ace sees me and ruins my plans.

"Mom!" he shouts, unaware not only that I'm suffering from the worst hangover of my life but also what a hangover is in the first place. "Isn't this awesome?" He's bouncing up and down, his arms spread wide, motioning to the strangers dotting my house.

I don't think it's awesome. I also have no idea what is going on. But I don't tell him that. "Yeah, dude. So awesome," I say, trying to force as much pep as possible into my otherwise hoarse and miserable voice. "Where's TK?"

"He's outside." He points through the open front door, his gap-toothed smile so wide I can see his molars. "We fixed the gate and now he's painting it."

"He's what?" My eyes open wide for the

first time all morning and my jaw falls to the dusty floor beneath me.

Ace just points out the open door to TK sitting on the pavement, painting the fence that's been on my to-do list for at least a year — probably three.

And dammit, even hungover, my insides melt and I feel all the freaking feels.

I slip on my flip-flops, which never leave my entryway, and make my way to the hottest handyman on the planet.

Yup.

The entire mother-effing planet.

He's so focused on the job at hand, he doesn't notice me approaching, and I take my time admiring him in peace. His hair is falling out of the bun on top of his head, a few paint-coated pieces framing his paint-splattered face. And lucky for me, it's hot outside. So the shirt he must've been wearing is now tucked into the back pocket of his old, holed-up jeans and his chest is glittering like freaking gold under a thin sheen of sweat.

Yum-my.

"You didn't have to do this." I pull his attention away from the fence. He jerks his head back and more paint splashes onto his jeans.

"I know, I wanted to." He smiles, looking

mighty proud of himself. He drops the paintbrush on the paint tray and saunters — yes, saunters, because a topless handyman with holed-up jeans and abs of steel freaking saunters — my way. "Sorry if all this noise woke you up."

"It's fine." I wave him off. "I don't know what I was thinking bringing Vonnie, Charli, Sadie, and Brynn together. They're terrible influences. I don't think I've ever been so hungover in my entire life. You probably think all I do is sleep."

"Trust me, Sparks, that's not what I think." He drops his gaze and lets out an appreciative grunt. His hands follow his eyes and his fingers graze my thighs at the base of my shorts. "And if this is what you wear hungover, I'll never complain."

Suddenly, I don't have a hangover anymore and I'm hyperaware that not only is my hair most likely a bird's nest of curls crowning what I'm assuming is a mascara-stained face, I'm also standing outside in full view of my neighbors and my house full of strangers in satin cami pajamas with no bra.

Not the best look.

And apparently my nipples agree.

An embarrassing, high-pitched — and involuntary — scream shoots from my lips, drawing even more attention my way.

"Holy shit." I cross my arms in front of my chest, turn, and run back into the house. Making the least discreet exit in the history of exits.

"You okay, Mom?" Ace asks when I come running through the living room he's managing.

"Fine!" I throw over my shoulder as I keep running until I'm alone in my room with the door locked behind me.

"Keeping it classy," I say to myself.

Because talking to myself seems like the natural progression of crazy I'm heading in today.

I slip off my pajamas, and if it wasn't nearing ninety degrees already, I'd put on sweatpants and a turtleneck. But it is and my desire to hide every inch of skin is outweighed by my desire not to die of a heatstroke. I toss on a flowy sundress I found pretending I wasn't well over the age of Forever 21's target audience. I do, however, wear my most modest underwear in case a gust of wind teams up with everything else conspiring against me today . . . and yesterday . . . and the day before that . . .

I unlock my door and peek my head into the hallway, making sure the coast is clear before I venture out. When I deem it safe, I force my steps to slow as I tiptoe into the bathroom.

I flip on the lights, and even though I don't want to, I look in the mirror.

My earlier assumptions about my appearance are right on point. Which sucks. I was hoping my Negative Nelly attitude would be wrong for once.

But no. I look a straight-up, hot-ass mess.

A bird's nest is a generous description of the disaster topping my head. It's more like a rat's nest that's home to eight rabid rats who spend their days fighting with one another. And my face looks like a raccoon who got pulled into the rat fight and was punched in its already black eyes, making the black eyes even worse.

I have to wash my face three times to erase all traces of mascara. And I don't even wear much makeup!

With the faint taste of tequila still in my mouth, I double up on brushing my teeth. I make a promise to myself as I rinse in the sink never to drink again. Like ever.

Well . . . except for wine. Because it's not really alcohol. It's more like an adult-aimed grape juice. And grapes are my favorite fruit.

Okay.

Maybe not favorite, but they are in my

top three.

Top ten.

Whatever.

I'm contemplating the benefits of con-cealer when a knock comes on the bathroom door.

"Yeah?"

"The security guys are done with the alarm," Ace tells me from the hallway. "They want to show you how to work it."

I open the door, hoping my zombie-like appearance doesn't scare away the security people. "Oh . . . okay," I say like I know what's going on.

"Come on!" Ace yells, even though I am right behind him. "Wait until you see the doorbell!"

"The doorbell?"

What could be so special about a doorbell?

Twenty-Eight

Doorbells can be really freaking fancy.

And TK has a lot of expendable income.

The first I know as fact, because the one attached to my modest, in-need-of-renovations home has a doorbell with more capabilities than my phone. And it's the same doorbell twenty-two people on *Forbes*'s richest one hundred list have. No, really, that's part of their pitch. And if I wasn't sold by the security features already, that would've sold me for sure.

It's also the same doorbell TK has, but that's not nearly as impressive as *Forbes*.

The second I'm just assuming because I glanced at the bill for the security system when the guy put it on the kitchen table and there was a comma in the price. I would've objected, but there were already holes in most of my walls from the touch-screen alarm boxes scattered throughout my house and video cameras at different angles on the outside of my house.

It takes the security guys (and one girl) over an hour to point out all the features and test me on arming and disarming the system and practicing pushing the panic button in case of emergencies. By the time they finish, the Advil and water have kicked in and my hangover is nothing but a memory.

Praise Jesus.

"TK." I grab his hand after he closes the front door behind the security team heading back to their vans. "You didn't have to do this," I start, and squeeze his hand in mine when he tries to interrupt me. "But I'm glad you did. I already feel safer and I really appreciate you doing this for us."

His mouth goes tight and he pulls me into his chest. "I'll do anything to keep you guys safe, Sparks."

It's a rare moment where TK is completely serious.

Then that annoying thing that's been happening more and more often when I'm with him happens — something inside me settles. An ache I wasn't aware I've been feeling for years disappears, leaving me lighter and happier than I thought was possible for me.

An ache I'm afraid will only multiply when this ends.

I don't say anything.

Instead I wrap my arms around his stomach and hold on tight.

"Ew," Ace says, ruining the moment with the efficiency and ease only nine-year-olds possess. "What are you guys doing?"

"Hugging." I state the obvious.

Ace shakes his head and rolls his eyes, not at all amused by my answer.

"Do you feel left out?" I ask, unwrapping myself from TK.

"Mom . . . ," Ace warns me.

"Is my Acey-Wacey feeling left out?" I start toward him, using the nickname I always used when he was little.

"Stop it, Mom." Ace holds his hands in front of his chest, backing away from me.

"I can't." I lunge at him, wrapping my arms around him as tight as I can, and swing him around, peppering his face with kisses. "I need to hug my Acey-Wacey!"

"Mom!" he screeches, trying, but failing, not to laugh and sound delighted.

"I can't stop!" I shout, letting my hands fall to his waist and squeeze his tickle spot. "I need hugs!"

"Make her stop!" Ace yells through the giggles he's trying so hard to mask in anger. "Dad! Help!"

Nothing could make me stop tickling and

being the annoying mom who has the audacity to kiss her kid.

Nothing, I thought, until I heard that one word.

Dad.

Holy shit.

My hands stop and all the strength drains from my arms. I look up at TK, who is staring, his eyes glazed over, his lips tipped up, at the back of Ace's curl-covered head.

And it's the most beautiful I've ever seen TK look.

Which is saying a lot.

Ace, unaware of how much saying that three-letter word means to TK, breaks free from my Jell-O arms, turns, and runs to TK's side. "Let's get her, Dad," he says again.

I know I want to cry and I'm pretty sure TK does, too. But instead, he gives a quick shake of his head, bringing himself back to the moment, and the small smile he had changes into a mischievous one.

Now this look? I know it well.

"Don't you dare," I warn the twins in front of me wearing matching expressions.

"Don—" I can't even finish the word before they both take off in my direction.

I turn and scream, but I only make it two steps before I'm upside down and slung over TK's shoulder.

"Put me down!" I pound my fists against TK's back a few times, but before I'm able to inflict much damage, I'm flying through the air until my back bounces off my throw pillow–lined couch.

"Get her!" Ace yells like a freaking war cry.

And TK, the big kid he is, doesn't miss a beat.

"Noooo!" I flail my legs and arms and try to flip off the side of the couch.

And shocker.

I don't get away.

TK grabs both of my wrists and pins them above my head and Ace, the freaking traitor, tickles my armpits.

Is it okay to call my kid an asshole?

Because I'm really tempted to.

I try to tell them to stop, but it's hard to understand between my painful laughter.

"No!" I scream, trying to free my wrists and buck Ace off me. "You're gonna make me pee!"

And it's not a lie.

Don't judge me. Ace was a really big baby, my pelvic floor might never fully recover.

"Ace, I'll never —" I screech louder when TK manages to restrain both of my wrists with one of his hands and his newly free hand goes to my ultrasensitive neck. "Please! I'm sorry!"

I don't know what I'm apologizing for, but I'll say anything at this point.

"No more tickling me?" Ace, the little creep, asks.

"No more tickling," I promise. I'm completely out of breath and my hidden abs are aching. They have officially tickled all the fight out of me.

Ace looks up at TK, who must have given him a nod of approval, because I'm freed from their grips.

"I can't believe you did that." I aim narrowed eyes at TK. "I'm a grown woman. You can't tickle me."

"Well then" — he looks at Ace, shrugging his shoulders and lifting his hands — "how'd we do such a great job?"

Ace dissolves into a fit of giggles, falling onto the couch at my feet, his little body shaking so hard, the cushion under my butt is vibrating.

I lean down and gently tug on one of his curls. "Traitor. See if I bake you strawberry muffins when school starts." I stick out my tongue, extra satisfied by my threat.

"Whoa, whoa, whoa." Ace sits up straight, looking so worried, I'd laugh if it didn't mean breaking character. "Don't you think you're taking it a little too far? Strawberry muffins are like . . . your mom staple."

And here I thought my mom staple was always putting Ace first and dedicating my entire life to him.

"I'll think about it," I say, knowing damn well I'll be up late making strawberry muffins for breakfast and my fabulous chocolate chip cookies (the trick is one-fourth cup more flour, salted butter, and dark brown sugar — not any of that light crap) for his lunchbox. "But speaking of school, you want to head to Target and get school supplies today?"

"Yeah!" Ace shouts, jumping off the couch with such height that for a nanosecond I question if I gave birth to a superhero. "I'll go get dressed!"

"Oh!" TK jumps up from behind me. "I love back-to-school shopping. Mind if I come?"

"Not at all." I don't say it, but I'm beyond thrilled not to have to deal with the crowds on my own. "But be warned, it's not fun like it used to be. It's a superstrict list about what to get."

"I know, I donate a lot of supplies to the Mustangs to pass out to schools around the city," TK says, like it's not the sweetest, most admirable thing he could do. "I still like it."

"Oh . . . okay." I don't make a big deal out of it since it's clear he doesn't want me to, but I almost tell Ace to go to Jayden's so I can jump TK's bones right here on my dusty living room floor.

"Ready!" Ace runs out of his room in the same shorts he had on before and goes straight to the front door.

Since TK has been here, my Volvo has been banished to the garage, only to be used when TK's Range Rover is gone. I'd be insulted, but I hate driving and buying gas, so I'm a big fan of this arrangement.

I slide into my flip-flops and TK pushes his feet into his Nikes, motioning for Ace and me to head out as he sets my alarm system.

"Damn," TK says right as he reaches the car. "Forgot my keys."

"Keys are a critical part of turning a car on." I laugh, digging my keys out of my purse and tossing them to him.

He runs up to my house, a view I very much appreciate, and is in and out so fast I can't help but be impressed.

And then we load into the same car, laughing at my lame jokes and TK's terrible singing voice, and run errands together.

Just like any other family.
Just like my dreams.

TWENTY-NINE

"How's school going?" Charli asks Ace.

"The best! Dad comes to school on Tuesdays to have lunch with me." Ace takes a giant bite of his relish-loaded hot dog. "All my friends think it's so awesome."

"Gross, Ace," I scold. "Don't talk with food in your mouth, nobody wants to see that."

I thought I'd be able to stop telling him that after the age of five. I was sorely mistaken.

Mom life is not glamorous and kids are freaking gross.

Ace takes an obnoxious amount of time to finish chewing and swigs a big gulp of lemonade. "Sorry, Mom," he says when he's finished. But the smile tugging on the corners of his mouth tells me I'll end up having to tell him the same thing at least three more times today.

But since this is our first time at a real,

live football game, I let it go.

Preseason is officially over.

What does that mean? Well, I'm still learning as I go, but what I do know is too many guys' dreams came to a crashing halt when they were cut. TK has been home a lot more, even though he's taken over Maya's room as his film study room and locks himself in there for a few hours a week, but we still have dinner as a family every night. Except the night before games. Even if it's a home game, they still have to spend the night at a hotel.

Last night TK handed over the keys to his Range Rover and had me drop him off at the team's hotel — the Marriott in Downtown Denver. He showed me the inside of his glove box, which was stashed with our parking pass to the players' lot and wristbands to go to some kind of room during halftime or something, and he laid the sweetest kiss on me for good luck. There were a few fans lining the entrance who snapped some pictures I'm sure are now floating around on the Internet.

But I'm too happy to care.

"TK said his agent is going to be here. I'll have to keep an eye out for him." I look over my shoulder, not knowing how I'm supposed to find a single person in this madness. "I think he said his name is Donny?"

Charli sputters out a laugh and almost sprays the lady sitting in front of her with beer.

"What?"

"Trust me." She uses her napkin to dry her face. "Donny isn't hard to spot . . . or hear."

I shake my head, always feeling one step behind everyone around me lately. "Whatever that means."

"You'll find out soon."

"Can we go see Mrs. Vonnie and Jagger later?" Ace asks when his hot dog is gone.

"I don't know if we can go up to the suites without tickets, but she said they'd meet us in the family room at halftime."

Vonnie is too fancy to rough it out with all of us normal folks and shares a suite with another offensive lineman's family. She told me she forced Justin to get a suite or she wasn't going to any more games once her boys became more interested in snacks than football.

"Sounds good," Ace says, too excited to be at the game in his Mustangs gear to care where he's sitting or who he's sitting with.

All of a sudden, music blasts from the speakers and fog billows out in front of the tunnel at the back corner of the field. A video starts to play on the jumbo screens at both ends of the stadium, the serious faces of Mustangs players crossing the screen one at a time. The noise around me rises from a steady hum to rip-roaring screams. Then, out of the fog emerge hundreds — fine, like thirty — of cheerleaders dressed in orange and blue (in what I'm assuming are supposed to be sexy cowgirl costumes) running to the field. They split into two lines, creating another tunnel, and stand in their places kicking their legs higher than my body could even dream and bouncing around with their pompoms in the air.

"Mustangs fans!" The announcer comes on the speakers. "Let's make some noise for your Denver MUUUSSSSTANGS!"

If anyone was still sitting, they aren't anymore. The screams reach eardrum-piercing levels, and everyone is jumping around, high-fiving their neighbors, beer and sodas sloshing all over the ground. I expect the next thing to come out of the tunnel will be the team. What I do not expect is a woman, in an actual cowgirl costume — or is it a uniform? — riding a horse onto the field followed by the Mustangs' mascot waving a giant Mustangs flag.

I, personally, think it's a little overkill on the Mustangs stuff. But judging by the reaction of the crowd around me, Ace included, I'm the only person who feels this way.

Then, finally, the team flows out of the tunnel. Some men are jogging, focused on the grass in front of them, while others are in a full sprint, jumping up and down and pointing to the crowd.

Charli is waving to Shawn, who is blowing her a kiss through the face mask on his helmet. Ace and I are both scanning the group of players, looking for TK. "Where's Dad?" Ace asks.

It still makes my heart skip a beat when I hear him call TK Dad.

"I don't know." I roll on to my tiptoes and squint my eyes harder. "I don't see him either."

"He's not out yet," Charli yells over the noise. "They are going to announce the starting offense."

I don't have to repeat what she says to Ace. I know he heard by the way his eyes start to sparkle and the flush rises up his cheeks.

The announcer starts with the linemen, saying each name as they run out of the tunnel, and fire blasts out of columns on the field at the mouth of the tunnel, startling me every time. He moves through the wide receivers and even the quarterback. The hairs rise on my arms, knowing not only that TK is coming up, but that he's last.

The song changes without warning, "We Ready" blasting from the speakers, and the fog gets a revival. The screams of the crowd change into a steady, synchronized chant of "MOOOOOORE" before the announcer's voice broadcasts through the stadium again, "Number eighty-two, TK MOOOOORE!"

The crowd goes berserk.

I mean, don't get me wrong, I've been out in public with TK, I understand how well liked he is in Denver, but I had no idea it was this.

Then, like I'm living in a dream, TK walks through the fog. His helmet in one hand, his hair down and swaying around his face, he bounces to the beat of the music to the top of the barrier tunnel. Then he drops to a deep squat, bobs his head around for a few more beats, and springs up, jumping off the ground with fire shooting out in sync with his movements.

It's amazing.

And I have to blink away the tears.

"Fuck yeah, TK!" a loud voice breaks through the noise and my thick wall of feelings. "My fuckin' boy! You better show them what the fuck is up!"

Ace might be nine, but my hands still earmuff his ears as I turn around, searching for the asshole shouting obscenities at a family event.

"What the hell?" I say to Charli, not doing so hot at the clean-mouth thing myself. "Could that guy be more obnoxious?"

"Yeah, he actually can," she says, laughter coloring her voice. "Poppy, I'd like to introduce you to Donny, TK's agent."

She aims her eyes over my shoulder and I see a man on the shorter side, not fat, but thick, sticking out like a sore thumb in a pinstripe suit and brown leather loafers.

"Charli, baby." He looks past me and Ace. "How the fuck have you been?"

"I've been good. How about you?" She smiles, used to his antics and language.

"I'd be better if that stubborn-ass husband of yours would dump his lame fucking agent and come my way. And if I knew what fuckin' surprise TK has for me," he says, still ignoring me. "I told him, I don't like fuckin' secrets. But TK does what the fuck TK wants. I just hope his bitch of a mother isn't here."

Oh.

Maybe Donny isn't so bad after all.

"You're my dad's agent?" Ace asks from beside me, proving my earmuffs to be one

345

hundred percent ineffective.

"I don't think so, kid. Who's your dad?" Donny answers, and it's clear he's just humoring Ace.

"TK Moore," Ace says, pointing to the 82 on his jersey.

I wish I had my phone out to record Donny's reaction as he processes what Ace is telling him because I know for a fact TK would've loved to see it.

"You've gotta be fucking shittin' me." He takes off his sunglasses and wipes the sweat that magically developed in the last five seconds off his forehead.

"Surprise!" Charli shouts, giving great jazz hands.

Donny turns his attention to me.

I'm in skinny jeans and the Moore jersey TK put on our bed before he left last night. I'm having a great hair day, my curls are huge, and my lips are painted red at Sadie's request (aka demand). And not to toot my own horn or anything, but I'm basically smashing this football girlfriend thing.

"Oh, fuck me," he mutters. "If this is gonna be another Pope scandal, I'm tapping out now."

"I don't know what you mean." I ignore Charli's and Ace's giggling next to me.

I know what he means.

Just because I nearly died of alcohol poisoning doesn't mean I could ever forget the Marlee/Gavin/Lady Mustangs saga.

Donny puts his glasses back on, knowing I'm full of shit. "Can you at least talk him into a fuckin' suite? I'm not going through one more season in this fuckin' snow. I got him his contract, I know he can afford it."

"I kinda like it down here." I also do not feel comfortable asking TK to spend what would most likely come to thousands of dollars on . . . well, on anything.

"Dammit." He opens his suit jacket and pulls out a small flask. "This shit's gonna be just like Marlee."

"Maybe even crazier." Charli offers her unhelpful opinion.

Ace laughs harder.

I glare at her.

Hmmm . . .

Maybe a suite wouldn't be too bad.

THIRTY

Football is the socially acceptable equivalent of a cult.

It seems like tons of fun and everyone around you is an avid follower of the religion.

Oops.

I mean sport.

They wear the colors. They memorize the prayers. They will shove a boot up your ass if you don't believe like they do — just ask the Chiefs fan who has been hounded since he sat his ass in his seat. And no matter your reservations, you get sucked in. Before you know what's happening, you're jumping out of your seat, cheering when the ball is caught, and booing when the refs prove to be blind and make the worst calls ever. As soon as you enter the church they call a stadium, you're a believer.

Until reality slaps you awake.

It's the beginning of the fourth quarter,

and much to my dismay, the score is tied 17–17. Some people might appreciate the closeness of the game. I, on the other hand, hate it. I'll take a blowout over this any day. You call it boring, I call it ulcer preventive.

Tomato tomahto.

The Mustangs have the ball, and I — with my vast knowledge of the sport — assume they're going to run it like they have for the majority of the game. Peter, the rookie quarterback who managed to snag the starting spot, turns his head to the left, motioning for TK to move out, then he looks to the right, yelling something else that causes the line to shift toward their sideline. He does his weird ritual of stomping his foot and clapping three times, then the ball is in his hands, and he's on the move.

I know the play isn't going well within seconds. A missed block? A missed step? I'm not really sure. But before Peter can fully scan the field, a defender — a very large defender — is charging toward him. Peter doesn't think twice. Before he's flattened to the turf, he launches the ball down the field. I figure it's a throwaway like he's done a few times already, but as I follow the ball, I see TK and a player in a red jersey bumping into each other, racing down the field.

I'm on my feet in a second. My eyes on the ball, my heart in my stomach, chanting the rosary in my head. I don't have to look down to know Ace is doing the same — without the rosary.

Because of the hit Peter took, the ball starts to lose momentum sooner than it should. And with TK and the defender running full speed, I let the prayers fade, positive it's going to be an incomplete pass.

But just as my butt unfolds the plastic stadium seat, TK turns and cuts to the ball. He stretches out his hands, his fingers channeling Spider-Man, and starts to pull the ball in.

The crowd, who has not stopped cheering and shouting this entire game — with the exception of halftime — shifts their volume up a decimal.

But even over the cheering, with crystal clarity, I can hear the sound of the other defender's helmet slamming into TK's, followed by the sickening thud of TK's body against the field. The defender barely looks fazed as he jumps up and pounds his chest.

You don't have to be a football fanatic to know it's bad. But the way the cheering instantly morphs into a collective gasp confirms it.

Even scarier is the way Donny whispers,

"Oh fuck," before screaming "Targeting! Throw your fucking flag, ref!"

I don't want to tear my eyes away from the field, but I can feel Ace shrinking next to me. I look down at him and he's no longer on his feet. He's sitting in his seat studying the fingernails he's already bitten to the quick, all excitement and color drained from his face.

I sit down next to him, pulling one of his hands into mine just as Charli sits down and does the same. I keep my eyes on the jumbo screen, watching as TK lays unmoving for a second before standing up and stumbling sideways. His teammates are at his side before he can fall again, helping him off the field. The camera stays on TK as he sits on the bench, but once he's circled with trainers and coaches, we're given a pretty view of the field as the players hustle to a huddle to make the most of the time-out called.

From our seats in the stadium behind the Mustangs bench, I can see as the person I'm assuming is a trainer or medic helps TK up and walks him to the tunnel.

I squeeze Ace's hand a little tighter, but I don't say anything. I don't know what to say. This is exactly why I hate this sport and I don't think Ace wants to hear, "I told ya so." And also, because I'm using almost all my energy to ignore the ignorant assholes behind us who I'm learning aren't just football experts but medical ones as well.

"That's gotta be a concussion for sure," one says to the other, their voices slurred from the beers they've been cheersing over since they got to their seats.

"You know how much higher the ALS rates are with NFL players?" the other one asks in response. "Like a shit ton. This is why I'm glad I decided not to play after high school."

"For sure, bro," the other agrees. "Shit's fuckin' brutal. I wonder how soon they can find CTE or if they have to off themselves first?"

"Are you fucking kidding me right now?" I stand up, leveling them both with a glare.

"Whoa. What's your problem?" the one with awful facial hair asks me.

"You." I lean forward, pointing a finger in his face. "You're my problem. Sitting back here, drunk as fuck, acting like you know everything about football and brain injuries. When in reality, I'd bet a thousand dollars your football career consisted of you warming the bench and your medical knowledge is nothing more than two episodes of *Grey's Anatomy.*"

I feel not only the heat rising in my cheeks but the unmistakable sensation of eyes and cameras trained my way. But do I make the mature decision to sit down and shut up?

Never.

"So how about, instead of running your mouths like imbeciles, terrifying my kid, who's already scared as hell . . ." I pause, clenching my fists to try to alleviate the shaking and catch my breath. "You shut." I lean in closer. "The fuck." Closer. "Up."

I level them with my best *try me if you want* look, prepared and willing to keep going, but I'm cut short when Ace taps my shoulder and shoves my vibrating phone in my hand.

I don't recognize the number as my finger glides across the screen, answering the call. "Hello?"

"Miss Patterson?" the deep voice on the other end asks.

"This is." I turn and sit in my seat, covering my open ear with my hand to hear him better. The assholes behind me are long forgotten.

"This is Jason Metcalf, the Mustangs' trainer. I'm here with TK and he's requesting for you and Ace to come down."

I don't even answer before I snatch my purse off the ground, motion for Ace to get up, and step over Donny. "We're on our way."

"Perfect, I'll meet you there," he says, clicking off before I can ask him where "there" is.

"Crap." I look between Charli and Donny. "I'm supposed to go see TK, but I don't know where I'm going."

"I'll take you," they say at the same time.

I nod my head and try not to hold Ace's hand as we walk up the concrete stairs. I laser focus on the man in the blue polo at the top of the stairs and move as fast as my legs will carry me, needing to see with my own two eyes that TK's okay.

But it doesn't prevent me from hearing Donny's raspy laughter behind me. "You're right . . . even worse," he says to Charli. "And I fuckin' love it."

Whatever that's supposed to mean.

"Dad!" Ace pushes past me into the medical room TK's being checked out in. "Are you okay?"

TK pulls a towel off his head at Ace's voice. I watch as his eyes go soft, seeing Ace run toward him, but I also see the way he flinches in pain when he sits up too fast. "Yeah, dude," TK says. "Just a little knock to the head."

354

I want to throttle him.

I want to jump his bones, kiss every inch of his gorgeous face, and freaking throttle him.

"Just a little knock?" I take a deep breath, not wanting to lose my mind in a room full of strangers. "I could hear the hit from my seat and you looked like you had fifteen shots of tequila when you stood up. That was not a little knock."

"It's just a slight concussion." Jason, the trainer, tries — and fails — to comfort me. "He'll be back on the field come Wednesday."

"I've fuckin' hit TK harder than that," Donny pipes in. "If he couldn't take a hit, he wouldn't be a Mustang. He's fine."

I feel the heat creeping up my cheeks as unfiltered rage starts to flow through my body at the way everyone seems to be downplaying the seriousness of a concussion. I mean, what the hell? I know I'm no doctor, but a quick Google search will yield you pages upon pages of brain-injury-related articles.

"Poppy." TK pulls my attention to him, probably concerned by the steam blowing out of my ears. "I'm okay. I promise."

He's not.

But I can tell Ace isn't either, and I don't

355

want to scare him any more than he already is.

So I drop it . . . for now.

"Okay," I whisper, my throat clogged and eyes burning all of a sudden.

Not surprising me at all, TK notices the change in my tone right away. And equally unsurprising, he does something about it.

"Hey, guys," he says loud enough to get everyone's attention. "Mind if I have a minute alone with my family."

His family.

I freaking *love* him.

Now I'm definitely going to cry.

I walk to an empty wall past the navy blue upholstered exam beds and stare unseeingly at a poster detailing the muscles found around the knee. I don't turn around until the trainers clear out, Charli tells TK to feel better, and Donny — a poet of vulgarities — parts with a classy, "You were a fucking beast out there today. That was a bitch hit and I know you'll be back on the field soon."

Awww.

Sweet.

The room we're in doesn't have doors, but it's tucked away in a corner enough so the voices all fade after a minute or two.

"Come here, Sparks."

I bite my bottom lip, breathe in through

my nose and out of my mouth, and turn around once I'm positive my composure is back intact.

TK's huge body is taking up the entire table he's sitting on, and Ace is standing right next to him, so close he might've, in fact, fused himself to TK.

"You scared me."

"I didn't mean to." He takes my hand into his and pulls it to his mouth, dropping gentle kisses on my knuckles and making Ace cringe so hard.

"I know you didn't," I say, proud of my even, nonhysterical voice. "It's part of this stupid game. I just hate seeing you hurt."

"She's a worrier," Ace pipes in. "She made me sit in a car seat until I was in second grade and still watches me walk to Jayden's house even though it's just down the street."

"Dang, kid, you're just gonna throw me under the bus like that?" I ask Ace, even though I don't care at all. I'm just glad the haunted look he's worn since TK went down is gone.

"She can't help it." TK wraps an arm around Ace's shoulders, leans to his ear, and stage whispers, "I told you, us Moore men make her crazy."

Since I can't argue with that, I roll my eyes and say nothing.

357

"Now." TK stands up, slow and with the caution my granny had after she had a hip replacement when I was seven. "Let me get changed so we can head out."

"You can go?" I look up at the small screen mounted in the corner of the room and see the game is still going on.

"Yeah, it'll be better because I'll miss press and fans asking for autographs upstairs." TK follows the path everyone else took a few minutes ago. "With the headache I have, I wouldn't be my best."

I don't argue with him.

For one, I know nothing of the rules or etiquette of injuries.

Two, I've wanted to get him home since I saw him run out on the field.

And three —

"Plus, it's a *schoooooool* night," I sing to Ace, whose only response is a quick roll of the eyes and subsequent terrified expression for daring to roll his eyes at me.

"I think they set up some after-game snacks already in the family room. You guys can sit in there and wait for me if you want," TK suggests before I can ask Ace if he took a hit in the head today too. "I won't take too long."

"Sounds good," Ace and I say at the same time.

Because while Ace might be getting a little too grown up for his own good, the family room has brownies and Cherry Coke. And neither of us will ever be too grown up — and I will never have the self-discipline — not to hoard chocolate and caffeine.

THIRTY-ONE

I roll off TK, my curls fanning across my pillow and my chest moving up and down as I try to catch my breath.

Seeing as TK is injured, I took it upon myself to do most of the work tonight.

"Jesus, Sparks," TK says, also out of breath, even though he just got to lie back and enjoy the ride. "That was fucking incredible."

"Glad you liked it."

"No, I loved it," he corrects me. "From now on, after every game, I'm gonna need you riding me."

My insides and my thighs clench at his words. So much so, I almost climb right back on top of him.

"Fuck," TK groans, and rolls on top of me. He pushes his hips down and I bite my lip so I don't moan as I feel him harden against me. "You can't look at me like that and not expect me to need to bury myself

360

inside of you again."

I don't fight the moan this time.

TK stopped fighting with me about turning off the lights, so even though the only light in the room is from the streetlights filtering in through my curtains, I still see his eyes darken.

"You're gonna kill me." He drops his head and covers my nipple with his mouth.

My back arches and my nails dig into his back.

"Wouldn't be a bad way to go," I tease once I can speak actual words again.

"You got that right." He laughs, but the laughter is cut short when he cringes in pain and rolls off me.

And I know as much as I don't want to have this conversation, I have to get it over with.

Maybe being naked and sated will help. I dive right into it. "I don't know if we can keep coming to your games."

"What?" he asks.

"Ace and me," I clarify. "I don't know if we can keep coming."

"Yeah, Sparks," he says with fire in his voice. "I got that part. Why the fuck not?"

So maybe postcoital wasn't the best decision?

"I told you how I feel about football. I

don't like it." I lay all my cards on the table. "It's dangerous and unnecessary and I feel physically ill every time someone gets hit."

"You didn't seem to have a problem with it at training camp." He stares at me, and even though his expression doesn't change, I swear I can see shutters go over his eyes.

"I got caught up." I reach for his hand and intertwine our fingers, even though TK's fingers are stiff and not giving in to me at all. "You were out there living the dream you told me about when we were kids. Ace got to run around, making new friends and watching his dad transform into a real-life superhero out on the field. I felt special watching you, knowing all these people worship you and want you and you're mine."

His fingers finally start to curl around my hand.

"But then, tonight, when I heard that hit and saw you go down so freaking hard, all I could think was, we just found each other again and it could all end because of a fucking game." I climb on top of him when I feel him start to stiffen again. "And if that wasn't bad enough, I looked to my side and saw Ace with tears in his eyes as his hero wobbled to the sideline and the guys behind us rattled off all the ways you'll probably die because of football. It was like a bucket of ice water being dumped on my head."

"I'm not going to die because of football," he says with an authority he doesn't have. "The helmets are better now than ever and the league is really coming down on concussion safety. I'll be fine."

"You don't know that." I run my fingers through his hair. "I don't want to make you choose us over football, but I also don't want you to make me watch you go out there and get tackled into an early grave."

"Poppy —" he starts, but I cut him off.

"No, let me finish." I lie down on his chest, not wanting to have to look in his eyes as I say what I have to say. "Ace wasn't lying when he told you I'm a worrier. And you weren't wrong when you said Moore men make me crazy. I am crazy about you and that's why I cringe seeing you get hit. I don't want to, but every time it happens, the stats for CTE and ALS and every other brain-injury-related disease run through my mind. I can't handle being at the stadium again." I lift up my chin. "I cussed out some random dudes! I clearly need some football girlfriend training before I'm released with the general public again."

His body starts bouncing beneath me even though I don't think I said anything funny.

"Oh yeah, Donny left me a very detailed voicemail telling me about the two guys."

"Are you laughing at me?" I slap his arm before he can answer.

"Marlee's my girl," TK informs me somewhat mysteriously. "She caused so many problems in the stands, Gavin started buying the tickets directly surrounding her seats since she refuses to sit in a box. You yelling at those guys? You're not the only girlfriend to do it. And I think it's hot."

Oh.

Well then.

"Hot or not, I can't yell at strangers in front of Ace!" My voice rises. "That's a terrible example to set for him. Plus, you know I can't fight. One day I'm gonna get slapped and then what?"

"You won't get slapped," TK says, his body bouncing again.

"You don't know that!" I yell at him, hoping these walls are as thick as I think they are.

TK stops laughing and moves one hand to my ass and the other one up to my hair, tugging it lightly to force my eyes to his. "Just come to one more game. Ace loves it and I've never, not in my NFL career, had the feeling I had running onto the field tonight knowing my girl and son were in the stands."

Dammit.

My insides melt at his words and the determination I've been clinging to fades away.

"Fine," I agree, but not happy about it. "One more game."

His eyes go warm, crinkling at the corners.

"Thank you," he whispers, dropping a quick kiss onto my forehead.

Then, without warning, he flips me on my back, spreads my legs open, and shows me just how thankful he is.

A couple of orgasms later, I'm pretty sure I'll agree to anything.

THIRTY-TWO

"Love you!" I yell to Ace's back as he hurries into school, no doubt trying to pretend he doesn't know who I am. "Have the best day ever and learn stuff!"

He breaks into a run.

Yup.

Definitely denying sharing my DNA today.

Whatever.

Embarrassing your kid is a privilege all moms have. It's in the Mom Handbook or something.

I pull my knit cardigan a little tighter across my chest and start my walk home. I don't know if this is going to be one of the Colorado falls where the chill comes early and doesn't leave until well into spring, or if this is a one-off and it's just too early for even the sun to do its job, but it's chilly.

Talking and laughing with Ace as he moaned and groaned about having to write in cursive this year and filled me in on the latest tales of fourth-grade gossip distracted me from the way my body still felt on fire from last night. But now, all alone with my thoughts and — holy freaking hell — memories, it's all I notice. I don't know if, after the way TK nipped and teased them last night, my nipples are still hard from that, the weather, or just thinking about TK. Or maybe it was the way TK made both Ace and me breakfast and woke me up by whispering in my ear and dropping a sweet kiss on my lips before he had to leave to get checked out, go to meetings, and watch film.

All are valid guesses.

Maybe it's a combination of them all.

My hips ache, my thighs feel as though I spent the day in the gym squatting and lunging, and even my back hurts.

My back has never hurt after sex.

But I've also never had so much sex in so many different positions as I did last night. Each step closer to my house is a feat and I decide to reward myself for walking Ace to school (even though he's convinced he's too old for an escort) with a hot bath using the Lush bath bomb I've been saving for the last couple of months.

Then, when I get out of the bath, I'm going to look up yoga classes. I'm thinking it would be beneficial for this new, sexy, bendy stage of my life.

I round the corner to my block and wave to Cole as he pulls into his driveway. He waves back, but it's terse and his smile doesn't reach his eyes. He's still friendly and we chat every now and again during soccer practice, but it's been different since that day at the park with TK.

Not that I mind. He's not touchy anymore and stopped sending right-on-the-verge-of-creepy messages through his kid, so that's a plus.

With my purple shutters and fence in sight and my teeth starting to chatter a bit, I speed up my pace.

I pull open my gate, which, thanks to TK, not only is a bright, fresh white but also no longer creaks when it opens. I don't know if it was part of TK's plan, but every time I open it, I think about him and smile.

I still can't quite believe the way things have happened, but I'd be a damn liar if I said I was upset about any of it.

Yeah, the flowers were creepy, but nothing has happened since and it got TK in my bed every night, which means orgasms every night and his beard against my face when he kisses me each morning. It's dinner with my family, Ace calling him Dad, lounging in the living room, laughing and creating memories. Every. Single. Day.

And I love it.

He hasn't talked about making it permanent or what the next steps are going to be. And I'm okay with that. I know what I signed up for and I'm not going to push for more. Plus, even if I tried, there's no way I'd ever move to Parker . . . ever. Saying I'm not your typical suburban housewife/stay-at-home mom is the understatement of the century. And I highly doubt TK is down for leaving his mansion to live in my tiny bungalow in the kinda hood.

I push open the front door and enter in the password, disarming and then arming the alarm system, and toss my sweater on the couch and leave my shoes sprawled out in the small entryway. I know it's easy enough take them back to my room, but since I'm wearing them to work in a couple of hours, it feels like a waste of time.

I walk into the kitchen, turn on the coffee machine, and measure out double the amount I would normally use. A night filled with lots of acrobatics and not much sleep calls for it.

Again, not that I'm complaining.

At. All.

I push the button for the coffee to brew, and as soon as I hear the wonderful humming as it gets down to business, my door-bell rings.

"What in the world?" I ask aloud.

Because when coffee time is interrupted and you can still feel aching between your legs, talking to yourself is totally acceptable.

I walk to the monitor mounted on the wall outside my kitchen to see who is outside.

"What the fuck?" I ask again, but louder and with some profanity this time. Because years might've passed since I've seen her and she might be slightly distorted from the doorbell camera, but one does not easily forget the face of a person who destroyed their life, broke their heart, or crushed their dreams.

And for me, Lydia Moore did all three.

So one more time for the people in the back — what the fuck?

Then, before I can fully process what's happening and what will happen if I let her in, she rings the bell again and then starts pounding on my door.

This, for some unknown reason, pisses me off.

Like, a lot.

And because of that, I stomp my way to my front door, punch in the alarm code, throw my shoes across the living room, swing open the door without thinking, and ask, "Why are you at my house?"

"Poppy, dear." She aims a condescending lip snarl I think is supposed to be a smile my way. "I see you're just as lovely as ever."

Then, like I won't hesitate to slap an old lady (okay, I'd never slap an old lady, but still), she pushes past me and into *my* house!

"Hmmm." She looks around my living room, scrunching her nose like she smells something funny. "How . . . quaint."

Okay.

She's really making me reconsider my "no slapping old people" policy.

I ignore her.

"What are you doing here?" I try asking again.

"TK isn't answering my phone calls," she says, as if that explains everything.

I stare at her, needing a little more information and a lot more movement . . . movement that moves her out of my house.

"He wasn't at his home either." She continues on. "I called Donny and he told me he was staying with you and sent over your address."

Donny. I'm gonna let him know about himself. And in doing so, there's a chance even he may cower from what's running through my head right now.

She's still talking when I stop thinking of

the ways I'm gonna cuss Donny out.

"I thought he must've been mistaken when I started driving through the neighborhood and pulled up to this . . . house . . . but . . ." She pauses, not catching on to or fazed by the homicidal vibes I'm emitting. "I guess he was right."

I wait for her to get in another insult, but she stops talking.

Finally.

"That's all fine and dandy, Lydia," I say, not missing the way the vein in her frozen forehead jumps hearing me call her by her first name. "But that still doesn't explain why you are at *my* house."

"Because of you, my son is not speaking to me."

So I guess she's just gonna ignore my question.

Also, really?

"*You're* the reason your son isn't speaking to you, not me." I step into her space, noting that besides a few grays she missed touching up her dye job, she looks nearly identical to the last time I saw her. Tall and lean (TK is not an anomaly in his family) with stunning green eyes and chiseled cheekbones. I might hate the woman, but I can't deny that even with the addition of too much Botox, she's beautiful. Her hair is

372

still pulled into her signature chignon, though I did note when she spun around to judge my house, it's more modern than the one she rocked ten years ago. She looks perfectly polished in a crisp, white button-up blouse, a beige cardigan, and wide-legged jeans cuffed at the bottom. The diamond tennis necklace Mr. Moore bought her for their fifteenth anniversary accentuates her slim neck, and pointy leopard-print flats make her long legs look even longer.

It might look casual, but I know.

She came dressed for war.

And here I am, Frumpy McFrumperson, standing barefoot in leggings (with bright purple flowers scattered across them) I bought from a mom at Ace's school for a fund-raiser last year and a scoop-neck tee with a paint stain on my boob.

Awesome.

"You most certainly are." She steps in, looking down her nose at me. "We had a lovely relationship until you showed up, meddling and lying, just as you behaved all those years ago."

"Lydia." I look up at her, refusing to be intimidated in my own home. A home that now contains touches of TK everywhere I look. "I don't know how that whacked-out brain of yours works, but what's going on between you and TK has nothing to do with me."

Her head snaps back like she can't believe I'd dare talk to her in such a manner before her eyes narrow on me.

"I saved him all those years ago when you tried to stop him." She jams a pale pink nail into my shoulder. "You tried to prevent him from achieving what I always knew he was destined for. And then, all these years later, you crawl out of the gutter you've been hiding in and try to bring him down again." She leans over me more and I curse my short legs. "I stopped you once and I'll stop you again."

I count to ten before I respond. Squaring off with angry, bitter mothers isn't something I specialize in. I'm not one hundred percent sure how to handle this. The only thing I know for sure is I can't let her see she's getting to me.

"That was a nice villain speech and all," I say, once I'm sure I won't just scream in her face. "But you're fighting a fight that doesn't exist. In my mind, hell, in my *life,* you don't exist. TK not only knows about Ace, but he loves him. And I might think you are quacked all the way out, but I know you love TK. You know how much a parent loves their child. And I know you know you can't win." I gentle my tone, trying to get in somewhere I know is impossible to penetrate. "You're TK's mom and he loves you, but he adores Ace and nothing you say or do will change that. If you were smart, instead of coming here and being a bitch, the move you should be making would be one to get to know your grandson."

"You are the same conniving little gold digger you always were."

Okay, so maybe calling her a bitch wasn't the best way to extend an olive branch, but this seems like an extreme response to what was actually good advice.

"Lydia," I sigh, already sick of this ride. "You really need —"

"Don't you dare tell me what I need," she says, cutting me off. "You have no clue what I need."

The adrenaline and anger I felt seeing her at my door are gone and I still haven't had my coffee.

In other words, I'm over this.

So I let her know.

"Think and do what you want. Your son kept me up way too late doing things I'm certain no mother wants to hear about and I have to go to work soon." I take secret joy in the way her eyes bulge out of her head and her mouth falls open. "I still haven't had my coffee and I want to take a long bath, so if we're done here, I'd like to get my day started."

"You little bitch!" she shrieks. Her face is cherry red and her knuckles are white. "How dare you! Just wait! TK has always been too good for you and now he's too good for that bastard son you're trying to pawn off on him!"

Oh, hey, adrenaline, welcome back.

My back goes straight and my claws come out. Say what you want about me, but mention my son one time and I will not hesitate to mess a bitch up.

But unfortunately for me, before I can get close enough to her to wrap my hands around her neck, my front door bursts open and slams against the wall so hard, not even the springy door stop can prevent the knob from going straight through the drywall. Then TK is in the doorway, his angry presence filling every inch of my house.

It's the freaking best.

Lydia retreats.

"Get out," TK growls.

"Honey, I was just — I —" Lydia stutters, but can't finish before TK is in her face, cutting her off.

"Don't care what you were doing, Mother," he says. "Told you I needed space.

Told you to give me that if you wanted back in my life. You couldn't do it."

"But I watched the game last night. I saw you get injured and you still wouldn't answer my calls." Her voice quivers and tears fall down her cheeks.

I watch, not at all moved by her waterworks.

And neither is TK.

"So because I still needed time and wasn't talking to you, you figure the way back in my good graces is to come and harass the woman I love?" he says, and any color remaining in her already pale face drains. "To call my son, who I missed nine years with because of you, a bastard?" He leans in closer to her now trembling frame and roars, *"Are you nuts!"*

I figure this is a rhetorical question because clearly she is, and has always been, nuts. Starting when she lied and tried to trick me into an abortion ten years ago.

But as much as I hate her, I love TK.

And I know TK loves his mom and will regret this.

So I decide to stop it.

I cross the small space and step in between him and his mom, placing both of my hands on his chest and moving him back a step.

"Enough," I whisper.

"But she —" he starts, his eyes still focused on Lydia, but this time, I do the interrupting.

"I know," I tell him, still whispering. "But I think she gets it, and if you keep going, you'll regret it."

His eyes finally move to mine. We don't say anything, but we don't need to. He nods once before shifting his attention back to Lydia. "Get out now and I'll think about returning your calls sometimes." He takes a deep breath, his body vibrating with anger under my touch. "But stay and fight this, and I promise I'll be nothing but a memory to you."

I don't look at Lydia while this is happening. Seconds pass in complete silence before I hear footsteps moving around us and then, finally, Lydia leaves my house.

I go to hug him, relieved this is over, but instead, TK's hands move under my arms and lift me away from him.

"TK —" I start, but he cuts me off.

"No." His green eyes, which are always lit with humor, are hard and angry.

My eyebrows knit together and chills go up my arms. "What's wrong?"

His mouth opens and his eyes screw shut, but he doesn't answer. Looking at the expression on his face breaks my heart. He looks so confused and angry. He looks crushed.

"I'm so sorry," I whisper.

It's like he doesn't hear me. He's in his head and the struggle raging in his eyes tells me it's a horrible place for him to be. But instead of talking to me, he turns around, and as fast as he was here, he's gone.

The door slamming shut causes me to jump. I move to go after him, but before I can, I hear tires screeching. When I get outside, all I see is TK's Range Rover speeding down the street.

I call Brynn when I go back inside, asking if I can come in a little later and early tomorrow.

Brynn being Brynn — meaning she's the shit — says yes.

Then I plant my butt in front of the TV and don't watch it.

This angry, unable-to-control-his-emotions TK is new to me.

When we were teenagers, it didn't matter what happened, TK never lost his temper. Not ever. He was always the rational one who'd calm me down when I'd been pushed too far. Now I've seen him snap a few times, and as much as I try to fit the pieces together to try to understand how he's angrier now, nothing makes sense.

And I don't stop thinking about it until I hear a car door close almost two hours later.

TK comes inside, his hair all over the place like his hands haven't stopped running through it.

"Hey." I walk to him, my steps hesitant.

"Hey." He closes the distance between us and wraps me in his big arms. "Sorry I left like that."

"It's fine." I release a breath I wasn't even aware I was holding. "Are you okay?" I ask after the thumping of his heartbeat starts to slow beneath my ear.

"I should be asking you that." He steps back but keeps his hands around my waist.

"I'm used to your mom being the worst to me." I smile, trying to lighten the mood.

It doesn't work.

"I'm so sorry she brought that shit to you." He looks so guilty . . . so sad. His normally bright eyes are dull and glassed over with unshed tears.

"Not your fault, so don't apologize." I grab the bottom of his shirt and invoke as much feeling as I can behind the words.

He closes his eyes and sucks his lips into his mouth, his fingers flinching at my sides, but he doesn't say anything.

So I do.

"I didn't text you, how'd you know to come home?"

"Donny."

Now it's me who's growling. "Well, maybe if he kept his big mouth shut and didn't give her my address, he wouldn't have had to send a distress signal your way."

TK finally cracks a smile.

"He does have a big-ass mouth."

"I've only met him once and I know that to be fact."

"My mom drives him nuts." He tells me what I don't find to be surprising. "I think he wanted there to be fireworks."

"Tell him next time he wants fireworks, I'll drive up to Wyoming and buy him some. But if he ever sends your mom on an ambush mission to my house again, I'll light them after I shove them where the sun doesn't shine."

Now that doesn't get another smile.

It gets laughter.

Body-bent, perfect-teeth-baring, eye-crinkling laughter.

And it makes my toes curl and my heart explode.

"Wanna have a quickie before I have to get Ace from school?" I ask once his laughter starts to die down.

He doesn't answer.

Instead, his hands go back to my waist and he lifts me up and throws me over his shoulder before running down my hall and tossing me on the bed.

I don't get my coffee or my bath before work.

But I do get a shower.

With TK.

So even though I leave the house with the ache more noticeable between my thighs, I do it admitting I'd happily spend the rest of my life with it never going away.

I also do it smiling.

Until I open my garage and see the same bouquet of flowers from my front porch in the alley behind my house.

Only this time it's bigger.

And beside it is a cut-up Moore jersey. The bottom half of the jersey's missing and the edges are black and charred from where it was burned.

I know the smart thing to do is to run back inside, tell TK, and then call the cops.

Hell.

I'm sure jumping in my car and running over it would be a better idea than walking straight to the flowers and searching for the card.

It's not hard to find.

The sender made sure it was sticking out

of the flowers and encased in a bright, you-can't-miss-me envelope.

I'll give it to them. This note is much more efficient and effective. And they did it in two words: *Dump him.*

THIRTY-THREE

"Whoever the fuck is doing this knows who you are." TK takes an angry gulp of his root beer — which, to be fair, I'd also be angry drinking, because root beer is gross — and glares at everyone in the general vicinity of his barstool.

As if all the poor customers at HERS had pitched in for the flowers.

I throw the towel I was using to wipe off the bar in a bucket and plant both of my fists on my hips. I've tried to be nice, to let him have his feelings, but he's driving me crazy.

I usually love when TK is off on Tuesdays, but he disappeared into the alley yesterday after I told him about the flowers. When he came back, he glued himself to me and he's been driving me crazy since.

"They know me? You think?" I don't bother hiding the sarcasm in my tone and TK's eyes narrow even further. "Did them having my address and name give you that idea?"

He ignores me and keeps talking. "We don't have the alley monitored, they must have known."

"Or the alley's already creepy, and adding burned football paraphernalia only adds to its natural ambiance." I walk around the bar, abandoning my job, and position myself between TK's legs. "You have to stop thinking about it. We filed a report, I'm not going to walk to or from work alone anymore. It'll be fine."

"I don't like it," is his well-thought-out and mature response.

"I know. I don't like it either." I wrap my arms around his neck and tangle my fingers in his hair. God, I so love his hair. "Maybe tonight after Ace goes to bed, we can try and distract each other."

I don't even get to do the sexy wink (which probably isn't sexy at all and might just look like I have something stuck in my eye) before his mouth is on mine. It's fast and hard, but it confirms my plans for tonight.

I roll to my tiptoes, needing his mouth once more and maybe for a little bit longer.

"Get out of here, TK, you're ruining the vibe of my bar," Brynn interrupts us.

I burrow my head in TK's chest, knowing if I look up, my cheeks are going to be bright red.

"You're such a liar," TK smirks, not at all fazed we got caught kissing at my job. "You should put a cardboard cutout of me in the corner, that's how much all your customers want me around."

I push out of TK's hold and roll my eyes at his ridiculous comeback while also wondering where I could get a life-size TK cutout for myself.

"I forgot what a cocky fucker you are." Brynn shakes her head, but the smile spreading across her face lets me know I'm not in too much trouble. "How you managed to land Poppy will go down as one of life's great mysteries."

She might be giving him a hard time, but that was so sweet I contemplate transferring my PDA to her.

"This is true." TK's voice and eyes soften. "I'm fuckin' lucky."

I don't know if most great writers drop an F-bomb into their declarations of love, but unlike most of the heroines in those stories, I love nothing more than a well-placed "fuck" . . . in every way.

"Okay." I look between the two of them. "Too many compliments and I don't know how to handle them. You" — I point at Brynn — "that was really nice of you to say and I promise I won't kiss my boyfriend on the clock anymore. And you . . ." I turn my attention to TK, who, now that I'm really focused on him, looks way too big to be sitting on the sleek, acrylic barstool. "Since you aren't at work, go pick up Ace from school."

Brynn is the shit for many reasons.

She created a kick-ass bar marketed and designed for women. She even put a photo booth outside the bathroom, for heaven's sake. She manages to wear dresses, sneakers, and buns and look like a freaking model. She comes into work every day with next to no makeup on and has a genuine compliment for everyone who crosses her path. You don't find that combination of beauty, success, and kindness in many people, so I don't downplay any of this.

But what I love her for the most is, after hiring me on the spot when I'd just showed up, she went out and bought a small desk, chair, and extra computer for the back room so Ace could come here after school while I work. She lets me take a break every afternoon to walk to his school and bring him to work with me. And every day, when we walk into the back room, she has goodies from

Fresh sitting on the desk, waiting for him.

Ace loves coming and he loves Brynn (he won't admit it, but I'm pretty sure he has a decent-size crush on her as well). But Brynn, like me, does not come close to TK in Ace's eyes. TK picking up Ace from school is the equivalent of the Spice Girls picking me up from school in that kickass bus they drove in *Spice World.* A freaking dream come true.

"I can do that." TK drains the rest of the root beer from his glass. "What time does he get out again?"

"Three thirty." I look at the time on the register behind the bar. "You still have a couple of hours."

TK came with me to pick Ace up a few times, but I just forced him into the car when it was time to go. This will be his first solo school pickup and I can tell he's nervous. The carpool line monitors are freaking intense. He's seen me get scolded twice already.

"Cool. Then I'm gonna head home and take care of a few things, maybe run to the store and step up your junk food game." He stands up and stretches his arms above his head, like sitting on the stool was even more uncomfortable for him than I originally guessed.

"We do not need any more junk food!" I wish I could hide the panic in my voice, but I am the kind of person who can eat healthy only if there's no other option. The second Oreos enter the house, I lose any semblance of self-control. And now that I no longer have to work in lingerie, my discipline levels are lacking even more than normal.

"Don't worry," TK says, knowing about my sweet tooth. "I'll get man snacks. You won't want any of them."

"A man snack?" I ask at the same time Brynn asks, "What the fuck is a man snack?"

"You know." TK shrugs, pulling his beanie out of his pocket and tugging it over his head. "Mountain Dew, beef jerky, oversize candy bars, that kind of shit."

I narrow my eyes. "Mountain Dew is disgusting, but I know plenty of women who drink it and you know I'll snack on some jerky and candy bars . . . especially the king-size ones."

This is also true. It doesn't even matter if I'm not a fan of the candy, hand me anything in its king-size form and I'll eat it.

"I know." He walks around the bar even though Brynn is right there and drops a quick kiss on my lips. "But it'll all be gone when you get home. Hence it being a man snack."

I shake my head, trying not to be mesmerized by the crinkle of his eyes and the lingering sensation of his beard against my face. "You're an idiot."

"You love it." He winks, turning before I can confirm or deny it. "Can I borrow your key? I forgot mine because you were rushing me out the door."

"It's in my purse in the back." I point to the office door. "Next time you forget yours, I'm going to put it on a necklace for you."

"I do look good in jewelry." He sticks his tongue out like a toddler before turning to walk away. "Later, Brynn."

"Later!" Brynn waves. "Tell Ace I said hey."

"Will do," he calls over his shoulder, oblivious to the way the heads of the customers turn and follow his fine ass through the front door.

I'm not oblivious.

But I can't be mad.

He does have a fantastic ass.

THIRTY-FOUR

I don't know what I was expecting a Lady Mustangs meeting to be like, but I can say, with one thousand percent certainty, I did not expect this.

It's my own fault, really.

Brynn, Charli, and Vonnie all tried to warn me. But did I listen? *Nooooo.* And this is what I get.

I figured after training camp and the couple of games TK's weaseled me into, not much could shock me.

Again.

So freaking wrong.

"I'm scared," I whisper into Vonnie's ear.

When we show up at the games, everyone is in their designer jeans, fancy purses, and blinged-out jerseys. And when I say bling, I don't mean a few rhinestones glued on. No. These things are cut and manipulated and doused in crystals. Not rhinestones, CRYS-TALS. This is not some Hobby-Lobby,

I-got-bored, crafting crap either. I'm talking spending hundreds and hundreds of dollars on a football jersey. They're tailored to fit perfectly around their curves, the V-neck is cut a little — or a lot — deeper, some have ruffles added to the bottom, others are turned into straight-up dresses worn with heels that are also bedazzled with a heart and their player's number on them. Dresses and stilettos at football games! I might be a slight hater because they are gorgeous, and I will never admit it to Sadie, but even I love a little sparkle.

So with all the extra-ness I've seen at the stadium, I didn't think there was a chance in hell it could be upstaged. I mean, HERS is just a small restaurant-bar in Five Points.

But when I walked in, after passing by all the Mercedes, BMWs, and Porsches lining the pothole-riddled street, not only was I met with the usual designer-covered women with their hair long and flowing and their faces polished, but there was also a camera crew.

Not like a "Say cheese!" camera. Like a "Put this mic on and let us interview you!" camera.

What. The. Hell.

"Girl, bye." Vonnie brushes me off. "You better order another cocktail and settle in, we haven't even gotten started yet."

My eyes bulge out of my head at this news. We've already been here for forty-five minutes. "How long do they go?"

"Feels like years, but usually two or three hours." Charli drains the remnants of her Skinnygirl margarita . . . which should've been the first sign I was in trouble — you know, after Brynn's repeated warnings of "Poppy, you're in trouble!" — since I've only ever seen Charli drink wine. Tequila should've sent sirens roaring.

"I thought you said Jane took over?" My eyes find Jane, but she doesn't look like she's going to take charge. She looks like she can't wait to get off the clock and drown in tequila her damn self.

"Jane brings clipboards." Vonnie points to the table in the corner covered in about ten clipboards.

"What does that even mean?" I hiss.

"Jane just sets up the activities," Vonnie starts to explain. "Tennis lessons are always there, you can sign up to host at your house for an away game, there's probably a painting and drinking night, then the rest are different volunteer opportunities. I always sign up for the food drive before a game and the fashion show. The first makes me feel like a good person, the second makes me feel fancy and drunk."

One could never fault Vonnie's reasoning.

"Okay, so if we just have to sign our names on clipboards, then how does this take so long?"

"They need footage to play on the news before some of the events and to add to the Mustangs website," Vonnie says in a way that I know I'm not the first person who has asked her.

"On the news!" I almost come out of my chair. I so did not sign up for airtime. "For what?"

"Brynn! Poppy needs another drink!" Vonnie shouts across the room and false-eyelash-rimmed eyes turn to me.

I wave to the room. "Afternoon drinking, am I right?" I half laugh, half mumble, fully mortified.

Then I turn and glare at Vonnie and Charli when I hear them snort beside me. "Assholes." But I can only hold it for a second before I'm laughing with them. "Why am I so awkward?"

"It's endearing," Charli says.

"Doesn't matter how awkward you are or aren't. After this you go home to TK Moore and all these bitches are jealous." Vonnie lifts her signature French martini with a splash of champagne (still classy AF) to her lips before saying, "Myself included."

"Vonnie!" Charli slaps her and Vonnie gives her a glare when her martini splashes over the rim and lands on her white sweater. Charli might be one of the only people on this planet immune to a Vonnie glare. She ignores it and keeps scolding her.

"What? You telling me you've never thought about TK's bearded face and thick ass before?"

"Once or twice." Charli blushes.

"Exactly. Anyways, she knows TK's fine. A woman tells me she thinks Justin is sexy, I tell her thank you and go to *our* home and get to have fun with his sexy self for as long as I want. I love my man, but I'm not blind. And TK could get it, shit, so could Shawn." Vonnie ignores the way color rises up Charli's cheeks and keeps going. "TK is delicious in that big, wilderness, caveman way where I just know his ass is taking charge in the bedroom, doing all sorts of freaky shit. Shawn is fine in the clean-cut, preppy way where I'd probably have fun turning his ass out."

"She's not wrong." I lift my glass and exchange cheers with Vonnie.

"*Brynn!* Drinks!" Charli stands up and crosses the room to the bar.

I can't even pretend not to be entertained.

I start laughing so hard, I have to push my seat back so I can lean over and clutch my stomach.

This lasts for only a couple of seconds, because before I know it, Charli's seat is filled and not by Charli.

"Hi, Poppy, is it?" asks a brunette so stunning that I have to blink a few times to make sure she's not a figment of my imagination before I nod.

"Y-y-yeah. That's me," I stutter like a fool.

"I'm Aviana West, no relation to Kanye and Kim." She tosses her hair over her shoulder and throws her head back, laughing like it was the cleverest joke ever. "Though I was on a show on E!, so we're kind of like cousins."

She winks.

Vonnie rolls her eyes so hard, I think I actually hear them hit the back of her head.

I stare.

I knew she looked familiar!

"Oh my god!" I slap the table. "You were on that one dating show!"

Trash TV is one of my many vices and I don't care who knows.

"Guilty." She smiles her movie-star smile she's probably been paid to endorse some teeth whitening kit on Instagram for. "But that was a long time ago. Now I'm married to Crosby West."

I stare again, but this time not in reality television awe but with a blank one.

"Sorry." I cringe, feeling a little bit like a bitch. "Unless I have a program in front of me, I don't know who any of the players are."

"Number sixty-five," she goes on. "He's an offensive lineman, guard." She keeps going when it's clear I don't recognize the name. Her smile freezes on her face for a second before she's flipping her hair . . . again . . . and back to her camera-ready routine. "Don't worry, I don't know much about the sport either."

Then, out of nowhere, Vonnie, who was completely uninterested, if not a little put off by Aviana's presence, bursts out laughing. "Ohh! I'm sorry!" She waves a hand at me before wiping at her eyes. "That was a good one, girl."

As I raise an eyebrow in question, Aviana glares and turns to me.

"Anyway." She waves Vonnie off, which I think is a mistake, but I decide to keep quiet. "I've been gathering some of the girls to see if any of them would be interested in being on a reality show."

Sirens, car crashes, massive explosions, all go off in my head.

My mouth falls open a bit and she takes that as a cue to continue on. "I still have some contacts from E! And they've been looking for a new city for one of their shows. I've just been raving about Denver, so they wanted me to test the water. See how you girls felt."

"Oh no." I shake my head so hard, I start to get a little dizzy. "No no no."

Her face falls a bit. "Really? I thought you would love it." Her eyebrows narrow in a way where she looks genuinely confused. "You know, with your background and all."

Sirens, car crashes, massive explosions, take two.

My back goes straight, and I note out of the sides of my eyes that Vonnie's does as well.

"I'm sorry?" I ask.

"You know, with stripping and stuff," she says like she's telling me the weather, and I can tell she doesn't have any ill intent. "There aren't set scripts or anything, but reality TV is a performance too. I thought maybe you'd want to get back into that."

I take a second to check my tone because I don't want to come off as a bitch and I definitely don't want to yell. "I wasn't a stripper."

Her perfectly filled and arched eyebrows

go straight to her hairline. "You weren't?"

"No. I was a waitress at the Emerald Cabaret, but it's not a strip club . . . and I still never stripped."

"Where'd you get she was a stripper?" Vonnie asks Aviana what I'm thinking.

"It's on all the blogs." She shrugs again, like this isn't a big deal at all.

Blogs.

With an *s.* Multiple blogs.

I suck in a sharp breath, feeling like my cocktail is going to reappear all over the table. "Blogs?" I whisper, not because I don't want other people to hear but because my lungs are frozen and it's all I can manage.

"Oh shit." Vonnie lifts her hand in the air and motions for Charli to come back.

"Yeah." Aviana pulls out her phone, her rhinestone-encrusted nails flying across the screen until she turns it to me. "See?"

I recognize the bold, hot-pink script of *Baller Notice* right away. It's burned into my brain from when Rochelle shoved it in my face to get me fired.

I take the phone from Aviana's hand and Vonnie leans over, reading along with me. I almost correct Aviana, I'm not sure a forum can really be considered a blog, but I also figure specifics aren't what's important here.

What's important is this "Is TK Moore dating a stripper?" thread with over three hundred comments, complete with pictures.

Pictures of me at training camp side by side with pictures of me in my Emerald Cabaret uniform.

"Oh my god." I breathe, scrolling through the thread, scanning over the comments like a madwoman.

Some are saying I'm pretty, some are saying I'm fat and fug. A few comments about TK liking the swirl and wishing they would've tried their luck. Then one stands out of the crowd saying I'm a single mom just looking for a check.

On one hand, I'm kind of glad they haven't pinged TK as Ace's dad. I don't need them all up in our history, something I'm pretty sure these Internet detectives are capable of. On the other hand, it pisses me right the hell off that I've been pegged as some money-hungry woman looking for a free ride.

I hand Aviana her phone back with a little more force than necessary.

"I'm so sorry." She tucks her phone under the table. "I swear, I had no idea you didn't know."

And I believe her.

Her tanned skin has a bit of a green

undertone to it now, and her eyes are glassed over like she might cry.

"TK's mom came by after the first game. She just dropped by my house unannounced and pretty much ripped me to shreds. She's hated me since I was a teenager and has worked her hardest to get TK to leave me. She thinks I'm scum." I hurry up when I see the confused faces staring at me. "Sorry, the point being, I've dealt with people thinking shitty things about me before. I really don't care what a bunch of strangers say about me on the Internet. I'm not talented enough and I lack the confidence to be a stripper. I don't think being called a stripper is an insult, I just wasn't one."

I force a smile, somehow becoming the comforter in this situation.

"And I think a reality show here would be awesome, I'm just not one for the limelight, but I'll totally be in the background, sipping a drink while you guys flip tables and shit."

Aviana starts to laugh, her coloring returning to her original shade of sun-kissed goddess when I realize Charli and Brynn are both behind me and heard the entire thing.

"Fucking Lady Mustangs," Brynn mutters under her breath. "I'm bringing a pitcher of margaritas over."

"Margaritas sound good," I say.

"Lady Mustangs!" Dixie's Southern twang calls out at the same time lights from the cameras positioned around the room turn on. "Welcome to our first meeting of the season!"

Then, like the glittered ghost of Sadie is haunting me, Dixie lifts a sparkly gavel in the air before slamming it onto the table and causing a mini explosion of glitter.

"What is happening?" I say out loud this time.

Vonnie's eyes dance with humor, and Aviana pulls her lips between her teeth to stop from laughing.

Charli lifts her freshly filled glass to her mouth and whispers, "Fucking Lady Mustangs."

Then the reality star, blogger, student, and stripper all start to laugh.

And cameras capture it all.

THIRTY-FIVE

"You look gorgeous," TK whispers in my ear just before we enter the private dining room in the basement of Beatrice & Woodsley, a restaurant I'd never even heard of before Vonnie texted me that we had reservations at eight.

"Thank you." My red-painted lips tip upward as I bask in his compliment.

I don't tell him I better look good, considering Brynn and Sadie invaded my house throwing dresses on me and yanking them off until they decided on the tight black dress with a high neckline and a higher slit, and shoved me in the highest heels I have. Then they pushed me into my bathroom and painted my face like they were Leonardo da Vinci and I was their muse in desperate need of work.

He links our fingers together and guides me into the room echoing with laughter and the sound of one or more bottles popping.

"Poppy!" Vonnie cries when she sees us walk in. "Girl, you look hot!"

"Yeah, you do," Charli agrees, wrapping me in a quick hug.

"So do you!" And I'm not saying it just to say it.

They look freaking amazing. Vonnie always looks beautiful, but right now, in an orange dress showcasing her tiny waist, full hips, and ample cleavage, she looks smoking hot. Her long hair is pulled into a high ponytail, and huge, diamond-encrusted hoops hang from her ears. Charli's wearing a long, flowy dress with so many different straps holding it up, I'm not sure how she didn't get tangled trying to put it on. It's so low-cut, there's no way to wear a bra (something I haven't been able to do since Ace was born) and has a slit so high she's at risk of flashing the room.

They. Are. Goals.

So I tell them.

"I want to be you."

"You going home with TK tonight?" Vonnie asks, and Charli rolls her eyes.

My brows knit together. "Ummm . . . yeah?"

"Then trust me, you want to be you," Vonnie says.

I look over my shoulder at TK, who is

standing by Justin and Shawn, ordering a drink from a waitress with hearts in her eyes. His wavy hair is down, semiparted on the side from where he ran his hand through it and tossed it back, and his beard is freshly trimmed. He's wearing tailored dark gray suit pants that come in just at the ankle with a plain white button-up shirt with the top few buttons open and brown leather oxfords even I would steal.

I almost fainted when he walked out of the bedroom.

He's that hot.

I look back at her. "You are not wrong."

"Can I get you something to drink?" the waitress asks me, no longer sporting the heart eyes.

"French martini with a splash of champagne." I tell her Vonnie's drink, because again, I do kind of want to be her. And I've tried her drink, it's delicious.

"Two of those," Vonnie says.

Charli already has a glass of champagne in her hand, so she doesn't order. The waitress jots down our order and hurries out of the room.

"Are you excited for your first Monday Night Football game?" Vonnie pulls out a chair at the table and I sit beside her, Charli on my right.

"I guess." I shrug and fidget with the wrapped-up silverware. "I'm not too jazzed to go to another game after the last one. But I like that they don't have to be at a hotel tonight and we're all able to get together."

I'd lucked out after telling TK I don't want to go to another game with the next two being away games, but that could only last so long. And tomorrow my luck officially runs out.

"We have extra tickets in our suite. You and Ace are more than welcome," Vonnie offers even though she knows my answer.

"Thank you, but I'll be okay with the other mere mortals."

"I made sure Shawn and TK talked, so we're sitting next to each other again," Charli says. "I'll be your backup in case you have to yell at anyone else."

"Oh god." I cringe, thinking back on my theatrics. "Do not let me do that again."

"I'm gonna egg you on! I've always wanted to do it." Charli laughs, but I know she's not kidding.

Fantastic.

Voices come from the stairway and we look to the door just as Aviana and Crosby walk in. Aviana looks her normal television-ready self, and even though she towers over me, she looks petite next to her guard husband.

Right behind them are Peter, the quarterback, and his girlfriend, Jacqueline Eriksson.

Jacqueline is model stunning. Literally. She's been in *Sports Illustrated* and walked in last year's Victoria's Secret Fashion Show. I know this because I still have the show on my DVR and I watch it when I get a little out of control with the carb intake. Her long blond hair in soft, glamorous curls glistens even under the dim lights, and her legs, which might be longer than my body, are exposed in her short, navy body-con dress.

"Hey, everyone!" Aviana shouts across the room, letting go of Crosby's hand and grabbing Jacqueline's, even though Jacqueline looks like a deer in headlights. "Come on, Jac, let me introduce you to the girls."

Since the Lady Mustangs meeting on Wednesday, we've all had a running group text. And Vonnie, who told me she wasn't sure about her, has warmed to Aviana. They are the ones who decided to take advantage of this rare Sunday night with the guys and get together.

"Jac, these are the girls, Vonnie, Charli, and Poppy." She points at us as she says our names. "Girls, this is Jac."

"Hi." I wave, half starstruck, half in awe, just as the waitress comes back, setting our drinks in front of us.

"French martinis with a splash of champagne," she says, color in her cheeks, obviously feeling self-conscious in a room full of people so pretty it's not even normal.

I want to squeeze her hand in solidarity.

"Oooh!" Aviana squeals. "I want one too!"

"Sure." The waitress nods and looks at Jacqueline. "And you?"

"I'll try one too," she whispers, color rising in her cheeks.

And dammit if her being shy doesn't make her even more endearing.

I need her to be a catty bitch. She's too pretty to be nice on top of everything else she has going for her.

I'm watching the waitress scurry away when strong hands are on my shoulders. I look up just in time for TK to drop a quick kiss on my forehead. And I swear I can hear a collective "aww" from the women around me.

"You gonna sit next to me, Sparks?" he asks, the crinkles next to his eyes on full display.

"Yeah." Now I'm whispering, because even in a room full of supermodels — fine, one supermodel — TK is still staring at me like I'm the only women in the universe.

I don't just love him. I *love* him.

"I really like them," I say into the darkness of TK's Range Rover as we navigate the Denver roads back to the house. The tint on his windows is so dark, the world fades away as we drive.

"I'm glad." TK keeps his eyes on the road, but one hand falls from the steering wheel to my bare knee. "They're good people. I lucked out with this team, I've heard some stories."

"Aviana is freaking hilarious." I think back to the way she tried to convince all of us to sign on for the reality show. Poor Jacqueline didn't even stand a chance — as soon as she said it sounded fun, Aviana leapt from her seat and called the producer she's been talking to. "I hope they do get the show. I'd tune in."

"I'm just glad Ace is with Jayden tonight." TK ignores my enthusiasm about a TV show that may never exist. "Because as soon as we get home, I'm ripping this off" — he tugs at the hem of my dress — "and burying my face in between your thighs until you're begging me to stop. Then I'm going to slide inside of you and stay there for the rest of the night."

409

My lungs seize and I say nothing.

I mean, what do you even say to that?

"You have no idea what that was like for me. Having to sit in that room, watching you in that dress, knowing I had to keep waiting until we could be alone." He groans and his fingers flinch around my thigh. "I almost tried to convince you to run to the bathroom with me."

"You're insane." I mean for it to come out strong and unaffected, but it's a breathy whisper.

"You make me insane."

I shake my head, biting my lip to hide my smile. "People don't say stuff like that, TK."

"I do." He tells me what I already know. "And you like it."

He is correct. I love it.

"I do not."

"Sparks." He turns his head, aiming a smile at me before focusing on the road again. "I could feel your legs tense and goose bumps cover them when I said it."

Betrayed by my own body!

"Whatever," I pout, not willing to admit what he already knows.

His soft laughter fills the car just as he turns onto my street, my purple shutters visible even at night thanks to the bright security lights TK had installed.

He slows to a stop and is out of the car, opening my door before I've even unbuckled my seat belt.

"You ready?" TK grabs my hand and pulls me from the car. His eyes travel down my body as if he's just seeing me for the first time. "Keep those on," he says when they stop at my gold, strappy heels.

My core spasms and my legs turn to jelly. "Okay."

Now TK's the one who doesn't say anything.

He tightens his grip on my hand and pulls me behind him up the path and through the door and turns off the alarm without letting go of me.

Then, he does what he promised.

And I wake up still wearing my shoes.

THIRTY-SIX

I thought the energy at the first game was off the charts.

I was wrong.

The energy tonight is so intense the hairs on the back of my neck haven't gone down and the butterflies in my stomach haven't settled.

"This is crazy!" I yell to Charli even though she's standing right next to me.

"Isn't it great?" She claps, bouncing on her toes as the guys run back onto the field after halftime.

As much as I want to deny it, I can't.

It's unlike anything I've ever experienced.

"It's the best!" Ace answers for me through a nacho-filled mouth.

"Don't talk with food in your mouth." I still manage to scold Ace through my excitement.

That mom life never stops.

Charli laughs. Ace shakes his head. I roll

my eyes.

I look back to the field and watch the guys jump around, loosening up like they've been sitting for hours instead of the ten minutes it's really been. I don't have to look hard to find TK. His ass is like a billboard in Times Square — impossible for me to miss. However, that's not why it's easy this time. He's walking toward the stands, crooking a finger at me and Ace.

"Cool," Ace breathes, seeing what I see. "Will you hold these?" he asks Charli, but shoves them in her hands before she answers and is halfway to the aisle before I register what TK wants.

I follow Ace down the concrete steps going slow and steady, a vision flashing in my mind of me meeting my demise if I try to skip down them like Ace. When I reach the bottom, Ace is leaning over, TK's hand ruffling his curls before doing the handshake they perfected last week.

I shake my head, but only to disguise the way my heart is threatening to explode out of my chest.

"Come on," TK says, turning to me.

I have no idea what he's talking about. I just know there's not a chance he's ruffling my curls.

I stare at him with a blank expression for

413

a second before he explains. "Kiss me," he says.

Oh.

That I can do.

I lean forward and touch my lips to his, keeping my hands firmly planted on the guardrail so I don't fall over.

Bloggers and fans be damned.

"Thanks, Sparks." He pulls away, tugging a curl before he puts on his helmet and runs to the sideline.

"Gross," Ace says.

I laugh and yank him into my side, laying a kiss on his cheek.

"Mom!" He wipes off his cheek and stomps up the steps back to our seats . . . which only makes me laugh harder.

I follow him, acutely aware of the eyes on me. Some are appreciative, some in shock, some envious. I add a little more swing to my step, trying to act unaffected. I know it works when I slide back into my seat and Charli gives me a high five.

"You better walk those steps," she snaps. "Jacqueline couldn't have looked better."

"That's a bit of a stretch," I say. "But I appreciate it."

The crowd starts to go wild and draws our attention back to the field, where the Mustangs are spread out, prepared to receive the kickoff. The cheering grows louder, rising in a crescendo as the Raiders' kicker makes contact with the ball. It sails high over the players' heads, soaring past the end zone. The crowd moans with disappointment, wanting to see a return, but changes its tune and starts cheering as TK, Peter, and Crosby jog onto the field with the rest of the offense. They line up on the twenty-five yard line, the O-line shifting back and forth until Peter is satisfied.

Peter does his quarterback jig and then, like a shot, the ball is in his hands and orange and black jerseys are going at it. The huge linemen are shoving and tugging at one another, trying to protect or attack Peter. TK's running down the field trying to best the defender keeping up with him. Peter fakes a throw but hands the ball off to Jaxon Cramer, the running back.

Jaxon makes it only a few yards before a Raiders' player wraps him up and brings him down. Even though it wasn't a big play, the crowd still cheers — happy for any forward progress.

The next play starts and Peter passes the ball to Jaxon again. This time, he doesn't go anywhere.

I know I claim not to know much about football, but I do know that even though they have four tries to get ten yards, they really have only three. Because of this immense knowledge of the sport, my hackles don't rise when the crowd starts to get a little restless.

"Throw the fuckin' ball, Bremner, you fucking bum!" the man one row back and a few seats over shouts.

"How about you go out there and try to do better?" I snap.

Okay. So I lied about staying calm.

The guy ignores me but Ace doesn't. Ace hides his face behind his hands, trying to conceal his laughter. He must not know the shaking of his shoulders and the snorts against his palms kinda give it away.

Back on the field, TK is running to Peter. He leans in for a millisecond before jogging out farther to the sideline. Peter stomps his legs and claps his hand — maybe doing the hokey pokey — before shouting for the ball. It's a perfect snap and the offense hold their men with pinpoint precision, giving Peter plenty of time to find his target.

But Peter doesn't need time. Just as the ball is snapped, TK takes off with his defensive counterpart. He sprints about ten yards and then cuts so suddenly, the defender trips over his own feet. TK crosses the field, his hand raised in the air. Peter spots him over the helmets of the linemen and fires the ball right into TK's chest.

The catch is effortless and well past what they needed for a first down. The crowd, already on their feet, goes ballistic. Jumping up and down, punching the sky and high-fiving their neighbors (hopefully not getting those two mixed up) and chanting "MOOORRRRRREEE." Next to me, Ace's curls are flying around, hitting me in the shoulder, and I can already hear the hoarseness setting in from his screams.

TK takes off down the field, dodging one defender at the fifty-yard line, then getting wrapped up with another. But because he's TK, he doesn't go down. He plants his powerful legs into the turf and digs in, wrestling and fighting for as many yards as he can get.

Then it happens.

Again.

Out of nowhere, the player who fell when the play began runs to help his teammate take TK down. I don't know if it's adrenaline from the game or an ego that's been bruised, but even though TK is wrapped up in a Raiders' player's arms and has nowhere to go, number 27 — the rat — lunges forward, helmet first, aiming right at TK's head.

I see it happening this time.

Probably because the last time has been playing on a wicked loop every time I close my eyes.

I step in front of Ace, hoping I'm wrong and just being paranoid but not wanting Ace to see in case I'm right.

And I know it all happens in a split second, but I swear to God, from my seat in the stands, it's a slow-motion movie.

The crack of the helmets, TK's helmet flying off him — his mouthguard not far behind — and his body going limp just before it hits the ground.

Unlike last time, there are no shouts from the stands. No moans of sympathetic pain.

It's dead silent. In a place where I can't hear myself think, you can now hear a pin drop.

So it's easy to hear players from both teams shouting to the sidelines for help while others immediately drop to a knee next to TK's unmoving body, even number 27.

I watch, frozen to the spot, as the Mustang coaches and trainers rush to the field, pushing players away, creating space for the medics already making their way to TK. The hit replays on the JumboTron, actually in slow motion this time, and competes with my mind. I screw my eyes shut, trying to block it out. Thinking to minutes ago when I dropped a kiss on TK's lips. To last night, lying in bed, his heavy thigh draped over mine as we fell asleep. Me stupidly agreeing to come to another game. Me pretending I could tag along for the ride while it lasted.

Ace's sniffling pulls me out of my stupor.

I turn around to look at him, hoping I was able to shield him from the worst of it, but his face is ashen and his beautiful green eyes are haunted as they focus on the screen above the end zone.

I reach for him, realizing Charli's hand is locked in mine, squeezing hard, trying to evoke a comfort that, quite frankly, doesn't exist. I try to smile at her before I pull my hand away.

"Let's go, buddy." I move the nachos from his lap and put his drink in the cup holder in front of him, but he doesn't move. He's staring, his eyes glazed over and unseeing, at the field, where TK's still lying on the ground, surrounded by teammates on a knee with their heads dropped in prayer. Color has returned to Ace's face, but it's green. I know he might seek emancipation if I pick him up and carry him out of this stadium, but I'm willing to chance it. "Ace."

His head snaps up, the sudden movement

forcing the tears brimming in his eyes to fall over.

"Come on," I whisper.

He nods, swiping at his cheeks, not wanting anyone to see he's crying, and puts on a brave face. He looks up at me, then reaches his hand to mine, locking our fingers together. "It's fine, Mom," he whispers back. "It's gonna be okay."

I know he's not talking about TK. I know he sees through me just as quickly as I see through him. And it makes me feel equal parts proud and guilty. We've been through a lot together, and as much as he looks like and worships TK, he's still my boy.

Always will be.

"I know." I nudge my head toward the aisle and tighten my grip in his. "Ready?"

He takes a deep breath, knowing without me telling him that this is our last time in Mile High Stadium. "Yeah, Mom." He smiles, it's weak, and his dimple is nowhere to be seen, but it's still a smile and I'll take what I can get. "I'm ready."

"Call me?" Charli asks, also forcing a smile, but all I see are the streaks in her makeup and melted mascara.

"Of course," I lie.

We haven't known each other long enough for her to catch the lie and I feel the stab of guilt when she leans in and hugs me, whispering in my ear, "TK's a beast. He'll be fine."

I don't say anything because I can't lie again.

And we both know he won't be.

Fucking football.

THIRTY-SEVEN

A small silver lining is that Mrs. Duncan is a huge Mustangs fan, so the phone doesn't even finish one full ring before she picks up.

"I'll meet you at your house," she answers without a hello. "Tell Ace I'm bringing peach cobbler."

"Thank you." I let out the deep breath I've been holding.

Just like last time, the Mustangs trainers called me to give me an update on TK and tell me to come see him.

But unlike last time, he's not in the training room. Instead, he's being transferred to Saint Joseph Hospital, where he'll be under observation overnight.

"Mrs. D says she's bringing you cobbler." I look at Ace in my rearview mirror. "And I'm sure she won't mind if you invite Jayden over."

"Jayden's at the game," he says to the window.

Crap.

I know he wants to see TK, but I also know the last time we were at Saint Joseph, we were saying our final good-byes to Maya. Seeing his dad in the same place will be too much. I suspect he knows it, too, which is why he didn't fight me when I said I was going to drop him off at home.

"Are you okay?" I ask him, even though I know he's not. "It's okay to be worried and sad."

"I'm fine." He keeps his eyes focused on the fogged-over window. "Tell TK I said I hope he feels better."

God.

My nose begins to burn as my vision clouds over and I damn near bite through my bottom lip trying to hold back the river of tears threatening to break free.

TK. Not Dad.

I want to punch my steering wheel and scream at the top of my lungs. I'm pissed at TK for putting us in this situation. Pissed with myself for letting TK burrow so deep into our lives that now I can almost see the hole forming in Ace's heart. I want to rip apart the freaking world.

I don't.

I tap my brake and check my speed. Because that's my job. Has been since I walked out of a clinic and away from my parents ten years ago. I hold myself together. I make sure Ace is safe, mentally and physically.

I slipped up.

But I know for damn sure it won't happen again.

Not ever.

We pull up to the house at the same time Mrs. Duncan opens the door to her Camry, climbing out of the car with a giant metal tray.

"Go help," I tell Ace.

He nods and opens the door, plastering a big, fake smile on his face as he goes. "I can carry that, Mrs. D."

"Why, thank you, young man," Mrs. Duncan says, doubt in her voice.

She knows he's full of it too.

Ace grabs the cobbler from her and pushes through the non-squeaking gate. My eyes follow him for a second before they meet Mrs. Duncan's worried ones.

"Here's the key. Ace knows how to work the alarm." I drop the key in her palm. "I shouldn't be gone too long."

Her warm hand wraps around mine, her grip strong even in her old age. She catches my gaze and whispers with a force I've never heard from her, "Maya would've liked him."

424

I close my eyes and shake my head, not wanting to hear this.

"No."

"Yes," she says. "I know you want to run. Maya knew it too, said you'd never get serious with anyone because that boy right there" — she points to Ace, who is watching us from the porch — "had your whole heart. But if she would've seen you these last few months, she would've known she was wrong. Ace has your heart, but TK has it too." She squeezes my hand tighter before letting it go. "Don't you run, girl."

"It's . . ." I stop, struggling to find the right words. "It's complicated."

"It always is," she says before turning on a kitten heel, joining Ace, and disappearing into the house.

I get back into my car and drive to Saint Joseph Hospital, fighting not to let her words sink in. Knowing in my heart that, as much as I've enjoyed these last few months, the inevitable has finally arrived.

I hate hospitals.

Even the parking lots are filled with so much sadness it threatens to break me before I step foot inside.

I walk in the entrance, ignoring the gift shop and the front desk. Walking with blinders as families huddle together, talking in hushed voices about loved ones suffering, thinking of plans to move forward after their lives have been ripped to shreds. Probably from some freak accident they never saw coming, not in a million years.

Not me.

I knew. TK knew. Yet here we are because I was too afraid to make him choose.

Too afraid he wouldn't choose me.

And now the decision's been made for us.

I push the elevator button to the floor the trainer told me on the phone. I ignore the older couple standing next to me with a young girl wearing a shirt that says big sister in bright pink with a matching bow in her hair, hating myself for the resentment their happiness causes me. Furious I let myself dream of a future where Ace held a baby girl in his arms, staring into her matching green eyes.

I swipe at the tears falling uninvited as the doors slide open. I move down the hallway, trying not to think of the plans that will never happen and focusing only on what needs to be said.

I have the speech rehearsed when I reach TK's room, but as soon as I pull open the curtain and catch sight of him, my mind goes blank.

He's lying back, his eyes screwed shut in a way I know to mean he's trying to fight pain and not sleeping. His big, strong body suddenly seems so small and frail in the hospital bed. His coloring is off and his hair is a knotted mess.

And he's still the handsomest man I've ever set eyes on.

There's a nurse in the room looking at the monitors next to his bed, then down to her iPad while she enters the information.

She notices me first.

"Can I help you?" She narrows her eyes, probably thinking I'm some rabid fan trying to get a piece of TK.

My mind, a swirling mess of chaos, doesn't have an answer. Can she help me? Ha. Nobody can help me. Nobody.

"Hey, Sparks." TK cracks his eyes open for a second but then groans in pain and screws them shut again.

My stomach twists.

I hate seeing him in pain, but I hate even more that I won't be helping him through this.

"Hey," I whisper.

I walk to the open side of his bed and ignore the annoyed eyes of the nurse while she finishes.

"If you need anything, the button for the

nurses' station is on the remote," Nurse Bitchy tells TK, throwing one more nasty look my way before she leaves.

I want to reassure her I'll be out of her way in no time, but I keep my mouth shut. She'll find out soon enough.

"Where's Ace?" TK asks after the nurse closes the curtain behind her, darkening the room again.

My hand is resting on the rail of his bed when he reaches out to grab it. His fingers graze my skin and just that small touch sends electricity through my veins. I pull away, stepping out of his reach before he can do it again.

"Mrs. Duncan is watching him." I school my voice, keeping it even and unattached.

"What's wrong with you?" TK asks with more than a small amount of anger in his voice.

"I can't do this anymore."

He blinks hard and jerks against the pillows supporting his head.

"I know." He struggles to keep his eyes open even in the shadows of his room. "I told you one more game and this bullshit happened. I know I'm not gonna get you to come to more."

"That's not what I mean." I want to go to him. My fingers are aching to touch his face

428

and run through his hair, but I shove them in my back pockets and stay where I am. "I can't do this anymore. You and me. It's not going to work."

"What the fuck are you talking about, Poppy?" He struggles to sit up, the pain in his eyes chased away by anger.

"I told you I'd never make you choose between me and football, and I'm not." He opens his mouth to speak, but I keep going before he can interrupt. "But I can't do this. I'm not meant for this life. I can deal with the blogs and the crazy fans pulling at you wherever we go. But what I can't do is sit by idly while you kill yourself every Sunday so you can live in some mansion in Parker."

"You're fucking ridiculous," he spits, his rage acting as a much more effective pain-killer than whatever the hospital gave him. "You're making shit up because you're fucking afraid and it's bullshit. You run when shit gets hard. You ran when you were pregnant. You ran when you saw me. And you're running now. That's your shit. Don't put it on Ace and me."

I fight the urge to flinch. I know they say words can't hurt you, but his words make my stomach lurch and the acid in his voice makes my skin burn.

"He called you TK." I surprise myself with

how strong my voice comes out. "I told him I was coming to see you and he said, 'Tell TK I said to feel better.' "

All anger and color drain from his face.

"He what?" he whispers.

And even though I told myself I would not touch him, under no circumstances would I comfort him, my feet move of their own accord. Sure, Nurse Bitchy might get pissed, but I climb into TK's bed, dropping my head onto his chest and curling into his side.

"I love you, TK, so, so much," I whisper, my tears falling onto his hospital gown unchecked. "I actually never stopped loving you. I hated you, but I still fucking loved you. And now I watch you come home limping. I see you closing your eyes and rubbing your head from the headaches. You used to be the voice of reason between the two of us, now you snap and get so crazy angry over everything. Something is not okay. You are not okay. I feel like I'm watching you kill yourself. And I can't do it. I can't watch as the man I've dreamt about spending my life with withers away in front of my eyes because of a game." I hiccup, trying to fight past the tears. "I love you too much to stand around and watch it, and I love you too much to ask you to walk away from football.

But if I stay, it's going to break me."

"But I need you. I need Ace." His heart-beat is pounding faster and faster beneath my cheek. "You guys can't leave me."

"You're his dad, and now that you know, I would never take him from you. But me and you? It's not going to work." I close my eyes, soaking up his heat and comfort for the last time. "We made the best kid and we got caught up in old feelings, but me and you just aren't meant to be. Time couldn't change that."

TK doesn't say anything, he knows I'm right. His arms tighten around me, almost to the point of painful, but before I can register any hurt — at least the physical kind — he drops his forehead to mine and the only thing I feel are his tears falling onto my face.

We lie in the hospital bed, unmoving, for what feels like hours, our tears merging together, our silent pleas and regrets float-ing around us, until the curtain opens and light from the hallway floods his room.

"Mr. Moore?" the doctor's hesitant voice says. "We have to take you for a CT scan now. Do you need a moment?"

"No." I push away from TK and scramble out of the bed. "He's ready."

"Poppy." TK reaches for me, but I'm too

far away . . . in every way possible.

"Go, TK." I don't try to fake a smile, it would only be a slap in his face. "Get better. When you're out, we'll talk and figure out an arrangement with Ace."

"Please," he whispers, his hoarse voice causing a fresh bout of tears to fall down my cheeks.

"I love you." I turn, pushing past the doctor and into the hallway, not caring what people think as I run with tears streaming and almost nonhuman-like sounds falling from my mouth.

I find a stairwell, not capable of waiting for an elevator or breathing in the same confined air as anyone else. My grief is too large, too consuming. I know I'll suffocate.

I won't survive.

I burst through the hospital doors and into the parking lot. Cold air and an unwanted memory hitting me hard. Thoughts of me bursting into the parking lot of the Emerald Cabaret filling my mind. Only that time, TK was falling into my life. Now I'm pushing him away.

I thought, leaving his hospital room, I had already broken.

But I was wrong.

I was still moving then.

Sharp pains shoot through my chest from

the pieces of my shattered heart. My legs give out beneath me and I fall to the cold concrete sidewalk outside Saint Joseph. My lungs catch fire as they fight with the tears stealing my breath.

I ignore the passersby and hide in the darkness of the night as I give in to the soul-shaking, body-racking sobs of a heart that will never be mended.

THIRTY-EIGHT

"Sadie, I'm fine." I slide a drink in front of her and hold her very disbelieving eyes. "I am!"

"You are so not fine." She brings the straw to her lips, sucking back some Diet Coke.

Okay. She's right.

I am so not fine.

When I got home from the hospital on Monday, Ace was asleep, Mrs. Duncan was gone, and Sadie, Vonnie, Charli, Aviana, and Brynn were all sitting in my living room. Brynn, bless her heart, came with a few bottles of wine she'd snagged from HERS.

So of course, this made me burst into tears . . . again.

Sure, Sadie was my girl and I knew I could always depend on her, but I'd never had this. I'd never had a tribe.

After the tears stopped, I told them my story with TK. Most of which Sadie had heard, most of which none of the other girls had a clue about. They sat there, not saying a word, just refilling my glass when it emptied and passing me tissues as I spoke.

By the time I was finished, Brynn's wine contributions were depleted and my personal stash had been opened. They didn't try to change my mind — well, not right out, at least — and Vonnie stayed after everyone else had left while I packed up TK's stuff for her to bring to her house.

TK called the next day. I told him where his stuff was, and since he was going to be out for the next few games and the team had an away game this weekend, we decided he'd pick up Ace from school on Friday and he'd stay for the weekend.

So not only did I lose my boyfriend, I'm losing my kid too.

And I'm flipping out.

"I'd be fine if you guys would stop watching over me like I'm about to snap!" I snap, realizing belatedly that I proved their point.

"Mmm-hmmm," Vonnie says from her barstool. "Tell us again how fine you are."

Charli, Sadie, and Aviana giggle. Jacqueline, who was not informed of the details of my jacked-up life before she was forced to come babysit me, looks uncomfortable.

"Whatever." I roll my eyes, thrilled it's Friday and busy enough so I'm not stuck with these well-meaning bitches all afternoon.

I load up my tray with half-priced drinks, thanks to happy hour, and escape as fast as I can without dousing myself with vodka and beer.

"Let me know if I can get you anything else." I shove my notepad into my apron and grab the now empty tray when I hear the bell over the door sound. I turn to greet the new customers, but when I'm met with a familiar face, the words die in my throat.

Now, the reason I remember customers at HERS is because I like them. The reason I remember customers from the Emerald Cabaret is because they gave me the creeps. There weren't a ton of them, but there were a few, and one of those few is Jacob from one of the last bachelor parties I worked.

Jacob and two other men walk in and stop at the hostess station. Jacob's eyes roam the restaurant and completely overlook two other waitresses before settling on me. A small smile touches his lips and the same feeling of unease I felt with him at the Emerald Cabaret snakes down my spine.

I mean, he's handsome enough, tall, blond hair cut short and neat, and a decent physique. He and his friends are all dressed similarly — nice trousers and button-up shirts with no tie or jacket — so I'm assuming they are coming in after work. Of course, two people are out with the flu today, so I have no choice but to quiet the alarm blaring in my brain that he might be a serial killer and cross the room to greet them.

I mean, really, what are the chances he was sober enough to remember that night and recognize me with my curls and real clothes?

"Hey!" I say with a little too much pep in my voice. "Would you like a table or a seat at the bar?"

"Bar's good," Jacob answers for the group, and I brighten, knowing I won't be alone with them since the only other people at the bar are my people.

"This way." I turn, guiding them to the bar, then gesturing my hand at the empty seats. "Take a seat wherever."

They settle, leaving a few empty seats between them and Charli, and I hand them menus. "Can I get you something to drink?"

"I'll have whatever beer you have on tap," Jacob's friend or co-worker or whoever the hell he is to him says.

"Me too," his other friend says.

"Good choice." I smile and mean it.

Given that HERS was built for women,

we have more martinis and wine than we do beer. But also, because it was built for women, the beer we do have is the shit. Brynn told me she finds a new local brewery every few months, does a tasting, and then orders from there. She said it's as much about buying local as it is supporting her brothers and sisters in small business.

Just another reason to love Brynn.

I don't have to write down their drinks to remember them, and when I look at Jacob, the glint in his eyes makes my stomach knot.

"You don't remember my drink?"

Crap.

"Sorry?" I decide in a split second playing dumb is the way to go.

"Serena, right?"

I mean, what are the freaking chances?

"No, I'm Poppy," I correct him, regretting giving him my name the second it leaves my mouth.

"I know. Poppy Patterson, TK Moore's new piece, which is why you weren't at the Emerald Cabaret last time I was there and asking for you."

I hear his friends snicker and feel my friends' eyes on me, but I can't tear my gaze away from Jacob. A smile, or more like a snarl, pulls on the corners of his mouth and he's watching me like I'm some wounded animal he's about to attack.

"What?"

He leans across the bar, his voice dropping a decimal. "If I'd known you went for extras in the parking lot, I would've left a bigger tip."

"What?" I repeat, trying to comprehend what the hell he is saying to me.

"I mean, you're hot in an urban, exotic way, but I can't believe TK Moore would turn down all the ass he's offered for you." He leans back on the barstool, his eyes dropping to my chest. "You must be working with something like magic. I wouldn't mind a taste."

Okay.

So no.

I try to count to ten, I really do, but I only make it to three.

"Are you fucking kidding me?" I screech, having it up to *here* with everything in my life.

The conversation floating around the room dies and all eyes turn to me. I vaguely hear the sounds of barstools pushing out, but I don't look away from Jacob. The cocky smirk he's been wearing since he walked in starts to fade and he looks a little nervous.

And rightfully so, since I'm two seconds away from a five-to-ten-year sentence.

"Did you seriously come in here to harass me? What the fuck is wrong with you?" I take a deep breath, but it does nothing to calm me down. "I don't know what you heard, but there isn't enough money in the world for me to ever do anything with you."

"Whoa." His friend, the kind, chubby one with an admittedly kick-ass mustache, butts in. "I think you need to calm down a bit."

Big mistake.

"Me, calm down?" I turn angry eyes to him and watch as he visibly shrinks into his seat. "Your friend here just called me a prostitute!"

Not that I have a problem with prostitutes, make your money, honey. But that's not the point here.

"You were a stripper." He makes the unwise decision to defend himself.

"I was never a stripper!" I pound my fists on the bar, and the empty glasses lined up fall over from the impact.

Before I can say another word, all of my girls are behind me and Brynn is at my side. Brynn might seem like a delicate flower, but you don't fuck with her bar or her people. And these douchebags are messing with both. She squeezes my hand but doesn't step in or fire me.

"You know Moore is gonna fuck you over,

right? He can get any piece of ass in Colorado, hell, probably the nation." Jacob regains some of his bravado. "You need to leave him before he leaves you. I wasn't the only guy in the club who wanted a chance with you."

Is he hitting on me?

"Are you hitting on me?" I'm not even about to try to work out his thought process on my own.

"I think you're hot." He shrugs, then leans forward again, taking my not yelling anymore as encouragement.

"Wait." My eyes go wide and I take a step back, thinking about the flowers I'd received. What are the chances a person who knows me as Poppy and Serena and hints for me to break up with TK randomly wanders into my job? Plus, it's clear to anybody with a set of eyes that this guy's out of his mind. "Are you the one who's been leaving the flowers and notes at my house?"

"What?" His back goes straight and all gloating leaves his face.

"I called the police," I tell him, my voice quiet but deadly. "You think it's funny? Threatening me and making me scared in my own house?"

He's white as a ghost when I finish, and

his eyes have tripled in size.

"No!" He shoots out of his seat, grabbing my arms. "I didn't do it!"

Brynn's no longer an idle support behind me. Before I can even register the pain from his fingers digging into my arms, liquid flies over my shoulder and into Jacob's face. "Get your hands off her now," she growls, her tone one not to be challenged.

Jacob lets go and his friends start pulling him away.

"It wasn't me! It was Rochelle!" he shouts, panic lacing his voice as soda drips down his face. "We've had a fling for the past few months. She's been fucking with you, leaving notes at your house, spreading all sorts of rumors on the Internet and shit. She called me last night and told me to come in today. Said you had a thing for me."

"That bitch!" Sadie takes the words right out of my mouth.

Dammit.

I should've known.

Now I'm even more pissed because I feel stupid!

"Get out," Brynn cuts in, pointing to the door after I stand frozen, saying nothing.

They don't hesitate, they take off running, the one friend who was quiet through this mess slapping Jacob on the back of the head as they go.

"Take Poppy home," Brynn whispers to the crowd behind the bar when the door shuts behind them.

I don't hesitate. I untie my bedazzled money pouch, hand it to Brynn, and walk to the office to get my purse.

When I push through the door and walk back into the restaurant, my girls are all waiting for me, worried looks marring their beautiful faces.

I know they think this is going to push me over the edge, but they're wrong.

What they don't get is I'm used to having crappy luck and getting screwed over. I wasn't used to going to nice dinners and waking up to my to-do list being taken care of.

"I'm fine," I say, answering their unasked question.

"You know what you need?" Sadie asks.

"Don't you dare." I point at her, stepping backward.

But before I can get far enough away, she lunges toward me, grabbing me with one hand and using her free one to cover me in glitter.

"I hate you so much." I stand still, glaring at her.

"You love me." She shrugs off my declaration, knowing it's a lie. "Plus, I invested in fine glitter, you're gonna sparkle for at least a month."

And as awful as my day — my week — has been, I start to laugh.

"Only you would think that's a good thing." I shake my head, thankful for her craziness.

"Come on, you sparkly bitches." Charli pushes open the door. "Let's take this party back to Poppy's."

We are halfway to my house, all of us laughing, even Jacqueline, when my phone rings in my purse. I recognize the number even though it's not saved in my phone so I slide my finger across the screen to answer it.

"Hello?"

"Ms. Patterson?" the friendly female voice asks.

"This is."

"Hi, this is Julie from Hamilton Elementary. I have Ace here and he's feeling a little worried. He said his dad was supposed to pick him up, but nobody came. Could you come in and get him?"

Ice slides through my veins before fire melts it away. "Tell him I'll be right there."

"Thank you," Julie says, her voice holding the barest amount of judgment.

I don't say anything else. I hang up and go straight to TK's name. I hit Call and listen to the phone ring and ring before his voicemail picks up. "Forget something?" I spit into the phone, hitting the End button and throwing my phone back into my purse.

"TK forgot to get Ace," I say to the worried — again! — faces watching me.

At this, a few things happen. Vonnie and Sadie get pissed. Charli and Aviana look sad. And Jacqueline walks to me, takes my hand in hers, and squeezes it.

"Go get him," Vonnie says, her no-nonsense voice taking over. "We'll meet you at your place and I'm taking Ace to have a sleepover with my boys."

"Vonnie —" I try to interrupt, appreciating her offer, but not going to take her up on it.

"No," she says, cutting me off and pointing a red fingernail in my face. "Ace loves playing with my boys and he'll be sad his jackass dad forgot him at school. You're going to find TK, cuss his sorry ass out, go home to an empty house, drink wine, take a bath, and sleep in."

"But . . ." I try, and fail, again.

"But nothing!" she yells, and for a moment I have to remember I'm the one who should be yelling now.

445

"Vonnie, I appreciate this, but you don't have to get worked up, I'll be fine." I reach for her hand but pull it away when I notice my words only served to piss her off more.

"Did I say you wouldn't be fine?" she asks.

"Well, no . . ."

"And I damn well do have to get worked up! You're my friend, this is what happens when people fuck with my friends. I get fucking angry!" She keeps yelling, ignoring the faces of strangers as they pass us, not even attempting to pretend they aren't listening. "Fuckin' TK. Always messing around, thinking everything's a goddamn joke. Piece of shit."

"I thought you like TK?" I meant for it to be a statement, but Vonnie's kind of scaring me right now, so it comes out as a question instead.

"So!" she booms, causing Jacqueline's hand to flinch in mine. "He's not my friend. He's my husband's co-worker. You're my friend!"

My sinuses don't even warn me before tears fog my vision and I have to suck in my lips so I don't cry.

I didn't even realize I was afraid of it until this moment, but now I know even if TK and I never get back together, I'm not going to lose my new friends.

446

I let go of Jacqueline's hand and pull Vonnie in for a hug.

Then because these bitches are so extra, everyone piles on.

On a Friday afternoon, we cause a massive traffic jam on a busy sidewalk just outside Downtown Denver.

And I laugh.

THIRTY-NINE

Before Vonnie took Ace to her house, she entered TK's address into the navigation app on my phone. Driving across town was the last resort. I was positive TK would answer his phone eventually.

But like always, I was wrong.

Now, parked on the street in front of his mansion — literal mansion — I don't know if I'm grateful he moved to my tiny bungalow or pissed he didn't push harder for me to come here. I'm pretty sure the landscaping alone costs more than a car.

I take a deep breath and turn onto his driveway, which loops around a fountain right on the verge of gaudy. I park in front of his door . . . well, doors. Two glass doors framed in wood that form an arch with an exquisite iron design decorating them. It's all so un-TK-like I would've laughed if I wasn't still raging.

I push the doorbell, which I know sends a

notification to his phone and is recording me, and wait.

Then I ring it again.

Lights are on throughout the house and his Range Rover is parked uselessly in front of his garage, so I know he's home.

Finally, I see him approaching through his door.

He's wearing sweatpants and no shirt. His hair is tussled on the top of his head like he's been sleeping.

And his beard is gone.

"Poppy?" He pulls open the door. "What are you doing here?"

"What happened to your beard?" I ask, momentarily forgetting the reason I'm here.

I haven't seen him without a beard since high school, and it's almost scary how little he's changed with it gone.

He runs his fingers down his face, as if he forgot it was gone, too. "Needed a change, I guess," he says, his lips turning up just enough for his dimple to show and looking more like Ace than ever.

Ace.

Focus, Poppy.

God. One meeting with a razor and he turns my brain into goo!

"What happened to you today?" I straighten to my full, still not tall height and narrow my eyes at him.

His eyebrows furrow together and he lifts his chin, not in a defensive way but in a way that conveys he has no clue what I'm talking about. "What are you talking about?"

I suck in a breath and take a step back. "You were supposed to pick Ace up from school." I cock my head to the side, watching as he screws his eyes shut and his hands fly to his head.

"Fuck, Poppy." He opens his eyes slowly. "I totally forgot. I'm so sorry."

This is not how I expected the conversation to go. I didn't expect to see the amount of remorse written all over his face or the self-loathing evident in his voice.

"TK," I whisper. "This is not okay."

"You think I don't fucking know that?" he snaps, catching me off guard by the sudden change. "You think I don't know I'm a fuckin' screw-up? That I'm not aware Ace hates me?" He clenches his fists, his knuckles going white as his face goes red.

And God.

I want to be so mad at him.

So fucking angry for already breaking his promise to Ace. For breaking his promise to me.

But I can't.

I can't look at this man, alone in a house

450

that might be big and beautiful but is so empty. I can't stare into his eyes and ignore the pain he can't mask as much as he tries. I can't deny the love I've had for him since I was fifteen.

"TK —" I try to cut in, but he doesn't hear me.

"You and Ace were the one good fucking thing I had and you left!" he shouts, and pulls out the hairband, letting his hair fall around his face. "Things got tough, and you left!"

I move toward him, wrapping my arms around his waist and staring into his eyes. "You aren't okay." I repeat the words from the hospital room, the words that have been nagging at the back of my mind for months. "Your mood swings give me whiplash. Like when I told you about Ace or when your mom showed up, you get mad to an extreme you used to not be capable of. You forget your keys or your wallet almost every day and now you forgot about Ace." He tries to look away, but I move with him, not dropping eye contact. "And I know how much you love him. When are you going to accept that something's not right?"

His body goes soft as he closes his eyes, the fight gone just as fast as it came, but he doesn't say anything.

"Do you really think these concussions have nothing to do with it?"

"This is the first season I've gotten a bad one," he defends himself. "Everyone forgets stuff."

"CTE isn't just concussions and you know that," I say. He stays silent, but he knows. "And I know it's scary and easier to live in denial. But even if you don't admit it to me, you have to admit something isn't right, even if it's just to yourself."

"I . . . tell Ace I'm sorry." TK straightens, pulling away from me and stepping back inside his marble-covered floors. "I'll call you."

"TK." I slump, realizing I got nowhere with him. "Please."

"I'll call you," he repeats before closing the door in my face.

Crap.

I turn and walk back to my car, hating how sad I feel, wanting to feel the fury from earlier.

I start the ignition and rest my head against my steering wheel.

It's safe to say that didn't go as planned.

FORTY

Five Weeks Later

TK didn't call.

He sent a few text messages and on the occasions when Ace would work up the nerve to call him, he'd answer, but that was it.

There was the time, a few days after I showed up at TK's house, that his lawyer called me to tell me he had a check for back child support and needed my bank information for future payments.

I told him to tell TK to shove the check where the sun don't shine and hung up.

Then I told Sadie and Vonnie and they told me they'd shove something up somewhere if I didn't call and take the "goddamn check."

I did as they said. Mainly because I was scared they'd follow through on their promise but also because as angry as I was with TK, I knew he was trying. And money was the only way he knew how to try.

Then we got on with life. Ace focused on soccer, I focused on Ace, and we both pretended we weren't disappointed every time the phone rang and TK wasn't on the other end.

In the surprise of the century, Lydia Moore reached out. It wasn't much, just a card addressed to Ace. It had a note about how excited she was to get to know him and baby pictures of TK that I hate to admit how much I enjoyed. She wrote her number inside, but Ace still hasn't called. And with TK missing in action, I can't say I blame him.

Oh, and Rochelle reached out. I think this is because Sadie put the fear of God into her and told her I had her and Jacob on tape going to my house and threatening me. It might've been because she heard from a blog that TK and I were over and she no longer hated me with the fire of three burning suns. I told her everything was fine — it wasn't — but if she ever came around my house again, I'd open my gun safe — I don't own a gun — and make her regret it. I haven't heard from her since.

"You want to take the boys to Bonnie Brae after the game?" Cole asks, scooting his chair a little closer to mine.

Ugh.

And Cole became a close talker again.

I scoot my chair away. "It's too cold for ice cream."

"Lunch?" he keeps on.

I gotta give it to the guy, he's a persistent little bugger.

"No thanks." I pull my sunglasses from my purse and put them on, hoping he'll get the point, expecting he won't.

He keeps talking. "Ace is doing great this season."

"Yeah," I agree, and watch Ace as he runs down the field, waving his hand in the air to show he's open. "He loves it."

"I guess being an athlete runs in the family." Cole huffs out an awkward laugh and I resist the very real urge to either roll my eyes or punch him in the throat.

He knows TK and I aren't together — his nearness proves that — but it hasn't stopped him from bringing TK up in conversations and subtly trying to get concrete evidence.

Luckily for him, Sadie's cleavage-baring, no-jacket-wearing self — even though it's nearly November and cold AF outside — materializes. I ignore his question and stand up, making my way down the sideline while still focusing on the game.

"Go go go!" I cup my hands around my

mouth and yell when Ace gets the ball in the goal box. He cuts the ball left, then right, beating the defender, plants his left foot beside the ball, and strikes it with his laces, sending it soaring into the top right corner of the net. "Yes!" I jump up and down, thinking this is *so* much better than football.

"Go, Ace!" Sadie's yelling as I reach her.

"You got here just in time." I shove my hands back into my pockets, colder just from looking at Sadie.

"You know I'm the Patterson good luck charm." She juts out her hip, the sun causing all the sparkles covering her skin and hair to wink.

"That you are." I link my arm through hers and pull her back to where I'm sitting and point to the extra chair I brought her.

"Thank you," she says, leaning back into the bright pink chair.

I point to the small duffel bag between us. "I brought extra blankets in case you get cold."

She unzips the bag, pulling out the fleece blanket and draping it over her legs. "See, this is why soccer mom Poppy is my second favorite Poppy."

"Who's your favorite Poppy?" I ask, like there really is more than one Poppy.

456

She turns to me, aiming a bright smile my way that makes me regret asking. "Drunk Poppy," she says. "She does some wild shit."

I don't have to look to know Cole is listening.

"A hat trick!" I ruffle Ace's hair before he climbs into the back seat. "You're a superstar!"

"It's not hockey." Color creeps up his cheeks, and not from running or the cold. "Next time don't throw your hat onto the field, and please don't steal other parents' hats to throw."

"Sadie stole hats, not me!" I defend myself, aiming a dirty look at Sadie.

She doesn't care about my glare or Ace's embarrassment. "One hat wasn't enough and I didn't have one. What else was I going to do?"

"You guys are nuts," Ace says with a hint of laughter in his voice.

"You love us." Sadie shrugs, fully embracing that she is, in fact, nuts.

"You're all right," Ace says, which is nine-year-old cool guy for "You're the best."

I turn out of the park's parking lot and notice out of the side of my eye that Sadie's looking at her phone and has gone completely stiff.

457

"What's wrong?" I ask, keeping my eyes on the road in front of me.

"Nothing," she answers too fast for it to be true.

"Sadie . . ." I use my mom voice on her.

"Aviana just sent a message in the group text." She drops her phone into her rhinestone-studded purse. "That's all."

She is so full of shit.

Aviana sends GIFs all day, every day, in the chat among all of us. Nothing she sends has ever made my back go straight.

Even though I don't want to, I drop it. I'll look at the text myself when we get home.

I turn up the radio when Ace hears his new favorite song and push the pedal down a little harder than normal. I don't even take the extra second to drive through the alley and park in the garage.

"Cool driving, Mom," Ace says when we come to a stop in front of the house. "I've never seen you blow so many yellow lights."

"I did not."

I totally did.

"Suuuuure." Ace slings his soccer bag over his shoulder and heads to the house.

"It's probably nothing," Sadie says as I dig through my purse, cursing all the receipts and unused napkins hiding my phone. "She just said to turn on ESPN."

I find my phone and swipe at the unread message notification.

Aviana:

Poppy. ESPN. Now.

I run into the house without even locking my car doors.

"Shower," I bark at Ace, who's looking too cozy on my couch.

"But, *Mommm,*" he whines.

I'll never understand the vendetta he seems to hold against personal hygiene.

"Now." I take the remote from his hand and point toward the bathroom.

I don't know what's about to happen, but I don't want Ace to see it with me if it's bad.

"Fine," he pouts, stomping away like he's not about to be ten.

"You're too old for that!" I shout after him, forgetting for a moment about the task at hand.

Sadie, not distracted, takes the remote from me, opens the guide (neither one of us knows the channel for ESPN off the top of our head), and scrolls.

"There!" I shout when she passes it. "Go up one!"

She does as I say.

We're standing in the middle of my living room, holding hands. Then, with what we see, we both fall onto the couch behind us.

There's an sc on the bottom-left-hand side of the screen, and a single man in a suit standing on what looks like a huge stage is talking. But that's not what made my legs give out from under me.

Behind him, on a screen stretching from floor to ceiling, is a picture of TK standing on the field in his uniform. I know it's an old picture, I saw it once or twice last year when I was flipping through channels. And it's not even the sight of TK that does me in. It's the words in all caps and bold print at the bottom of the screen.

TK MOORE RETIRES

"Holy shit," I say out loud.

Sadie's hand tightens around mine while the man in the suit keeps talking. "After a month spent in a Southern California clinic that focuses on brain injuries, Moore has decided to end his career in a move that has shaken the league. Moore is in his sixth year in the league, and only his second in his new contract. Because the NFL does not offer guaranteed contracts, he is walking away from millions of dollars. This story is just developing and we'll report on it as we get more information."

Sadie turns off the TV when a commercial comes on. We both sit there, saying nothing at all. The only sounds are our heavy breathing and the running water from Ace's shower.

"Holy shit." I stare at the blank TV screen, not knowing what to think.

"You can say that again," Sadie says, and because I have nothing else to say, I do.

"Holy shit." I turn to her, convinced we're wearing matching expressions with wide eyes and open mouths. "What does this mean?"

Sadie stays quiet for a minute, biting her lip like she's not sure she should say what's on her mind. "I think you need to go ask TK that."

I nod, my hands fidgeting nonstop in my lap. "I think you're right."

"Now, Poppy," she says when I don't move to get up. "I'll stay here with Ace."

"Maybe I should give it a day." I push my hands onto my knees to stop my legs from bouncing.

"No." She uses my mom voice on me. "Now."

"Fine," I pout, sounding a lot like Ace did a few minutes ago.

461

I pick up my purse from the spot on the floor where I dropped it and check to make sure my keys didn't fall out and end up under my couch somewhere. Same thing with my phone.

In other words, I'm procrastinating.

"You have everything!" Sadie yells, and points to the door. "Go!"

"Geeez." I stick my tongue out at her, now definitely acting like Ace. "So bossy."

"Poppy!" she shouts, her cheeks burning red.

"I'm gone!" I pull open the door, laughing at her as I go.

I pull the door closed, taking my key out to lock both locks.

With my keys in hand, I turn to walk to my car.

But I don't get far, because after one step I'm toe to toe with TK Moore.

FORTY-ONE

I don't know if I'm more startled by him being here or that he looks even more handsome than he ever has — something for which I both thank and curse the Lord.

"Jesus, TK!" I shove his chest, acting mad, but really just wanting a reason to touch him. "You scared me!"

"Sorry." He grins, his dimple popping out on his still-beardless face. "Didn't mean to."

"What are you doing here?" I ask him once my heart rate has dropped and my breathing has returned to normal.

"I came to see you and Ace." The smile fades away and he shoves his hands in his pockets, rocking back onto his heels. "I can come back another time if you're busy."

Where I fidget all the time, TK does it only when he's really nervous.

I was going to lie. Maybe say I was going on a date or something else more believable, but seeing how nervous he is and knowing how hard this must be for him, I don't. "I was actually going to see you."

The dimple reappears along with the creases around his eyes. "Lucky me."

"We have a lot to talk about, TK," I say, my tone serious. "You disappeared for a month. Do you understand how hard that was on Ace?"

And me? I think, but don't say.

"I was scared. The last time I saw you, I fucked up." His voice drops and lines I haven't noticed before crease his forehead. Lines that show his age and pain. "I messed up with you and with Ace. Justin called me, telling me he had to hide Vonnie's keys so she couldn't come over and murder me."

That makes me smile. Vonnie was almost as upset as I was and she let everyone know.

"And I knew you were right and I was fucking up, but I didn't know why." He takes a hesitant step toward me. "I stayed up all night looking up CTE. Reading about the early warning signs, watching interviews with older players, reading interviews from the widows of players who died."

His voice hitches and it's all I need to hear to close the rest of the distance between us. I take his hands in mine, hoping he accepts the only comfort I can offer.

"I found a clinic." He links our fingers

together, a small smile touching his lips. "I wasn't sure it could work, but I stayed up all night trying to find success stories, and when I knew Donny would be up, I called him and had him get me in."

"Why didn't you tell me?" I try to fight back the frustration I feel. "I would've supported you."

"I know you would've, but I was skeptical. I didn't think it'd work." He takes a deep breath that causes me to brace. "And if it didn't, I thought you and Ace were better off with me out of the picture."

"TK." I close my eyes, feeling as if someone has shoved a knife into my heart. "That's not true."

"You don't understand where my head was. I read all of these stories about men who were unrecognizable when they died. They became physically abusive, cheated on their wives, lost all their money. I didn't want to do that to you and Ace."

"But you're here now," I reply, stating the obvious.

"I'm here now." The memories haunting his face fade away, leaving the green eyes I could live in staring back at me. "I feel better than I've felt in years. So I'm here."

I take a deep breath and try to take a step back. Since he's been so honest, I know I have to open up, too.

"I don't want you to resent me." I look at my shoes when TK doesn't let me pull away. "First I come barging into your life, throwing a kid at you, then I forced you to leave your beautiful house to move into my tiny house, and now you quit football for me."

"Stop." TK wraps a hand around the back of my neck. "You didn't make me choose."

"I might not have told you to choose, but I forced your hand." I close my eyes, guilt bringing me to the verge of tears.

TK drops his mouth to my ear and whispers, "Look at me, Sparks."

I missed hearing him call me that more than I let myself admit.

"You didn't make me choose and you didn't force my hand." He holds my face between his hands, wiping away the tears as they fall. "You just showed me what was important in life. You gave me the purpose I'd been trying, unsuccessfully, to find in football."

"But you walked away from so much money." I hiccup, sounding like a blubbering idiot.

"I have a great financial advisor who made sure I put most of my money away and invested wisely. Donny is good at his job, and after I signed my last contract, he had

466

me put in place an eight-million-dollar disability insurance policy I'll collect." He smiles at me when my jaw drops open. "Plus, my house is worth more now than when I bought it, and I already have a buyer on the hook."

"Holy crap." There's a lot to unpack. "You get eight million dollars for quitting?"

"Not quitting. Leaving the sport because I was injured."

"Okay." I shake my head, still stuck on the other thing he said. "You're selling your house?"

"I hated that house, my mom pushed me into getting it."

"I knew it!" I shout, interrupting him. "That house was so not you."

"I know." He smiles before dropping a quick kiss to my forehead. "And it's too far from you guys. I found a house a few blocks from here. It's got two extra rooms, a decent-size yard, and is close to Ace's school."

I blink.

"You . . . you what?"

"I found a house," he repeats, cocking his head to the side and studying my face. "Is that not okay?"

I shake my head, trying to activate my brain again. "I mean, it's fine. Is this place too small?"

Now it's his turn to look confused.

"I didn't think you'd want me back in after everything that happened."

"What happened was you got hurt, listened to my fears, and got help." I put my hands on my hips. "We love you and miss the hell out of you. Come back home."

"You love me?"

"I already told you I love you!" I go to shove his chest again, but he grabs my hands instead, pulling me into him and wrapping my hands behind his back before dropping them.

"I was concussed. I thought I imagined it."

I roll my eyes, knowing he remembers and this isn't the last time I'm going to hear about him being "concussed."

He looks down at me, his eyes going soft. "Say it again," he whispers.

I don't hesitate.

"I love you."

"Good." He smiles, dropping his mouth to mine, kissing me softly. "Because I love you too."

He goes to kiss me again, but I pull away before he can.

"I have one condition if you move back in."

468

A guard shutters his eyes and his shoulders tense. "What?"

"I'm gonna need you to grow your beard back." I run my fingertips along his bare cheeks. "I liked how it felt."

He doesn't answer and his eyes don't go soft again.

Instead they fill with something that makes my toes curl and my thighs clench.

Then he kisses me until the door opens behind us.

"Disgusting," Ace says, startling us both. "Just promise not to ever kiss in front of me again. Okay, Dad?"

My vision goes watery again and I watch TK's arms go around Ace as he pulls him in tight.

"Can't promise that, dude," TK says. "I kind of planned on showing you both how much I love you as often as I can. So I'll probably be kissing your mom a lot and embarrassing you in front of your friends when I eat lunch with you at school. That all right with you?"

"So you're back?" Ace asks, trying not to sound too hopeful.

"I'm never leaving again." And it's not just words, it's a fierce promise, a vow I know he will never break.

"Good." Ace smiles, his cool nine-year-old persona firmly in place. "Mom was going nuts without you."

I feel my eyes bug out of my head, betrayed by my own flesh and blood! I open my mouth to deny it, but TK beats me to it.

"That's all right, I was going crazy without you guys too."

I suck in a sharp breath and blink hard.

And when I open them, staring back at me is my family.

It only took ten years.

Freaking finally.

"It's starting!" Aviana shouts at the crowd milling around HERS. "Be quiet!"

I sit down next to TK, staring at my ring as it catches the light, still not quite believing I'm getting married. "She's insane," he whispers in my ear.

I smile and nod, because he's right.

"I can't believe she found enough people for the show." I keep my voice low as the lights go down and the opening for *Love the Player* starts to play.

"I can." He looks at me like I'm crazy. "Dixie has been vying for fame since she put that ring on her finger and Aviana should really get into the business with how well she pitched this shit."

"You know Dixie's ass is gonna be the villain and get kicked off after the season ends," Vonnie says, not caring who hears her.

"Damn, girl!" Justin's eyes double in size

as he looks over his shoulder for Chad. "You know I still have to get along with her husband, right?"

"And?" She rolls her eyes and takes a sip of her martini. "That has nothing to do with me."

"You need another drink?" Jenna, the waitress Brynn hired after I gave my notice, asks.

"I'm fine for now, thank you." I smile at her, understanding how she feels being stuck in a room full of Lady Mustangs.

"Girl, you better stop nursing that drink." Vonnie arches a brow and purses her lips.

"I have to," I pout. "I have to go home and study some more, I have a huge test in my psych class tomorrow. Plus, TK's mom is coming into town tomorrow afternoon."

Vonnie's eyes go wide and she doesn't have to even open her mouth for me to know exactly what's going through her mind.

"It should be fine. We've talked a few times. She's obsessed with Ace now and we'll play nice for him." I answer the unspoken questions.

"Look at you." Sadie slides in next to me. "Being all responsible and engaged and shit."

Now it's my turn to roll my eyes.

"I can't believe you're here and still haven't made time to come see the house."

Since leaving Maya's house isn't an option for me, TK hired a design company to do all the changes I could've ever wanted. I even redid Maya's room. I almost didn't, but I know she'd want me to fill her room with more babies, not keep it as some shrine to her.

"You guys are always holding hands and kissing. It's gross." Sadie scrunches her nose. "Plus, Brynn promised me free booze if I came and kept her company tonight."

"Then it looks like you're slipping on the job." I point out the obvious.

"I was sitting at the bar for the last hour. Trust me, I wasn't the company she wanted." She wiggles her eyebrows.

I'm trying to be discreet and see what the hell Sadie's talking about, when the sound of shattering glass pulls my attention to the bar anyway.

"What the fuck?" Brynn screeches, her eyes focused on Maxwell. The two bottom shelves behind the bar are broken, and shattered bottles cover the counter beneath them. "Get the fuck out of here!"

TK comes unfrozen first and crosses the room. I follow him, but when he grabs Maxwell and walks him to the door, I walk around the bar to help Brynn.

We get all the glass picked up, the liquor cleaned, and through it all, Brynn doesn't say a single word. Then, when it's all finished, she turns and walks to her office, slamming the door shut behind her.

"What the hell happened?" I ask TK, who came to help with cleanup after he got Maxwell to leave.

He shrugs. "No clue, Max didn't tell me anything."

"That was crazy." I've never seen Maxwell so much as raise his voice. This is so out of character, I can't begin to wrap my mind around it.

"Yeah," he agrees. "That's a nice way to put it."

"I think I'm ready to go home." Being around the Lady Mustangs is taxing on a good night . . . and this was not a good night.

"You sure you have to study?" His fingers stroke his now fully regrown beard.

I bite my lip and rub my thighs together.

"I mean, I've already studied a lot."

He grabs my hand, pulling me behind him as he gets my purse from the table and drags me out the front door.

When we get home, the only studying I do is the way his mouth feels on me and how he feels inside me.

And it's a subject I'm going to dedicate the rest of my life to mastering.

ABOUT THE AUTHOR

Alexa Martin is a writer and stay-at-home mom. She lives in Colorado with her husband — a former NFL player who now coaches at the high school where they met — their four children, and a German shepherd. When she's not telling her kids to put their shoes on . . . again, you can find her catching up with her latest book boyfriend or on Pinterest pinning meals she'll probably never make. The Playbook series is inspired by the eight years she spent as an NFL wife.

CONNECT ONLINE

The employees of Thorndike Press hope you have enjoyed this Large Print book. All our Thorndike, Wheeler, and Kennebec Large Print titles are designed for easy reading, and all our books are made to last. Other Thorndike Press Large Print books are available at your library, through selected bookstores, or directly from us.

For information about titles, please call:

(800) 223-1244

or visit our website at:

gale.com/thorndike

To share your comments, please write:

Publisher
Thorndike Press
10 Water St., Suite 310
Waterville, ME 04901